"It's not so clear what's true and what isn't in *The Chinatown Death Cloud Peril,* but that is half the fun. This high-energy novel is written with a confident hand by an author who understands what it takes to write a good story and keep readers mesmerized from page one and yearning for more when it's over. . . . It's a novel filled with rich characters, high adventure and fantasy—just like classic pulp fiction."

—*USA Today*

"While the tale veers between fact and fiction, the writing itself is pure pulp. The lurid details and swashbuckling language are torn from the pages of 'Amazing Stories,' 'Phantom Detective' and 'Terror Tales'— sensational 1930s magazines. . . . We haven't seen writing quite like this in a very long time."

—Associated Press review in the *San Francisco Chronicle*

". . . breezy pulp pastiche."

—*The Village Voice*

"There's more than enough blood, cruelty, fear, mystery, and vengeance here—along with nostalgia and literary gab—to appeal to fans of Michael Chabon's *The Amazing Adventures of Kavalier and Clay* and Alan Moore's Victorian fantasies."

—Bob Lunn, *School Library Journal*

"Like the pulpsters he reveres, Malmont doesn't let the facts get in the way of his storytelling, and the result is a fun, if wildly improbable, pulp joyride."

—*Publishers Weekly*

". . . pure pulp."

—*The Washington Post*

"As someone who cut his literary teeth on Lester Dent's Doc Savage books, who's an ardent fan of Walter Gibson and pulp writing in all its incarnations (okay, and who frequents Greenwich Village's White Horse Tavern), I was halfway through this novel by the time the shipping envelope hit the floor and had finished it not long after. Rest assured, though, you don't need to fall into any of the above categories to thoroughly enjoy author Malmont's marvelous work. It's a rip-roaring yarn the likes of which we haven't seen in a long while."

—Jeffery Deaver, author of *The Twelfth Card* and *The Cold Moon*

"The very definition of a ripping yarn, with infamous villains, nefarious plots, and hair-breadth escapes. That the square-jawed heroes are also writers—pulpateers—makes the game a whole new kind of thrill ride. Pulp fiction at its best."
—Glen David Gold, author of *Carter Beats the Devil*

"Readers . . . are sure to be delighted and amazed."
—Mary McCoy, PopMatters.com

"A genuine page-turner."
—Kenneth Terrel, *US News & World Report*

"Malmont, a first-time novelist, has an obvious passion for the pulp novels of the '30s."
—James McGowan, *Times Colonist* (Canada)

"*The Chinatown Death Cloud Peril* is an homage to our literary past and to the readers who savored tales of derring-do."
—Oline H. Coghill, *Sun-Sentinel*

"Paul Malmont's debut novel *The Chinatown Death Cloud Peril* is both homage to the pulps and the men who wrote them, and a lightning-paced, intricate adventure novel in its own right. . . . *The Chinatown Death Cloud Peril* is a pulp at heart . . . and Malmont wallows in the possibilites of the genre. . . . As an action-adventure novel, *The Chinatown Death Cloud Peril* is a thrill ride the likes of which are rarely seen in mainstream publishing. . . . It's a testament to the power of a ripping good yarn."

—Blogcritics.org

"A witty work of rip-roaring adventure that is just as exciting and enchanting as the works that inspired it. You don't have to have read pulps to enjoy *The Chinatown Death Cloud Peril,* but if you have ever thrilled to heroes such as Doc Savage, the Shadow, Conan or John Carter of Mars, this is a wonderful novel that you cannot afford to miss."
—*Mongomery Advertiser* (Alabama)

"In *The Chinatown Death Cloud Peril,* Paul Malmont does for pulp writers of the 1930s what Michael Chabon did for comic book writers of the same era in *The Adventures of Kavalier & Clay*: he brings them to life."

—*South Bend Tribune* (Indiana)

"A riot of retro-themed adventure."

—*The Sacramento Bee*

"One of the coolest freakin' things you'll enjoy this year."
—aintitcoolnews.com

THE CHINATOWN DEATH CLOUD PERIL

Paul Malmont

SIMON & SCHUSTER PAPERBACKS
New York   London   Toronto   Sydney

SIMON & SCHUSTER PAPERBACKS
Rockefeller Center
1230 Avenue of the Americas
New York, NY 10020

First Simon & Schuster paperback edition 2007

SIMON & SCHUSTER PAPERBACKS and colophon are registered
trademarks of Simon & Schuster, Inc.

For information about special discounts for bulk purchases,
please contact Simon & Schuster Special Sales at
1-800-456-6798 or business@simonandschuster.com

DESIGNED BY LAUREN SIMONETTI

Manufactured in the United States of America

1   3   5   7   9   10   8   6   4   2

The Library of Congress has cataloged the hardcover edition as follows:

Malmont, Paul.
The Chinatown death cloud peril / Paul Malmont.
p.   cm.
1. Gibson, Walter Brown, 1897-—Fiction. 2. Dent, Lester, 1904–1959—Fiction.
3. Authors, American—20th century—Fiction. I. Title.
PS3613.A457C47 2006
813'.6—dc22   2006042205

ISBN-13: 978-0-7432-8785-2
ISBN-10:   0-7432-8785-1
ISBN-13: 978-0-7432-8786-9 (Pbk)
ISBN-10:   0-7432-8786-X(Pbk)

To my son, Nathaniel,
for getting me up early all those mornings so I could write this
and bearing with me while I did

To my wife, Audrey,
for my sons, and for so many other wonderful ways you have shared
your life with me

To Forrest Barrett
and
William Putch,
old teachers gone but never forgotten

THE CHINATOWN DEATH CLOUD PERIL

My little son is crying out for nourishment—
O Alice, Alice, what shall I do?

—Edgar Rice Burroughs

We know how Gods are made.

—Jack London

INTRODUCTION

IT IS called the Pulp Era.

An era is like a book in that it has a title, its own unique exposition, characters, a beginning, a middle, an ending, a theme, and maybe a moral. And just as heroes and villains in a book do not realize they are in a story, so you cannot know the title or themes of the time in which you live. You may think you know. You may even hope to contribute to the story line, or be a witness to the ending. But even if you did, you would not know. Only after those days have passed can one discern the form, voices, and meaning of those days. Then the era can be given a title because titles are how we refer to times passed and stories told. The Pulp Era.

In other times and places—Imperial China, for example—an emperor could declare his own era while he was living in it. When Li Shimin, Emperor of the Temple and Library, decided that China was in a period of divine richness, then from that day on everyone was living in the Divine Richness Era. At least until the next emperor decreed the dawning of a new era.

In China this prerogative was considered a literary expression on the part of the emperor. The known world, after all, was his, and he could tell his story about it as he saw fit. As this known world is mine to tell about as I see fit. I am the Emperor of the Light and Darkness, and this is the Pulp Era.

You may recognize some of the heroes and villains of this era, but recognizing a vaguely familiar face is not the same as rediscovering a long-lost friend. I will introduce you to some old friends of mine, and make their days come alive again. I will let their voices speak and let their hearts fill with life one more time. An era, like a book, can be forgotten. Days, like pages, crumble into dust. Stories, like memories, fade away.

In this account I will offer you these lives, their stories, their shared events, that time with as much truth as they deserve. But saying that I will tell the truth about them is not the same as saying that I will tell you truth. In order to exercise my imperial prerogative I have to let shadows fall between fact and fiction. These friends, several of whom were writers, would have been among the first to remind me to never let the facts get in the way of a good story, and so I will not. The reader will determine what is truth and what is fiction.

In the end it's just a story.

But if you ask me, it's all true.

Issue 1:
Curse of the
Golden Vulture

EPISODE ONE

"YOU THINK life can't be like the pulps?" Walter Gibson asked the other man. "Let me tell you a story. You tell me where real ends and pulp begins." The cigarette in his left hand suddenly disappeared.

The young man, whose most distinguishing characteristic, in spite of his stocky build and shock of red hair, was his powerfully forward-thrusted jaw, blinked in mild surprise at the magic trick, then nodded agreeably. "All right," Ron Hubbard said.

The cigarette, a filterless Chesterfield, reappeared in Gibson's right hand. He took a long sip from his whiskey and washed it down with a sip of beer and an involuntary shudder. He was getting drunk and it was too early. He knew it. He didn't even want to be here tonight. Well, he did want to be in the White Horse Tavern drinking. But he didn't want to be here drinking with the youthful and ambitious president of the American Fiction Guild, who had been hectoring him relentlessly to speak about his writing at the weekly gathering of pulp mag writers in the Grand Salon of the old Hotel Knickerbocker. John Nanovic, his ed at Street & Smith, had begged, pleaded, and in the end agreed to pay for a few of this evening's drinks if he would agree to do it. Nanovic had told Gibson that it was important for him, as the number one bestselling mag writer in America, to take an interest in the new writers, the young writers. To help groom them. Gibson felt that what Nanovic really wanted him to do was to find his successor in case he stumbled in front of a trolley car some drunken evening. Ultimately he had to admit that it was a fair concern for an editor to have about him.

So, here he was having drinks with Lafayette Ron Hubbard, a writer of moderately popular but pedestrian (in Gibson's opinion) westerns, and at twenty-five, fifteen years younger than he. One of the new writers. One of the young ones. They were seated at a small table next to the bar and treating themselves to waiter service. Hubbard was one of those writers who acted like they really cared about writing and had launched into a theory that the sort of adventure pulp Gibson wrote was somehow less valid than the westerns and two-fisted tales he wrote because at least his stories were based on history or reality.

Gibson knew the kid was impressed by him. Hubbard had practically been begging him for a sit-down for weeks. Every now and then Gibson would see Hubbard looking around the saloon as if he could recognize somebody he knew who might come over and interrupt the conversation. If that had happened, he might then have the opportunity to say to them, "Excuse me, but can't you see I'm having drinks with Walter Gibson? That's right, the guy who writes *The Shadow Magazine*. Well, I know *The Shadow* byline is Maxwell Grant, but that's a company name, a Street & Smith name. Trust me. Walter Gibson is Maxwell Grant. Walter Gibson writes *The Shadow Magazine*. We're just talking about writing." But he recognized no one and no one recognized him.

Gibson had seen several writers that he knew come through already; the Street & Smith building was just up the road at Fifteenth and Seventh, and the tavern was popular with writers who had just been roughed up by eds and by the eds who had applied the beating. George Bruce, the air-ace writer, had been and gone; Elmer Smith, the rocket jock, and Norvell Page, the fright guy, were still drinking in a corner. But he hadn't invited either to join them. As a rule Gibson didn't like other mag writers; he found them too self-denigrating yet self-important at the same time. He much preferred the company of the magicians whose books and articles he often ghosted.

He kind of liked Hubbard, though. The kid was eager and acted like he thought his shit smelled like roses, a confidence most other writers lacked. In a one-draft world a man had to believe that every word he wrote was right. Gibson knew he had quickly muscled out old Arthur Brooks, a man Gibson had no use for whatsoever, who as head of the Guild had run the organization as a lazy gentlemen's social club. Hubbard had plans for the Guild, but Gibson didn't really care to know what they were. He knew that Hubbard had lived in New York for several years a while back with a wife and a daughter, and that they had all moved back to Washington State for a while, and that he had left them behind in Washington and come back to New York alone just a few months ago. Gibson could only venture a guess why; the Depression had made it so that sometimes a man couldn't afford to bring his family with him when he went looking for work. But the last thing Gibson wanted to do was ask another man why he had left his wife and child.

"What's real? What's pulp? Right, Ron?" He unbuttoned his collar and loosened his tie knot. "Okay. Here's a story. For the sake of argument, let's call it the Tale of the Sweet Flower War. This is a story filled with blood and cruelty and fear and mystery and love and passion and vengeance and villains," he said. "It began with the arrival of a strange mist which rolled in from the harbor and seemed to fill the streets of Chinatown. Those who were superstitious felt it was the cloak of death. Those who weren't superstitious, and their numbers were few, only felt it was another reason to hate living here." Walter spoke rapidly; the hard emphasis of his consonants tended to resemble a staccato drumbeat, and his fingers twitched mildly as he spoke, involuntarily typing his words onto the table or against his leg or into the air as fast as he spoke them. Gibson's energy always seemed to keep him in motion. His friend Harry Houdini had once told him he seemed to vibrate, even when he was standing still.

"Here Chinatown? Or San Francisco's?" Hubbard asked with a vaguely worldly air that implied he had traveled some in his time and knew both intimately: a warning to Gibson that he'd better have his facts straight.

"New York. Here." The tone of Gibson's voice let Hubbard know not to interrupt the storytelling again unless it was something important. "The deadly fog rolled over the tiny enclave thirty years ago during the great tong wars, when the red flag of war flew over the tallest building in Chinatown."

"Tong?" Hubbard made the same mistake again and winced a little, knowing that Gibson's next breath would have explained it.

"Ancient organizations with mysterious roots going way back in Chinese history. Brutal, cruel, and sadistic. Mostly they imported opium, slave girls, and indentured workers from China.

"In 1909, the year of the menacing mist, the biggest tong in America was the On Leong group. They controlled everything in the matter of things Chinese from Frisco to New York. There were other tongs around at the time, but the only serious rivals were the Hip Sing. Their boss was a fella about your age, everyone knew him as Mock Duck, and he had a habit, when he got into a brawl, of whipping out two pistols, closing his eyes, and firing blindly until everyone was dead or running for their lives. You can laugh if you want, but legend had it that this was a very effective street-fighting technique.

"Well, those that said that something sinister would emerge from the shadow which had fallen over Chinatown were right. One day Sweet Flower came to town. Now she was, by all accounts, a beautiful and delicate virgin. She had remarkable long, slender fingers and could play a variety of Chinese instruments with skill and grace. A slave, of course, smuggled in by a slaver and probably destined for a life of prostitution. But one of the On Leong leaders saw her, fell in love with her, and he had his men steal her from the slaver. Or rescue her, if you prefer. And, he married her. She was sixteen, and on her wedding night he possessed her in every way that a man can possess a woman. And she was happy with her station in life.

"At first, all the slaver wanted was proper restitution for his loss. But the On Leong man refused to pay for what he considered to be true love. He told the slaver to go to hell. The slaver went to another tong, the Hip Sing. A truce was declared and the two parties sat down for formal negotiations. Now this was at a time when the tong fighters, the hatchet men, the *boo how doy,* were killing each other at the rate of two or three a week. So for these two tongs to actually sit down together in the same room and hold a peaceful discussion . . ." He made a futile gesture. "Chinatown did not hold its collective breath."

"The negotiations did not go well for the Hip Sing. Once again, they were told in no uncertain terms where they and their demands could go. All things considered, it's pretty remarkable that any man walked out of the tearoom alive that day. That night, however, was a different story. While her husband slept, someone broke into their house and cut off each and every one of Sweet Flower's slender and delicate little fingers."

"Mock Duck?"

The White Horse Tavern served its own blend of scotch, and each bottle was topped by a cork with a white tin horse rearing up. There was a cork on their table now; it was usually given to the customer who had put the polish on a bottle, and he had, several drinks ago. Gibson picked it up now, idly playing with it.

"Maybe. It was probably the vile slaver. And, in fact, Mock Duck delivered him over to the On Leong for whatever justice they chose to administer. But it wasn't enough and over the next couple of months, over fifty men from both sides were killed, and hundreds more were crippled or maimed in the fighting. Now what's really incredible about this is that we're talking about a neighborhood that takes up maybe a square mile and is made up of only a dozen or so streets. So relatively, it's a truly gruesome amount of men carving each other up."

"Hundreds! C'mon! That's pulp."

Gibson cleared his throat. "In those days the center of Chinese social life was the old Chinese Theater. It's still there; you can go down and see it for yourself. It's all boarded up now.

"At the time of the Sweet Flower War there was a famous comedian named Ah Hoon. Famous among the Chinese. An ugly clown of a man. Loyal to the On Leong. His grand finale was, and this supposedly laid them in the aisles, an impersonation of Mock Duck firing his guns blindly until he would roll over, ass over teakettle. Guess you had to be there, right? That's what the Hip Sing thought too. They were losing this war badly and now they were being made fun of in public by a clown. Word went out that Ah Hoon was a dead man and he would never see the sun rise after his next performance.

"Even though City Hall never went out of its way to keep one Chinaman from killing another, the rising tide of blood was starting to offend the sensibilities of the rest of the city. This bald-faced death threat was just the opportunity the cops had been looking for to show that they could handle a few uppity Chinese. That night they turned up at the theater in force. There were probably more Irish in Chinatown altogether that night than there were in all the bars in Brooklyn. The chief of police himself escorted Ah Hoon from his apartment to the theater. I imagine a load of innocent Chinese men took a whopping nightstick to the head for looking this way or that to some cop's dislike, but there was going to be law and order on Doyers Street.

"Poor Ah Hoon didn't even want to do his act that night! When he heard he was a marked man, he wanted to take the next train out of town, but the cops and the On Leong made him take the stage that night. They had something to prove. He didn't. But he waited in the wings and sweated through the acrobats leaping over each other. He agonized through the singer's songs, trying to peer into the darkness to see where the bullet or knife or hatchet was going to come from. He probably came close to having a heart attack every time the gas lamps sputtered and popped downstage. But all the time the cops and the On Leong men reassured him that all would be well. He was protected. He would live.

"Can you imagine anyone having a better reason to have stage fright than poor Ah Hoon? He walked out onstage that night and the first person he saw front and center was Mock Duck, grinning up at him.

But there were the American police to the left and right of his mortal enemy. Ah Hoon took a deep breath, wished he were in a faraway place, and dove into his act. He didn't change a word and by all accounts he was very, very funny that night. Even Mock Duck laughed at the impersonation. When it was time for the curtain call, the police swept him offstage before his first bow and an encore was out of the question. The point had been made: Ah Hoon had survived the performance.

"Well, the On Leong men went wild that night. Fireworks exploded in the sky over Chinatown, their brightness dimmed somewhat by the eerie fog. Hip Sing men were burned in effigy and humiliated in songs and jeers. To the On Leong men, the survival of Ah Hoon had proven that the Hip Sing were no longer the threat they had once posed and that the war was won. Meanwhile the cops hustled Ah Hoon to a cheap room in a cheap hotel next to the theater. They had rented it just to ensure that nothing would happen to tarnish their reputation as protectors of the weak and innocent and funny.

"The apartment had just one room. Everyone on the floor used the same washroom at the far end of the hall. The other apartments along the hall had been cleared of occupants for the night. Didn't matter if they had paid in advance, lived there for years, or had no place else to go. They were rousted. There were no closets in the room, but several small cupboards. There was a bed. There was one window, but it had been jammed into a stuck position for years. A two-inch gap let a little air into the stuffy room, but the window could be neither forced open wider nor lowered more. Three stories down was a dead-end alleyway barely the width of a broad-shouldered man. Three cops were positioned at its mouth, preventing any entrance. Opposite the window, about three feet away, was the solid brick wall of a building. That particular side was unmarred by a single door or window, featureless and rising another four stories beyond Ah Hoon's floor. Cops on foot and horseback blocked the front and back entrance to the hotel. Ten officers stood in the hallway outside Ah Hoon's room. A big Swede cop of impeccable moral fiber, at least of no discernible vice, was placed before Ah Hoon's door.

"An hour after sunrise, the chief of police led a phalanx of reporters, photographers, reformers, and politicians past the few remaining On Leong revelers, into the hotel, up to the third floor, down the line of ten cops standing at attention, and up to the big Swede. The chief of police himself proudly opened the door to introduce Ah Hoon to the rest of his life and announce to the world that the resolve of the Hip Sing tong had been broken and that peace would reign forever and for all time in Chinatown.

"The bullet hole had made a perfect dot in the center of Ah Hoon's forehead, giving the appearance of a third eye. He sat cross-legged on his bed, stiff and cold in a pool of his own drying blood. Legend has it that it wasn't even a bullet hole, it was the touch of a demon.

"Flies were already buzzing curiously about his head, which faced the single window. Still opposite a solid brick wall. Still jammed at less than two inches open. And as the chief of police roared his outrage and the flashbulbs popped, and as the word spread through Chinatown like a flash fire that the Sweet Flower War was over and the Hip Sing, not the On Leong, had won, and as an entirely new celebration began, the wide-eyed expression on Ah Hoon's face seemed to say one simple thing:

"Now that's funny!"

Gibson closed his fist around the tin stallion and reopened it. It had vanished. "The winds changed that morning, and after months of coldly clinging to every nail and stone and board, the Chinatown death cloud rolled back out to sea and vanished as completely as the life from Ah Hoon's body." He closed his fingers into a fist again and then opened them suddenly. A fresh cigarette, tip glowing, now lay crooked between his first two fingers. A simple French drop with a flourish for dramatic punctuation. His tale was told. He inhaled the smoke deeply and waited for the reaction. He could tell a lot about a fella by the way he reacted to a story or a magic trick. They either bought it, didn't, or tried to find some little flaw that could let them feel like they hadn't been conned into enjoying it when they really had. He figured Hubbard for the last type.

"The cops were in on it."

Gibson was right. "They weren't. And you forgot what I asked in the first place," he reminded Hubbard, the booze making him sound more arrogant than he wanted to be. "I asked you to tell me what's real and what's pulp."

"Well." Hubbard thought a moment. "The way Mock Duck fired his guns sounded kind of pulp."

Gibson shook his head. "True story."

"When all her fingers got cut off?"

Again Gibson shook his head.

"What happened to Sweet Flower?" Hubbard asked.

Gibson shrugged. "No one knows. Some say she may have killed herself. Others suppose her husband kept her sequestered in his house until he died. But no one really knows."

It looked like Hubbard was about to speak again when he was suddenly interrupted by a strong cough from the bar behind him. When they looked to see who had coughed, the man began to speak.

"Actually, it's not fairly common knowledge, so I'm not surprised you passed over this, Mr. Gibson, but Sweet Flower, considered defiled, was driven from the house of her husband and ended up living at the mercy of others."

Gibson looked at the tall man leaning against the bar placidly smoking his pipe and found himself gritting his teeth. What the hell brought *him* out tonight?

"It's a trick question," said a man from behind them. "Because the whole story is true. If it were pulp it would have a better ending."

Dent.

"It's real if it's a lie. If it's a pack of lies," Lester Dent said with definitive superiority, "it's a pulp."

Gibson tried not to let his expression change. Dent. Here. Tonight. What were the odds? Everyone said he was a teetotaler anyway. But here he was in the White Horse hoisting a mug of beer and looking as smug as an ape on a pile of bananas. Of course there was a good chance that Dent had dropped off his latest *Doc Savage* manuscript at Street & Smith earlier and decided to celebrate with a beer. For a moment Gibson wondered just how many books Dent was up to, then decided he didn't care. At that moment.

"Not to say that there can't be true stories in pulps, but most true stories don't have good endings. Pulps need great endings. Mr. Gibson's tale doesn't have a good ending. In fact, it has no ending. The problem with the Tale of the Sweet Flower War is that Mr. Gibson ends it just when it's about to turn into pulp."

Gibson felt his blood rising. "I can't believe you're going to lecture me on what makes great pulp. I am pulp."

"You're not pulp. The Shadow is pulp. Doc Savage is pulp. In fact, I will tell you what makes pulp. Of course there's blood, cruelty, fear, mystery, vengeance, heroes, and villains. That's just a good foundation. To make true pulp, really great stomach-churning, white-knuckle, turn-your-hair-white pulp, you have to fill it with a pack of outright lies. Secret identities and disguises." Dent began ticking off the items on his fingers to emphasize the point he was making. "The Yellow Peril. Super-weapons. Global schemes. Hideous deaths. Cliff-hanging escapes. These are the packs of lies you won't find in any slick or glossy or literary hardcover bestseller. Horrors from the grave. Lost lands. Overwhelming odds. Impossible heroics. Unflagging courage. Oh, and I almost forgot! Gun-totin', lingo-slingin' cowboys." He looked at Ron with a mischievous smile, knowing that Hubbard was guilty of perpetrating more than his share of outlandish cowboy tales. "Can't be a true pulp without a genuine gun-slingin', tabaccy-spattin' cowboy, right, Ron?"

As if charged by the sudden burst of electrical tension in the air, Hubbard's gregariousness had increased substantially. He was practically bursting with joy at the fact that Lester Dent knew his name. "That's right, Mr. Dent!" he said loudly and eagerly, nodding like Nipper responding to his master's voice over the Victrola.

Mr. Dent? What was it about the guy that made the kids like Hubbard call him Mr. Dent while he, Walter, was always Walt or Gib or, God forbid, occasionally Wally? Sure, Dent had a good ten years on

Hubbard, but Gibson was still a few years older than Dent. It had to be the height.

Gibson, who barely cracked five eight, had never grown accustomed to being the short man. Gibson had heard from eds and other writers that Lester was the athletic type who liked sailing and mountain climbing. Gibson didn't know if it was true or not but Dent certainly was broad-shouldered as well as tall. Sitting in a chair now as Dent loomed nearby only encouraged his sense of resentment that Dent had shown up here to ruin his night. Dent hadn't even bothered to take his overcoat off. And Christ, he was smoking his damn pipe like some longhair! Couldn't he smoke cigarettes like a normal man? Only eds and socialists smoked pipes.

"Walter." Dent nodded after a long pause in which he seemed to scrutinize Gibson through his thick glasses. His broad mustache twitched in the vaguest manner. Dent, thought Gibson, was tweaking him. Gibson felt the alcohol pulsing through his veins. It was a sensation that began at the back of his neck. He shouldn't have started on the shots so early.

Dent's eyes then flicked back to Hubbard and his hard expression seemed to soften. "It's all about the formula. Just throw enough of the right lies into the mix and add a great ending, and that's the formula for a pulp."

Dent spoke with a flattened midwestern intonation. Gibson tried to remember if he knew whether or not Dent was from Illinois. Dent's inflections were more rough-hewn, he decided, even less sophisticated than Illinois. Arkansas, possibly. Then he remembered. Missouri. Nanovic had told him that once. Definitely Missouri. "To make the Tale of the Sweet Flower War pulp you would have to find out that Ah Hoon's enemies had released a venomous snake into the room through an old mouse hole; what everyone thought was a bullet hole was actually a bite, and the cops never even looked for the serpent, which remained coiled behind a radiator."

"Excuse me. So the Sweet Flower War. It's true? Both of you know about it?" Hubbard asked, looking concerned.

Both men nodded simultaneously.

"What I want to know is how come I never heard of it?" He looked from Gibson to Dent. "And do you know what really happened to Ah Hoon?"

"I don't have a clue. Then again I've never tried to pass the Sweet Flower War off as a pulp. But if I wanted to know for sure, I'd start by going down to Chinatown and doing some research. Right, Walter? You used to be a newspaperman. Weren't you the cub reporter who exclusively interviewed Al Capone behind bars? You know how to research a story. And you used to know how to get that ending." He looked directly at Hubbard. "That's the kind of work you have to do if you want to be a good enough writer to get yourself out of the pulp biz and into the glossies, slicks, and hardcovers. Where the real writing matters."

Gibson took a long drag on his cigarette and blew the cloud in Dent's direction. He knew Dent's beef with him, but he was not going to rise to the bait. He just wasn't going to do it.

"Well, that Sweet Flower yarn. It's a helluva story," Hubbard said to them. "You fellas, uh, mind if I take a crack at writing it? I believe I'd like to."

"Well, I'll tell you, Ron," Gibson said, "the reason the Sweet Flower War was on my mind tonight was that it just inspired a big part of the Shadow story I just dropped off today. *The Art of Murder.* There's a locked-room murder in it which was inspired by the Sweet Flower War. And Lester, you'll be happy to know that I propose a solution. A pulp solution."

In his latest book, his 217th, The Shadow, the hero who knows what evil lurks in the hearts of men, had set out to solve a series of murders which had taken place in the Metropolitan Museum of Art. Priceless antiquities arriving from distant lands had been stolen from a locked vault deep within the museum, while guards inside the vault had been found dead come the morning. Slinking from dark corner to dark corner without making a sound, ink-black in his greatcoat and slouch hat, becoming nearly invisible by merely acting invisible, The

Shadow had penetrated the museum, eluded the well-meaning guards, and entered the vault, where he had, earlier that day as Lamont Cranston, his millionaire playboy alter ego, made a big show of donating a lost Rembrandt. The door had slammed shut behind him: The Shadow had been betrayed by one of his very own agents, the dedicated and devoted who owed him their lives, men and women whose vigilance constantly provided him with information from every corner of the city, and who carried out his orders without question. Except for this one, who had turned rogue.

Sometime before the dawn the vault door had opened and the sinister crime lord behind the plot had entered and, to his delight, laid eyes upon the murdered corpse of The Shadow, enemy to the criminal demimonde. As his hands had fallen upon his new prize, The Shadow's eerie laugh—a haunting, piercing, maddening sound which rattled in the black minds of the guilty—had filled the air around him. But the corpse remained still. The crime lord shut himself in the room, knowing it would be safe. At that moment, The Shadow revealed the key to the mystery. A secret panel under the floor flipped up and The Shadow leapt out, nickel-plated .45s drawn. The corpse in The Shadow's coat had been none other than the traitorous agent, who had been lying in wait under the floor. When he had attacked, The Shadow's justice had been swift and merciless, as it would now be with this evildoer. The struggle to the death began.

In the morning, when the museum guards opened the locked room, three dead bodies were found inside beside a note from the mysterious Shadow explaining all, identifying the villains, and giving directions to the location of the rest of the stolen art. In the resulting confusion and general throng of visitors to the scene of the crime to examine the secret hiding spot, no one had noticed as one of the corpses suddenly arose and vanished into the crowd. Later, no one would be able to say for sure whether there had actually been a third body.

"Trapdoor? Not bad. It's pulp." Dent puffed on his pipe. "Of course, I went completely pulp when I proposed a solution in the very first issue of *Doc Savage.* I had a Mayan with a rifle scale the girders of the unfinished top floors of the Chrysler Building and take a shot at Doc Savage, who was ten blocks away. Of course, he missed because his target was a decoy statue. I'm sure you read it, Mr. Gibson. It was just six years ago. Right after the Golden Vulture disappeared."

And there it was. The Golden Vulture. He'd brought it up. All of a sudden Gibson could sense Dent's particular dislike of him. It was there in his penetrating gaze, and Gibson felt a sudden rising pang of guilt, which he tried to force back down with angry self-righteousness.

"The Golden Vulture," Hubbard interrupted. "What's that?"

"Like the Sweet Flower War, it's a story that's become a legend. And like the murder of Ah Hoon, it's something only two people know the truth about. The one who held the gun and the one who got shot."

Gibson leapt to his feet. He was quivering with anger. "Why don't you call a spade a spade and tell me what you want to say, Dent?"

Dent took a step forward from the bar and drew himself up and over Gibson, looking down at him. "I just did. Anyway, it's all just spilled ink, Mr. Gibson," Dent said. He put his beer stein down in front of Hubbard, who, having been oblivious to the tension, was now registering an expression of complete surprise at their open hostility. "I believe I'm done," Dent said. "I'll see you around."

"Not around, Dent." Gibson put the palm of his hand on Dent's chest. For a moment Gibson thought that the brick wall he could feel under Dent's jacket and shirt was muscle, but then he realized what his palm was on. If Dent had placed his hand on Gibson's chest, he would have felt the same thing. A Street & Smith–issued notebook was always next to a pulp writer's heart. "Behind. You'll always be behind me. The number two. They're not making Hollywood movies of Doc Savage. Doc's not on the radio. The Shadow is. My Shadow." People were starting to look over at them. Gibson saw men he knew recognize him, whisper about him. He didn't care. It was time to put Lester Dent in his place. "And you can forget about cracking the glossies. You ain't gonna see your name on the cover of the *Saturday Evening Post* or the *New Yorker*. 'Cause you're just a nickel-a-word pulp monkey like me, selling daydreams at wholesale prices to soda jerkers in Boise and schoolboys in Kansas City while your house name, Kenneth Robeson, gets all the glory! So take that, and your Doc Savage oath, and blow it out your pipe."

Gibson knew Dent would take the first swing. When he swiped at him, Gibson was going to try to punch his lights out with one hit. He even had the spot on his chin that he was going to go after. Then the big man would probably pummel him into a pulp. He had only been in a few scraps in his life, two of those in the army and one in the Bowery, but those had been years ago. On the plus side he had come out of those dustups better than the other guys. Instead of making an aggressive move, Dent looked passively down at the floor for a moment. For some reason this made Gibson even angrier. Why wouldn't the guy just put his mitts up?

"I may not be Jack London, or Ernest Hemingway, but I will make it out of the pulps and into the glossies," he said. He put on his hat, his eyes almost disappearing beneath the brim. Then he nodded toward Ron. "Ron, it was nice seeing you."

Ron cast about for something to say. "How about coming by the Knickerbocker on Friday?"

"Your pulp writers mixer? I just might." Dent puffed on his pipe to make sure it was burning. Without looking at Gibson he said, "That soda jerker and that schoolboy? They're good people. Until I get out of the pulps they'll get my best month after month. I know you're happy to just do pulp—that's the big difference between us—but are you still giving your readers your best?" He walked slowly around the table, deliberately in no hurry as he headed toward the door.

"Holy . . . ," muttered Hubbard as Gibson dropped into his chair and swallowed another drink.

"Yep." Gibson sighed. The anger was evaporating. The gaze of the spectators was moving on. "A regular Algonquin roundtable here at the White Horse Tavern. Without the sex. Or the witty banter. But mostly without the sex."

"What the hell was that about?"

"*The Golden Vulture.* It's his beef with me."

"So what's the Golden Vulture? A legend? A statue like the Maltese Falcon?"

"It's a story. Just a goddamned book." He wanted to say that it was something that he felt bad about but he couldn't bring himself to admit it. "When you get the number one and number two bestselling writers in America together, there's bound to be some rivalries. Some misunderstandings. Some shit."

"Why don't you try and straighten things out with him?"

Gibson shrugged. "Because I'm still number one and Doc Savage is still number two."

"You mean Lester Dent?"

"Of course."

He waited for Hubbard's contemptuous response. Something deserved that would just wither his spirit. He still felt like he needed the pounding from the fight with Dent that he hadn't received. Combat might have vindicated him, at least restored his honor. Instead he had received nothing from his rival but a lecture. His own notebook felt heavy in his breast pocket against his chest. He carried it out of habit, but had he made any entries in it lately? Weren't all the notes and observations in it kind of stale? Maybe Dent was right. Maybe he hadn't been delivering his best lately.

Instead the young man asked, "Do you guys really make a nickel a word? 'Cause I'm only making two and a half cents. What do you think I can do to make more?"

Gibson decided at that moment, as Hubbard spoke, that not only was Nanovic going to pay for all the drinks tonight, but the ed was about to drop a substantial down payment on his future bar tab.

"I got a boat back in Washington. Sure do miss her," Hubbard rattled on. "You know, I went to China once. It was okay. You get better Chinese food here, though."

Gibson smiled to himself. Like any pulp writer worth his salt, Hubbard told his tales well and half-believed his own bullshit. Believing was essential.

"Tell me all about China," Gibson said. And as the other writer launched into what was sure to be a wildly entertaining story full of plausible lies, gratuitous distortions, and outrageous half-truths, he ordered another round.

EPISODE TWO

Howard Lovecraft knew he was going to die. It was a horrible thing to know.

He had always been obsessed with his death. Even as a child he had imagined, in evocatively vivid detail, what his funeral would be like. The eight-year-old Howard had envisioned an open-casket viewing in the small Providence chapel his family attended. There would be lots of candles, an imported pipe organ (the chapel only had a tinny piano), and a tiny mahogany coffin lined with red silk. He would be serenely beautiful in a very adult black suit with long pants, and nestled on a soft, white satin pillow. There would be no wailing or cries of despair, only gentle weeping and perhaps a whispered apology from Howard's father for the way his choices in life had led directly to his son's present state.

In his teens, perhaps to compensate for his growing shyness and awkwardness in all situations not directly involving any family member, Howard had imagined his funerals as grand expressions: New Orleans jazz parades with a solemn procession accompanied by a somber *thomp-thomp* cadence on the way to Swan Point Cemetery, the citizens of Providence lining the streets, and then a boisterous explosion of music and celebration upon its return. There had been a somber midnight burial accompanied by a distant bagpipe player shrouded in graveyard mist. He had even conceived of an elaborate and very satisfying Viking funeral to be launched in fiery fury from the shores of the Cape; its light would be a beacon to the cod fleet through a long, dark night. In later years, after he had forgotten most of his fantasy scenarios, he still would occasionally recall this one fondly and with approval. He had in the end, however, made other arrangements.

Lightning was followed, after a count to ten, by thunder. The heart of the storm was five miles away. Wisps of Bing Crosby's voice reached him like puffs of a gentle breeze from a distant land. Someone had tuned the RCA a floor below to a Broadway song review show and Bing was singing a Cole Porter tune that had been big last year, "You're the Top." Howard couldn't remember what show it was from. It might have been a movie, as well. Howard didn't go to the theater or the pictures.

Howard desperately wanted a cigarette. The last bout of wracking spasms had ended and the pain had receded somewhat. He knew the agony would return, worse each time, forcing him to curl up into a moaning ball, but before it happened, he needed a smoke to steady and prepare himself. He forced himself to climb out of the uncomfortable bed. His cigarettes sat on a table on the other side of the hospital room. The green and white tiles were refreshingly cool against his feet. His legs were a little wobbly, but he crossed the room with the stability and dignity requisite of a scion of the Phillips line. His mother would have been proud of how her little boy was holding up under the strain. He had been very proper. A good Phillips. She would have liked to have known that he had risen to the occasion.

He lit his cigarette and willed himself to the open window, where he exhaled his first lungful out into the night. The cold rain fell in great sluicing torrents, spattering heavily across the parking lot. If he put his hand out into the night air, even if only for an instant, he would draw it back as wet as if he had plunged it into the pitcher of water near his bedside. The next bursting crack of lightning was followed by an ominous flickering in the lights in his room. Dependable as ever—a mere rumor of heavy weather could cause the Providence power system to collapse. He watched, fascinated, as the lightbulbs struggled to regain their brightness for a moment, only to dim again. Electricity delivery in Providence was not an exact science; it was more of a game of chance. The lightbulbs seemed to settle into drawing less electricity than before, and though they flickered erratically, the light they provided seemed somewhat steady. He let the cool, damp air caress the long, gaunt face that children had always taunted him about, calling him "horse" or "Man o' War."

The cigarette tasted good. Great, in fact.

He wanted his mother.

For a moment he thought he heard her voice, but then he realized with disappointment that it was her sister, his Aunt Annie, in the hallway. She was pleading with the doctor for more information about her nephew's condition. She wasn't convinced about the stomach cancer diagnosis. Howard smiled grimly. Of course she was right; no one gets stomach cancer in three days. He had had to lie and tell her that for months now he'd been feeling pains in his gut which he'd been ignoring. She still didn't understand how he could become so ill so fast. That's what she was pestering the doctor about in the hallway. Aunt Annie was sweet and good but not the smartest of her sisters, and now she had grown old as well and the afflictions of her age were often upon her mind. She and Howard had lived together in Providence in the devastating years since his mother had died raving beyond the bounds of human sanity in the asylum.

Howard had given Aunt Annie complicated instructions to be executed upon his death. He was worried that she was nearing a point of hysteria which would incapacitate her when he needed her the most. For the first time in his life, now that he was dying, he had real plans.

Outside, standing at the edge of a pool of light from a streetlamp, a man was looking up at the hospital. At Howard's room. His hat was pulled down to conceal his face and his open coat blew around him in the wind. A haunter, Howard thought. A haunter in the dark. From far off he thought he could hear a man laughing wildly; someone must have switched the RCA to *The Shadow.* It was Sunday night, after all. The man staring at his room was swallowed by sudden darkness the next instant when the lights of Providence dimmed again. The strangest thought emerged in Howard's mind—that perhaps it had actually been The Shadow. His old friend Walter Gibson's Shadow, come to pay his last respects. A flash of lightning illuminated the area where the man had been standing, and Howard was startled to see that he had vanished completely from sight. He cursed his imagination, the instrument which he had called upon so many times in the past to deliver him to literary greatness but which had only offered up a dark mythology that the world had ignored resoundingly. So many times, as he sat down at the typewriter, he had begged for the story that issued forth to be about something that was, well, if not normal, then at least something that normal people wanted to read. But in the end, he wrote what he was miserably and helplessly compelled to. And now, as he waited to die, with no more words to write, his own mind did not have even the dignity to offer up hallucinations of his own creation, only The Shadow. Although this was mortifying, he had to admit that in the end, that vision was ultimately preferable to his own creation, the great dark god Cthulhu, with his dripping tentacled mouth and dreams which caused madness.

Madness.

His father had died insane as well. For five years when Howard was still a young boy, his father had been locked away in a hospital in Chicago. For five years Howard had been told that his father had been paralyzed in an accident and lay in a dark slumbering coma. For five years while Howard had prayed every night that his father would awaken and return home refreshed, his father had staggered around a gray hospital room, naked and shorn and screaming at phantoms. Aunt Annie had finally told him the truth about his father and the cause of his terrible dementia, syphilis, only in the past year. She could bear the shame alone no longer.

Howard closed his mind against the sound of Aunt Annie's voice in the hallway. Stomach cancer. He had assumed he would die in the grip of madness as his parents did, but as another great crashing wave of pain broke over him, he realized he had rarely experienced such mental clarity. He had to protect his aunt the way she and her two sisters, including his mother, youngest of the three, had protected him about his father. He had been able to grow up under the romantic delusion that his noble father was only trapped in a dark spell like an old king in a legend and that any day might bring his return. His aunts and his mother had given him hope at an age when he had needed hope. When he could still believe. Now he could protect Aunt Annie. By dying.

The six-minute smoke. That's how they advertised his Lucky Strike cigarettes, and he was three minutes into it. There was another flash, the bolt of lightning clearly visible across the skyline. The thunder followed quickly—five seconds. Two and a half miles away. The hospital wing was quiet now. Aunt Annie had followed his doctor out of earshot, still pleading with him to help Howard.

Death would be cold.

He looked at his reflection in the mirror: his long face, always somewhat equine, was now a skull barely covered by a thin layer of barely living tissue. His eyes were wild circular orbs, gleaming and alive against the dying flesh. He felt the emotion roll up from deep inside him; it rocked his body as much as the pain had a moment before. Tears began to fall onto his cheeks. Sadness. He felt sadness and regret for the moments off his life. He missed ever knowing how it felt to be loved by a father—his father. He wished he had made a success out of his marriage, had been a better husband, had found a way to love Sonia and be loved by her. Why a divorce? There had been love there. Where was she now? Chicago? Cleveland? Back in New York? And how would she find out about him? And what would she think? Would she shed more tears than he was shedding now? She had wanted a different path for them than the one he had chosen and clung to. A writer. As if that career could restore his family name to the station his mother had dreamt of. Perhaps had he risen to the stature of Mark Twain. But what a mess he had made of that. Not even good enough to be considered a second-rate Poe. He had written the worst tales for the lowest of the low—the pulps—and even they had shunned him. If only he had had the sense to stop early on. Become a professor of English or a journalist or anything but a failure to his family. He had always thought there was more time. There should have been. If only his path hadn't forced him to translate research papers from science to English at the Providence Medical Lab. He never would have discovered that damned island. Never would have made that nightmare trip. Never would have entered the abyss. Never would have had to find himself facing the cold. If only—

If only his mother were still alive.

"Howard." He heard his name spoken aloud and it startled him. He twisted around, the motion painful. The voice hadn't belonged to his doctor.

His eyes fell upon the figure of the person who had called his name, his murderer. The man suspended himself in the doorway on shaking arms. Rainwater dripped from his soaked coat. He clutched a dripping felt fedora in one clawlike fist. His head was bare and water drops slid easily over his bald, fleshy scalp. Howard could see that their skin shared the same nearly translucent yellow coloring, arteries clearly visible beneath. The man's deadening eyes were shining and desperate, like cold, hard anthracite. Jeffords. Howard realized instantly that it had been Jeffords he had seen outside in the flash of lightning, and not any Shadow, and he knew why the glimpse had caused him to shudder. In another instant the thought crossed his mind that the two of them might be mistaken for a pair of syphilitics and he was afraid that people might think he had died like his father after all.

"You sneak son of a bitch," Jeffords hissed at him. To Howard, Jeffords didn't look nearly as afflicted as his own reflection had. Of course, Jeffords had been farther away when all hell broke loose and was a more robustly healthy man to begin with than Howard had ever been. "Where is it?" Why, he might live on for days yet. In agony, Howard pleasantly assured himself. But he would still be able to perpetrate great harm to Aunt Annie in that time. That's what Howard could protect her from. Jeffords. And Towers.

Paul Malmont

Howard sighed. He thought it would be an extremely defiant gesture to light up another cigarette now and have a puff before answering; to show Jeffords that he was no longer afraid of him. But the cigarettes were still on the table and he was still by the window. And he was still afraid of Jeffords. Terrified. He held his hands open to indicate that he had nothing for Jeffords. "Gone," he said simply.

"You misguided bastard!" Jeffords took a couple of steps into the room and looked around as if he expected to see what he was looking for just lying around. "Don't bullshit me."

"I'm not," Howard explained. "It wouldn't have done us any good anyhow. Don't you understand that? Look at us. We never had enough time. None of us did."

A look of understanding, horrified understanding, dawned across Jeffords's face. His shoulders sagged as if all hope were being crushed out of him. He looked at Howard as if trying to make sense of this strange, dying little man. He clapped a hand to his forehead. Jeffords always prided himself on being a problem solver, Howard remembered. He was now a problem for the man to solve.

Howard felt he had to make another attempt to explain himself. "Short of going back to the isle, destroying *this* was the only thing I could think of."

"The only thing! The only thing! Christ, Lovecraft! I might have thought of something." He took a couple of steps closer.

"Your thoughts on the matter were perfectly clear." Howard could see that Jeffords's despair was beginning to turn into something more menacing. He wished he would hear Aunt Annie's voice and the doctor's in the hall again. He swallowed hard; even that was painful. "I was saving it from you."

"You've killed us both," he said. "You're a goddamned murderer."

Howard stared at him. Then he shrugged. "I didn't take us to the isle."

Jeffords leapt at him. Howard was so surprised he could only blink. Jeffords's hands wrapped around his throat. Howard was still so uncomprehending of the actual events unfolding upon him that he had time to think that Jeffords's hands were soft and smelled like Ivory

30

soap and Burma-Shave. This was in the time that it took for their bodies to fall, ungainly, to the floor. Howard's elbow cracked upon impact, bearing the full weight of his own sickened body, and Jeffords's. The shock and knowledge of the imminent awesome pain made him open his mouth to gasp in air. That's when he understood he was being choked to death. He found his body's urge to struggle. The pain in his chest grew. He could feel his body panicking; his legs began kicking. His arms began pawing at Jeffords. Something exploded in his chest. Still his mind resisted.

"I'm going to hunt you down in hell, Lovecraft." Jeffords's face was turning red from the exertion. It made his sickly skin glow orange, like that of a deranged jack-o'-lantern.

Howard's gaping mouth began to turn up at the edges. He was trying to grin. Saliva drooled from the corners of his mouth. His chest began to convulse. Jeffords pulled his hands back, unsure of himself. Howard sucked in a gale of air, which instantly escaped from him in a whooping laugh.

It was the best he had ever felt. Jeffords was looking at him queerly. Howard owed him an explanation for his good humor.

"I've got other plans," he whispered, his voice a croak. There were red spots floating in his vision. He could barely see. He couldn't breathe well at all. It wasn't even his windpipe; some mechanism in his chest was not drawing air. He could feel his grin, though. He had a lot to look forward to.

He heard a scream which sounded as if it came from the bottom of the deepest ocean. Aunt Annie. She was so far away. He could feel Jeffords lift himself from his body. His body instinctively tried to draw itself into a fetal position, trying to find some kind of protection from the pain without and within. Some of the redness cleared from his vision. He saw Jeffords's feet running away from him. He saw Aunt Annie and the doctor, their faces aghast, in the doorway. Saw Jeffords push past them. The doctor in pursuit. Aunt Annie's hand in his. She looked like his mother. His mother should have been here when he died. He should have been with her when she died.

"Our Father, who art in heaven," she began softly. Tears were beginning to fall from her eyes. He could feel his writer's mind, ever present, struggling to preserve all the little details of the moment. There were shouts down the corridor. Aunt Annie smelled of lavender. The floor needed grout in between the tiles. Agony was beautiful. "Hallowed be thy name."

He shook his head at her. She stopped praying. His mouth moved, trying to form words. She leaned in. She was weeping now; it would be hard for her to understand him. He knew she felt as if she had failed her sister and failed their entire family line. He clutched her hand harder, trying to reassure her, staring into her eyes. From far away he heard music. She understood that he needed to communicate and stifled her sobbing.

"Is it cold?" he asked her, desperately. "Is it?" Everything depended upon that.

She nodded. "It's very cold."

A moment before he died, he wished the moment of death would bring some clarity or enlightenment or revelation. But there would be nothing.

That was his last thought.

It was cold.

EPISODE THREE

WORD ON the street was John Campbell had work for writers. And that was the word The Flash needed to hear.

The Flash paused by the newsstand at the corner of Seventh Avenue at the edge of the Street & Smith building to look for Campbell's mag. This particular newsstand, run by a set of old Italian twins, had all the mags put out that month—not just by Street & Smith, the biggest publisher in the world, but Popular, Frank A. Munsey, Clayton, Thrilling, Culture, and Pro-Distributors Publishing. There were over two hundred mags decorating their stalls this month. Two hundred titles. The newsstand looked like an ink truck had crashed into it. A sharpster could tell instantly how well any given mag was selling by where it stood on the racks of this newsstand. If that same sharpster knew whether or not a certain mag was hot, said sharpster might have an angle on squeezing more than a penny a word out of that mag's ed. The Flash considered himself a sharpster.

Astounding Stories, Campbell's mag, wasn't hanging on a clip from a clothesline out in front like the very best-selling titles, the hero books like *Doc Savage* or *The Shadow* or *G-8 and His Battle Aces,* but it was clearly visible, full cover on display, on the first rack above the slicks like *Collier's* and *Vanity Fair* and the *New Yorker,* and the chewing gums and chocolate bars. On the same row as *Astounding* were some of the other bestsellers that month, titles that were flying out of newsstands, soda shops, and drugstores all across America: *The Spider, Thrilling Detective, Adventure, Thrilling Adventures, Amazing Stories, Blue Book, Weird Tales, Dime Mystery, Phantom Detective,* and the granddaddy of them all, still going strong after more than forty years, *Argosy.*

The cover of each and every mag on the newsstand was a brilliant four-color explosion of breathtaking action captured forever in a frozen moment of suspense: the instant before a righteous fist impacted against a gnarled and snarling face; a plane spiraling disastrously toward earth as its hero struggled to untangle his parachute from its tail; Art Deco skyscrapers crumbling under a devastating alien onslaught. The Flash loved the mags' cover art, though he knew how much it was derided within the industry and without. He knew it was what sold the mags to begin with and then kept folks coming back to find out what was in them. Ten *million* of them a month. Each buying an average of three mags. That meant that thirty million pulps, give or take, were being read by America each and every month! It was the cheapest and most popular form of entertainment in the country, and as long as the covers beckoned from the newsstands, it would continue to be so.

Behind the first row were the mags that still sold consistently well but just were not gangbusters. Their bold legends were clearly visible but most of the artwork was covered by other mags. The Flash was disheartened to see that many of these titles were westerns and two-fisted tales—his bread and butter. *Thrilling Western,* for example, had done well by him and he by it, but it would never pay more than two and a half cents a word. Same for *All-American Stories* and *Thrilling Wonder Stories.* None of them had broken out while he had been writing for them. Probably none of them ever would.

The third row of mags were all pulled up from behind the second row so men could see the mags that boys couldn't bring home. In addition to the mushy *Love, True Love, Romance,* and *True Romance* titles were *Spicy Adventure Stories, Spicy Mystery Stories, Spicy Detective Stories,* even

Spicy Western Stories published by a man named Donenfeld. Their cover artists were inventive in coming up with endlessly daring ways to put glamorous and scantily clad women in harm's way. They knew how to deliver the goods. These were the mags that had imperiled the entire industry recently, as Mayor La Guardia was so offended by their lurid scenes that he was threatening to have the garbagemen rip them from the newsstands as they executed their rounds. Some of them were making good on the mayor's threats. Some newsstand owners had recently taken to ripping the covers from the pulps before placing them on the racks, as if that would help. The Flash had certainly never written for any of the mags on this row, but their covers had given him plenty of stimulating moments. Every writer he knew had a stash of the men's mags in one of his desk drawers.

He had also never written, nor would ever condescend to write, for the final row. This was the row whose titles were mostly blocked by the arousing arrangement of the men's mags before them. Here were the shudder and menace mags like *Terror Tales, Horror Stories, Strange Detective Mysteries* (Who was strange? The detectives or the mysteries?), *Eerie Stories,* and others. Dreck. The bottom of the bottom of the literary barrel. This was the ghetto where that Lovecraft fellow had tried to eke out a name for himself. An assortment of dark perversions and decadences, never permeated by the light of a well-written phrase or inspiring insight. Many of these mags were the literary equivalent of the filthy eight-page Tijuana bibles the old Italians hid under their newspapers and would sell you if you asked for the "funnies." He supposed that somebody must be reading them. Publishers ran their mags on a slim profit margin that didn't allow for much misjudgment of the public's desires. If a mag slipped only one month, it could be gone from the stands the next, its publisher bankrupt, its eds pounding the pavement and looking for work.

He knew in his bones he was destined for the top tier. After all, he was The Flash. Sometimes (when an ed demanded) he was also Kurt von Rachen, L. Ron Hubbard, and Frederick Engelhardt. But he liked The Flash best of all. Of course it wasn't a name he published under, like the others. It was a nickname given to him by his agent, Ed Bodin, because he could write so damn fast. He liked The Flash a hell of a sight better than Red, which was what he had most often been nick-named until he embarked on his writing career, on account of his shock of thick red hair. But these days, Red was gone and no one in New York or Hollywood need ever know that he had existed. There was only The Flash.

Fact is, he earned the name outright. He was blazingly fast at turning out stories. Like a machine. He wrote faster than anyone he knew, except maybe Gibson. And Dent. It was just like when he had been a boy in Montana and could read earlier and faster than anyone else. He took great pride in his ability to write fast, and to hell with writer's block. Sometimes he felt like he was a river of words, that they flowed out of him with unimaginable force to soak the pages churning through his Remington. It was as if his imagination was fed by a deep spring. He had every confidence that the wellspring would never run dry. Why should it? It hadn't yet. He knew his mind and never doubted it.

Gibson's story about the Sweet Flower War had been pretty damn good, all right, he thought. He could use a killer story like that to bust things wide open. But if both Gibson and Dent had drawn on it, they'd know where it came from if he wrote it again, even if he used a pen name. Still, it was tough to let that one go. Really good stories were hard to come by.

These days, every two weeks, he had a new story to sell to the mags. It wasn't easy. It was righteously hard work, tougher than laying tracks or stowing cargo had ever been. But he did it because he loved writing. He loved using his mind and his fingertips to move mountains, shape the universe, wreak havoc. Rewriting? If a fella knew what he was doing the first time, he wouldn't have to rewrite. Muses? Hell, fear of starvation was the name of his muse. He didn't hold with the theories about motivation, which he overheard other writers talking about at his Knickerbocker gatherings; his characters *knew* what to do. They knew from right and wrong, good and evil. That's all you needed to know about someone to know what they would do. Besides, there wasn't time for motivation. Not when the eds were trying to chisel a guy. The only way to make money in this industry was to write as best a sharpster could, as fast as he could.

His writing had attracted attention too. He actually had a small but loyal group of readers. The eds heard from them occasionally when they would write in and demand more Hubbard. Even if a few of those letters were actually written by The Flash himself, that didn't devalue the bona fide original and unsolicited letters that the eds would receive. His dim glow of fame, within the limited sphere of the mags, had at least made it a little easier to sell stories. When eds received a Hubbard story, they didn't have to read it too carefully anymore. His name on the cover page was a mark of recognized quality. They could publish it easily and it would help sell. Which was the name of the game. So that was one thing he had over both Gibson and Dent: although they were top sellers, nobody in America knew who they were; they were hidden behind house names, Maxwell Grant and Kenneth Robeson. He, on the other hand, was becoming known by his own name.

The top tier, that was his destiny. He knew he'd get there. He loved the pulp business like no one else he knew. Most of the writers he knew were cynical about it, embarrassed by where their fortunes and talents had abandoned them and damned by their ambitions. They longed to be published in hardcover. Read in libraries. Discussed in cafés. They longed to be lionized like the legendary Street & Smith writers: Horatio Alger, Upton Sinclair, Theodore Dreiser, and, most of all, Jack London. The Flash didn't crave the stature of those alumni, or even of Dent and Gibson. Particularly those two men, he felt, were his peers, who owed their elevated positions to the benefits of age and timing more than talent. When he looked desirously at another's career, and chose to emulate its course, the writer could only be Edgar Rice Burroughs.

Tarzana. The thought of it practically made him sigh with longing. Burroughs's ape-man had practically ushered in the pulp age, as publishers sprang up all over the place to try and produce a successful imitation. Through careful control Burroughs had parlayed the character in the funny papers, movies, toys, and games, not to mention a seemingly endless string of new novels and their lucrative international translations. With the money he had made doing this, he had turned around and bought himself a kingdom. A whole valley in California! Just outside of Los Angeles. He built and sold houses on the land to the suckers who wanted to get out of the city. He ran the town council. He was king of the pulp jungle.

Just before the decision to move back to New York had been made, The Flash had been in Hollywood writing a serial movie adventure, *The Secret of Treasure Island.* He had made the pilgrimage to the promised land of Tarzana and seen for himself what it had to offer. It was peaceful and bucolic in the California way. Fragrant orange trees basked in the warm sun, shading the little backyards behind the small houses Burroughs had built and sold.

He could do better, he had decided as he strolled down the elm-lined sidewalks of Tarzana. He had tried to meet Burroughs but the people at his gatehouse said he was otherwise engaged. Imagine being too busy to meet The Flash! He suspected that Burroughs, now an elderly man, might be jealous of The Flash's youth and vitality. Burroughs was richer than Croesus. He had created an empire. By simply writing! Now why wouldn't The Flash himself aspire to do the same?

Tarzana.

To get there he knew he first had to jump from the second row to the clothesline. *Astounding Stories* looked like it might finally be the way. Campbell had already moved it from the second row to the first. It just needed a push to get to the top tier. Then maybe The Flash could land a hero mag for himself.

He turned from the newsstand. It was much colder in New York than it had been a few months ago in Hollywood. A fell winter wind blew off the dank Hudson River, which he could see just west of him. The wind stung the ears and eyes, and he turned up his collar, wishing he had had time to pack a heavier coat. Upon his return from Hollywood, he hadn't even made it up the stone path from the front gate to the white door of his house in Bremerton, Washington, before his wife, Polly, had turned him away. He had had an affair with a starlet, and a jealous former lover of hers had written his wife a letter, ratting him out. He loved his wife and loved being married, and he didn't feel he deserved to be banished from their household just because he had done something stupid out of loneliness. The suitcase he had brought with him to his hotel in New York was the same one he had been carrying when she had appeared in tears upon their front porch. In it then, and now carefully arrayed on his cabinet in the hotel, was an untouched brand-new teddy bear for his son, Ron Jr.; and a china doll for his daughter, Catherine.

Damn, it was cold. He looked at the faces of the men hovering outside the Street & Smith building—anxious men, expectant men, hopeful men. Men who hoped to be able to slip a story to a passing ed in exchange for a few bucks or a break. He realized that no matter how many times the radio played "Happy Days Are Here Again!" or Roosevelt spoke about the next New Deal, the Depression was not over. Especially not for these men. These were the penny-a-word men. Most of them had other jobs and were here on their lunch hour. Some of them spent an entire day out here, trying to scribble stories in notebooks as they waited. The Flash felt a moment of dread. This was the fate that awaited him if he fell to the third row, or farther. Even a guy with talent could end up like Lovecraft. In truth he knew that his moments of weakness, as with that actress, could put him out here on the street faster than failure to anticipate the public taste ever could.

He walked past the line of men, aware that they were staring at him. A tall, gawky teen tried to foist some pages on him but stepped back at the last moment. The teen looked at his face eagerly and then his face fell as he realized that The Flash wasn't an ed. Just a writer.

Francis Scott Street and Francis Shubael Smith had founded the company which took their names in 1855. The firm had made its home in this seven-story, block-long building fifteen years before The Flash was born. Even outside it was possible to feel the deep and persistent thrumming vibrations of the enormous printers, rolling and pounding below the street in the basement; and the binders, which folded the cheap pulp paper into four sections to make a book. Farther up the street he could see the trucks at the loading docks, and the teamsters tossing the bales of freshly printed pulps into them. Some of them were down to their undershirts, even in the chill air, and their coarse language and rough joking reinforced for The Flash that the pulp business was hard work. From the discipline and determination it took to write pulps to the aggressive tactics it took to get them published and onto the newsstands, it was a man's job. He knew of no women pulp writers—even the romances were written by men—and he couldn't name a female artist or ed to save his life. Not that there weren't women in pulps. There were assistants and secretaries.

God, that actress! What had he been thinking?

He put his hand on the door and opened it up. The security guard inside waved him on in. His tenure as president of the Guild had granted him certain privileges; easy access to the Street & Smith building was one of them. The reception lobby was faded and dark. The walls were brown from years of cigarette and cigar smoke (The Flash detested smoking). The carpet was worn from years of shuffling feet. The wood desk was scuffed, and the club chairs were leaking stuffing. In spite of the scent of smoke, he loved it all. He headed for the elevator.

She had had long, loose blond hair and staggering blue eyes and she smelled like an orange grove on the Malibu shores at sunset. She was California incarnate. When he had first been introduced to her on the set, she had been dressed in the wardrobe of an explorer, with tight beige jodhpurs and a crisp white blouse that accented the dark tan of her cleavage. Later he would find that skin to be smooth and warm, covering muscles toned by years spent splashing through the surf. She was utterly without restraint, introducing him to situations and sensations he had never even dreamt of. Her red lips and sharp tongue had peppered his body with kisses; she had devoured him in every way. He had tried to match her enthusiasm; after all, he was a young man in his prime. Not even his own wife had made him feel so powerful in bed as this fierce Hollywood creature.

With a practiced twist of the wrist, the uniformed operator stopped the elevator at the second floor. The cacophony that hit The Flash when the door slid open made him wince. A man wearing a vest and ink-stained apron stepped onto the elevator, carrying a heavy tray of spent lead slugs and space bands. The Flash saw dozens of men just like him sitting in front of machines with giant rollers—the linotype machines. The men were endlessly keying in letter combinations to create the lines of text which would be used to make the molds for the pages the presses waited to print. Hubbard watched with fascination as the man at the station nearest to him slammed a lever back to force his finished page mold, all the letters backwards, into the next level, where molten metal would flow over it and create a mirror cast. This was the room where the type became hot, where the words became real.

The linotype man took the ride to the third floor, the sorting room, where his tray of slugs would be cleaned and sorted by men standing at wooden bins and prepared for the next round. The man gave him a dead-eye look. He didn't care that The Flash was a writer. He didn't care about the pulps. His father when he worked here probably hadn't cared about the mags that they had then, called "dime novels," and even earlier than that, the "penny dreadfuls." If Street & Smith decided tomorrow to print Bibles, he'd show up and carry letters for the Bibles. Just a job. The man exited at the next floor with a bored look at The Flash. Then the operator drew the door shut and the elevator rose again, ascending to the publishing floor, where The Flash stepped off. Campbell's office was at the far end of the long, dark wood-paneled corridor. To his left was the archive, which held the fifty years of man-uscripts published by the house. On his right were offices for writers, artists, and eds. The floor above him, the top floor, held the manage-ment offices, where guys like Henry Ralston worked. The money men. The men who owned The Shadow and Doc Savage.

He shook the tangle of thoughts of Polly and Hollywood from his head. It was time to be The Flash and The Flash was here to sell. He strode with confidence down the hall.

He passed a life-size poster sign of Walter Gibson holding a typewriter. The advertisement boasted that Street & Smith writer Gibson had been recognized as holding the record for writing the most words ever, over a million, about a single character—The Shadow. The man's output was staggering. And so was his impact. Before The Shadow's appearance, all the top tier mags were detective stories. Within a year of The Shadow's first issue all the bestseller mags were heroic avengers who did more than solve a crime; they combated it. It was as if the nation as a whole had decided in one collective moment that they were tired of justice being served after the fact; they wanted it dished out in advance. They didn't want someone to just look out for them, in the middle of this Depression; they wanted someone to protect them. And the pulps were more than willing to accommodate them. According to the poster, Walter Gibson had achieved greatness on his Smith Corona. The Flash sniffed at the numbers. He was easily turning out a hundred thousand words a month, in his estimation. Okay, they weren't about a single character, but he was certainly on track to set some sort of record. If only he had a hero mag, then he would earn the record and the endorsement money.

He sure wished he had a killer idea like that Sweet Flower mystery. He had to admit that he wasn't very good at tracking down stories like that and using them the way Gibson and Dent seemed to. That was one of the reasons the Street & Smith style suited him so well; here most of the ideas, sometimes even the outlines, for stories of the sort he wrote were provided by the eds. It was just the writer's work to put the words to them. He relied much more on his imagination than his life to just make up the goods. So far the words kept bubbling up.

"John Campbell?" He knocked on the door. On its window were stenciled the words ASTOUNDING AND AMAZING. He knocked again. The Flash's palms were sweating. He needed to win Campbell over. He needed something big. Something bold. Something with great heroes, horrifying villains, and beautiful dames. Something astounding and amazing. He heard a rustle from behind the door, a smooth whisper of pages turning.

"Yeah?" The door flew open and the young ed appeared. He was big man, nearly as tall as Lester Dent, and barrel-chested. The Flash caught a glimpse of paper everywhere, both the yellowish browns of cheap pulp and the richer whites of typewriter stock, as if both the newsstand and the men peddling their stories on the sidewalk below had exploded in a blizzard of scattered pages and spilled ink across every available surface in Campbell's office including the floor.

"Ron Hubbard." He stuck out his hand. Campbell took hold of it and gave it a powerful shake. To Hubbard he appeared to be one of those types that advertisers liked to call a man-on-the-go.

"Hubbard," he said. He was either Hubbard's age or younger. "I hear you're a writer."

"As a matter of fact," said The Flash, matching Campbell's grip with vigor and confidence, "I am."

EPISODE FOUR

"AND NOW," the tall thin man with the thatch of white hair announced, his voice ringing out fiercely, "I will attempt to save this sinful woman from the eternal inferno of hell itself!"

The woman held on to a velvet rope for dear life. Below her was a pool of roiling fire. A tendril of sputtering flame climbed busily up the rope, leaving charred strands behind. The woman recoiled in fear and tried to pull herself up but it was clear that her grip was slipping.

"Of course, as every righteous soul knows, the path to salvation lies through the fire." He threw his arms wildly toward the woman, and fireballs leapt from his fingertips. The rope snapped and the woman dropped into the roiling conflagration far faster than anyone could possibly have anticipated. Books and movies have convinced people that a rescuing hand can reach a falling person in the nick of time, but the truth is that the speed is breathtaking and that the moment of rescue is nearly impossible. Voices cried out in terror from onlookers male and female. The fire vanished in a cloud of smoke and heavenly birds flapping into the darkness, and great gasps were heard. The woman floated in the air in the very spot where the flames had been an instant before. She was dressed in a gown of shimmering light, which surrounded her in angelic radiance. The man gestured and slowly the woman descended, as if controlled by a mysterious energy emanating from his hands.

As her feet touched the floor, the audience at the Majestic Theater erupted in rapturous applause. Elderly women fanned themselves excitedly with their programs. Couples turned to each other to express their astounded disbelief. Gibson applauded along. He had seen Blackstone perform the Salvation of Miss Molly illusion dozens of times, and it never failed to impress him with its artful deception and its ability to captivate and impress an audience.

The fireballs from the fingertips were a dazzling new wrinkle, however, and an inspired flourish. He made a mental note to try to figure out how it was done as soon as possible. A flash powder effect was common enough, but he had never heard of one being detonated from what he assumed was some kind of handheld or wrist-attached apparatus. Flash powder was extremely volatile stuff. Anytime the size of a load of powder was doubled, its explosive force multiplied eightfold. Just four ounces, handled recklessly, could do more than remove a limb or an extremity; it could dismember a person. To keep quantities of the explosive somehow attached to reservoirs on his person in close proximity to an igniter was an invitation to disaster for a lesser magician than Blackstone and a reminder to Gibson why his old friend's name was on the marquee.

The bewitching showgirl, one of the bevy of show beauties, bowed and slipped quickly off the stage, no doubt to make another costume change. Blackstone theatrically dabbed some droplets of sweat from his brow with a silk and drank in the applause as he transformed the innocent piece of cloth into the dancing handkerchief, one of his signature pieces. The premiere so far had been brilliant and Gibson could see how much his old friend was enjoying himself.

Gibson had been introduced to Blackstone soon after ghosting biographies for Houdini and Thurston about a decade before. The two had become friends and had collaborated on seven books and dozens of magazine articles about magic over the years.

As Blackstone held the stage, alone in a single spotlight, Gibson could imagine the hullabaloo backstage. Blackstone's team of technicians and performers numbered around fifty; the intense stillness of the man onstage belied the havoc that Gibson imagined was happening mere feet from his back. Blackstone adjusted his bow tie, drew a finger across his thin mustache, then held up his hands in a call for silence, his long fingers spread wide. "Ladies and gentleman," he said in a strong stage voice. "We have a great treat for you tonight. The name of the Great Raymond is known to many of you, as it is throughout the world, as one of the legendary magicians of our time." There was a smattering of applause as some audience members placed the name, although Gibson recognized that Blackstone was being gracious to a brother magician.

Maurice Raymond had been an eclectic yet middling professional magician at his career's apogee, which was more than a few years past now. Just one of that great number of mediocre but serviceable magicians who had sprung up out of nowhere in the previous decade during magic's explosive boom in popularity, performers with no discernible original style—and more importantly, no signature tricks—of their own. Their survival seemed to depend upon presenting budget-conscious versions of the fantastic illusions created by the masters—Thurston, Houdini, Blackstone—to a populace who would never be able to afford to see them otherwise.

"As you may know," Blackstone continued, "this master showman has recently retired from the stage in order to pursue certain occult studies of the deepest and most profound nature."

Once again Harry Blackstone was being charitable. Raymond's shows had declined in quality because of his unwillingness to develop new tricks, and he had quit touring because producers would no longer bankroll his moth-eaten productions. Even though magic shows were not as popular as they had been ten years ago, the public still expected to see new and fabulous extravaganzas, but the Great Raymond had emptied every trick he could from his dusty old bag. Blackstone had surmised to Gibson that with fewer magicians around to crib acts from, Raymond had been unable to sustain his show. Furthermore,

Gibson knew, as Blackstone did and the audience surely did not, that the Great Raymond was ailing.

Blackstone continued in the spotlight, his Michigan accent flattening some of the rounder sounds, "We are thrilled that he has been gracious enough to loan us a special pleasure for the duration of our American tour. She was trained in her mystic art by the greatest of all mentalists, El Cheiro, far from civilization, high in the Peruvian mountains. She has read the minds of kings and queens, emperors and shahs, viceroys and chancellors, presidents and prime ministers. And tonight, ladies and gentlemen, she just might read yours. For seven years she has been one of the star attractions of the Great Raymond's show, as well as his partner in wedlock, and we are proud that she has deigned to join the Blackstone Spectacular for a limited engagement."

Gibson knew she was now part of the show because with Raymond's show in mothballs, Blackstone had been able to sign her at a farm foreclosure price. And she was worth so much more.

"Please give one of your legendary New York welcomes for the woman whose mentalist abilities are sure to convince you of the existence of higher planes of reality, of the existence of worlds unseen and unknown, of the existence of spirits who see all and know all."

A low, mysterious melody began wafting from the orchestra pit, summoning imagined memories of far-flung tropical islands floating on the black Pacific Ocean in the deep of night. "I bring you the astounding, the shocking, the mystifying, the enlightening, the terrifying, the Dragon Lady from the Tibetan Orient, Pearlitzka!"

The spotlight winked out on Blackstone, and another light, hung above the stage, blinked on. It shone into the eyes of the audience. A woman was silhouetted in its beam. Her arms were held high, her back was arched, and her legs were poised in a dancer's position. Light fabric extended from her wrists to the sides of her body, giving her appearance some slight resemblance to a Chinese fan. Gibson could see the rise and fall of her breasts neatly outlined in the light.

"Spirits from the nether regions speak to me of things seen and unseen, of the knowable and unknowable." The girl's husky voice seemed to float out of the air around her. Her arms drew to her side and she turned downstage, a sylph in the light, and bowed. As she stood upright, the house spotlight caught her in its clutches and revealed her to all. Gibson's heart skipped a beat as the light drew out her features.

The woman looked like an Asian of uncommon beauty. Her exquisite baby-doll face was painted white with greasepaint, great swooping teardrops of red Oriental makeup accenting her almond-shaped eyes. Her black hair was piled on her head and held in place with a number of long, thin metal spikes. Her long curved nails were lacquered red. The silk Chinese dress with open sleeves was slit up its side, occasionally revealing the breathtaking legs of a dancer. The silk clung to her skin in a smooth, coolly sensual way.

A stagehand wheeled a rectangular object onto the stage. It was one of the ticket stub boxes from the lobby.

"The spirits will select some of you this evening and tell of things past and present and future." Her voice was light, strong, and clear. "For some of you the things they have to say may be enlightening; for others, terrifying. Only the spirits can know what they know and why they know it. It is for us, the living, to determine what we shall do with the knowledge they choose to share." She unlocked the stub box and extended her arm into it. The audience tittered expectantly; few things enlivened an audience like allowing them to participate in a magic show. Whether being hypnotized, choosing cards, or inspecting chains, the civilians loved to be part of the act.

If they thought about it for two seconds, Gibson thought, they could figure it all out. The box was obviously just a ruse. All the stubs would have the same seat number on them. She could call any number she wanted to, when it came down to it; whoever she called up would obviously be a plant. But the audience was here to be entertained, and surrendering the human desire (or was it an American desire?) to know how everything worked was key to the theater.

"The spirits have spoken!" Pearlitzka called from the stage. Gibson watched everyone look around. "Will the person sitting in seat E2 be kind enough to join me onstage?"

A hand tapped him on the shoulder. "Hey, buddy," a voice whispered in his ear, "that's you! You're in E2!"

"It's only a letter and a number, E2. It shouldn't be hard to find yourself. Of course I could just let the spirits come bring you to me." Her voice had a ring that tickled the base of his spine. He stood up suddenly and waved.

"There he is. There's the one whom the spirits have chosen!" Gibson's palms were sweating, and he swallowed, nervously. He looked back to the exit, which got a laugh. Then he shrugged and gamely marched up the aisle toward the orchestra pit, where an assistant was waiting to direct him up the stage steps.

The beautiful young woman had his hand in an instant and gave it a surprisingly reassuring, and strong, squeeze. Her hand was small and soft. She smelled of sandalwood and jasmine. She looked younger onstage than she had from the auditorium. Her makeup was perfect. Completely in control of the stage, she turned both of them so their bodies faced the audience.

"Do we know each other?" she asked.

He shook his head. There were twitters and whispers from the audience before him. It was hard to see past the footlights and make out faces.

"Do you have a name?" she asked.

He nodded. This time there were guffaws.

"Well, don't keep it to yourself. How about sharing?"

"Walter Gibson," he said sheepishly, and the audience rewarded him with some light applause. He wondered whether if he had said the name Maxwell Grant, it would have garnered more applause than his own name did. Here he stood, the number one bestselling writer in America, creator of the most popular show on radio, and no one even knew who he was.

"You don't mind if I call you Walter, do you, Walter? All right, Walter. Let's see why the spirits have chosen you this evening." She took several steps back from him. He glanced down into the orchestra pit. Some of the musicians were sneaking looks up the slit of her dress. "You work with your hands, they tell me."

"Yeah," he said, not in the least surprised.

"You're not a laborer. You're some kind of skilled craftsman, a sculptor or carpenter. Something that combines the mind and the hands, right?"

"I suppose."

"Wait, it's coming to me. It's not about making something physical; you're more in the nature of an artist or a writer."

He nodded. "I'm a writer."

The audience applauded. She peered at him closely, scrutinizing him. He knew what she was doing. Shotgunning. The technique, adapted by magicians from an old spiritualist routine popular at the end of the last century, required throwing a large amount of random information at the mark and letting them pick out what seemed personally relevant. In their astonishment they would tend to forget about all the other questions and choices that were presented to them and focus on the ones that seemed to concern them. For example, stating that a dead relative was trying to contact a mark was usually a safe place to start because everyone always has a dead relative. Then it was a matter of calling out relatives until a match was found. If one rattled off enough relatives, sooner or later the right one would be hit upon. Shotgunning was occasionally referred to as the Barnum Effect, because it played off people's vanity and desire to believe that someone would actually want to have meaningful contact with them from beyond the grave. People tended to believe a lie told to them about themselves if it was a flattering lie. And to tell a person that someone they had loved was trying to break the boundaries between heaven and earth just to tell them where the fried chicken recipe was hidden was quite flattering indeed.

Her green eyes were lively but critical. Her approach, which had started off in typical fashion, had become fairly specific. She was an expert shotgunner. Maybe the best he had ever seen. "The spirits tell me you carry one picture in your wallet at all times. Do they tell me truly?"

"Yes." How had she known that? He was beginning to feel vaguely uneasy.

"And that picture is . . . I see . . . There is someone far away. Some-one who loves you. The spirits are showing me a little boy. He wears shorts and is holding a baseball."

Reluctantly Gibson slipped his fingers into his wallet and pulled out a photo. The audience broke into applause.

"A little boy, ladies and gentleman. Walter, the spirits want you to know that he . . . Robert . . . thinks of you often and sends his love."

The audience applauded with great enthusiasm. He tucked the pic-ture back into his wallet without saying a word or even glancing at it. Pearlitzka tried to take his hand. He wriggled his fingers free. She seized it and led him in a bow. He turned to leave but she held on to his hand. She looked at him and a puzzled expression crossed her face. She held up her free hand. "It appears the spirits have more for Walter from the world beyond," she said.

"That's okay," he said. "They've said quite enough."

She was silent for a moment. A long moment. Long enough for the audience to begin to grow uneasy. The orchestra vamped. She studied him closely. "Someone you know is dying," she said at last. Her voice had dropped into a much lower register. "He's dying." She closed her eyes; the spectral voice made his flesh shiver. "He's dying right now and he's so afraid. It's so cold."

The audience began to murmur. Someone coughed, nervously.

"No," he said with a shrug. "I don't think anyone I know is dying."

"The spirits are afraid," she said, and her voice was hollow and cold. "The spirits want you to know that . . . he refuses to cross over. His soul is trapped between our plane and theirs. They are trying to help him but he won't go. He won't admit he's dead. He says he was mur-dered! You have to help him! There are lives to save. You have to help."

He could feel the audience slip away from her. He looked at her face and realized she had lost the thread of her patter; she seemed dis-tracted. "Help who?" he said, loudly. "The only one dying here is me!" The drummer rapped out a rim shot for him; the sound of it plucked at her stage instincts.

She recovered in an instant and looked at the audience. "Obviously a comedy writer!" she told her audience with a wink, and they applauded. But her hand had turned cold and damp with sweat. She released him and he retreated to the safety of his seat as quickly as he could, while she summoned the next willing mark to the stage.

His heart was pounding. He felt a tap on his shoulder. It was the man sitting behind again who had alerted him to his fate a little while ago. "Hey, pal," the man said, "too bad she's married, huh?"

"Yeah," he replied, angry at the man and angrier at Pearlitzka. "Tough."

EPISODE FIVE

"**H**OW DID you know about my son?" he demanded.

"What?"

"Robert! How did you know I had that picture in my wallet?" he said to her later, back in his apartment. She was naked and glistening in sweat which had soaked even into her loosened hair, giving her a wild leonine look. He was naked too and lying on the floor, where he had landed after falling off the couch.

"The spirits," she said, still trying to catch her breath. Litzka was beautiful. He thought so now as he looked at her in his apartment. How could he have helped himself? Of course she wasn't an Oriental. She was from Mount Carmel, Pennsylvania. The makeup was a disguise, again created by her husband to play upon certain feelings he knew American men had toward Asian women, which ultimately served to further misdirect them. Without the stage makeup her Kewpie-doll face had an innocent, open, vulnerable appearance. Except for her eyes. Her eyes were wise and experienced.

"I don't buy it."

"I am a little bit psychic, after all," she said, with a mildly offended tone. "Just last month the spirits warned me not to get on a train and it got trapped in the Rockies for three days because of an avalanche. And they were trying to tell me something about a friend of yours."

"Litzka," he said, sitting up. That was what most people called her instead of the mouthier Pearlitzka. Actually, her real name was Pearl Beatrice Gonser Raymond, but she hadn't gone by that in years—not since the Great Raymond had anointed her Pearlitzka. "I don't buy your psychic bit. I never have. I'm serious. Now how did you find out about my son?"

She sighed, finally—hating, as all magicians did, to divulge even the tiniest secret. "That's easy. I went through your wallet when we were in Silver Springs."

Silver Springs. Florida.

He had never meant to start an affair with a married woman. He had never wanted to make time with the wife of someone he knew. But he had. In Silver Springs.

Blackstone's company was preparing a series of shows in Miami for the snowbirds, the rich New Englanders who traveled to the southland to winter. This yearly destination was always a lucrative engagement for the tour, so Blackstone's customary demands for flawless execution were always greatly amplified. Among his many concerns: his backers spent the season in Miami and, despite their participation, this was the only time during the year when they took an active interest in the show that always reaped them a profit. Facing such myriad distractions, he was unable to spend as much time with Gibson as he had anticipated when he first suggested that Gibson come to Miami and cowrite a new book with him. So Gibson had spent much time watching rehearsals in the showroom of the Eden Roc Hotel and much more time at the hotel bar. He had spent so much time there, in fact, that the hotel had invited him to leave his typewriter on the bar so he could walk right in and begin his work.

He had met her once before at a Society of American Magicians meeting, when she had first appeared on the arm of Raymond, and he had agreed with the assembled brotherhood that the old magician was lucky to have found himself such a dish. But he hadn't realized how that pale, pert face disguised her mischievously bright and clever spirit until they had spent time in Florida. She was new to Blackstone's company and was having trouble breaking into the tight-knit group. Gibson was an outsider as well. And that was the first thing they had in common.

He had tried avoiding her for several days. But the attraction was too apparent to both of them, and so to make sure that he would not add any more pressure to his friend's hectic production, he slipped out of town.

He had driven his Ford Tudor north, away from the coastal cities, toward the sparsely populated wet wilderness which lay inland beyond the swamps and Seminole Indian jungles until, late in the evening, when he could drive no farther, he discovered Silver Springs. A simple hotel sign had compelled him to turn off the road. He had never been to this oasis before, had never even known of its existence, but as he stood watching a heron rise over the waters bubbling up from deep beneath his feet to form the Crystal River, he felt as if this wild place were his very own.

Upon checking in he had discovered that a Hollywood movie crew was staying at the small hotel, which clung to the bank of the deep springs. Evidently the waters of Silver Springs were so clear that they were perfect for underwater photography, better than anywhere else in America. He spent the next day watching the crew film swimming scenes, and that night he spied on Johnny Weissmuller and Maureen O'Sullivan as they dined at the Angebilt Hotel's restaurant. They were sleek, sophisticated, glowing from their tans. Gibson knew many famous magicians, and theater and radio actors, but there had been something about being in the presence of bona fide *movie stars* that captivated his attention. He had watched their every move all evening long, fascinated to see them in color, and to hear Weissmuller speaking in complete, articulate sentences. O'Sullivan smiled at Walter more than once. She had a slight Irish accent. The chimp who played Cheetah had pissed on the dance floor and chased the singer from the stage.

That night there was a knock at his hotel room door. Litzka stood in his doorway, hair damp and wild from the tropical rainstorms that swept through Florida on a daily basis. Her eyes were filled with desperation and longing. Her lips trembled. The thought had crossed his mind to just close the door on her. She wouldn't have spoken a word if he had; she would have just left.

"You chose the only woman in the world you can't run away from," she had said.

He had let her in.

"What would you have done if I had taken the picture out?" he said to her, casting off the memories of Florida.

She shook her head. "That picture has been in your wallet for years. I knew you wouldn't." She flung herself on him and he kissed her roughly. "Weren't you surprised, though?"

"It's not what we rehearsed!"

"That's what you're mad about? That I improvised? Really, Walter?"

"You were really improvising up a storm tonight," he said. "Between that and your message from the grave, I just felt like I was out there flapping like a screen door in a twister."

She looked down and seemed to be studying her red-lacquered fingernails. He heard a scratching from the other side of his living room. "China Boy is messing up my pulps."

With a sharp cry meant to startle the bird, she leaped up and ran across his apartment to where China Boy was scratching the cover off a recent issue of *The Shadow.* He watched her strong, naked body with fascination. "Bad China Boy!" She picked him up and tucked his head under his wing. "Go to sleep." She gently rocked the chicken back and forth and it stopped moving.

"That bird's a pain in the ass!"

"He's showing an interest in your work. I think you should encourage that."

Gibson shrugged and pulled himself onto the couch, wrapping the blanket around himself. "I'm pretty hungry. If he does any more damage around here I might just fricassee him."

She gasped with mock horror and put the sleeping bird in the basket she used to transport him from place to place. Everyplace to everyplace, Gibson corrected himself; she went nowhere without her lucky bird. The scraggly bantam had been part of her act until, at the height of their career, Raymond had decided that the psychic chicken act just didn't suit the dignity of their status and had sidelined him.

"Sorry," she said to Walter as she straightened up the damaged mags. "Why are they called pulps?"

"Well," he said. "It all began with a wasp."

"A wasp?"

"The kind that stings you, right?" He was still angry with her. But maybe she was right about him and he could share a little more of himself with her. "You see, paper used to be very expensive, much more like a cloth than what we have now. In fact, paper was made from the cotton fibers in rags and worn-out clothing. It was expensive and slow to make. Then one day a Frenchman, René de Réaumur, noticed wasps building a nest in the eaves of his house. He studied the wasps as they chewed up wood. They were mixing it with chemicals in their saliva, which created a moist mass of fibers that, when it dried, resembled the paper made from cloth. He experimented with sawdust and chemical glues until he came up with a fairly good facsimile of what the wasp was spitting up. When he pressed it through a roller, it made a nice sheet of paper.

"Now a lot of people since have put their two cents' worth in and come up with some pretty fancy ways of making paper nicer, and more expensive—adding bleaches, for example. But for our mags to be cost-effective they need to be cheap, and that means hiring the cheapest writers, using the cheapest ink, and buying the cheapest paper. The paper we use is pretty much like the original wood pulp process inspired by the wasp. Hence, the pulps."

"Oh." She brushed a loose feather from her arm. She came back to Gibson and stretched out along his side. "Pulps have a bad reputation. Like actresses."

"That's because they're both fast and cheap but they look good doing it."

"Hey!"

"I don't aim to educate or enlighten, so by that measure I guess pulps don't pass as literature. But if it's entertainment you want, a little bit of showbiz, I got that over literature any day of the week. And as long as I can write and be read, and get paid for it, I'm a happy man."

She snuggled her head into the crook of his arm and for some time they simply dozed. Hovering just above the place where dreams begin, he let the memories of Silver Springs swirl around him.

"What's he like?" he heard her asking him now, and his consciousness raced up to meet her. Dawn light was burning away the night and made her gleaming eyes seem even more penetrating, as if she really could read his mind. And for all he knew, when it came down to it, maybe she could.

"Who?" He was groggy.

"Your son. Robert?"

"I don't know. I haven't seen him in years."

"Why not?"

He tried to talk but couldn't. His throat had closed up on him. He was only able to give her a mute shrug.

"Why not?" she said again, insisting.

"I can't talk about it," he managed to croak.

"No, Walter," she said, "you *won't* talk about it."

And suddenly she was getting dressed, pulling on the garters and affixing the clasps to the stockings, the gold silk Chinese gown she had worn to the premiere party gliding smoothly over her body. "You won't talk about it."

"What do you want me to say? What do you need to know about me? Do you need to know that I'm a bad man? That I turned out not to be the man I thought I once could be? I'm just the man that I am. The kind of man who walks out on his wife and son and never sees them again? The kind of man who steals another man's wife?"

"You didn't steal me!"

"What more do you need to know about me? My desk is over there. There are some personal papers in the drawers. I'll go back to sleep and you can sneak over and have a look! They'll tell you all about my divorce. Look for the words 'alienation of affection.' What that means is that my wife stopped loving me because I wasn't happy being a newspaper reporter and I made her life miserable because I was miserable."

She stared at him in silence for a long moment. He thought she would say something, but she didn't. He could see in her eyes that he was changing from someone she knew to someone she didn't recognize and didn't want to be in the room with.

"I'm sorry," he said. "Litzka! Honey! Wait!"

She was already at the door. The basket with the slumbering rooster swung from her hand. He went to the door to stop her.

"Hang on a second," he said. "I didn't mean it like that, and just wait!"

But she stepped into the hallway. She turned to look back at him and for a moment he remembered again how she had looked in that doorway at Silver Springs months ago and how she had whispered, "I love you," as she slid past him when he hadn't closed the door on her.

"Do you believe I'm a little bit psychic?" she asked him suddenly.

"No."

"Then I must be a complete liar," she said and turned away. He slipped on his trousers and then ran down to the hall where she waited for the elevator. Then he stood there mute, dumb, as the cage rattled wearily down toward them. He kept searching for something to say, knowing that there were words in his head that could make things right. Where had his words gone?

She entered the elevator and refused to look at him even as the doors closed. He stood there and listened as it descended the shaft; he heard the echo of its doors as it opened onto the lobby of the Hotel Des Artistes, where he rented the biggest apartment.

He waited for a long moment hoping that the elevator would spring to life again and rise and the doors would open to reveal Litzka and she would listen to him. Because he knew what he would say to her.

He had the words now.

EPISODE SIX

NORMA DENT held a martini in her hand as she hunted for Dutch Schultz's lost treasure.

"Who shot you?"

"I don't know."

"How many shots were fired?"

"I don't know."

"How many?"

"Two thousand."

Last year he had been gunned down at the Palace Chophouse in Newark. Sometime prior to that, his accomplices were now admitting in testimony, he had buried a steel chest full of, according to those same accomplices, stacks of thousand-dollar bills, jewels, gold, and stock certificates estimated to be worth millions of dollars. Stolen from the honest, decent citizens of New York, as well as some of its dishonest and corrupt ones.

"Please crack down on the Chinaman's friends and Hitler's commander. I am sore and I am going up and I am going to give you honey if I can. Mother is the best bet and don't let Satan draw you too fast."

"What did the big fellow shoot you for?"

"Over a million—five million dollars."

Five million dollars in treasure.

He had been shot in the stomach. It took him four agonizing days in his hospital bed to die. Newark cops had been with him the entire time, writing down his ramblings and confessions as he slipped in and out of feverish delirium. The transcript had finally been published in the *New York Herald,* despite the best efforts of the police to keep it from the press. While they may have hoped his words would provide insight into the underworld, Norma knew they contained the key to his treasure.

"Control yourself."

"But I am dying.

"No, you are not."

"Then pull me out. I am half crazy. They won't let me get up. They dyed my shoes. Open those shoes. Give me something. I am so sick. Give me some water, the only thing I want. Open this up and break it so I can touch you. Danny, please get me in the car. Please mother, you pick me up now. Please, you know me. No. Don't you scare me. Please let me up. If you do this, you can go on and jump right here in the lake."

The lake. Was that a clue? Norma wondered. His accomplice, Lulu Rosenkrantz, had claimed that he and Schultz had buried the treasure near a grove of pine trees near the town of Phoenicia in the Catskills. The atlas open on Norma's lap indicated that an Esopus Creek ran between Phoenicia and Kingston, the only body of water directly in the vicinity that Lulu Rosenkrantz claimed to have visited. Schultz alluded to water more than once in his ramblings. Water was the key, she decided. The treasure was buried near the creek, which in the mind and on the lips of a dying man could become a lake.

"Police, mamma, Helen, mother, please take me out. I will settle the indictment. Come on, open the soap duckets. The chimney sweeps. Talk to the sword. Shut up! You got a big mouth! Please help me up, Henry! Max, come over here! French-Canadian bean soup. I want to pay. Let them leave me alone."

She felt her face flush with the thrill of discovery. She took another sip of her martini. The gin was crisp with the scent of juniper. The doctor had told her it was okay now for her to drink occasionally, so she made sure to follow doctor's orders.

Norma Dent loved treasure hunts and this promised to be a big one. It didn't matter to her that she had never found any treasure; the thrill was in finding clues, tying loose ends together, trying to get into the mind of someone who could stash their secrets away. Together the Dents had embarked on a number of quests. They had explored the ingeniously booby-trap-rigged shaft on Nova Scotia's Oak Island, presumably the resting place of Captain Kidd's wealth; hiked the fields of Georgia's Chennault Plantation in search of the lost gold of the Confederacy; and sailed the *Albatross* across the sapphire-blue waters of Cuba seeking the Spanish golden tablet. Each time she felt as if she had come closer than ever before to realizing her dream. Now here was a treasure practically in her own backyard. The winter had been long and heavy, so the creek might be frozen over, the ground hard. But it could be right there waiting for them. But then again, it was so much effort.

She sighed and laid the newspaper clipping across the atlas, then closed the old book. She swept an errant lock of her long blond hair out of her face and tucked it behind her ear, feeling the surging treasure passion recede. Maybe in the spring she'd be ready. Or by summer.

A sharp metallic snap echoed through the apartment, interrupting the steady rat-a-tat-tat beat of Lester at his typewriter which was the daily background noise of her life. Suddenly she could hear the traffic from West Seventy-sixth Street below her, the distant hoot of steamships on the Hudson, and the ratcheting clank of the elevators in the hall. The apartment, which seemed so warm and alive while he was writing, instantly chilled. She waited expectantly, knowing what had happened. Lester had been typing so hard and so fast that one of the strikers had snapped off and whizzed across the room. Whenever this happened she always half expected, as she did now with a wince, that the flying sliver of metal would impale Lester. At least he wore glasses, so his eyes were protected. She waited, knowing for certain what was happening in his tiny office. Lester, still writing his story in his head, would remove the page he had been working on and place the broken typewriter on the floor to the right side of his desk. Then he would turn to the left side of his desk, where he kept several cases of new typewriters. He would open up a new box; place it on his desk; roll in the page of paper, which made very reassuring clicks; then begin to type again, trying to get his fingers to catch up with his mind, which was already racing pages ahead into its story. Or if he were out of type-writers and Elizabeth, his secretary, was around, he would simply dic-tate as she wrote in shorthand. But she was off today, and Lester would fend for himself. Norma listened for the sound of a new box opening. Instead, she was startled when Lester cleared his throat in the doorway behind her.

"How are you feeling?" he asked in his low, deep voice. She still felt his soft rumble in her toes—the same way she had when she had re-sponded to an ad for a Western Union clerk back in Carrolton, Mis-souri, and Lester had answered the phone. God, she thought, that was thirteen years ago. Lester almost never raised his voice over that whis-pery rumble, yet she never had trouble hearing him, even in a crowded restaurant or on the noisy elevated train.

"I'm okay," she shrugged, sipping at the martini. She saw him fur-row his brow in concern. She knew it had been difficult for him to un-derstand how so much more of her mind and heart had suffered than her body. The blood, the physical pain—he could understand that, she knew. He could act on that, and he had. During the emergency of the miscarriage and the traumatic recovery afterward, he had responded swiftly, with decisive, caring purpose. It was only later, during the long fall and the cold of early winter, that she could sense his occasional frustration and impatience with her. Because he didn't understand. It had happened to him too, it was true. And she knew she had to ac-knowledge that he had lost too. But what had he really lost? A figment of a future? Not a life that he could feel within him the way she had.

She had wanted four children. She had ended up with four miscar-riages. Her doctor had told her that her uterus wouldn't support life, that it was a hostile environment. What a horrible thing to say to a woman.

On the coffee table she could still see the edge of the cover of the one present she had allowed herself to purchase when she first realized she was pregnant this last time. It was a children's book which had been published just around Christmastime: *And to Think That I Saw It on Mulberry Street*. It had been purchased in hope. Now it was buried under a mound of *Doc Savage* magazines which she had meant to read but hadn't.

She had lost another life in blood, and this time nearly lost hers as well. And in the months since the miscarriage, while her body mended, while she spent her days in dark places removing that child from her dreams of the future, she had grown angry at Lester for being there too much and not being there enough. It wasn't that he was angry with her, but maybe she wanted him to be. Maybe she wanted him to scream at her, tell her it was her fault, that she had made a mess of everything because of who she was. Recently, while making a pot roast (because cooking seemed to be the only thing she did lately), she realized that she had been waiting for the past six months for him to blame her. She wanted him to be angry with her, yell at her to stop wallowing. She wanted him to deck the doctors with a patented Doc Savage double-fisted haymaker to the jaw and set everything right. But that wasn't Lester. Although strong and dependable and loving with her, he had never been a forceful person. And in the end it wouldn't have fixed her.

So she had dug herself out of her hole. Somewhat. She had begun by focusing on things other than her loss. For example, making sure that Lester had proper meals at the right time was an important step. It was a small goal she could achieve on a daily basis, and a more realistic goal than finding a lost treasure.

"I'm going to go out tonight," he said, "to a Fiction Guild meeting at the Knickerbocker."

"Okay." She nodded. "I have ham steak for dinner."

After a hesitation in which he only blinked three or four times, he said, "I thought we might go down to Chinatown this weekend and visit Mr. Yee's." And by that she knew that he couldn't care less about ham steaks or pot roasts.

Mr. Yee's was one of their touchstone places in the city. On their first night in New York four years ago they had taken the wrong train and ended up in Chinatown in a blizzard. It was as far from La Plata, Missouri, as either of them had ever been; it might as well have been China, as lost and lonely as they were then. Mr. Yee had been one of the few brave souls to keep his restaurant open and had welcomed them graciously. Treating them as his special guests, he had brought forth to their table a large tank holding live fish and asked them to make a selection. She could still remember how grateful she felt that someone could be nice to her in a city that everyone had warned them about. He had been as thrilled to have customers that night as they had been to find a warm and friendly place: his restaurant had only been open a week. They talked to him for hours, and listened, as he told them all about how to get around their new adopted city. Mr. Yee had been their particular friend ever since, and Lester consulted with him often on the Chinese details that gave the Doc Savage books a special level of authenticity.

He chewed on his pipe stem and waited for her to answer. He wasn't used to her taking her time to make a decision.

"Let's move to New York so I can be a pulp mag writer for Street & Smith. They've already hired me to write a Shadow story for them and I did it. It's called The Golden Vulture. *Walter Gibson, the fella that usually writes* The Shadow, *just has to sign off on it and they're gonna run it. John Nanovic says there could be a whole lot of work for me up there."*

"That sounds nice. Let's go."

He would go to Mr. Yee's without her if she didn't want to go; she knew that. Lately he had been going out more and more on his own. He had recently come home in a foul mood from an evening at a bar where some of his fellow pulp writers went. He was disinclined to discuss his night, but he had spent the next day looking through his old story file instead of writing. At the end of the day he had mailed off several stories to the *Saturday Evening Post*. She wished he could be satisfied writing *Doc Savage*. He was more successful than almost any other writer in America. But she knew how much he wanted public recognition of his talents under his own name, how much he despised being forced to publish under the name Kenneth Robeson. He craved, with a depth she could only imagine, the vindication of being published in one of the so-called classier magazines. She understood that about as well as he understood her pain, she supposed. After so many years of marriage it was good that they still had things they needed to learn about each other.

"Is this about something you're writing?" She always liked to help him research his stories, help open the doors which lead to adventure. Well, she used to. She hadn't even been able to bring herself around enough to be able to read the last three issues of *Doc Savage*.

"Sort of."

There was something else, she was sure of it. But his face was nearly impassive. She looked at the yellow corner of the children's book on the coffee table. A pang of sadness and fear stabbed at her, but she said, "You know, I've missed his dumplings. That sounds nice."

She hoped it would be. She hadn't left the apartment in six months.

Episode Seven

"DID YOU know Howard Lovecraft?" Dr. Elmer Smith asked him. The Flash shook his head, as did the other men at his table. Bob Hogan, who wrote the *G-8 and His Battle Aces* hero series, shrugged; his angular, bony shoulders bounced up and down beneath his suit. "Who was he?"

"He wrote a few things for the shudders."

"I never even heard of him," Hogan said.

"Yeah, he never broke through," Smith said. "And he didn't live here in New York. He lived in Providence." He was a heavyset man; his girth was an occupational hazard. Doc Smith was a pulp writer, but he was also a real scientist, a chemist, who created tasty mixes for the Dawn Doughnut Company. He could always be counted upon to bring fresh samples of his newest creations to the Knickerbocker get-togethers. Tonight the big boxes of blueberry dunkers were being received with great enthusiasm. Not so much for the coffee-strawberry.

Smith wasn't the only one afflicted with an expansive waistline. The Flash looked around the room. Fat and hemorrhoids were the plagues of his field. Even the skinny men in the room shared another common misery with the fat ones: their shoulders were all stooped and the head of each and every one hung from his neck so it looked as if the room were full of strange, gray vultures. This was the ultimate reward for hunching over a typewriter for long, hard hours. The Flash shifted his weight, straightening his posture, feeling the tendons crack in his neck as he did so. When he was rich he would have a masseuse and a chef on staff. And he would dictate his stories from a comfortable position, perhaps on a sofa, to a secretary.

Smith continued, "His stories were all about ancient horrible monsters from outer space who have been on earth in a state of suspended animation for eons waiting for the day when their leader would arrive and help them to take over the world. Meanwhile, while they sleep, their dreams have enough power to drive men insane. Very strange stuff. Full of reanimated corpses and shuffling dread fish creatures and mysterious, fog-bound islands that don't appear on any chart."

"Sounds surefire. Surprising that stuff didn't sell," The Flash said with a tone of enlightened disdain. He reached for a blueberry doughnut, his third, but he hoped that the other men hadn't seen him take the first one and would think it was only his second. He looked around the room. The turnout tonight was quite good; he nodded to himself. Four tables full of writers, drinking coffee and talking about writing. Some of them were very successful, like Hogan and Smith; some were just starting out, like his friend Al van Vogt, who had recently moved to New York from Canada to rustle up more work. Then there were the grizzled old veterans like the Brit, Talbot Mundy, who claimed to have tramped around the whole of the Empire, hunted tigers in Afghanistan, fought in the Boer War, and published his first adventure story in *The Scrap Book* in 1911. The Flash had been reading Mundy's stories since he was a little boy and was always thrilled whenever he could spend time in the man's company.

A low rumble made the chandeliers shake and tinkle. It had been a while since they had been cleaned well; the Knickerbocker was no longer in its prime, and dust trickled down in a slow flurry. He covered his coffee cup. Knowing that the vibration was caused by the subway which ran under the hotel didn't exactly reassure him. The shudder felt too much like the earthquakes he had known so well back in Washington. He didn't trust the subway and only took cabs or the el. Tonight he had taken the trolley to the hotel on the corner of Forty-second and Broadway. Once upon a more elegant time the Knickerbocker had been part of the social pulse of the highest levels of the Manhattan elite. Now it was just another stop for the merchant class.

"He and Robert Howard were good friends," Smith continued his impromptu eulogy.

"Aw jeez! Was he a suicide too?" asked Norman Daniels, a man who was often hired by publishers looking to imitate the success of *Doc Savage* or *The Shadow.* Howard, a *Weird Tales* writer who over the last ten years had authored a series of bold adventures about a mythical land traveled by a fearsome, amoral barbarian named Conan, had put a bullet into his brain with a .38 Colt revolver last year outside his home in Texas. Rumor had it that he had been upset by the irreversible coma his mother had slid into. He had been only thirty years old.

Smith shook his head. "Some kind of cancer, I heard. But here's the weird thing they both had in common." He lowered his voice and the men at the table leaned in to hear him. "They both lived at home with their mothers."

They all looked uncomfortably at each other, aware why Smith had lowered his voice. One by one they all snuck glances at Cornell Woolrich, the skinny, nervously fey detective writer who had begun his writing career in *Black Mask,* the pulp started by H. L. Mencken that had launched the career of the West Coast gumshoe pulp writer Dash Hammett into the stratosphere. Hollywood made movies of Hammett's stories and real publishers put his books in libraries and bookstores. Woolrich's star was rising as well; he now sold almost exclusively to the slicks, and there was gossip of a nice novel deal in the works (a novel, The Flash thought, how great would it be to have the stories he wrote considered fine enough to be novels instead of just pulps), but he still stayed tight with his pulp friends. The great Fitzgerald himself had taken an interest in Woolrich's writing and had tried to persuade him to make a move to Hollywood. Woolrich refused to leave the Harlem hotel he lived in with his mother, who sat by his side now, possessively brushing imagined lint from his ill-fitted suit. The Flash had to admit that some very strange people were attracted to writing as a profession. They couldn't all be as normal as he.

He wondered why some of these other fellas wrote. Smith, for example, had a great job and with his skills as a chemist could find all kinds of interesting work even if the American public suddenly rejected tasty doughnuts, so why was he here? There had to be better hobbies. And the same question applied to the perennial second-story man Emile Tepperman, over there under the chandelier with all the crystal missing. His meager monthly returns, cashwise, couldn't compensate him for the effort he put into his silly Purple Invasion stories. He even seemed content with his place providing filler for other magazines. Maybe one Friday night he, The Flash, might introduce the topic of muses and see what these men had to say about that subject. He was sure it would be interesting. But tonight he had prepared a different topic for their discussion. It was time to introduce it.

The Flash excused himself from the table and moved to the lectern at the head of the room and raised his arms. "Gentlemen, gentlemen! Can I have your attention, please?" Smith clanked his spoon against his coffee cup and others picked up the call to attention. The Flash waited for the room to settle down and all eyes to be upon him. "Thanks all for coming and thanks for all getting your dues in to me on time. Let's thank Dr. Smith for the doughnuts!" Everyone applauded. Smith heaved himself up and took a bow.

The Flash continued, "There's no real news on the Guild front this time out. We're always looking for new members, of course, so if you've got any buddies, bring 'em along." A latecomer was entering the room. He removed his fedora and The Flash grinned. Lester Dent had come after all.

The big man looked a little lost. The Flash gave him a little wave, inviting him to join their table. Dent nodded and made his way to the table. The Flash could see the other writers sneaking furtive, envious looks at him. Of the men in the room, probably only Hogan and Woolrich had achieved a somewhat comparable level of financial success. Many of the men in here were second-story men, the guys who wrote the filler tales that ensured each book was the proper length each month.

Then he started to worry that his beckoning gesture to Dent had been too eager and enthusiastic. Had he looked foolish? It was important that he represent the Guild with dignity. Until he had campaigned for and won the presidency, the Guild hadn't functioned as anything more than a glorified social club for men who, by the very nature of their work, spent their days in isolation. In the few months of his tenure he had been able to institute a few changes, including the circulation of a newsletter and the quiet distribution of a few Guild dues bucks to some established writers who had hit a streak of bad luck. He wasn't trying to turn the Guild into some kind of commie labor union and he had no intention of going up against the powers that be at Street & Smith in any kind of negotiation. When it came to wages, it was every man for himself. He just thought that it was a good way for guys who had crossed a certain professional threshold to look out for one another.

The Flash continued as Dent took a seat at his table, next to Smith. "So let's get down to why we're really here tonight. Taking over the world!"

It got a great laugh and he grinned. If he had acted like a giddy fanatic when he had seen Dent, then it had been forgotten.

"A lot of us write about how to do it. Death rays. Vast armies. Rocket-powered missiles. Plagues. Lots of our characters have designs on the world. Our masters of menace: The Octopus, Doc Death, Doctor Satan, Dr. Yen Sen, Shiwan Khan, Fu Manchu, Wu Fang. What I want to discuss this evening is, what does someone do with the world once they've achieved their goal of world domination? Why do I think this is a relevant topic? Even to those of us who write cowboy stories?

"Hitler."

There was a snort of derision from somewhere in the room. The Flash shrugged. "I know it seems ludicrous. But since he shredded the

Treaty of Versailles and moved troops into the Rhineland and has started building his forces, it made me start thinking that if someone could make a run at it, he could. If not the whole world, then three continents at least—Europe, Asia, and Africa. So, in trying to figure out if it is really possible for someone like Hitler to do it, I decided to backtrack and ask the question of all of you, would it be worth it? Could you, in fact, rule the world?

"Of course, I mean in the pulp sense. Say you managed to take over the world. What happens the next day? What kind of organization would you need to manage it? Would you have to be accountable in any way to anybody? How would you suppress an uprising of opposition which occurs on the other side of the world? Could you enjoy it? In short, to come back around to its relevance to Hitler, is ruling the world actually worth the effort? Go to it!"

He sat down as the room began to buzz with conversation again. He didn't know if they were discussing his topic, but he certainly hoped so. He shook Dent's hand. "Lester Dent! Glad you could make it. You know everybody here?" The Flash was thrilled that Lester had come. Adding him to the Guild would only burnish its reputation, which would help improve the image and status of its members, and by extension, its president.

Lester nodded. "Sure." He tore a chunk of fried dough from a dunker and before any of the surprised men at the table, Smith included, could stop him, he had popped it into his mouth. Conversation at the table stopped. He chewed unsuspectingly for a moment and then his jaws stopped moving. "Is that mint?"

Smith nodded. Dent shrugged and swallowed. Then he took a second bite. "You fellas talk about writing here. I've got a question for you. Anyone know the origin of the expression 'and the horse you rode in on'? As in, 'to hell with you and the horse you rode in on'? I was writing that today and I got to wondering where it had actually come from."

"Nick Carter?" The Flash said, reminding them of the first Street & Smith hero, who had fathered their profession. "From the days of the real Old West."

"I first heard it during a poker game in Texas," Smith said. "So that could be it."

"Like everything else," Hogan interjected, "it's from Shakespeare. 'Some hilding fellow, that had stolen the horse he rode in on.' Not sure which play, though."

"Thanks, Bob. Maybe I'll try and work that tidbit in. Somehow." He pulled out his pipe and a leather tobacco pouch. Unlike his hat and suit and watch, which looked new and expensive, The Flash noted, both the pipe and pouch were old and worn. Dent packed and lit the pipe. Its stem was well chewed. He pointed it at The Flash. A thin tendril of smoke leaked out of its small opening. "You know, Mrs. Dent and I made an accidental detour into the Reich last summer on our trip to Europe."

"Sounds like fun," The Flash offered. He wished he had been so adventurous as to visit Germany. Dent must have come up with some great story ideas there. He decided he should travel more.

"Nazi soldiers shot up our car and chased us back across Bavaria."

"Oh."

"Let me ask you something, Lester." Hogan was scratched at his balding head. "I always wondered how you came up with Doc Savage."

"Well. Nanovic wanted a new Shadow series. Only better. So I took some of that and then I came across some articles by an old Street & Smith writer named Richard Henry Savage, who fought in Loring's Egyptian army in 1861. He turned in some fine stories of his time over there, and when he came back he became an engineer, a lawyer, and a playwright. So he was kind of interesting too. I don't know, maybe that's it. Soon after reading about Savage, I woke up with an image of Hercules riding on the running board of a car down Broadway toward some great adventure. Sure, laugh at that. It's kind of funny. But it's important for kids to know about Hercules and I don't know if they even teach mythology like that in schools anymore like they did when we were young.

"Like I said, when I woke up there he stood, bigger than life, as big as myth, standing in front of my eyes with a brown wool coat over his shoulders instead of a lion's hide, a ripped shirt revealing skin tanned during exploits in equatorial jungles and deserts. And my fingers began to get that itch." Every man at the table nodded knowingly. "Then I had to use my imagination."

"Is there much of you personally in there?" Hogan asked him.

Dent shot the man a look of scoffing derision. "You mean like that Miller fella in *Tropic of Cancer*!" That got almost as big a laugh from the table as The Flash's crack had. Almost. "Hell no! I make stuff up. That's what they pay me for."

"I meant," continued Hogan, unperturbed, "for example, that Doc's own father created a physical and mental regimen designed to turn him into a superhuman. He turned his own son into a science experiment. Do you think he has any problems with that?"

"Why would he? His father made him a hero."

"But do you draw on your own life to make stuff like that up?"

"I see what you're saying. No. My own father couldn't read a book and didn't care if I learned to. So no." He smiled, gazing into the bowl of his pipe as if reading tea leaves. "Not in the least."

No one seemed to want to pick up the dropped thread of conversation. "How do you think Ah Hoon died?" The Flash heard himself asking Dent.

"What's that about?" Smith asked, curious.

The Flash quickly explained the story of the Sweet Flower mystery up to its unresolved ending. For a moment he felt as if his telling the story had revealed an ending, but when he got there, the story trailed off just as it had when Gibson told it. The ending The Flash thought he was going to come up with just wasn't good enough. He shrugged and bailed out with a cryptic-seeming "We may never know."

"Hooey," Dent snorted. "There's an ending to this story, maybe even a great one. I don't yet know how Ah Hoon was killed but I've been turning it over in my head a great deal. And I tell you what. I'm going to find out. That's what Walter Gibson should have done before he even started telling that story. I'm gonna find out and I'm gonna bring it back here and get up in front of all of you and tell you what happened."

The Flash now wished he had kept his mouth shut. Why hadn't he just thought of solving the Sweet Flower mystery himself instead of asking Lester Dent's opinion?

"And then"—Dent grinned and puffed on his pipe contentedly— "I'm gonna write up the greatest pulp ever."

EPISODE EIGHT

"So, Walter Gibson did not create The Shadow, eh? But one could say that The Shadow created Walter Gibson," said George Rozen, with his tone of Viennese presumption. He was painting a cover for an upcoming issue of *The Shadow,* and blood seemed to flow from his fine brush as if it had pierced an artery in the hand that was holding it. "Without Walter Gibson would there still be a Shadow? Without The Shadow, would there be a Walter Gibson?"

"I don't know about that," Walter replied, "but without The Shadow there would certainly be no Maxwell Grant." Walter had cleared some old canvases from his desk and was lying on it while Rozen painted. He didn't have much to offer the talented painter by way of inspiration or motivation, but the two men enjoyed each other's company. He had been in a foul mood since Litzka had deserted him and he didn't particularly want to be alone with himself. He could have gone to the Fiction Guild meeting at the Knickerbocker, but he didn't particularly want to be around anyone else either. Sequestering himself in his office while Rozen painted was the perfect compromise. Rozen's work could be a focus for both of them, offering conversation-free seclusion and the security of companionship at the same time. Except that for some reason Rozen was feeling expansively garrulous today.

Gibson watched as a little bit more of The Shadow disappeared under paint. Strict with its resources, Street & Smith made all its artists get as much use out of stretched muslin as possible. This meant that the gloriously violent covers like the ones Walter had moved out of his way and the dozens more lying around the studio had all been painted over at least twice, and all were destined to be painted over at least once more. Then they would be thrown out.

Rozen was the only artist ensconced on this floor, on editors' row, but great sunlight poured through the large south-facing windows all day long, and Gibson had pressed Nanovic until he had given up and allowed Rozen to paint up here instead of in the large bullpen on the third floor with all the other artists. The argument was easy to make. Rozen was the best artist Street & Smith had, he painted the covers for the biggest mag the house had, and he deserved the light.

The Shadow glared righteously at Gibson from the paintings, silver-black eyes flashing vengeance and retribution. There were dozens of canvases around his office, so the malevolent pupils blazed at him from every corner of the room; he shifted his head slightly to get a different perspective. The steely eyes above the character's hawklike nose followed him. Walter shuddered and closed his eyes for a moment. The image of The Shadow's glare hovered before his closed lids—alive, penetrating, and judging. He gasped and opened his eyes, suddenly shaking. There had been a few times since the creation of The Shadow that he had felt as if the character were real—this brief flicker had been one of those—and it always made his blood run cold. It meant The Shadow wanted something.

He dragged his gaze from the old paintings and turned to watch the silver-haired old man concentrate on his art. The artist had originally based his conception of The Shadow on the profile of one of Street & Smith's art directors, but over the last few years the character had taken on a life of its own.

"Where do you get that?" Walter asked him. "The inspiration?"

The old Austrian shrugged. "From The Shadow. Same as you, right?"

The only artist in town who gave George Jerome Rozen a run for his money was his own brother, Jerome George Rozen, the second-best cover painter at Street & Smith. All Walter or his ed, Nanovic, needed to give Rozen was a thirty-second story rundown and then he was off to the races, creating the luminous and disturbing covers that did as much to sell the mag as the stories themselves did. More, in some months.

"Well, if he's lurking around, I haven't heard from him lately."

Gibson knew that his efforts of late hadn't been his best. He'd even hired a ghost for the first time, a guy named Tinsley, to pick up one of the two books he had to deliver each and every month. That's why Dent's needling had really worked its way under his skin. He had been having problems with endings in particular.

"Not since Kent Allard, yes?"

"That's right. That whole Allard thing."

"What brought that on?"

"I still don't even know."

"I think The Shadow spoke to you, is what I think."

"I'm sure that's it." The painter either missed or ignored Gibson's sarcasm.

That Allard thing. An incident of creative impulsiveness he was still doing penance for. One morning it had come to him in a burst which Rozen might call inspiration and the result was *The Shadow Unmasks.* For seven years, readers had been told that The Shadow was actually secretly Lamont Cranston, playboy about town. In *The Shadow Unmasks,* Gibson had taken his readers' expectations and thrown them out the window. What they discovered behind Rozen's cover was that it had all been a lie. Cranston, it was revealed, was merely a disguise. The Shadow's true identity was Kent Allard. Possibly. The implication was that Allard was only a disguise as well. Maybe seven years of success had made his eds complacent: Nanovic claimed to have read the tale, but Gibson suspected he hadn't. When it ran, the vocal reaction from the fans was loud. Very loud. They didn't like it. They considered it an outrageous betrayal akin to Arthur Conan Doyle's pitching Sherlock Holmes over Reichenbach Falls. By the time the scope and extent of the outrage were clearly expressed by the incoming mail, several more issues had run with the Allard subplot and it was too late to turn back. There would be no stopping of the presses.

Street & Smith's management had been furious. Nanovic had taken a lot of heat and had passed most of it along to Gibson. He continued to, in fact. The scrutiny he was under was intense. The only reason Gibson kept his job was that the mags sold better *after* the Allard revelation than before! Gibson was glad of the success; it felt somewhat vindicating. The only problem was that when someone asked him why he had done it, why he had messed with a successful formula, he had no answer for them. He had no idea what had compelled him. The whole Allard thing was just there for the telling and he had told it.

Since that incident he had felt a vague unease while he was writing, as if he doubted his own process. It hadn't been as easy to let the powerful torrent of words conduct his fingers. If he were to be honest with himself, the torrent had slowed considerably. Maybe he could crank out 100,000 words a month right now—more than most writers and just enough for him to keep up with work, but compared to his usual output, a mere trickle. It wasn't just the distraction of the affair with Litzka, with all its inherent emotional turmoil; he had been feeling this way for some time now. In fact, the compulsion, the need, to inflict some sensation on himself, to stab at himself or pummel himself in order to feel anything, emerged at the same time as Kent Allard. He had begun the affair with Litzka hot on the heels of Allard's first appearance. Nineteen thirty-six had been one for the books. Nineteen thirty-seven was shaping up to be one hell of a sequel.

The Shadow's eyes were following him again. The words, the images, the stories—they weren't his to control anymore; they were just coming from someplace within and he didn't know where or how. At the same time he also knew not to question the process too deeply or it might just vanish altogether on him. Then where would he be? Out on his ass while Nanovic, his ed, tossed the mag, *his mag,* to some two-and-a-half-cent hack like Hubbard.

The thought of Hubbard getting his mitts on *The Shadow* made Walter grimace. He could almost feel the kid's triumphant gloat. Hubbard was an okay writer, and blazing fast, but his ambition was greater than his talent and he had none of the skills needed to wrestle The Shadow to the page. Walter shook his head to clear it. Between Litzka and his writing problems he had enough to worry about. He didn't really have time to worry about Hubbard or whether or not The Shadow's eyes were watching him. "Scotch?" he asked, knowing the answer.

"Of course." Rozen was from the Old World and had developed no puritan sense of impropriety about drinking before the sun set. Or even before the clock struck noon. Gibson heaved himself off the desk and pulled a bottle of White Horse scotch whiskey from the drawer where he had stashed it. He splashed the brown liquid into two vaguely clean glasses and handed one to Rozen. Then the two of them stood back to look at the cover for *The Shadow of Death.*

"Christ almighty," Gibson breathed. "That is one son of a bitch of a painting."

It was one of Rozen's favorite themes, The Shadow face-to-face with Death. In his paintings the characters mirrored each other's nature. Many times they had met before; Death had lurked in tarot cards, behind Broadway curtains, in warehouse rafters, whispering in the ears of cruel-mouthed thugs. If The Shadow lacked an arch-nemesis within the pages of the mag, he never lacked for one on the cover. Against a background of flames and smoke, the two rivals challenged each other once again. One eye glittered, rolling loosely in the ivory skull. A skeletal hand held the book of Life and Death and with a bony finger he touched the word *Shadow,* written in flame on the page of Death. The Shadow seemed like a dark Lucifer about to take the throne of fate with a .45 and a sneer while Death appeared on the verge of taking his retribution upon the hero for usurping his role on Earth and sending more souls to hell than he. Only a slight turn of The Shadow's head gave any indication of his recognition of his mortality. He might prevail this time, as he had before, but he was only human; sooner or later his enemy would have him.

"Brother," Gibson said, impressed. "I wish I could write what you paint."

"At least no codes this time," Rozen replied, stirring up some red paint. Gibson loved codes and often included them in his stories. When he did, he liked Rozen to place messages on the cover for his readers to solve. Rozen hated painting the intricate symbols or numbers and letter sequences that Gibson required at those times.

"Don't tempt me."

"So, Walter. How about we finish up and go to Rosoff's for some steak and beers?"

"I can't," he said. "I have to go to a funeral."

"Whose? Anyone I know?"

"Howard Lovecraft. Ring a bell?"

Rozen shook his head. "A writer?"

"He tried."

"I never heard of him."

"Not many did. I have to go up to Providence for the funeral. I wasn't even going to go because I didn't really know him all that well, although he could write letters like nobody's business. But his aunt sent me a telegram asking me to attend. His will asked for me specifically. So . . . At least I can get some writing done on the train."

"A new Shadow book?"

"Probably. I'm far enough behind that I ought to get crackin' on one, that's for sure. I don't know, George. Maybe I'm just tired of writing about The Shadow. Maybe I just need a break. I've been doing it steady for seven years now."

"Ha!" Rozen grinned. "The Shadow won't let you."

The comment made Gibson give a little jerk. "What do you mean?"

"Without you? *Pfft!* No Shadow. Maybe he won't like that."

"I kind of miss investigating and reporting. I used to be quite the reporter back in my Philadelphia days. You know when Al Capone was being held at the federal prison there before his sentencing I was the only reporter he allowed to come interview him? It's true. He was a big Houdini fan and had read the autobiography I wrote for him, *Houdini's Escapes,* and he wanted me to do the same for him. Got him to tell me the really great stuff. His whole life story from Brooklyn to Chicago was right there on the paper. I was like his priest and he was the sinner making a confession."

"I have never heard of this book. What happened to it?"

"Well, unfortunately, old, sick, fat Al confessed a little too much. After the first few articles were published in the paper, his lawyers were able to seize my notes and do God knows what with them. Probably burned them. To be fair, the things he told me about would have had his ass in the electric chair before the ink dried on the book. Ah, the stories I could tell you, brother, if only I weren't afraid a lawyer would jump out of that spittoon there and serve me. But you know what? Every Christmas I get a card from old Al over in Alcatraz, so don't believe he's as brain-addled and feeble as he lets on to the papers. He's a canny son of a bitch."

"If that kind of writing excites you, then you should find a way to do it. If your muse lets you. Of course, I would miss our collaborations. No one else here will take a drink in the afternoon."

Taking the hint, or taking it as a hint, Gibson refilled their glasses. "It ain't easy finding a subject as interesting as Houdini, or Blackstone, or Capone to write about. They broke the mold when they made those guys. To be honest, I'm more interesting than most of the famous people I meet now and I wouldn't want to read *my* autobiography. So until I meet someone who really captures my attention I'll keep making up characters to write about."

"So how does a reporter from Philadelphia arrive at all this?" Rozen made an exaggerated gesture of showing off the entire office. It looked as if a bomb had recently been detonated in its center.

"Houdini again. Okay, so about seven years ago Street & Smith decided to start advertising on the radio. They sponsored a program called the *Detective Story Hour* and every week they would take a story from one of the mags and turn it into a radio play and put it on the air.

And the host of the show, some actor, decided it would be clever if he called himself The Shadow. He'd put out these messages to his agents. Say things like, "Agent 57, be on alert. Report to me immediately any skulduggery in the Bowery," and things like that. And you know how people are about the radio. They started wondering if The Shadow was real and whether or not, at least, he had a mag of his own. So Ralston and Nanovic cooked up a little story for their new hero series, and they had liked my Houdini book, and they knew because of my magic articles that I could write really fast. They sent me a telegram making me an offer. I caught the train up and here I am. At the mercy, as you say, of my muse!

"Now I'm stuck. Pays too well for me to be doing anything else, but not well enough that I don't have to do it."

Rozen nodded in commiseration and picked up his paintbrush to add a few sparks here and there. Gibson poured himself another drink and sat on the edge of his desk. To this day he attempted to maintain the illusion that The Shadow was real. Each month's story was printed "as told to" instead of "written by" Maxwell Grant. He looked out the window toward lower Manhattan. The winter had been so brutally cold that sheets of ice had formed on the Hudson River all the way to the Battery. Folks said it was the same on the Brooklyn side with the East River. He had never seen a winter in New York cold enough for that to happen.

He wanted to call Litzka before he left and try to explain himself to her. But he knew she would then want to see him this evening, and he had to go to Providence. She would think he was pushing her off again and get even more mad at him. It might be better to wait until he came back to talk to her. He thought about sending her some flowers at the theater, but the things he needed to say to her couldn't be said with a card and flowers. For a second or two he envied Lester Dent; now there was a man who seemed to have made a good, strong marriage and wasn't plagued by the absurd impulses of women.

Rozen cleared his throat, indicating that he was finished. "So," he asked, stepping aside, "how would you know if this person or that person is worth writing about should you meet him? How do you know if someone is a Houdini or a Capone? Do you know, as your Shadow knows, what lurks in their hearts?"

Who knows what evil lurks in the hearts of men? The Shadow knows. It was the catchphrase of the day. It was on the lips of every American. Thanks to the radio shows, they now knew to follow the statement with The Shadow's signature maniacal laugh. Walter thought for a moment about the inspiration of the phrase. There had been a German magician of the previous century, Alexander Herrmann, who billed himself as "the man who knows." What exactly he knew was up to the audience to divine, but that simple sentence had outlived the man and Gibson had always wanted to write about a character who lived up to that title. When he finally had been able, in his first description of The Shadow, to begin the sentence, "Who knows," he had been surprised to see his fingers type, "what evil lurks in the hearts of men?" It sounded sinister and right.

Gibson stared at the painting. The Shadow's eyes were going to give more than one kid a memory that would last a lifetime. Years from now those kids, grown to manhood with The Shadow long forgotten, would wake up from nightmares and wonder where those piercing eyes that haunted them came from. He knew.

"Yes," he finally answered.

Issue 2:

I Am Providence

EPISODE NINE

THE LEGEND of Zhang Mei, the Dragon of Terror and Peril, begins in this way:

The man who would be his father was a Manchu and he rode from the west, from the Nulu'erhu Mountains, across the windswept, snowy plains of Lianoning Province behind Zhang Zuolin, the warlord. With him were three hundred militia men, temple-trained in Northern Shaolin mountain fighting techniques. *Chua'an fa* had turned their muscles into wood and their skin into iron. No sword could cut them and no bullet could pierce them.

They swept into the village of the woman who would be his mother just past dawn and put to the sword all the men who had accepted the god of the ocean men. The man who would be his father took the woman who would be his mother to be his second wife. His first had produced no sons.

When the moon was new and black, the warriors, including the man who was his father, rode out from the village. Zhang Zuolin turned his men south toward Beijing. Toward the war. Toward the foreign invaders.

It was the year 4597, the Year of the Rat. And the men of the Fists of Righteousness and Harmony rode to glory.

EPISODE TEN

"YOU KNOW why the streets of Chinatown are curved?" Lester was asking, or rather telling, Norma. Trying to listen, she neatly sidestepped a slop-smelling gap in the cobblestones. She was wearing her smart brown leather button-up boots today and was not about to get rotting cabbage leaf on them—even if that meant she occasionally had to put all her attention on where she was stepping and ignore Lester's ongoing travelogue. She was wearing the gray wool dress she had bought last winter at Gimbel's; it made her feel very attractive. And nothing in Chinatown, no stain from sauce or slime or oil, no drop of cabbage-filled puddle water, was going to stop her from feeling that way about herself today, finally.

"To confuse the hell out of all the demons," he continued, oblivious to her street gymnastics, although he always seemed to have a helpful arm out for her, instinctively. He was wearing a brown tweed suit which she had bought him, and which she thought made him look very dashing. She felt they must seem quite the pair.

The shadows of the low buildings hung heavily over the sidewalks in the late afternoon. Her long legs kept pace with his swinging stride as they left the Quong Yuen Shing and Company store and headed south on Mott Street. Lester loved doing research in the little market and it was always their first stop upon entering the exotic enclave below Canal Street. While Norma fingered the delicate silks and carved ivory and jade figurines, he would prowl beneath the store's ornate bower, carved from oak and stained with years of tobacco smoke, discovering exotic herbs and medicine and testing the bemused patience of the owner with questions about their Chinese names and powers. Astragalus (*huang qi*) for the heart; ginseng (*ren shen*) for fertility and diabetes; skullcap for hay fever; angelica (*dong quai*) for anemia; and licorice (*mi gan cao*) for infections, hepatitis, and colic. Bia Yia Pian pills and Ping Chua pills for strong lungs; Bu Zhong Yi Qi Tang for the health of "delicate" areas. The stranger the better, as far as Lester was concerned. It was all ammo for the gun. Clark "Doc" Savage Jr. was, among many other things, the greatest chemist in the world, and it behooved his creator to know as much about as many interesting substances as possible.

Lester towered over most of the men on the street around him, and he forged easily through the crowd. "That's the headquarters of the On Leong tong." He pointed out a nondescript building across the street. "They protect the laundrymen."

"I thought the tongs were gone."

"Not gone. Just rehabilitated."

There was never any room to move in Chinatown. The streets were narrow and clogged with Chinese, mostly men, who seemed to have a total disregard for anyone's personal space. Every now and then a sullen-faced Chinaman would careen off Lester like a small marble hitting a big one.

A new blue Packard squeezed past a double-parked horse-drawn cart; the horse didn't even twitch an ear at its horn blasts. Two men were unloading eviscerated whitish-pink pig carcasses from the back of the cart and tossing them into bins. Other men were rolling the full bins of porcine husks to different destinations within their enclave, the cobblestones causing the hind legs to rattle against the sides of the bins like thick drumsticks.

Across the street a bloated Irish cop, his uniform too tight, his face as red as the crimson on the many prosperity banners which hung in shop windows, was angrily berating a fishmonger. Norma could not tell what he was so angry about, but she thought that his tipping over a bushel of crabs was uncalled for. An elderly woman rushed from the fishmonger's stall pleading loudly and carrying some fish wrapped in paper. The cop patted her patronizingly on the head, took the fish, and swaggered up the street.

Norma turned to Lester. "You should get his badge number and report him."

She saw the tiniest crinkle of a wince at the corner of his eyes. He didn't want to do it; it would interrupt his plans. He didn't want to, but he would.

"Never mind," she said. She didn't want to turn their excursion into an incident. "Let's not get involved."

His quickening resolve turned into relief, and as they headed away from confrontation, he picked up his discourse on Chinatown. She could tell that Lester was excited to have her out. He spoke rapidly as if he were trying to distract her, keep her mind from turning inward. She didn't mind; she appreciated his efforts on her behalf. And it was good to be out, stretching her muscles.

He turned them left onto Pell Street, passing around a steam cart selling huge white puffy rolls full of sweet pork. Pell was even darker and narrower than the cramped thoroughfare of Mott Street. The stores were smaller, more Chinese, more mysterious; red banners hung from doors and windows, adorned with gold symbols of blessing or curse. Chinese gods sat in windows holding sticks of richly smoking incense.

Lester pointed out another building, taller and newer than its surroundings. "Another tong building," he said. "We're in Hip Sing territory now. This is their street."

"It doesn't feel any different."

He looked at her for a moment before realizing that she was making a joke. His face relaxed and his mustache crinkled as he grinned. "Hard to believe what a man will decide to fight for, isn't it? But a few years back these streets were red with tong warrior blood and visitors some-times had to step over the bodies to go about their business."

It never ceased to amaze her how much Lester knew about so many things. He never stopped investigating or reading and his curiosity was limitless. Once he discovered an interest in a subject, he would obses-sively devour all he could about it until he was an expert. The knowl-edge he acquired flowed from his mind into his stories. Not only was Doc Savage a chemist and a scientist and a global explorer; the men who kept his company were also remarkably accomplished in the fields of electricity, architecture, engineering, and law. Lester always tried to sneak information he thought boys needed into his mags. Millions of American boys knew about the malaria-resistant and ultraviolet prop-erties of quinine, the writ of habeas corpus, the benefit of calisthenics, the virtues of Eastern meditation, the cultures of South America and the Caribbean, the steel cage construction of the skyscrapers, the his-tory of the lost Maya, the physics of positive and negative electrons, and the use of the word *superamalgamated* as an expression of amaze-ment through Doc and his band of merry adventurers: Monk and Ham and Renny and Long Tom and Johnny. But most of all they knew about friendship, courage, and loyalty.

These were the qualities she was most proud of Lester for working into *Doc Savage,* and exactly the qualities which were missing from his other stories, although he could never see that. She knew he put down the Doc Savage series as mere formula, but she thought there was an integrity to the work that made it better than he thought it was. Lester Dent wasn't happy being Kenneth Robeson; he wasn't even all that sat-isfied being Lester Dent. He wanted to be John Steinbeck.

They walked on past the utterly unthreatening building. She was disappointed that no one even glowered at them. At the intersection of Pell and Doyers, Lester paused.

"Where are we going?" she asked. "Mr. Yee's is down farther."

She saw the look in his eye again, the one he had had in the living room a few days ago. Something was eating him. He was obsessing about something he wanted to know about. She looked at his fingers and they were twitching, already typing out words on an imaginary typewriter.

"I ran into Walter Gibson the other night," he said, his eyes wandering down the street looking for something.

"I hope you gave him a piece of your mind."

"Maybe a little piece."

"Good! I would have punched him."

"Maybe it's time to let bygones be bygones."

"Bygones. He nearly ruined us. He tried to keep you from having a chance at writing."

"First of all, by getting Nanovic not to publish *The Golden Vulture,* which I got paid four hundred fifty dollars for, by the way, he may have done me a favor. I didn't have to be his substitute writer."

"Some favor."

"If I had been writing Shadow stories, I never would have come up with Doc. And think how different our lives would be."

"He still had your very first story squashed, which was wrong of him to do because it was your big break. Thank God you were talented enough to land another break. But I don't see how you can forgive him."

"Oh, I'm not trying to forgive," Lester assured her. "I want to get one up on him."

"How?"

He stared down the block for a long moment. "I just want to take a look at something, real quick," he said at last. She nodded, but he didn't even notice. He was writing. He set off down Doyers and she hurried to keep up. He headed toward an aged building standing by itself by an alleyway. She followed, still fuming about Walter Gibson, whom she had never met and knew only as the man who had denied her husband his first steady writing job.

The old building was boarded up with rotting black planks which smelled of oily pitch. The remnants of a faded marquee still clung stubbornly to the bricks over the row of double doors. Any glass in the windows had long since been pried away and covered over with tar paper; any trace of elegance in its façade was erased. It stood as an aching spot to be avoided, like a sore tooth. As an indication of its diseased state, the sidewalk before it was empty, as if the locals allowed the awareness of its existence to intrude upon their single-minded missions and purposes and avoided it instinctively by crossing the street or finding alternate routes. Even in the middle of one of the busiest neighborhoods in the busiest city in the world, it exuded vapors of quiet desertion. They were almost entirely alone as they approached it.

"What is it?" she asked. Her pulse was quickening; her thoughts of Walter Gibson were fading away. Lester's interest in the building was infectious. She felt a surge of treasure-hunting excitement, a feeling she could never get by sitting on her chesterfield doing research. She felt the weight of the last six months melting away.

"The Chinese Theater," he replied.

"It's beautiful!" she exclaimed.

"I guess it kind of is." He showed only a passing interest in the building, preferring to investigate its surroundings. "It ran Chinese plays and operas for almost thirty years. The Salvation Army then tried to run a soup kitchen out of it, but nobody came. In the end it was a burlesque house, until La Guardia closed all of those down about five years ago. And now it's just abandoned.

"You know there are secret tunnels leading to and from this spot? They run all under Chinatown. A tong man could sneak in, whisper a garrote around a rival's neck while he watched the show, and *shneek!*" He made a deathly horrific face. "Meet your ancestors. Then it's back into the tunnels. The Irish cops think they've got a lid on it up here, but it's down below, where they'll never go, where you can find the real Chinatown. The gambling, the brothels, the opium dens, the slavers. It's happening in rivers and torrents below us."

"Sounds like a brilliant story."

"Story! It would need to be a novel! An exposé ripping the cobblestones off Chinatown and getting the first real look into the demimonde."

"That's your plan for getting back at Mr. Gibson? A novel?"

"No," he said. "I'm just trying to find the ending to a story." He looked the building up and down. "The boardinghouse was over here," he muttered.

"What boardinghouse?" she responded. But he didn't answer. Now that he was engaged, no matter what the outward Lester said or did, the inward Lester would be preoccupied with writing the next book. The words would have to be in place when he sat down at the typewriter so they could stream out in an uninterrupted flow onto the page. He walked off to the left side of the building, still muttering to himself. There was a gap about two feet wide, big enough for garbage cans and not much else, separating the windowless wall of the Chinese Theater from the tenement building on the other side. Lester stood in contemplation.

Norma lost interest quickly in his woolgathering. He could have the boardinghouse, whatever it was, all to himself. She was falling in love with this old, faded beauty. She walked along the front of the theater, running a hand along what was left of the ornamentation which had once adorned its pillars; once powerful long, thin dragons had wound their way around them but they had been chipped at and worn away to the point that they had become nothing more than mere worms.

Long, heavy beams had been posted with spikes over the front doors to the theater years ago. The beams were rough yet soft, slowly rotting away under the constant assault of the city's elements. Gaps appeared between the planking, and wondering if she could see anything beyond, she stepped up to the hole, mindful not to actually touch the smelly wood, and tried to peer into the darkness. She assumed that the closed doors of the theater would be behind the boards, but the blackness between the cracks indicated that at least one of the doors had swung open or fallen off its hinges at some point. She could make out vague shapes in the gloom but nothing that she could recognize properly.

Deep in the darkness something golden winked at her.

Something glittered, like a lone firefly just seen out of the corner of the eye—a momentary flash that had probably never really happened at all. Startled, she pulled her face back and looked around as if she had done something wrong. She leaned her head back to the position it had been before. She saw the flash again.

Excited, she reluctantly pulled herself away and ran to the side of the building where she had left her husband. Lester was trying and failing to scale the gap between the buildings by placing his hands and feet against the opposing walls and forcing himself upward. He was grunting with exertion and red-faced with frustration. The sight almost made her forget her own discovery. She watched in befuddled amusement as he strained and skidded obsessively against the bricks.

She was going to tell him not to rip his suit but she felt it would only be adding insult to his somewhat embarrassing struggle. She knew she'd read about this someday and it would all probably make sense. Watching Lester in this small space jogged her memory. There was a bigger alley on the other side of the theater. Set into the wall of the theater on that side was a stage door. She backed away from Lester, hoping no one they knew was in Chinatown that day; then she trotted quickly past the front of the theater to the other side.

The alley was dark. Distant sounds of pots being rattled came down from somewhere in the windows high above her. The shrill, high-pitched yammer of a faraway, very angry Chinese woman echoed through the air. The stage door was just to her left, but the alley continued on until it ended at the door of another building. A red light-bulb above the doorway was lit, as if the people behind that door were ignorant of the daylight.

She tested the doorknob on the stage door. To her surprise it responded with an affirmative twist and click. She gave the other door at the end of the alley another look and decided that no one was going to come out that portal anytime soon. She gave the door a little push and it opened with a rusty squeal onto the darkness of the Chinese Theater. As she stared into the gaping darkness spreading before her, she took a step back. Why had she come out? She should never have left the safety of her home. It wasn't too late. She could turn now and get Lester and return. To what? The chicken thawing in her sink? The pace of her heart was quickening. She didn't want to cook. She wanted to see.

The thick, sweet smell of ages-old incense greeted her as she waited for her eyes to adjust to the contrast of the auditorium's darkness against the light pouring in through the door. It seemed as if much, if not most, of the light was absorbed by a decade's worth of dust leaping into the air as she introduced oxygen into its vacuum. She stepped farther into the theater. Above her was a balcony floor. At its edge the room opened up to a cavernous yawn. Most of the seats were gone, but individual rows still remained like teeth in a jawbone. Torch lanterns that had been twisted in an attempt to wrest them away once upon a time were still affixed to the walls. The stage raked up from the brick proscenium arch. Thick rope hung like hemp cobwebs from the rafters. Tattered canvas backdrops and rotten set pieces lay scattered about the auditorium, some of them quite large—relics of performances decades old. But towering over all in its exotic glory was the object sitting center stage, her glittering attractor. She walked compulsively toward it, passing through pagodas painted on aged wood, across a muslin scrap depiction of the Great Wall, and emerging from a bamboo grove to see it clearly. So this is what it feels like to discover treasure, she thought.

The statue was gold, of that she was certain. She hadn't worked at the jewelry counter of the Rike's department store when she was sixteen and not come to know gold when she saw it. The figure of the man seated on a drapery-covered throne was nearly a dozen feet tall, she guessed. In appearance and presence it was horrible. Its angry face was dominated by a gaping mouth which forced its chin down to its chest. The body was draped in robes. In one hand the statue held a vase and in the other an upright sword which spired over its head. Both also appeared to have been forged of gold.

She stood before it at the lip of the stage gazing up as it seemed to look over her at an invisible congregation. How long had it sat here waiting for an audience? Well, it had her now.

"Hey!"

She spun around, choking back a gasp. Lester stood in the doorway. "That is the ugliest Buddha I've ever seen!"

"It's not a Buddha," she said. "It's treasure. A real treasure."

"It's just an old piece of set dressing."

She climbed up onto the stage. "Look how old it is. It's practically ancient."

"I don't think you ought to mess around with it," he cautioned her.

She knew that if it had been his discovery, he would already have been prying samples off to bring to a jeweler. She felt a small, fierce stab of pride; this was hers! She rubbed a hand slowly down the statue's arm. "There's not a speck of dust on it. Everything else is covered in dust, but this is spotless." She held up her fingers for him to inspect.

"Someone's been cleaning it," he said, looking toward her feet. From where she now stood she could see that recent footprints had been left in the thick dust. They came from and led back to the stage left wing, but they seemed to stop short of the statue. A wide expanse of dust surrounding the pedestal of leaping lions was undisturbed. She was about to tell Lester this when something insectlike hummed past her ear. As if the entire world had suddenly grown thick and slow, she saw Lester's expression change from concern to shock as his gaze moved from her to somewhere past her left shoulder.

The man emerging from the shadows of the wings was Chinese, but he had about him an attitude that was markedly different from the humbled westernized men on the streets just outside. He was dressed in a black variation of the standard gray pajamas that many Chinese men wore; around his waist the shirt was cinched with a tight yellow sash.

His contempt for them was palpable. He swung a length of chain in a long arc by his right side. It hummed in a hypnotically threatening way. In the same instant she took all this in, she realized that he must have already launched this at her once, that what had flicked past her ear had not been an insect but had, in fact, been the tip of the swinging chain.

"*Nee how ma,*" she heard Lester greet the man. Everything was happening so slowly and too fast at the same time. She wondered why Lester would be asking a man who had just tried to whip her with a chain how he was, and then she realized that the chain had moved so fast that Lester probably hadn't seen it. She heard the chord of the chain deepen and knew it was a moment away from lashing out again. She felt the speed of the world return to normal as her head snapped around to Lester.

"Don't just stand there!" she said simply. And then she flung herself toward the edge of the stage. In motion, she could feel the last of the chain as it whisked past her hair. There was a hollow metallic clang as the chain struck the statue.

They were frequent dancers at the Rainbow Room and Roseland. Lester was accustomed to the weight of her body in motion; his hands caught her waist and he used her momentum to swing her to her feet. She could see that the Chinese man had a grip on the long chain which stretched out from his hand in a straight line. Its other, more lethal end, a spike about seven inches long, was embedded in the soft gold of the statue. His expression hadn't changed at all.

Lester spun her around, in control now. They sprinted for the door. They heard the chain hit the stage but there was no time to look back. They burst into the gloom of dusk. She could hear the man angrily slam the door open again, for their impact had caused it to swing back closed. The sidewalk was still ominously empty. They raced toward Pell Street, to people and to the welcoming neon sign of Mr. Yee's. She looked back. The man was gaining on them.

They plowed into the human traffic at the intersection. Lester kept a viselike grip on her hand. Her calves were beginning to ache from running in heels and she began to have trouble catching her breath. Lester pulled her into the street. Cars squealed to a halt as they darted across. The uneven cobblestones didn't help her balance, and Lester nearly threw her up to the sidewalk. She couldn't run another step. She knew Lester knew too. She wanted him to keep running but she couldn't speak.

Lester did the last thing she, and probably the man chasing them, expected. He stopped. The man was so close behind them he didn't have time to react. Lester drew his arm back, his large hand clenched in anger, and he threw the first punch Norma had ever seen him throw. She could hear the threads in the shoulder of his jacket tear apart as his arm snapped out and his fist made contact with the man's jaw.

The man's face stopped instantly, but his feet continued the skid he had begun to try to stop himself. The impact threw his head back as his legs propelled his body forward, until, for a moment, his body seemed parallel to the pavement, suspended at the end of Lester's arm. Then he collapsed to the ground. There were murmurs of surprise from the bystanders. At least, Norma thought as Lester grabbed her again, he had knocked that nasty look off the man's face.

Lester was staring at the end of his fist, still suspended steadily in space several feet away from his nose. He gave a low whistle of amazement. In the stillness of the moment the eerie, floating, melodyless tune seemed to be the only sound in New York.

"Let's go." She snatched a handful of his jacket.

"Did you see that?" he said as he stumbled after her through the crowd toward a familiar destination.

"So lovely," she had time to reply.

"Mr. and Mrs. Dent!" Mr. Yee greeted them outside his shop enthusiastically, waving off the small crowd of spectators. Norma looked back and saw that the man had managed to crawl off into the shadows somewhere. Life had returned to normal so quickly that except for her throbbing legs and Lester's ripped jacket, there was no outward indication of any trouble. *"How boo how?"*

"No," Lester said, massaging his swelling knuckles, *"boo how doy!"*

Mr. Yee's ever-pleasant demeanor never changed. "The *boo how doy* are long gone, Mr. Dent."

"I'm telling you, Mr. Yee," Lester replied. "Mrs. Dent and I just met living history in all his glory. An honest-to-God hatchet man. In fact, I knocked him ass over teakettle!"

He began to tell the story of the chase but Norma interrupted. "Mr. Yee? Where are your dumplings?" She caught her breath and drew *And to Think That I Saw It on Mulberry Street* from her handbag. She had wrapped it in colored crepe paper. "I have something for them."

"Of course, Mrs. Dent, please come in off the street." He ushered her into the building, where hugs and squeals of delight from little Monk and Ham, Mr. Yee's dumplings, greeted her.

EPISODE ELEVEN

THE BOY, who was known only as Gousheng, dog food, left his village behind him and set off on the harvesters' path through the rice paddies. The evenly spaced sprouts were growing in water that smelled dank and old. It was the smell of his grandmother, who worked these paddies. He hated his grandmother, who, in addition to smelling like cow dung, was shrill and quick to anger and favored his cousins before him because he was a bastard and his mother was dead.

The summer day was brilliant and clear. The sun was high in a sky with few clouds. If his cousins or friends were with him, the day's fun would be to try to knock one another into the knee-deep, muck-filled water. This contest could last for hours.

A water buffalo gazed sagely at him, a huge wooden yoke upon its back. The ticks on its flank were swollen nuggets, the size of his thumb. The boy knew what the weight of the yoke around the beast's neck felt like. It felt like his grandmother's burning hatred.

He came across the ridge to a copse on the far bank of the paddy. He stepped easily up the hill and looked around. From here he could see no one from his village. The buzzing of bees and the distant cry of cranes were the only sounds he could hear. The old women of the village (there were no old men, or any men, only boys) said that the thicket was haunted by demons and that no one should ever go there. So he escaped there whenever he could, for he knew no one would follow. He crept deeper into the grove of trees, pushing into the darkness for the clearing he knew lay ahead.

The temple was ancient, older than any old thing he had ever seen in his village, which meant that it was older than anything he had ever seen. There were stones embedded deep in the earth, grass growing up nearly over them. The clay tiles of the roof were gone in places. He knew there were no demons here.

Inside the temple were old stone statues of gods that he had never heard of and that no one worshipped anymore. Most had toppled from their bases ages ago and lay crumbling on a hard wooden floor. Their hands embraced holes carved through the centers of their chests in some ancient symbol of heavenly illumination. The large statue, still upright against the back wall, fascinated him in particular. This god's face was not serene and meditative, like the faces of the others. It was wrathful. He liked to pretend that he was this god's priest, and the caretaker of his temple, and here the people of his village could come to him for the interpretation of the whims of the gods, and he would instruct them that the gods would favor them if they were to drive his grandmother from the village or harness her to a yoke.

The sound of the horse snorting interrupted his daydream. He ran from the temple. A strong hand grabbed his shoulder and threw him to the ground. The sun was behind the demon and made it hard to see him when the boy looked up from the ground. His head hurt. He kicked out at the demon, his foot connecting with wooden shin armor. He couldn't fight this. He thought about the beautiful day, the secret grove, his temple with its gods, his one god in particular, and he thought of his grandmother and the yoke on the water buffalo and realized he had nothing much more to live for and that this was a nice place to die. He smiled and closed his eyes, for he knew his life was over.

"Your father, who was my cousin, has died," spoke the demon into his darkness. His voice was hard and commanding, but gentle. "I have come for you. You will sit behind me in my saddle and we shall ride from here together."

"I shall never return here?"

"No," said the demon. "You will find a new home."

"Would my grandmother be able to find me?"

The demon laughed. It was fearsome and warm at the same time. "You will never see your grandmother again."

The boy opened his eyes. "I will come with you," he said, and the demon held out his hand to help him up.

And so the boy, who had been known in the village only as Gousheng, dog food, was adopted into the clan of the warlord Zuolin and took his surname, Zhang. But he was also given a name that honored his father's spirit as a warrior who fights against the foreign invaders. His new name was now Zhang Mei. But he would not be known as the Dragon of Terror and Peril for many years yet.

Episode Twelve

"Jesus Christ!"

Walter could tell that Hubbard was a little impressed by his personal Pullman car.

"Holy jeez!"

He knew it was impressive.

"Son of a bitch!"

He had bought it to impress. "Like it?"

"Hell!"

"I couldn't tell." He threw his hat on the banquette. "Well. Come on in and make yourself at home. It's not the distance to Providence that wears you out. It's all the stops at nowhere in between."

It had taken a couple of days to get the car hitched up to the New York and New England Railroad, over from its usual place on the Seaboard Air Line Railroad, where Gibson used it to make frequent runs down to Miami. Often on those occasions when he wasn't heading south, the railroad would rent the car out for him. This arrangement had already paid for the car. Yesterday, Friday, the car had been floated on a tug from the Oak Point rail yard in the Bronx to the New York Central rail yard at Seventy-second Street on the Hudson, where they were now boarding it to get to Providence and Lovecraft's funeral tomorrow.

A Negro porter opened the door separating the living quarters, which they were in, from the sleeping quarters, and said, "Welcome aboard, Mr. Gibson," with his smile of familiar affection.

"Hi, Chester," Gibson greeted him back. "How're the ladies?"

"Same as usual, Mr. Gibson. They all want me richer or deader. Or both." Chester traveled with the car; tending to it often meant living in it. In the year since Gibson had hired him, Chester had kept the car as neat and trim as any ship.

Through Orson Welles, Gibson had met a number of people involved in the Federal Theatre Project and the Works Progress Administration. One of them had mentioned a talented young writer who had the misfortune to be both a Negro and a prison parolee but was on the straight and narrow and would work honestly and hard. Gibson had hired him with the words, "There's typewriters in the car and lots of paper and lots more spare time. A man could put all that to some kind of use." Gibson didn't know whether or not the man had put it to good use because the car was always immaculately prepared for him whenever he arrived.

Chester hopped off the train to get their luggage from the nearby cab. He moved with an old, slow limp. The story was that he had fallen down an elevator shaft at some point in his life, before prison, and busted his leg up.

Gibson hung his coat on a hanger and put it in the small closet. He hadn't traveled recently and the scents of varnish and polish made him smile. It was one of those particular combinations of favorite smells that he always remembered that he had forgotten once he remembered it.

"God damn!" There was a heavy thump behind him as Hubbard stumbled around the car. Being in a coach was kind of like being on a boat. There was never quite enough room and it took some getting used to.

The walls of the lounge room were paneled with dark cherrywood, and the Persian rugs on the floor were deep red, so even though the glow of the oil lamps seemed to be swallowed up, the room remained comfortable and warm. A leather banquette, a pair of leather club chairs, a sideboard with liquor decanters, and a small bookcase stocked with books on magic made up most of the furnishings. There was a small workbench supplied with tools of the trade where Gibson could tinker with magic tricks. If he had any time on this trip, he intended to continue his efforts to re-create Blackstone's astonishing exploding fireball effect, which had stymied him for months.

Unless he could bring himself to write.

At the end of the room, beside the corridor to the main cabins, galley, and head, was another small desk set. A typewriter sat on it with a fresh sheet of paper in the roller. Thanks, Chester, he thought. Thanks for reminding me. Next to the typewriter lay a neat stack of the latest mags in case he would rather read than write.

Gibson went straight to the desk and opened one of the drawers. Good. He was pretty sure he had left a half-finished manuscript here after a trip to Chicago many months ago, and seeing the papers confirmed that he had. One of the reasons he was taking the overnight train was that it took a roundabout route and made many stops, so it wouldn't pull into Providence until late morning, giving him plenty of time to work on this book. Or start a new one. He flipped to the back page and read the last sentence to see if it would remind him what he'd been writing: "Lamont Cranston had a premonition of Death." For a moment he stared at the words, which appeared halfway down the page. He turned the phrase over in his mind, whittling it down until just one word remained: *premonition.* Had Litzka really had a premonition of Howard's death?

He put the thought out of his head and instead focused on the work that had to be done. He'd be able to finish the book on this trip. And maybe he'd start something new. Something different.

If only Hubbard gave him a break.

"How much did you spend on this? Are you still making payments? Can I borrow it sometime?"

There was something else rolling around in the drawer. At first

Gibson thought it was a cigarette, but it wasn't one he had rolled. He picked it up and sniffed it. Reefer. Interesting. Without putting it down he looked at the mag on the top of the stack. It was the recent issue of *Bronzeman,* one of the only Negro pulps. This particular mag was actually published in Harlem. Underneath the striking image of a handsome Negro—face turned to the sun, sleeves rolled up, indicating readiness to work or to join the revolution—was the list of names of this issue's story writers. He saw Chester's name and smiled, guessing that Chester had been planning to throw himself a little debut party. Looking at the reefer stick and the mag, he knew that Chester would probably be moving on soon. Gibson would read the story and congratulate Chester, but the two of them would never speak of the marijuana that went missing on the run to Providence.

He'd smoked the stuff once or twice before and hadn't seen any demons. Anyway, maybe this would help him relax. After all, he hadn't slept for nights, ever since the theater, and Litzka and her disturbing premonition. And the booze just wasn't cutting it.

Sleep? Hadn't he been thinking about writing all night moments ago? To sleep or write, the writer's eternal boxing match. If sleep weren't such a damn good fighter, there would be a lot more books to read.

"Do they make these to order or can you buy them from a showroom?"

He wasn't quite certain how Hubbard had managed to invite himself. He certainly was a persuasive and ingratiating little son of a bitch. If writing didn't work out for him, Gibson suspected politics would. One minute Gibson was in his office making travel arrangements and the next Hubbard was offering to tag along. As the president of the American Fiction Guild, Hubbard felt it was important that a representative pay his respects to one of their fallen own.

"You ever read Howard?" Gibson asked, surprised that he didn't already know whether Hubbard had any knowledge of Lovecraft.

"Sure. Nothing that comes to mind right now. But folks say he was good. Doc Smith says he was great."

"Yeah." Gibson felt like telling him that he didn't have to lie.

Howard's stories were hard to find and even harder to like. Gibson moved to the sideboard and held up a decanter of scotch. Hubbard nodded and Gibson poured.

"Yeah," Gibson continued. "He was good. Could have been the next Edgar Allan Poe. He was that good." Lovecraft—just another writer passing from obscurity to oblivion.

"What happened?"

"Well, I guess most Americans think we already have one Poe too many."

"Oh." Hubbard settled easily into one of the club chairs. "How'd you meet him?"

Gibson looked out at the sun setting over the Hudson River. The ice was thick and silvery in the pinkish light; boats wound their way through channels hacked through it. "Our wives," he said. "Our wives introduced us."

"You're married?" Hubbard was surprised.

"I was."

"I know what that's like."

"You're divorced?"

Hubbard shook his head. "My wife threw me out. She heard I had an affair with an actress out in Hollywood."

"How'd she hear that?"

"Well, it was true, for one thing. What a mistake! Walt, I'm telling you . . ." He stopped, carried away with his memories. "My lawyer calls it a trial separation. She'll take me back when she cools off. I hope so anyways. I miss my damn kids."

"Didn't want to go back to your actress?"

"Well, the picture didn't really do what everyone hoped. So . . ." He trailed off for a moment. "I s'pose she's screwing the next writer by now. So's Hollywood, for that matter."

Gibson smiled and loosened his tie. Hubbard could be an agreeable person when he wasn't trying to shine a fella on.

Hubbard sighed. Then he gave a dismissive flip of his hand. "So how'd your wives introduce you?"

"When I was married, I used to get lots of fan letters." He paused, then decided to back up a little bit. "Lovecraft was a huge letter writer. He spent as much time writing letters during the day as you or I do writing our stories. Anything or anyone that struck his fancy would get a letter. So he started writing me because he liked my codes which I stuck in some of the books. I was working on one of those at the time, so I sent him a special code key for it. I gave him his own layer so everyone who had the code key that I published in the story would read it one way, but only he could read it another. I've done that occasionally for other people who are interested in the codes. It's a good brain teaser for me to write one code that has two keys. Y'know, I'd just stick in something personal like, 'Hi, Howard. Ain't scotch swell? Drink more scotch.'"

With a whistle and a shudder, the train began to move. Gibson continued, "Howard was a really smart guy. Self-taught about biology and math, in particular. He had always wanted to be a scientist, but he'd had to drop out of college and I guess he was embarrassed about that so he tried to make up for it by learning and doing these little experiments.

"He loved the codes and he would keep writing me. I got a letter a week, mostly about writing and how frustrating he found it. He never asked me to read his stories, which he could hardly ever get published. But he talked about them and he spoke about writing as if he were a bestseller.

"After a while I was getting so busy with my books that my wife started reading and answering my mail. She came across a letter from Howard telling me that he and his wife were moving to New York and she was going to open a hat store. Well, among other things, my wife loved hats. I think for about three months she single-handedly kept that store open. So, she and Sonia, Howard's wife, were getting together and eventually we went out to visit them in Red Hook and I met Howard.

"It was obvious that this was a nervous guy. I guess his family was blue-blooded. So Red Hook was a real comedown for him and I think he really resented it; all the immigrant Italians distressed him in particular. I don't think he had ever been really exposed to anything even vaguely foreign or exotic. I think he was humiliated by the poverty of their apartment and their neighborhood and their life. He was kind of a momma's boy and Sonia really tried to mother him. She didn't exactly cut his steak for him, but fairly close. We had drinks a couple of times after that. He was just miserable in New York. I think he hated that his wife had to work. Even though he was where the mags were, he couldn't get his stories published on any kind of regular basis. I mean, even *Weird Tales* has a limit to how far they'll actually push 'weird.' And his stuff was weird. Y'know. Poe weird." He trailed off.

"I tried to get him a gig before things got too bad. *Weird Tales* had a license from Harry Houdini to print some of his true adventure stories. And by true, I mean completely made up. Harry asked me if I could do it, but I was too busy with The Shadow. So I recommended Howard. So he met with Harry and wrote a crackerjack little story called "Imprisoned with the Pharaohs." Well, we all thought this was going to be the big one. He waited for it to be published so the eds could really discover him.

"Of course, first *Tales* decided it was a good spring issue fit, and it was winter. Then in the spring they decided maybe it was a better summer story. So they sat on it. Howard didn't get that things like this happen all the time."

Hubbard nodded; he had stories all over town that were waiting for publication for one reason or another.

"I told him to get busy and write another story. And another. And another. Take the fact that he got paid well for this one as a sign of encouragement. He really wanted to see that story in print, more than anything. Really thought it was going to break his career in a really big way. But it just took too long. And when it finally did get published, it didn't even get the cover.

"The bigger problem was that Harry hadn't read the story before it was published, and he didn't like it. In the story his character keeps fainting from sheer terror. He found that rather unmanly. Houdini never faints! And he never asked Lovecraft to write for him again.

"I don't think Howard could take it here anymore. He left Sonia and moved back to Providence. I'd get a letter from him every now and then. He took a job writing science papers at some research lab. Once or twice a year he'd publish a story in the shudders and he'd let me know. I'd write him back in our code, y'know, just a short, secret note of congratulations."

"What happened to his wife?"

"I don't know. My marriage . . ." He let it hang, unwilling to talk to Hubbard about it. "Lose the wife, lose her friends, y'know?"

Hubbard nodded empathetically.

Gibson rose, swaying gently with the rhythm of the train. He could hear Chester in the main cabin unpacking his bags.

"I'm going to try and get some work done," he said, moving to the desk set.

"Sure thing," said Hubbard. "Pretend I'm not here."

Gibson took a seat and lit a cigarette.

"What's your story called?" Hubbard was stretching out on the sofa with one of the books from the cabinet: *The Great Raymond Presents 200 Tricks You Can Do!*

Gibson took a long drag on his cigarette and stared at the cover of the book in Hubbard's hands. Seeing the cover of the book he had ghosted with the elderly magician five years ago gave him a pang of guilt.

"*Murder Rides the Rails,*" he said, trying to remember more about the unfinished book.

Hubbard stuck out his lower lip in thought, as if he had heard better. He thumbed through the book. "I saw Lester Dent at the Knickerbocker. Said he was thinking about trying to solve the Ah Hoon mystery."

"Mystery. History. I wish him luck."

Gibson looked at that last line again.

. . . premonition of Death.

He took a long swallow from his glass. Why was Lamont Cranston having a premonition of Death? Where had Gibson been intending to take that thought? His glass was empty, so he rose and went for a refill, turning the words around in his head. Should he have called Litzka? Maybe he'd compose a telegram to her and have Chester pass it along to the conductor to be sent at the next stop.

"What do you think happened?"

"To what?"

"To Ah Hoon. What do you think happened?"

"I think for the purposes of the story I was telling it doesn't really matter and if old Lester Dent wants to try and dig up something, then that's his story to tell. I'm ready to start the next one."

"What's your secret?" Hubbard asked a while later from behind the book. Gibson gritted his teeth. Just because a man's not typing and is staring out the window watching the Hudson Valley open up to him doesn't mean he's not writing, he wanted to blurt out.

"How do you keep cranking out the words? You gotta have a secret is what I figure. I mean, I can write a lot. But you. Everyone says you're like a machine."

Gibson shrugged. "Sure, a machine," he said. "I don't know about secrets but there's some tricks I keep in mind that keep problems from getting in my way and stopping my flow.

"Don't worry about getting it right, just get it on paper. Never, ever try to describe New York in its entirety, only by blocks, neighborhoods, or atmosphere. I never use the word *occasionally* because I can never spell it right.

"When you write about a dame always start with what her legs look like. 'Dashing' is the quickest way to describe a hero. 'Hirsute' is the quickest way to describe a villain. Never take a job from an ed who says he'll pay you better next time around after you earn your stripes; he'll never respect you and he'll just toss you scraps from there on in. And he'll never pay you better. Never.

"Don't try and write a whole book at once. Throw everything you know on the page. Only write a story that you really know, because only you can come up with the right ending. Don't steal a story; you'll be found out. Keep writing. Don't stop. Ever. Because there's always the chance that you won't start again."

. . . a premonition . . .

He had it! The book had been started before the Allard thing. But Gibson must have already been toying with the idea in the back of his mind and let it spill out onto the page. Lamont's premonition had been about his death as a character. That would never do. His fingers began to move against the keys. He struck out the line and started a new sentence.

"Although The Shadow wore many disguises, he would always be Lamont Cranston, and when he laughed, weak men would experience a premonition of their death."

"That's better," he muttered to himself.

Hubbard arched an eyebrow and then returned to his book.

Gibson wrote like the train itself—relentlessly, driving forward into the night. Long after Hubbard had turned in, he slammed away at the typewriter keys. The pages began to pile up. The skin on his fingertips cracked, then bled. When he finally lit the reefer cigarette early in the morning, he watched with interest as the thin paper turned red from blood which hissed and bubbled away into tiny wisps of steam as it burned.

EPISODE THIRTEEN

THE PIGS had screamed all night.

Mei had been unable to sleep. Even if he hadn't been so excited, the sounds of the tormented pigs would have kept him up anyway. So he was alert to the sound of someone creeping down the hall to his sleeping chamber.

"He's coming," Xueling whispered from the door.

Mei threw his cover off and leapt up. He was already dressed.

Of his eight adopted brothers, Xueling was the closest in age to him. He was also his closest friend. The two studied many things together, from history to sword fighting to riding to languages such as French (it was important to know the language of diplomacy) and English (it was more important to know the language of the foreign invaders).

They padded silently together through the halls of Shenyang Palace. Mei was bigger and faster than Xueling and most other boys his age, and Xueling had to quicken his pace to keep up. Dawn had yet to arrive and everyone but the guards was asleep.

There was a man awake, however, standing near the entrance awaiting the sun: Mi-Ying, the diplomat from Beijing, who counseled their father on the intricacies of dealing with the Russians and Japanese who flocked to his court like goldfish to crumbs.

"Your father is triumphant. The foreign invaders have been driven from the land. It is only a shame that you are not old enough to be at your father's side at his victory," he said to them.

"There are many battles yet to fight," Xueling said back to him coldly. "Though China is divided by civil wars, an emperor will sit in Beijing yet again."

"Indeed." The diplomat nodded and took a step aside so the boys could pass him. His eyes were dark and mercenary, and malice and contempt lurked behind his thin, unctuous smile. Mei could feel the man's hard eyes driving into his back as he retreated into the dark of the hall.

They entered the courtyard with its eight pavilions. The sky was lightening and the stars were winking out. The cool dew on the flagstones made his feet tingle. They ran up the stairs of the Phoenix Tower. At the top of the turret they could see the vast palace below them, across the city, even to the land beyond.

Slaughtered pigs on raised platforms lined the wide, tree-lined road which led toward the palace gate. The heralds had arrived yesterday at noon the previous day with word of the victory. Each house had been commanded to produce an animal for the feast. The pigs were decorated with painted symbols of victory, flower blossoms filled their eyes and mouths, and colorful flags were staked into their flanks. Many were draped with firecrackers.

"Look," said Mei. His eyes were sharper than Xueling's. He pointed into the distance. A cloud rose on the horizon. "Dust," he added. "Our father comes. He will be at the gates by midday, at the head of an army of triumph."

"Someday," his brother said, "we will ride with him into Beijing, and China will be saved."

Mei nodded. He knew Xueling was wise for his age. Xueling could grasp the vastness of China's history and dilemmas at times when he could not. But then he also knew that there were things he saw that Xueling did not. He knew for example that devious Mi-Ying profited from the dealings he recommended to Zuolin. Mei also knew that Mi-Ying hated them all. He knew this because he recognized his grand-mother's cruelty in Mi-Ying's eyes. Xueling would not know hatred like this. Xueling was as oblivious to this side of human nature as the dead pigs had been to their fate.

The two boys turned to watch the sun break through the great cloud rising in the east. The Emperor of the Northern Lands was returning home to his sons.

EPISODE FOURTEEN

"OPIUM? SO that's what that smell I smelled was?" Lester asked. "Yes," Mr. Lee nodded. "*Fook yuen*. Opium. There is a notorious opium den underneath the theater for many years. Men descend through the door at the back of the alley." He sat back and contemplated Mr. and Mrs. Dent. "You should not have gone into the theater. It is a very bad place. You are very lucky you were not hurt."

Mr. Yee's restaurant wasn't the fanciest restaurant in Chinatown but it wasn't one of Chinatown's many cheap noodle houses either. There were always fresh red cotton cloths for every table and the savory green tea was served in painted porcelain pots, not tin. The aromas of fresh garlic, scallions, and vinegar filled the air. Every now and then a rich smoky blast of sizzling peppers would issue forth from the kitchen, causing guests to clear their throats. Dozens of framed pictures of China's landscapes and history, and of Chinese immigrants in America from the railroad age on, hung on the walls. Candles burned at the foot of a small Buddha statue in a shuttered box at the back of the restaurant.

An old man sat at a table near the front window, having dinner with a much younger man. Neither of them spoke to, or even seemed to acknowledge the existence of, his companion. Next to them, on a table near the door, sat a fresh metal pail. A flyer was pasted to the pail. Every now and then a person would open the door, drop some change or a bill into the bucket, and then leave. On the other side of the window, Chinatown had neatly made the transition from late afternoon to night. The women had taken their shopping home and the men were out running the errands that men do after dinner.

Monk stared Norma down over the last few pot stickers on the plate. The boys' mother had died in labor giving birth to the second child. Norma had nicknamed the children Ham and Monk after two of Lester's most popular characters, Doc's comic relief companions. The names seemed to suit them. In the books Brigadier General Theodore Marley Brooks, or Ham, was a fussy and supercilious lawyer who carried a sword sheathed in a dandy's cane. Gorilla-shaped Lieutenant Colonel Andrew Blodgett "Monk" Mayfair was his opposite in every way except his brilliance; his field was chemistry. The elder boy, Ham, who was eight, was fastidious and somber and unusually erudite for a child. Monk, who was four, was strong and messy and thought nothing was funnier than tweaking the sensibilities of his older brother, to his father's amusement. In return, they had dubbed Lester and Norma Mr. and Mrs. Doc.

Although Monk had probably eaten three times his weight in pot stickers during his short life, he wanted nothing more than one of the savory, steamed wrapper-around-pork-rolls which lay on a bed of cabbage between him and Norma. He made moon eyes at it and then her, and back and forth, trying to get some indication from her that it would be safe to attack the pot sticker. What complicated matters was that he had already managed to cadge one from her, but it had slipped from his hands and landed with a slightly greasy plop on the tiled floor. The look he gave her now was intended to make her aware that he understood the responsibility of being entrusted with the next pot sticker, and that its fate would be entirely different.

Meanwhile Ham, also sitting at the table, studying the *Doc Savage* magazines Norma had brought him, would periodically look up with disdain at his brother's scheming. Norma took great delight in stretching out the suspense for both boys.

"The *boo how doy*. The highbinders. The hatchet men. They don't really exist in Chinatown anymore," Mr. Yee explained to Lester. "There has been a truce between the Hip Sing and the On Leong for almost ten years, and the smaller tongs such as the Sam Yip and others have really died away.

"Look over there." He indicated the two men at the front of the restaurant. "My uncle is a Hip Sing man. Does he look like a fearsome gangster to you? I am a Hip Sing man. Am I not your brother? Why, right this moment my uncle and his friend, a diplomat from the consul general's office here in New York, are discussing the upcoming Unity Parade in which we Chinese here in this land will show our solidarity with our families fighting the Japanese back in China. The consul general himself, a great man, will be the grand marshal," he added proudly, "and he will take the money we have raised back with him to our people who are in desperate need. It was not until mere months ago that the remaining warlords and the Communists set aside their difference with the old Imperialists and began to fight the Japanese invasion. And that only happened because Chiang Kai-shek was kidnapped by the last warlords and forced into an alliance at the threat of his life. Meanwhile, Japan advances every day and the Chinese people go hungry."

Norma looked toward the two men, who were still stoically eating. Any discussion appeared to be taking place on a purely metaphysical plane.

"Unlike in China, the old feuds have died out here. The face of Chinatown today is one of unity. Being peaceful and prosperous together in the Chinatowns across the Golden Mountain is the only way we have to convince your government to lift the Exclusion Act and bring our refugee families here."

"What's a Confucian hat?" Monk asked.

"Exclusion Act," his brother snorted. "It means no Chinese in America. Unless you're born here. It's the law."

"Father wasn't born here," Monk said defiantly.

"Through the graces of my uncle who already lived here, I entered," their father told them. He gazed toward the front of the restaurant for a moment, recalling his journey. "I sailed across the Pacific Ocean and then I had to make my way all across Canada, which is almost as big as the whole America, and much colder. And I was just a little older than your brother when I did it. By myself."

"They can't make us go back to China, can they?" Monk asked, plainly worried.

"Of course not!" said Norma. "I would never let them take you. Because you're my dumplings and I love you. And your father makes the best pot stickers in the world and I love them too!"

"Which do you love better? Pot stickers or dumplings?" Monk was laughing. Ham looked up from his magazine, invested in the answer as well. Norma laughed at Monk and the great pot sticker–dumpling debate was joined.

While Norma and the dumplings teased each other, Lester turned to Yee. "You ever hear of a fella by the name of Ah Hoon?"

"Ah Hoon?" Mr. Yee began to laugh in a most good-natured manner. "Ah Hoon!"

The old man at the table by the front caught Yee's eye with a gesture so subtle that Norma nearly missed it. "Excuse me," he said, rising, wiping away a tear. He went toward the table.

"Who's Ah Hoon?" she asked Lester. She had never heard him speak that name before.

"It's just something I'm working over." She knew that Lester was superstitious about letting anyone read anything of his until he was done with it. He felt that the act of its being read would trigger something in his mind that said that the work was done; it had been read; it was over. Apparently the story of Ah Hoon fell into that category because "something I'm working over" was his stock response to questions about his writing.

Monk was kicking at the pot sticker under the table. He made contact and it skittered slickly across the tiled floor.

"Go get that!" Ham was imperious, assuming his father's mantle of control.

"You get it," Monk said with defiance.

"That's all right," Lester said. "I'll get it."

He stood up. Monk looked enviously at his height and said, "I bet if you had a son he'd be taller than you."

Lester smiled and tousled the boy's hair. "You're probably right." He walked toward the pot sticker.

"Are you ever going to have some boys?" Monk asked Norma.

She felt her lips purse for a moment. Both boys looked at her, earnest and eager for a response. She looked at Lester as he sauntered across the restaurant and felt something break in her chest. His whole life revolved around creating stories for boys, and he would never have his own to share them with. She realized a truth about the rest of her life. She smiled at the boys, to reassure them. "No," she said. "I don't think so."

They looked disappointed.

The front door slammed open. The sound startled her, and she reflexively choked back the tears which she had been verging upon. As she turned her head to look, she saw Lester in mid-bend toward the pot sticker, and Mr. Yee speaking with the old man at the front table.

"Hey!"

It was the fat cop they had seen harassing the fishmonger earlier in the day. His face was overly pink and oily, as if he had been drinking. He swaggered through the door, his silvery, greedy eyes swiveling around. She saw Ham grow tense and wary, and Monk quickly slid off his chair and slid up to her side, under her protective arm.

"I heard there was some street fighting outside earlier and one of them punks was from here. Come on, Yee. Give it up. You speakee English better'n any other Chink down here."

"I don't know what you mean," Yee said politely. "A man fell down outside. That is all."

The old man at the table continued to eat, oblivious, while the younger man glared at the cop. Yee placed a hand innocently upon his shoulder as if to reassure him. From the creases which appeared in the man's jacket, Norma could see that he was actually applying pressure. She realized that he was keeping the man seated, and she wondered what exactly the young man was capable of. "There was no fighting here."

The cop had already lost interest in Yee and was casting his gaze around the room. His eyes lighted upon the pail of money. "That's some collection you're raising there, Yee. Church building?"

"It's the fund for the defense of Beijing," Yee replied.

He reached his hand into the pail and it came out with a fistful of bills. "Think of me as the *auxiliary* defense league."

The young man at the table brushed Yee's hand aside as if it were a stray branch and leapt to his feet with a shout. Yee barked at him.

The cop broke into a big grin. "Your friend sure looks like he could be the kind to start a rumble in the street." He reached in and pocketed another handful. "Anybody want to change their story here?" He reached in again. The rustling of the paper bills made the change scratch unpleasantly on the bottom of the pail. "I didn't think so."

"That money is for widows and orphans." For the first time the cop seemed to notice the presence of white people and he seemed to be especially surprised that the woman had just snapped at him.

"Lady, this is between me and the Chinee," he snapped at her. But his voice wavered.

Lester took a step toward him. Norma tried to stand too, but Monk held her fast. She pulled the little boy closer. She could feel his heart pounding against her side.

"Like she said, the money is for widows and orphans. And you ain't either. I want your name and badge number."

The cop took a step closer. "You're so tough, why don't you tell me your name."

"My name," Lester said, "is Kenneth Robeson. I want you to put that money back before I report you to your superiors and the mayor's office and the papers."

"Okay, Robeson, let some of that steam out of your collar." The cop was nervous. He hadn't expected to be challenged, and certainly not by a white man who loomed over him. "Look, I'm putting it back." He twisted back to dump the money in the pail.

"All of it," Lester commanded.

"Sure," said the cop. Then he suddenly charged at Lester, drawing his truncheon from a ring around his belt.

Norma gasped. Lester didn't move a muscle. The cop raised his arm and was opening his mouth to say something or yell something when his whole attitude changed in an heartbeat. His eyes opened wide in fear and he seemed to lose control of his legs, which flew out from under him. His arms flailed around; his club knocked into his mouth. Off balance and moving fast, he crashed to the floor, his head banging, then bouncing, off the tiles.

Norma looked down. Mashed onto the sole of the cop's shoe at the tail end of a long and greasy skid mark was a slick residue of cabbage and pork and dough, the sad fate of the lost pot sticker. There was a sudden quiet in the restaurant. Even the cooks in the kitchen stopped cooking and came to the door. Lester bent down over the moaning cop. "Can you hear me?"

The cop shook his head from side to side.

"Okay. I have your badge number now. I want you to stay out of this restaurant forever, do you hear me? Leave the Yees alone. Or so help me I will be hanging your badge over my mantle by spring. Hear me?"

The cop nodded.

"And I want you to act more decently to the Chinese folk on your beat. Treat 'em nice."

"Les . . . Kenneth," said Norma. "It's enough."

"Okay." He turned to the cop. "Do you want me to call an ambulance?"

The cop shook his head. He crawled to his hands and knees and staggered to his feet. He had his hand over his head. He fumbled toward the door.

"Remember what I said. You won't come back here, right?"

The cop nodded.

Norma watched as Lester remained motionless as the cop staggered into the night. Lester slid the tip of his shoe across the slick floor streak of squashed pot sticker.

"Boys, when it comes to pot stickers or dumplings," he said, with a wink to Monk and Ham, "I gotta tell ya, I'm coming down on the side of the pot stickers."

EPISODE FIFTEEN

I T WAS summer in the Year of the Monkey. The solstice had passed a few weeks before and the days were long and hot. The men fighting and dying were hidden by the dust of the battle.

Blood streamed down the blade of Mei's *pudau* and onto the wooden hilt. It was warm and his fingers stuck to it. He had lost sight of Xueling and Zuolin soon after the charge. Now he fought on only to reach the river. The river was life.

Troops loyal to Beijing had ambushed Zhang Zuolin's army as they prepared to cross the river. It was a preemptive strike, intended to keep the warlord from bringing the war to the gates of the Forbidden City itself. The surprise attack was a desperate attempt to catch Zhang's army while they were still spread in a line, unable to create formations quickly.

Fortunately, Mei's own division was only several miles west on a parallel course, preparing to ford the river at a different point. Messengers reached him within an hour of the ambush.

Though it was not his first battle, he was already coming to be known as the Dragon of Terror and Peril, but Mei's heart had pounded fearfully in his chest as they crested the hill above the fray. Down the hill in the small valley soldiers swarmed like ants and he could not see if his adopted father had survived the attack, if men he knew had fallen. He felt as if he would scream for the battle that was lost. At last the signal had been given and they had raced out of the trees to the attackers' unprotected rear flank.

The surprise worked. Mei and his men had plunged into the mass of confused and terrified soldiers like a shark cutting into a school of fish. The entire rear of the Beijing army collapsed in an instant from a unified organism of destruction into individual cells of fear. The traitorous ambushers were trapped between pincer claws. Mei's brother, Xueling, had led his cavalry toward the river after the charge in order to seal off retreat. That position would now be fortified. That was where safety lay.

Mei felt as if his body had never performed as strongly before and never would again. His horse had been cut out from under him at the height of the charge, its front legs sheared away at the joints. He had miraculously landed on his feet in the midst of his enemies. Slashing and blocking as he had practiced so many times, he made men fall before him. The straps of his armor bit like razors into his back. He knew he had to reach the river and Xueling. His blade was dulling from impact. It bit deeply into the side of a man, grating on rib, and fastening deeply into the spine. He threw his foot against the man's body to dislodge him from the weapon.

Something hit him with the force of a mountain falling. The chest of a runaway horse. He curled into a ball as he fell and the hooves fell harmlessly about him before the horse galloped off. He could die here now, he knew. A sword could fall, a spear could pierce; he had played his part. Men had fallen at his hand.

He heard the sound of his death rushing toward him. It was as horns calling above the din. Slowly he brought himself to his knees. He could hear water now and smell the moss. All around the battlefield men stood. Zuolin's men, Xueling's men, the men of the Northern Lands, his men. A cheer was rising. Hands grabbed him and helped him up. A face he recollected was speaking to him. He knew the man, he realized, one of his own soldiers. He was speaking with great excitement. Mei waited patiently for his words to make sense and suddenly they did.

"Beijing is taken!" the man shouted. He was a peasant, such as Mei himself had been once. This man's lowly life could have been his. Instead, while this man would return to his village and his rice paddy tomorrow, Mei would ride with his adopted father and his adopted brother into the great city of Beijing. "The enemy runs! We are victorious! China is united!"

Mei looked back. His own path toward the river was visible as a line of corpses fallen as bamboo is knocked aside by a bear moving through a forest. He had reached the river.

EPISODE SIXTEEN

"YOU KNOW, it's almost not as heavy as you would think a coffin
would be."

Someday, Gibson thought, how he and Hubbard and a perfect
stranger ended up carrying Lovecraft's casket through the dismal rain
and icy mud at the Swan Point Cemetery to the Phillips family plot
might make a funny story.

Someday.

Right now he was having too hard a time keeping his feet from sliding out from under him to think about a story.

"You think there's a latch on this thing?" the stranger wheezed.
Gibson hoped he was not about to burst into one of his coughing fits.
Not now. Not while supporting his share of the casket. "He's not . . .
Nothing can flop out, right?"

"You feel anything shifting inside?" Hubbard snarled. "Just keep it
steady."

Might.

Gibson would have to begin the story when the stranger suddenly
woke up coughing and gasping in the back pew of the Providence
Chapel during Lovecraft's service and nearly startled him and Hubbard

to death. It was easy to be scared in the small chapel because even though it was day, the sky was dark, and for some reason the shabby chapel had lost its power. Until the stranger made his abrupt appearance Gibson and Hubbard had been the only guests in the dark, dark, very dark chapel, listening to the ancient minister evoke the prophets. Fortunately the stove had kept the room warm.

Actually, the story really would have to start with Hubbard falling asleep, Gibson thought, as he slipped on a patch of grass and heard Hubbard curse quietly behind him. "Sorry," he said, winded.

"You all right?" If Hubbard was half the writer he was, then he probably exercised about half as much. And half of nothing is . . .

Hubbard had fallen asleep and the church had been empty.

That's where it should start. The service had started with only him and Hubbard in attendance. Then the mustachioed stranger with the high forehead had awakened, coughing. But before that, the minister had begun the service. That was about the time Hubbard had fallen asleep, after muttering something about organized religion being a crutch for the weak-minded.

He was coughing again now.

"Pal, how about you? Are you all right?" Gibson asked him. He stopped, acting as if the coughing had interrupted his progress. In fact, he was grateful for the break. "You been coughing up oysters all afternoon."

The man inhaled, nodded, and began coughing again. The other two men juggled the coffin against his spasm. The stranger was much taller than Gibson, and the burden of the coffin tilted unfairly toward Gibson. Fortunately, nothing shifted inside.

"Lung damage," the man wheezed. "Tuberculosis."

"Now?" demanded Hubbard, leaning away.

The man shook his head. Gibson could see exhaustion in the dark circles under his eyes. He seemed young, probably around Hubbard's age, but he had put some miles on his lanky frame. He had the weary, defeated look of so many American men his age who had finally lost hope but hadn't yet slid into despair. He cleared his throat with a mighty effort and regained control of his breathing. "It hit me a few years ago when I was in the navy. Had to retire and move to California. Nice and dry there."

"Retire?" Hubbard asked. "What're you? Forty?"

"Thirty." Gibson could believe it if one gave the man the benefit of imagining him with a sleep, a shave, and a haircut.

Hubbard appraised him for a moment. "Retired," he finally said. "Well done."

The stranger shrugged. "Welcome to Easy Street."

"I'm ready whenever you are," Gibson said. His arms were aching and his fingers, already stiff from a night of typing, were beginning to go numb. He knew they were going to ache too much for him to write tonight. Oh well, he could work on Blackstone's magic trick.

"Right," the stranger said. He wore workman's clothes—dungarees, a sweater, and a Salvation Army–issue peacoat.

"Okay," Hubbard grunted. They continued their slog toward the wrought-iron gate and the few plots beyond. "Aren't your friends and family supposed to be your pallbearers?" Hubbard complained.

"He was kind of a hermit. Lived with his aunts. Then one died. So, just an aunt. I wonder why she's not here." Gibson had half-feared and half-hoped that Sonia would make an appearance, but she hadn't. It made him feel worse for Howard. "At least somebody he knew showed up, though. Right?" He indicated the stranger.

"To be honest, I don't even know who we're burying," the stranger said.

Gibson stopped and stared at him. "Then who the hell are you?"

"I helped dig the grave."

"You're a grave digger?"

"Well, I'm not *the* grave digger. I dug this grave. Look. I'm stuck in Providence, which is a strange land. I needed some cash. One thing I've learned is that graves always gotta be dug. Once we get this fella planted, I get fifty bucks, which gets me down to New York City."

"What's in New York for you?" Hubbard wanted to know.

"Not my ex-wife."

"Ah." Hubbard seemed skeptical.

They moved through the gate and set the coffin with a thud upon the slats over the grave. They all massaged their hands.

"At least it has stopped raining," said the stranger. Gibson nodded in agreement, although the skies were still dark and foamy. Along the path they had taken, the ancient minister was slowly approaching.

Hubbard groaned and rotated his shoulder in its socket a few times. "I specifically became a writer to avoid working," he said, grinning at Gibson.

"You're a writer?" the stranger asked.

"As a matter of fact, I am," he replied. "Ron Hubbard."

The stranger shook his head apologetically. Gibson noted that even in his destitute position he carried himself with the rigid dignity and force of a military officer.

"Ever read *Adventure Magazine* or *Two-Fisted Tales?*"

The stranger nodded and shrugged at the same time. "Sorry, pal. Never heard of you. Ever write for *Astounding Stories?* I read that."

"Great," Hubbard sighed. "Look. You heard of *The Shadow?*"

"Sure. Everybody knows *The Shadow.* You write *that?*"

"No. He does."

"Seriously?" the stranger asked. "You're Maxwell Grant?"

Gibson ground out his cigarette. "Now there's a name you'll never find in the Irish sports pages. I'm Walter Gibson. Maxwell Grant's a nom de plume." He held out his hand and the stranger shook it. His grip was firm and steady. This man was no rummy or hophead, Gibson decided. Gibson waited for a few seconds after releasing his hand. The man seemed disinclined to provide any more information. "So what's your name, pal?"

"Driftwood," he said, without hesitation. "Otis Driftwood."

Gibson smiled and was about to speak when Hubbard butted in. "I know that name! Are you a writer?"

"Naw, I'm in high society. Can't you tell?"

"Yes," Gibson said. "You're obviously an opera lover."

Driftwood gave him a sly smile. "I'm kind of trying to keep a low profile these days. Trying to keep out of the funny pages, if you know what I mean."

"G-men?" Hubbard asked. "Revenuers?"

Driftwood shook his head. "Business associates," he said. "Like I said before, I was in the navy. I was a gunnery officer out of Annapolis. I got TB.

"I'm from Missouri originally, but the hospital the navy discharged me to was in Arizona because it was hot and dry. After I recovered enough, I decided to move on west to California. Another fella who mustered out with me, a marine, said he knew of a silver concern in the San Jacinto mountains and wanted to stake a claim. But he needed some partners to help him finance it and work the mine. Well, I had a little discharge money, and some disability money coming to me. Plus I can squeeze a nickel till the buffalo shits.

"We went to work. The high mountain air was good for me. I mean, it was really hell at first. Like trying to suck air through a straw. But it really helped build my lungs and my strength back up. Turns out I wasn't the only investor, though. My partner had dug up some real un-savory types in Los Angeles, gangsters or what have you. This was be-fore we had headed up into the mountains. I don't know why he went to them. I think maybe he owed them some money from some gam-bling debt, which maybe was why he had ducked into the marines in the first place. I don't know. I sure as hell didn't know about any of that.

"I learned quick and in a few weeks I was running the operation on-site. Y'know how silver is mined? It's not like panning for gold dust or crushing it out of rock. It's really difficult. First you dig through the rock looking for the kind of ore that just might, I say, might, contain silver. Then, if you've been lucky enough to find it, that mined ore gets crushed and mixed with water into a slurry. Then you wash that over amalgamation tables which are coated with mercury. The silver sticks to the tablets while everything else—the tailing, it's called—gets sluiced off into the river. So it's not exactly like pulling big hunks of silver out of the ground. It's slow going and the returns are small at first, but eventually the silver starts accumulating.

"At first I guess they started harassing my partner because the mine wasn't paying off. Then it wasn't paying off fast enough. Then it turned out that it was going to pay off big-time. One week we banked fifty dollars in silver. The next week, nothing. A week later we banked ten grand!"

Hubbard stared at him with wide eyes. Driftwood nodded.

"That's right. And it looked like that was going to be just the tip of the iceberg. Boys, there I am. I am thinking that I have got it made in the shade. My ship was come in. I am going to be living the life of Riley from here on in. I guess my partner felt the same way because he telegraphed his associates to tell them of the great days a-coming.

"I was in the pit when he drove up. I could hear him talking to my partner. My partner starts putting up a stink and this is where I hear the whole story for the first time. My new associate wanted the mine. Not just my partner's share. My share too. The whole tamale. So I started climbing out of the pit, figuring I'm going to add a little muscle to the mix, turn this fella around and tell him where to get off. Well, I didn't even get to dust myself off before I noticed what he had brought as a bargaining chip. A Thompson sub. Ever seen what a machine gun can do to a man at close range?"

The two men shook their heads.

Driftwood ran a hand over his weary face. "It chews a man up. I took a few steps right back into the pit. The man lobbed a few spits of lead after me but it's dark down there and there are places to hide. Finally the sun went down and I made it out of the pit and into the mountains, dodging wildcats and rattlesnakes the whole way."

"Jesus," said Gibson. "How long ago was this?"

"About three months ago," Driftwood said. "I took it as a sign that it was a good time to see the rest of the country that wasn't particularly California. Been shacking up in Hoovertowns. I got rolled in Boston. I haven't shaved in a week and I'd give a tooth to make it with a woman.

I'm diggin' graves in the middle of winter and I ain't a silver tycoon. But I am alive."

"Keep sinking lower and next thing you'll probably be a pulp writer," Gibson joked.

"You don't suppose this fella's looking for you?" Hubbard asked. "Seems like he got what he wanted."

"That's what I'm hoping. I just figure to keep my head down for a little while longer. Never really been to New York, so that's kind of where I'm headed."

"That's where we're from," Hubbard said.

"Not from here?"

"No," Gibson said. "Came up for this. He was a writer too, like us. And a friend of mine."

"That's good. It's good to have friends," Driftwood said. "If I had died in those mountains my friends wouldn't have even known it, let alone made it to the funeral. I think you owe it to your friends to at least let them come to your funeral. You think working in a graveyard has made me a little bleak? You know, I actually used to do a bit of writing myself."

Gibson nodded. "Really?" Everyone was a writer, he had found. The quickest way to find out about somebody was to ask him about his novel. Everyone was always writing one, or about to.

"I used to write the newsletter for EPIC—End Poverty In California."

"You're a red?" Hubbard blurted.

"A socialist," the stranger countered with indignant defensiveness. "If Upton Sinclair had won that election, California would have been leading this country out of this Depression this very day."

"As if the New Deal isn't bad enough," Hubbard replied. "Now why not just give abandoned factories to a pack of poor people and let 'em try to make whatever they want?"

"Production for use is so much greater than that."

"Speaking of product," Gibson said, looking down, "nice hole."

"Thanks. It gets easier when the torches thaw it out."

Hubbard wouldn't drop the subject. "All I know is no one is giving me a free typewriter or free paper to do *my* work! And I've been as poor as poor can get," he said. He put his hand on the casket as he shifted his weight out of a muddy spot.

"Gentlemen," the old minister croaked as he shuffled through the gate. "We are all there is."

"Isn't Howard's aunt coming?" Gibson asked.

Gibson looked down at the headstone, which leaned against a tree, already prepared. He lifted the wet muslin from the cover to read the inscription. Under Howard's name and birth date, and the blank spot that would be filled with the date of his death, was a simple epitaph:

I am Providence.

"Unfortunately the cold weather has restricted Miss Gamwell to her home," said the minister, "but she has invited all the attendees to her house for a small reception."

Gibson looked at all the attendees and they both shrugged and nodded. "Sure," he said.

"Then let's begin, shall we?"

Then, without warning, Hubbard slipped and fell into the muddy grave with a graceless thud, and Gibson suddenly knew he had his ending.

EPISODE SEVENTEEN

ZHANG MEI strode angrily down the street and the citizens cleared a path for him. He was a fearsome sight, tall in his officer's uniform with his saber smacking heavily against his thigh. He only hoped someone would stumble into him; then he would take up his sword and vent his rage upon that unfortunate, clumsy soul.

He hated Beijing. It was filthy. It stank. Rats and dogs ran with carefree abandon through streets that were slick with the grease and refuse which overflowed from the open *benjo* ditches. The constant smoky aroma of cooking horse flesh hung thickly in the air. The people were eating horses because the supply of pork and beef from the countryside was thin and constant harassment by pirates and foreigners such as the Japanese had made the seas dangerous for the fishermen.

He hated the Beijing bureaucrats who swarmed over the palace. Their life's work was self-preservation; many of the ministers and counselors had survived the regime changes of the past two decades, steadily accruing power for themselves until no gate could be opened or dish served without their say-so. To Zuolin's face they were respectful and obsequious, agreeing with every decision, flattering every thought. They showed him all consideration due to the ruler of the various coalition factions occupying Beijing: his own men from the Northern Lands, the western provincials and Christians, even representatives of the popular Dr. Sun Yat-sen's Imperialists from the South. Yet behind his back they schemed and plotted and undermined him at every move.

His adopted father, accustomed to a martial life, seemed to accept their pledges to execute his orders without question. This was Mi-Ying's province, and the thieving diplomat seemed to pull as many strings behind the courtyard as Zuolin did upon it. Mei's dismayed warnings to Zuolin and Xueling about Mi-Ying had been waved off—Mi-Ying's actions were considered sacrifices necessary to attempting to bring order to China. If Mei had been emperor, he thought, these diplomats, even the Americans, but especially all the Chinese ones such as Mi-Ying, would learn to fear him before being put to death. Fear was the only way to control them.

He passed under the Gate of Supreme Harmony, glaring back at the bronze lions guarding it, and marched across the square to Wenyuang, the Imperial Library. This was the heart of the bureaucracy. He had nearly as much contempt for the bureaucrats as he had for the diplomats. Of all the bureaucrats he hated, the one he most despised was Lu Zhi, the librarian who controlled the Sikuquanshu, the Four Treasures of Knowledge, the Encyclopedia of the Universe—what Mei most wanted access to in all of Beijing. The peace had brought him time to pursue knowledge beyond what his brother found useful. What he could learn from the Sikuquanshu! If only Lu Zhi would bend to his will!

Although the librarian was neither the most powerful bureaucrat nor the most subservient, something in Lu Zhi's nature disturbed Mei greatly and kept him from peace. He entered the vast building, the scrolls and paintings lost upon him in his wrath. Today he would settle the score with at least one of the irritating civil servants.

He found Lu Zhi in contemplation of a new book in the publishing gallery. The sight made him quiver. His hand fell to the hilt of his sword.

"Lu Zhi," he called. His blood was rising. The battle was engaged.

Paul Malmont

Lu Zhi turned. "Master Zhang?" His visit was unexpected.

"You have driven me mad," he said to her. She was the most exquisite sight he had ever laid eyes on. "I have come to ask you to be my wife."

And, in another Year of the Rat, she said, "Of course."

Episode Eighteen

"I s it me?" Hubbard rubbed his hands on his arms. "Or is it colder in here than it was outside?"

"No," replied Gibson through teeth he was clenching to keep from chattering. "Aunt Annie's house is cold as hell!"

"Fellas," said Driftwood in a low voice. "She's coming back."

Annie Phillips Gamwell, the last of Howard's kin, lived alone at 66 College Street in a dilapidated Victorian house on a block that wouldn't have seemed out of place in Red Hook, Gibson noted with sad irony. The street itself was heavily trafficked and irritatingly noisy. An ice delivery truck was parked across the street from the Gamwell house, and the cars and cabs that wanted to pass it had to pull into the opposite lane, honking loudly and rudely as they did.

The withered old lady had invited them into her foyer and then left them standing there, shivering, as she wandered off down the dark hallway to put the kettle on for tea. Evidently she must have thought they had followed her, for she had begun a conversation with them in the kitchen which she continued as she came out of the dark corridor toward them.

"The Phillips plot has been in that cemetery for generations. It's traditional for anyone of our line, or anyone who married into it, to be buried there. Although his father isn't," she said dismissively. "Howard's surname may have been Lovecraft but he was a Phillips as far as we've always been concerned. So we're glad to have him home where he belongs." Her eyes looked up, as if following a thought that had drifted away from her. When she found it, she spoke again. "Howard was deathly afraid of being buried. He thought he might wake up while he was down there. Would you men take a drink in the parlor?"

"Oh, no, Miss Gamwell," said Gibson. "We just stopped by to pay our respects. We don't want to trouble you anymore."

"Please," she insisted. "You've all come so far, from New York City! And then being out in the cold and rain like that." She pointed to the parlor again. "Please help yourself. I hear the teakettle whistling."

"I don't hear . . . ," Hubbard started to say, but Driftwood gave him a gentle poke in the ribs. Gibson looked at the other two men and nodded. He didn't know about them but he really wanted a drink. Several, in fact. "Thank you," he said after they nodded in resigned approbation.

She creaked back into the gloomy passage, her black dress merging into the darkness so her silver head seemed to float by itself in the air. It reminded Gibson of the old school of French theatrical magic where assistants—dressed completely in black on a black stage, making them nearly invisible to the audience—would lift objects at the command of a sorcerer. To the awed spectators it appeared as if the objects were levitating. *Magie noire.* It was the foundation of the illusory ability of The Shadow to move through the pervasive darkness of the criminal underworld so effectively. Black magic is real, he thought. Not pulp.

As she completed her vanishing act, the men entered the shabby parlor. The heavy drapes were drawn against the gray day. Gibson went to a dusty liquor cabinet and poured some bourbon out of a heavy decanter into three glasses. His fingers left marks on the grimy crystal.

"Well, I didn't hear any teakettle," Hubbard complained.

"She's an old woman, Hubbard. Cut her a little slack," Gibson replied.

"I don't think anyone's been in this room for years," said Driftwood as he took a glass. "Between the damp outside and the dust in here, this town is gonna kill my lungs."

Gibson picked up a telegram which sat on the coffee table. It had been sent from Chicago. MY CONDOLENCES STOP SONIA. The simple expression, devoid of any emotion, made him feel sadder for Lovecraft than had any part of the service. He set the telegram down.

"This has been one hell of a strange day," said Hubbard. "You know, I have a crazy aunt, and her house always smells like ammonia too. Ammonia and lavender sachet. I always wonder where the smell comes from."

"I don't know if it's the cool air or what," said Driftwood, "but I got the feeling we're being watched."

"Well, if we learned anything today," said Hubbard, "it's that there ain't nobody interested in Lovecraft but us."

Gibson poured himself a second drink to keep the first one from growing lonely.

"Listen," said Hubbard. Gibson turned his attention to the creaks and sighs of the old house. There was a distant murmur of a low voice. "She's talking to herself. Must be hard to suddenly be all alone."

Her distant and muted voice suddenly broke off. The house seemed incredibly still. They could hear floorboards groan outside the parlor. Gibson suddenly found his heart racing. He looked at Driftwood, who, in spite of the cold, had broken into a sweat. Hubbard's normally florid face had suddenly gone pale. What are we afraid of? Gibson thought. What if what turned the corner wasn't an old, grieving woman but one of Lovecraft's ancient and horrible things from beyond space and time and human comprehension?

"Tea biscuits?"

Gibson exhaled with relief. The other two men shifted their weight, visibly relaxing. Gibson felt the tension leak out of him as suddenly as it had come upon him. He had a recollection of Lovecraft's Brooklyn home as having the same dread atmosphere. He thought of how much vibrant effort Sonia had put in to dispel the gloom with bright furniture and clothes and light, never realizing that perhaps the murk was Howard's own atmosphere.

"No thanks," he said. The other men politely accepted, each taking a handful. Driftwood especially seemed hungry. She placed the tray on a small end table. They stood looking uncomfortably at each other for a long moment.

"I knew your nephew in New York," said Gibson finally. "And his wife too. Does she know about Howard?"

"Of course she knows," the woman said crossly. "She wasn't much of a wife to him in life, so why should she care that he's dead?"

She rubbed her hands together as she spoke. The gesture appeared miserly but Gibson saw her wincing as she tried to work some relief into her joints.

"Miss Gamwell, it seems a bit cold in here. Do you need some help with your heat?" Driftwood asked. "We could build a fire or check your boiler—is it in the cellar?"

"No!" she exclaimed.

"It'll only take us a few moments."

"We like it cold," she insisted.

He looked down at the pattern on the rug, embarrassed for her.

Hubbard said, "I'll have another one of those biscuits, if you don't mind." He reached over toward the end table but stayed his hand for a moment before picking up an object which lay to the side of the cookie tray instead. "Hey, Walter," he said. "The Shadow's been here!" He tossed Gibson a small shiny item.

"You're right! It's a Shadow decoder ring." He smiled at the object in his hand. It was a cheap tin device that used a simple type of code called a substitution cipher. A disk of alphabet letters rotated around an inner ring of identical letters. All a kid needed to know to decode a jumble of letters was the offset key—3, for example—and whether to turn the wheel to the left or right. If the first letter in a jumble was A, then turning the A three clicks to the right placed it over D, which would be the actual first letter. "Julius Caesar invented this code."

"But did he invent the salad?" Driftwood cracked.

"Latin's not hard enough, he had to put it into a code?" Hubbard shuddered. "I hated Latin."

"That was one of Howard's gewgaws," the old lady said. "You can have it if you'd like."

"Oh, that's okay," said Gibson. "I've got a shoebox full." He held out the ring to her but she refused to release her hands and take it. After a moment he put it down on the table.

"I guess we should be going," he said. "Thank you for the drinks." She stepped aside to let them pass and they headed into the hallway. Gibson reached for the doorknob.

"Thanks," added Driftwood. "I'm sorry about your nephew's death. Cancer is awful."

"Cancer!" the woman scoffed. "Howard was murdered."

"I'm sorry?" Gibson stopped turning the doorknob. His hand began to tremble. He felt as if he were back onstage with Litzka. "How do you mean, 'murdered'? I thought he had stomach cancer."

"I mean murdered as in somebody done him in. Killed him, deliberately."

"Who?" Hubbard challenged.

"Mr. Jeffords. He owns the Providence Medical Lab, where Howard worked. I saw him at the hospital when Howard died. That ugly, bald man was choking Howard and then he ran off and Howard died. And I know why he won't leave the Medical Lab again. Because he has what Howard has. Had."

"What do the police say? Have you talked with them?"

"Bosh! The police. The only thing more corrupt in Providence than our politicians is our police. Jeffords is a rich man. That's who the police listen to. When I called the police, they talked to the doctor and I know he told them I was a senile old woman and not to believe me and that Howard was dying from stomach cancer. That's Providence for you; only thing that gets more sleep than its dead is its police. But he was murdered. I saw it."

"Why would someone do that?" Driftwood asked.

"Because something happened at the lab. Something that made him ill. And he was going to tell people. But then he was murdered."

Something bumped in the cellar, startling the men.

"What was that?" asked Hubbard.

"Rats in the walls," she said. She put her hand to her throat and toyed with her thin strand of pearls. "I'm sorry, gentlemen. I'm afraid I'm just a very overwrought old woman and it's a difficult time."

"Of course," said Gibson.

She turned and looked back down the dark hallway again. "I know your coming today means a lot to Howard," she said finally.

"You sure there's nothing we can do for you?" Driftwood asked with concern. "It's very cold in here."

She shook her head. "Thank you. Thank you for coming."

Gibson was going to ask her more, but she turned abruptly and walked down the corridor, disappearing into the gloom.

Hubbard looked at the two of them. "Brother, I wish your train could drop us off right at the front door of the White Horse Tavern. We get back, that's where I'm heading. I feel like it's going to take a month of drinking there to get this out of my system."

Driftwood nodded. "I hear that."

Gibson opened the door and the three men moved out to the porch. The yellow Checker Cab they had come in was idling at curbside while its driver smoked a cigarette. The skies were still gray and lowering. Gibson closed the door behind them. He shook his head. "Howard was afraid of his own shadow," he said. "I can't imagine him getting involved enough in anything where someone would want to kill him."

"What exactly did he do at the Providence Medical Lab?" Driftwood asked.

"Ghostwriter. Turning all that science jargon into English. Not exactly the stuff conspiracies are made of." He pulled out his pocket watch. "It's four o'clock," he said to Hubbard. "The train's not pulling out until eleven-thirty. Want to meet me there at eleven?"

"Okay." Hubbard seemed a little uncertain. "I thought you guys might want to grab a bite to eat or a couple of beers."

"Can't," Gibson said. "I've got just enough time to drop in on an old friend."

Driftwood grinned. "A girl in every port."

"Something like that." Gibson smiled back every bit as broadly. "You want the cab?"

"I'm on foot," said Driftwood. "I'm off to find a soup kitchen."

"I saw a pub about a block back," said Hubbard. "How about that beer?"

"You're buyin'?"

Hubbard winced. "Sure," he said. "Come on. I'll meet you at the train."

"Right." Gibson held out his hand to Driftwood. "Otis, it was nice to meet you. When you get down to the Empire City, look me up. I'll either be at Street & Smith or, as Ron said, boozin' it up at the White Horse."

"A pleasure, Walter." Driftwood shook his hand.

Gibson climbed into the cab and watched the two men walk down the sidewalk. He looked back at the house. He knew what Driftwood had meant when he described the sensation of being watched. Even now, outside the house, Gibson thought he saw the parlor window curtain sway as if stirred by some vague, unnatural breath.

"Where to?" The cabbie was uninterested.

Gibson rubbed his hands together. They were still chilled but the cab was warm and it felt great to get some heat. He felt sorry for the lonely old woman and wondered how she would ever manage. What became of people like her, he wondered. How did people cope with being abandoned?

Robert would know. Why not just ask him?

The thought hit him like a sledgehammer to the stomach. An old woman must understand that loved ones are taken. A wife might understand that a husband could go. What would a young son know? His son. Robert. An emptiness beyond knowing?

The driver cleared his throat.

"You know where the Providence Medical Lab is?" Gibson said.

Issue 3:
THE NIGHT WATCHMAN

EPISODE NINETEEN

T HE DOOR to the Pullman flew open with a crash and Walter Gibson, his suit torn, his hair wildly disheveled, slumped wearily against the doorjamb.

"Jesus, Walter! I guess her husband got home early, huh?" Hubbard said, putting his scotch down and rising from his club chair as Gibson dragged himself into the train car.

"I hope you got in a few good licks yourself!" Otis, in the other chair, stood too, while Chester moved swiftly to Gibson's side to help him aboard.

"Whew, that's some smell," Hubbard's happy commentary continued. "What'd you do? Fall into an outhouse?" He put a handkerchief over his mouth. "I ever tell you about the time I did just that thing . . ."

Chester helped Gibson peel off his torn jacket. Driftwood snatched a cloth napkin and poured a few ice cubes from the ice bucket into it. He wrapped it up and gave it to Gibson, who put it against his bruised and bloodied nose.

"What happened, Mr. Gibson?" Chester was worried. "Someone try to roll you?"

Gibson flopped down in his club chair, grateful for the cool pack against his face. His head was throbbing. In fact, his whole body ached. Driftwood poured him a drink, which he accepted. The three men gazed at him with concern.

"I, uh, invited Otis to hitch a ride down to New York with us. I hope that's copacetic?" Hubbard looked like a puppy who had piddled on an heirloom rug.

Gibson nodded. He was actually happy to see some friendly faces. He inhaled the alcohol's fumes through his nose, trying to get rid of his own stench, which seemed to be adhering to his nasal membranes. He wasn't usually one for gulping booze, but tonight he poured the contents of the glass down his throat and felt it explode in his stomach. At that moment, with a whistle and a lurch, the train began to move. Just in time, he thought. Providence was going to kill me if I didn't leave.

"Mr. Gibson?"

"I'm all right, Chester," he said. "I could use a bite to eat, though." He wasn't hungry at all, but he didn't want the men hovering over him like a bunch of nursemaids. Chester nodded and moved to the end of the car where a small galley stood, and began to poke around in the cabinets. Gibson knew he was all ears.

Driftwood removed the ruined jacket from the banquette and sat down. "Brother Walter," he said. "I bet you got some story to tell us!"

"Well," he said, "I took the cab to the waterfront."

"There must be someplace in Providence that's nice," Gibson had said to himself as he got out of the Checker. "I just haven't seen it yet."

The cab drove away from the lab as soon as he had paid his fare, its driver insisting that the train yard was close enough for Gibson to walk to and that he had a wife and a Sunday roast to get home to. The wind that blew in from the harbor was so cold it made his cheekbones ache, and he turned his face into his shoulder to try to shield it. He had been cold all day and it was wearing him out; even the brief trip in the cab hadn't been enough to allow the warmth to penetrate the chill which seemed to have settled deep within him.

It suddenly occurred to him to curse Lester Dent. In a way it was really that big hick's fault that he found himself here, investigating the mystery of a murder that probably hadn't even happened. If Dent was serious, as Hubbard had told him, about finding an ending to the Sweet Flower War story, he would have it over Gibson forever. Lester had been right in that, at the least, he should have had some sort of ending for the Sweet Flower story. Even though he had just been telling the story to Hubbard, it had been lazy of him not to take the time to come up with one. Being caught without an ending offended his pride as a onetime journalist, to not mention as the best-selling pulp author in America. He just couldn't possibly tell another story without an ending at the White Horse or the Knickerbocker. People would say he had gone soft.

He looked around. His cabbie had told him that this was where the Providence Medical Lab could be found, but all he could see were long, low, windowless buildings which fronted the stinking inlet. He went to the doors of several buildings but found no signs, no markings, save for street numbers. He rubbed his hands together and blew on them for warmth. He looked up and down the street. Where there was a wharf, there were longshoremen, and where there were longshoremen, there was a tavern, and where there was a tavern, there was information. Gibson located the blinking neon Beverwyck Breweries sign within moments. Waterfront bars always seemed immune to Sunday blue laws. He turned up the collar of his jacket, thrust his hands deep into his pockets, and walked briskly to the tavern.

At first he thought that maybe a fire had swept through the establishment and that the owners had simply swept up a little, restocked the icebox, and opened for business. On second thought he decided they hadn't swept up. The room was long and narrow. The bar, which ran the entire length, cut into nearly half the room, leaving only enough space for a few tables at the back. Otherwise, the few men who were here perched on stools. Their weather-beaten faces turned to look at him in a single motion. He couldn't have been more unwelcome if he had suddenly walked into any one of their living rooms.

The bartender gave him an appraising eye, which told Gibson that he had been pegged for an easy mark. Gibson ordered a pilsner from him and leaned against the bar. The radio was tuned to a hockey game over the CBC from Montreal: the Canadiens against the New York Rangers. He looked at his watch. Moments from now in New York, Orson would begin broadcasting this week's episode of *The Shadow*. He thought how well it might go over in this crowd to ask the bartender to change stations. Maybe not so well.

"You lost?" The voice was deep and salted with New England air. He hadn't even been served his drink and it had started.

Gibson looked at the wharf rat and his pal. The bigger man who had spoken was older and toothless, weathered like a mast of spruce. The little man next to him had several more teeth, and the cord of muscles in his neck twisted down to the top of his shoulders like huge snakes. Gibson looked quickly from one to the other, trying to figure out which was the dumb one and which was the dangerous one; these types usually ran in pairs. In this case it looked as if they were both dangerous. Their eyes glittered with a certain kind of wanton amoral lunacy. There were few crimes these men could commit and not escape from on the next boat sailing.

"In town for a funeral," he said. He had found through his early years as a reporter in Philadelphia that the easiest way to stay out of trouble in a situation like this was to be straightforward and unpresumptuous; common ground would eventually appear.

"There ain't no cemeteries around here," the big one said in a thick Oyrish brogue. "What was it? A burial at sea."

Funny, Gibson thought, from all the hair he would have pegged him as Russian. "You're right," he said, "the funeral wasn't around here. But the man who died worked around here at the Providence Medical Lab. Know where that is?" The little man blinked in surprise while the other one seemed to scrutinize him more closely.

The bartender set his drink down in front of him. "Shove off, fellas," he said. "Let the man drink to his friend in peace. It's the Lord's day, after all."

The two men looked at each other and shrugged. The little one pulled down his wool cap to just above his eyebrows. "We was catching the next tide anyways," he growled to the bartender. He put a hand on Gibson's shoulder. Gibson could feel the power of a life spent stowing loads and hauling sheets in his grip. He looked at the hand out of the corner of his eye. It was so covered with scars and tattoos that it was impossible to tell whether any original flesh was left. He could see an ink drawing of a severed head, dripping blood from its neck. The knife that did the cranium in was stuck gratuitously from temple to temple, to indicate that beheading wasn't enough. The man drew close and Gibson could smell the liquor on his breath. He tried to keep his breathing easy and his gaze level.

"Keep a weather eye out for the night watchman," he growled.

"Who's that?"

"Ask 'im," he said and tilted his head down the bar. Gibson did not take his eyes from the man's face to look; he'd be damned if he'd turn away from him for even an instant. Finally, the wharf rat released his shoulder, and he and his hairy Irish friend swaggered into the encroaching evening. A few moments passed and the bar wound back up to normal speed like a clock after its chimes have been struck.

Gibson motioned for the bartender to draw close. "Who's the night watchman?"

The bartender concentrated on polishing his glass. "Ignorant sailors," he said, moving away.

Gibson choked down a swallow of his thin beer and looked around. There was an old man sitting at the far end of the bar. Gibson met his eyes briefly. A moment later and the old man was at his side, settling onto a stool. "Want to know about the night watchman, so?" he asked. Gibson acted as if that thought had never crossed his mind before.

"I guess."

The old man cleared his throat to indicate how dry he was. Gibson nodded at the bartender, who filled a glass from a cask of rum. Gibson watched the old man's Adam's apple bob up and down as he threw down the liquid. It seemed to be the part of his body that functioned the best; certainly the blossoms spreading across his nose and face spoke to certain inadequacies of the liver and kidneys and blood, not to mention spleen and gallbladder and probably stomach. His retching cough completed the picture of health.

"It's why we all been getting off the waterfront afore the sun goes down of late, so?" Gibson wasn't certain if a response was needed; he kept his expression open. "Eve'y night walkin' the docks, swingin' his lantern. They says they found something on Harmony Isle and brought it back and he's come to find it."

"Found what?" Gibson whispered conspiratorially.

The old man leaned in. His breath was about the worst thing Gibson had smelled since leaving Philadelphia. "A curse."

"Was this something they brought back to the lab with them?"

The old man shrugged. He looked out toward the warehouses. Gibson tried to follow his gaze. Between the warehouses he could see the light reflecting off the surface of the inky black harbor. In the distance he could see a dock to which a long, low boat was made fast. A fog was coming in with the wind and the opposite shores were disappearing in the gloom.

"They used to have Indian sacrifices on that island, did you know that? For hundreds of years them savages would paddle out there and make sacrifices to their heathen gods. Human sacrifices. I heard of stone altars still got markings on 'em and each corner points to the four corners of the compass. The magnetic compass! Now you tell me how them redskins knew about that, I ask you."

Gibson shrugged and the old man continued. "Four good men shipped to Harmony Isle. Went out on the *Zephyr*. A few nights later, the *Zephyr* came back, but not the crew. A few weeks after that and the night watchman begins walking up an' down these here docks in the dead of night, scarin' off decent souls."

"Did the night watchman kill the crew of the *Zephyr*?"

"Goddammit, don' you understand nothin'?" His voice rose. "I told you about the curse!" He emphasized the point by smacking his palm down, rattling the bottles.

"Hey!" the bartender shouted at Gibson. "Can it!"

"Look, I'm sorry," Gibson said.

"I don't give a rat's ass!" exclaimed the bartender. "We like things quiet here. Now get the hell out before I beat ya!" His eyes were bulging. The old man began mewling that he had no place else to go. "Out!"

"Sure." Gibson tossed a few bucks on the bar and backed out into the night. No one seemed inclined to follow him and the vicinity appeared as abandoned as before. He could hear the foghorns in the distance, and the lapping of the water against the pilings, and the distant clanging of channel buoys. To the south the train whistle blew. He pulled the belt on his overcoat tight and put his hat on. He took a deep breath of cool, damp, fish-scented air and looked around. The fog drew eerie coronas from the yellow street lamps, which in this part of town were still powered by gas.

The Shadow's menacing laughter caressed his spine. He leaped around in near terror. It emanated from the bar. How about that, he thought. He had fans up here, or at least The Shadow did. It never occurred to him before to ask himself why The Shadow laughed. Gibson knew when he laughed, of course. Both in his mags and on the radio the laughter signaled the audience that The Shadow was about to strike. It was meant to drive fear into a criminal's heart, to let the evildoer know that the weed of crime he had tended had yielded bitter fruit, to mock his feeble plans. The laughter faded into the mist but left Gibson feeling far colder than the winter night.

The train whistled again. He felt he ought to start walking toward it. But then again, that boat was just tied up out there on the dock. And no one was around. Not even the night watchman. Or any watchman, for that matter. And since he hadn't been able to pry the location of the lab out of anybody, at least he could still investigate something. Anyway, there was almost no chance at all that a quick examination in the near dark would yield any information. Almost.

The fog was coming in thick and fast now, and the sun had completely set. The auras around the lamps had a physically solid look to

157

them now, as if they were pale yellow globes with candlelit centers one could harvest.

The wharf was part of a wooden boardwalk which ran behind the warehouses and connected buildings as far as he could see in either direction. Through the mist he could see dim lights of long jetties which jutted out at intervals from the boardwalk. The *Zephyr* was tied up at the end of its dock; the tide was low and its railings bumped against the boards. The transport boat was nearly seventy feet in length and fifteen wide at the beam. He guessed it drew about seven feet. Light waves rocked it gently.

He walked toward it, his footfalls tapping hollowly on the wood. The scents of salt foam and creosote filled his nostrils. The fog grew thicker and thicker as he drew closer.

The boat had begun its life as a fishing trawler on its way to being a runabout. Its cockpit was lofty and protected, its prow wide and high. There was plenty of room on the rear deck for cargo or for men to work. Gibson looked the boat up and down and shook his head. He clambered aboard and peered into the hold, where only gear was stowed. The deck boards creaked under his weight.

He opened the door to the cockpit and entered the small, glass-enclosed cabin. It felt great to be out of the wind for a few moments. He ran his hands through his hair, thinking he must be out of his mind. What was he doing on this boat? It was Providence, that was all. Dead writers, crazy aunts, superstitious drunks—a terrible environment for an imagination like his. All he had to do was get back home to New York where it was normal and when people went to a funeral that was the end of the story, not the beginning.

He looked at the navigation station. There was a spyglass, and a stack of charts with a compass and a protractor arranged upon it. He walked over and examined the yellowed chart at the top of the stack. It displayed the section of Long Island Sound somewhat south and west of the boat's current position. There were endless handwritten notations on the chart, the markings of voyages undertaken, then forgotten, over-written, crossed over with lines from other voyages. He looked up from the chart to the window and tried to imagine his chart to his voyages, his markings.

Gibson froze. Someone else was on the boardwalk.

He picked up the small telescope and put it to his eye.

"What'd you see?" Hubbard asked.

He took a bite out of the steak sandwich Chester had cooked up for him. Moments ago he hadn't been hungry, but now it seemed he had never been so hungry in his life. He swallowed and looked at the three men.

"I saw The Shadow."

EPISODE TWENTY

H E COULDN'T imagine anything more beautiful than their son. Not the dawn mist rising blue on the distant Thousand Lotuses Mountain, not the eight ancient treasures in Yunguang Cave, nor the waves breaking at Golden Stone Beach.

Zhang Mei named him Shaozu, a name which meant that he brought honor to his ancestors. He had his mother's green eyes, brilliantly aware of his surroundings even at birth, and a smile which must have come from Mei's father, for it was neither his nor his wife's. Only Mei could bring out the biggest, widest smile on Shaozu's face, sometimes by tickling him, or throwing him high into the air; sometimes by merely smiling at him first.

Mei knew Xueling and his brothers thought it unseemly for him to spend so much time with the boy. Until a boy was five or six—in other words, old enough to begin to learn to ride and fight—his upbringing was best left to the one who stays at home and the women of her family. But Mei couldn't help himself. His brothers had always had a father; they had never known what it was like to be alone in the world. At play with his son he felt as if his father was finally with him and at peace within him. Zuolin, his adopted father, seemed to understand. He too loved the new baby.

In the morning the governess would bring the slumbering boy to them and he would lie between Mei and Lu Zhi, and Mei would admire his long lashes and chubby fingers and breathe in his scent, and he would know that his son was his destiny. He wanted to grow old for his son so he would be able to offer him wisdom and comfort the many days of his life. He wanted to watch his son grow strong and confident and become a scholar, perhaps, like his mother. But not a warrior.

He waited for the baby to awaken so he could listen to Lu Zhi tell them both the legend of the time the Monkey King created a contest between the Wind God and the Sun God which neither could win (the Monkey King was so clever!) and so both had to live among men. Later, as he watched his son sleep, he would puzzle over the enigma that was his nation: how to bring it peace, how to rule it? He did not want his son to die young, even for glory. He wanted a rich and safe life for him.

He wanted the wars to end.

EPISODE TWENTY-ONE

GIBSON COULD feel his blood roaring through his arteries. A breathless dread seized his chest. This was no painting or vision or story. This was neither longshoreman, nor the effects of bad beer, nor even the dismal atmosphere of Providence. As certain as he was of the fear that gnawed at his spine, he was certain that he was in the presence of his Shadow.

It was the way his Shadow coalesced out of the night, standing in the open doorway of one of the low warehouses, absorbing the dim light from the space beyond. A great black overcoat swirled around him and blended into the darkness, blurring the distinction between where the night ended and he began. His nose was neither as long nor as hawklike as Gibson had imagined it to be. But the eyes: Gibson had described the eyes perfectly—lethal, spectral, glittering. That the man was an Asian was little more than a mild surprise. For years Gibson had written that "Ying Ko" was the name the denizens of Chinatown called The Shadow when he moved among them. It had never meant anything to him before; it was merely a bit of exotic embellishment. But here on the docks of Providence The Shadow had revealed another layer of his identity to Gibson: beyond Lamont Cranston, beyond Kent Allard, he was Ying Ko. He was Chinese.

He sees me, Gibson thought, and his breath caught in his chest. Then he realized that the man was only peering into the mist and the fear which had gripped him began to ease. An instant later the shadowy figure spun around and swept smoothly into the building, his coat filling the door frame with blackness before it closed altogether.

Gibson sat down heavily in the pilot's chair. He wanted a cigarette but he knew any light from a match might give him away. He thought about how close he'd just come to being apprehended and his hands shook. When he thought of the man's piercing gaze, the chill set in and he could not warm himself enough to be rid of it.

The first time The Shadow had appeared to him was on the night he had left his home, his wife, and his son. He had felt as if someone were following as he walked down the street away from his house, felt eyes upon him. He had found a room in a cheap hotel near the Main Line and watched the trains go by. Despair was a yawning black pit which devoured everything he might have been able to feel. He had wondered what it would feel like to throw himself under the train wheels.

He had tried for so long to explain to his wife why he felt compelled to move to New York to be a writer, until that night when there were no more explanations. Nothing he had said had motivated her one bit; she did not want to leave Philadelphia. There hadn't been a fight that night, like all the others; he had just nodded after her refusal and walked out. He had been so mad at her that it wasn't until afterward that he realized he had also walked out on Robert. In his anger, he wanted his boy's sadness to make her feel even more guilty.

Sometime during that night (and afterward he was never quite sure if it was while he was awake or sleeping) the shadows had coalesced into a human shape. He had felt the sensation of a watchful presence again, as he had walking down the street earlier. And all of a sudden there was something in the shadows, whispering promises he couldn't quite make out. When, a week later in their office at Street & Smith in New York,

Nanovic and Ralston had asked him if he had any ideas about how to turn the host of the *Detective Story Hour* radio show into a book, he suddenly understood those promises and was able to say that yes, he knew what to do: he would open his story with a man on a bridge in despair and with the dark figure which emerges from the shadows to save him.

He heard the train whistle again, far away and lonely, reminding him of another train and another time. He'd had enough. It was time to stop pretending there was a story here and go home to New York. He hadn't known Lovecraft well enough, really, to waste an entire weekend coming to his funeral, and Lovecraft certainly wouldn't have come down for his had the roles been reversed. But being away meant he wouldn't have time to talk with Litzka. That's what he needed to do. Talk with her. Maybe there was time to straighten things out with Litzka. Hell, he didn't even know what the tour schedule was. For all he knew the show was already packing up.

He knew this feeling of not wanting to go home. He had felt it before. It was the feeling that had driven him from Miami to seek out Silver Springs. It was what had kept his feet walking forward that night when he had left Charlotte. And Robert. And Philadelphia. Only now he didn't really have a home to avoid. Sure, he had an apartment. In a hotel. He could pack that up and be on the road in a day. But where would that get him? Just to another waterfront in another town. One thing he knew was that running around Providence pretending to be a reporter again was only a waste of time. Altogether this was turning out to be a completely fruitless trip. He realized with deep satisfaction that he wanted to go home.

He stepped out of the cabin and onto the deck. Perhaps he should write a sea tale, like Joseph Conrad. He didn't know as much about ocean-faring life as he would like; maybe this would inspire him to research the field a little more deeply. He could buy a boat. Or just take this one. Throw off the lines and head for the horizon. A warm horizon. He would call for Litzka when he arrived at Bora-Bora or Fiji and, maybe, she would come. He sighed. When he stepped off the boat, his little adventure would be over.

He clambered up the rope ladder and reached the dock. He carried with him the sensation of the boat, bobbing on the waves. He looked toward the warehouse that the man had emerged from; its door was closed once more. He had to pass it to reach the alley which led to the street that ran in the direction of the train station. He put his hands in his pockets and kept his head down, to try to give the appearance of someone who was just taking a nighttime waterfront stroll on the boardwalk, should anyone happen to notice him. He stopped near the door and tried to keep his head from turning. He couldn't resist a look. There, under a buzzer, was a small brass sign which read Providence Medical Laboratory. Found it, he thought. He listened at the door but heard no sound from within. He put his hand on the doorknob. The train whistle blew again. He pulled his hand from the knob and began walking briskly up the alley.

The blow to his head knocked him to his knees. As the red stars cleared from his eyes he saw two pairs of scuffed work boots through the blur.

"Hey, Shorty! I warned you to keep a weather eye open for trouble, din't I?" he heard the wharf rat growl.

One of the pairs of boots disappeared. A moment later a strong hand gripped his wrist, twisted his arm up behind his back. His head was yanked back. There was a cold knife at his throat. He could feel hands rifling through his jacket, looking for his wallet. They would do well, he thought; he had over a hundred dollars on him. The worth of his life. If only he had seen it coming, he thought. If only he had had a fighting chance.

"Got it!" he heard the wharf rat tell his pal, excitedly.

"The picture," Gibson gasped.

"What?"

"The picture of my son! Give it to me. It's all I have!"

"You want this?"

Gibson's head was yanked back and he could see the picture of Robert, taken when he was six.

"You ain't gonna need it where you're goin'," was the reply. "Cut his throat and drop him in the bay."

165

He felt the pressure of the blade on his throat suddenly grow. He wanted to see the picture one more time but it had been removed from his view.

He heard a sharp but distinct crack behind him. The pressure on his neck suddenly disappeared but some tremendous force threw him, prostrate, to the wood boardwalk. He tried to move away and ended up rolling across the boards.

The big man fell to the ground with a thud where Gibson had been a moment before. Gibson looked up. The wharf rat was held by his neck in the grip of the black-clad man Gibson had mistaken for The Shadow. His companion was groggily drawing himself to his knees. Then he took off, running toward the lights of Providence.

Gibson's wallet dropped from the wharf rat's hand and fell to the boardwalk. The Chinese man's speed and power were incredible. Gibson watched, astonished, as an instant later he had lifted the wharf rat into the air and thrown him neatly into the bay. Gibson could hear him splashing and coughing in the cold water. The mysterious man reached down and picked up Robert's photograph, which lay near Gibson's wallet. He looked at the picture for a long time and his hard, dark eyes grew even more narrow. Gibson pulled himself up to a sitting position, rubbing his head as the man approached. Suddenly his hand flicked out; Robert's photo pinched between two fingers. Gibson took it from him.

"Thanks," he said. His voice was raw and hoarse.

The man nodded back at him. He seemed on the verge of saying something—Gibson wondered if he even spoke English—but instead he drew his coat tightly about him and in a moment he had disappeared into the night. Gibson could hear the man's footsteps fading away as he staggered to his feet. Then he was alone on the boardwalk. The splashing of the wharf rat had stopped. He had either found his way to shore or drowned. Gibson didn't really care either way. The side of his head was throbbing. He slipped the photo into his wallet and tucked it back into his pocket. Not that it mattered to him now, but the money was still in the wallet as well.

The door to the Providence Medical Lab was open. A wedge of light broke through the fog. Gibson felt the warm flow of blood against his face and on his throat. He needed to appraise his wounds, and a medical lab could provide any first aid supplies he might need.

"So you had to go inside?" Driftwood said.

"I didn't really have a choice," Gibson said. He polished off the sandwich. "For all I knew I was bleeding to death. There was no way I was going to make it back to the train. No way at all. At the least I could find a phone to call for help."

The train's rhythm was soothing and he put his feet up on the footstool. Of course he hadn't told them about his thoughts of Litzka, or his doubts. It was his story and he told it the way he wanted to.

"How did you know he wasn't going to do you in?" Driftwood wanted to know.

He massaged his sore shoulder. He couldn't describe what he had seen in the man's eyes. "I just knew."

"So you went inside?"

"Yes, I did. Though now I wish to God that I hadn't."

EPISODE TWENTY-TWO

Z HANG MEI mixed the powdered herbs thoroughly into the soup. The soup and the powders needed each other to work properly. Eaten by itself, the soup would only nourish. Taken by themselves, the herbs would only cause diarrhea. But the powder, combined with the right amount of dog meat and a certain type of bean, would create distress in the eater's belly and soon after, death. It was a technique he had learned from a monk who had been brought to Shenyang Palace when they were young to teach them these secret arts. Xueling had had no stomach for it. Zhang Mei had turned out to be an excellent student in this, as he was in all the ways of death. It had been the monk who explained that one who had complete mastery over an art was known as a dragon and that Zhang Mei was the Dragon of Terror and Peril. Zhang Mei took no pleasure in his talent or his title; he was only pleased that he was able to serve his adopted father to the best of his abilities.

He wished that this soup would be fed to Chiang Kai-shek, the general of Dr. Sun Yat-sen's Nationalist Kuomintang troops. The little general was brusque and dismissive to his adopted father's face. But the general had ridden out that very morning to join his troops in an expedition against a small force deep in the western lands who called themselves Communists but were in reality colonial tools of their Russian masters. It was just as well that he had left. Dr. Sun Yat-sen was a popular man in Beijing. If both he and his general were to die on the same night, it would be apparent to all that their deaths were assassinations. Zhang Zuolin was playing a dangerous game. The battles had not ended. They had only become much, much smaller.

The secret meeting with Dr. Sun Yat-sen was at Zuolin's invitation. The doctor's Army of the South had grown powerful and fearsome, driven by officers, including Chiang Kai-shek, created at his own unique military academy. It had recently become apparent that he only had to give the word and the army could crush the combined forces of Zhang and his old allies.

And yet, the word was never given. Dr. Sun Yat-sen perceived greater threats from abroad: Russians, through the Communist insurgents, and the antagonistic militarization of the Japanese. He claimed to hold his army back to defend only against these predicted conflicts. However, the threat of his war machinery was enough to cause the members of Beijing's ruling council to consider offering the doctor the opportunity to rule over them all—before he killed them in battle—and by extension over China. This new position would see him elevated over even Zuolin. This point was what Zuolin had offered to discuss with the doctor in the secret meeting.

Mei instructed the servant on the position of the soup bowls before the guests. The man said he understood and he shuffled out of the room. He would taste each of the soups in front of the men to vouch for their purity. It would only make him ill much later in the evening, out of the sight of the true targets.

Mei paced the quiet halls. Few in the building knew of the meeting. Mei felt anxious, and not about whether the poison would work or whether his adopted father's plan would unfurl properly. Something else was gnawing at him.

He heard voices from a waiting room and walked silently toward it. On the other side was Mi-Ying, the diplomat. He was discussing shipping permission with one of the diplomats from the Japanese consulate. It seemed as if there were more Japanese in the palace some days than Chinese. Their tone was warm, nearly brotherly in nature. Mi-Ying was offering promises of influence, most beyond his grasp.

Zhang Mei swept the curtain aside, startling both men. Mi-Ying stood without even a formal greeting and looked at him levelly. Zhang Mei glared back. "This is not the night for diplomatic fornication," he said.

"My lord! We are only conducting the business of state," Mi-Ying protested. "My only interests are China's interests."

Zhang Mei had no rejoinder. He had not actually interrupted anything duplicitous and all the men knew it. He had only succeeded in embarrassing himself, and perhaps clarifying the enmity of Mi-Ying.

Zhang Mei let the curtain fall and strode away. He chewed his upper lip while the nagging feeling grew into a solid thought. He had heard the rumors: that were Dr. Sun Yat-sen to bring his army to bear in a new civil war, Zuolin would draw on Japanese clout. He couldn't imagine that Zuolin would call on such a devil for power, but at the same time he knew that there was no force in China that could stand up to Dr. Sun Yat-sen and his general, the little Chiang Kai-shek. What deals had Zuolin made with the Japanese?

Perhaps Dr. Sun Yat-sen was right. Perhaps the greatest threat to China lay within and without at the same time. Perhaps he was right. He would like to speak with the well-educated old man and perhaps discuss such matters with him. But it would never happen.

By now, the soup Zhang Mei prepared had been set before him.

EPISODE TWENTY-THREE

"THE DOOR to the lab was hanging open," Gibson continued his story. "It squeaked quietly on rusty hinges as it swung to and fro in the soft breeze. The slight sound carried up and down the lonely boardwalk. Other than the lapping waves of the rising tide against the pilings, everything was still. I took a deep breath and went in.

"Turns out I should have held that breath. The stink of the lab hit me first. It was thick and oily, like the garbage in the alley behind a fishmonger's. The smell of fish makes me retch anyway, so this was infinitely worse. I fumbled for one of my silks and put it over my nose and mouth, which helped a little bit. At least I could breathe."

"Silks?" Driftwood looked curious.

"I'm always carrying a couple of magic tricks on me just in case."

"In case what?"

"In case I need to perform a magic trick."

"Oh."

"I looked around. There were a few lights on. Mostly in the back. This place is long and low, like a warehouse. Most of the space is open, but starting about two-thirds of the way back, there are stairs up to the second floor, where all the offices are.

171

"I took a few steps in. It was a wide aisle. On either side were long rows and rows of metal shelves which held jars and bottles of all different shapes and sizes and full of a variety of powders and liquids. Then there were medical cabinets full of specimens. One shelf was just full of jars, the size of the jar of olives that the White Horse keeps under its bar, and each jar was filled with eyeballs suspended in a solution, all just staring at me. One jar had all brown eyeballs. One had all hazel eyeballs. One was full of blue eyeballs.

"I don't know how long the place has been in business, but it seems like quite a while. Maybe twenty or thirty years. Lot of old military surplus chemicals in old containers on those shelves. Pretty clear that they buy old stuff from Uncle Sam and sell it along.

"Through the shelves I could see a lab space in the middle of the building. As I walked toward it my shoes started crunching through glass. There were broken jars everywhere. Several shelves had been knocked over and their contents had spilled all over the floor. These are heavy, heavy shelves and cabinets and when they were stocked up they must have been very difficult to budge. As I drew closer to the lab I could see that even more of them were knocked back from the core. It reminded me of a daisy which had opened, with the lab as its hub of florets and the rows and rows of fallen cabinets flung out from that as its rays. It was like coming upon the scene of a bomb blast. But there was no crater.

"Once I got to the center of my strange blossom I realized that, in fact, my instincts had been right. There had been some kind of detonation in the building. At the epicenter of the flower lay a rusty hundred-gallon drum, probably about four feet high and two feet in diameter. I know the type. The army uses them to transport everything liquid, from gasoline to chicken soup. When I was stuck in the mud of St. Mihiel at the end of the Great War, we used empty ones just like it for latrines and campfires sometimes. Like all the others, this had once been a military-issue drab olive color. But it was so old that much of the paint had stripped off, exposing its rusted skin. It rested on its side; a rupture along its seam had violently flayed the metal open so it looked like the curled-back lips of an open mouth. This was the source of the energy which had thrown the lab into disarray.

"You know how smells can bring back stronger memories than almost anything else? I had lowered my silk for a moment and another smell hit me which brought back more military memories from my days in France. None of those memories, or smells, are particularly pleasant, but this was one smell I hoped I would never remember again as long as I lived. It was the smell you discover coming upon a battlefield a day or so after the fight at the height of summer. It meant there were dead bodies there.

"There were seven dead men on the floor. They wore white lab coats and were stacked neatly against one another in a line. Their bodies were frozen in contortion; their backs were arched and their arms were curled up. In one man's twisted hand was an unlit cigarette, clenched between his fingers. Death must have come suddenly. Their faces were hollow, leathery, desiccated. They looked for all the world like dead roaches left in a nest after an exterminator's visit. It took me right back to the battlefields.

"Aunt Annie was right that something bad had happened here. I slowly approached the canister. It was empty and bone-dry. The area around it was covered with a fine, gray powder, about the granularity of flash powder. Do you know that stuff? No? I have some in that cabinet I can show you later. Just imagine gray flour. It was light enough to puff out from under my shoes as I took steps. I wanted to see if I could find out this drum's story. There was probably a stencil on it somewhere, so I looked. Believe me, I was careful not to touch it. I found what was left of the stencil just below the ruptured seam. I recognized the typeset: Property of the U.S. Army. Sealed on March 4, 1917. Over twenty years old.

"I have seen some horrible ways to kill people in war, but the gases were by far the most horrible. By the end of the war there were some pretty strange chemicals being used on the field. It was as if the French, the Krauts, and the Americans all knew that the war was ending and they wanted to try out all their different toys before the grown-ups took them away. On the other hand, each side was so desperate to score decisively that they were willing to throw everything they had at each other. You see atrocities toward the end of a war that you could never see at any other point. The smell of rotten lemons, the withered and dried-out postures of these scientists, brought memories back to me I wish I'd never acquired. I have seen this horrible gas used before.

"I've seen it with my own eyes before. My division was supposed to rendezvous with a supply truck hauling some, but the truck must have hit a ditch or trench because it went off the road. I drew patrol with some buddies and we had to go after it. What we found was a scene remarkably similar to the one I found in the lab. Three men were dead. Two poor sons of bitches who lived we brought back to base, but they died on the way. The other—Private Woods from Oklahoma—well. We brought him back, but what the gas did to him was worse. The MPs took him away. We heard stories about what happened to him, but I always thought they were pulp."

He paused and finished his drink. The swaying of the car was relaxing him, finally. "Hard to believe, I know. But bear with me because it gets stranger. I heard someone crying. Crying in the lab.

"The sobs were soft and broke my heart. Like the sound of a child crying at its mother's funeral. They came from near the staircase which led from the first floor to the second. I called out, 'Who's there?' And, 'Is anyone there?' After I spoke, the sound stopped completely, though I thought I heard the scrape of hasty footfalls. My heart was pounding again. But I went toward the direction the sounds had come from instead of away.

"There was another dead man on the staircase. Unlike the scientists, this man wore a suit. He had obviously been dying from exposure, and slowly. His skin was hollowed out and thin, but his tie had been knotted this morning. But it wasn't the gas which had killed him. His blood, which was everywhere, was still wet. It was the long, thin blade plunged deep into his chest which seemed to have done him in. The hilt of the blade was carved wood with jade inlays. Chinese craftsmanship."

"Jeffords?" Driftwood asked.

"Yeah," Gibson nodded. "He was ugly and bald."

"But why would the Chinaman kill him?" Hubbard questioned.

"I don't know. Maybe he expected to find more than just a bunch of dead men there."

"Like what?"

"More gas."

Driftwood chewed his lip as Gibson continued. "There was someone behind me. You only need to be attacked from behind once in a night to be a little sensitive about a sneaking presence. I spun around.

"What was left of the man who stood there was a massive, shambling wreck. Oily folds of greenish skin hung from its outstretched arms. Shreds of a shirt and tattered pants hung from it in a parody of decency. The top of its head had flattened and drooped back as if the skull had softened and lengthened. Its eyes were wide and terrifying and a sickening slurping sound issued from the gaping maw that should have been a mouth. I realized that the liquid which flowed from its eyes was tears. In its hand it held a hanging lantern.

"I had found the night watchman.

"I don't know how much faculty the man had had before his exposure to the gas. I think he may have been feeble to begin with. Whatever his previous mental state had been, there was no reasoning with him now. His blind fury and grief had reduced him to trembling.

"The night watchman pointed at the body on the stairs and tried to speak. Its mouth encircled a word that I could barely distinguish.

"'Daddy,' I realized it spoke.

"I tried to reason with it. I shook my head to indicate that I had had no part in this. But the motion only seemed to snap it out of its stupor. It lurched toward me. I tried to dodge but I slipped in the blood and fell to the staircase. I could feel the hot, slimy hands fumbling to get a grip on my neck. There was tremendous strength in the grip. He won't just choke me, I realized. He was going to completely crush my throat.

"The night watchman stank like a tidal pool at low tide, like rotting crustaceans and seaweed. I felt an electric stab of fear bolt from my

175

stomach and spread into my body: panic was setting in. I twisted and at the same time pushed against the creature's bulk. It slipped on some of the blood and stumbled back toward the lab. At least I could breathe. The creature regained its balance.

"I put my hands out to push myself up as it charged toward me. I felt the knife in the corpse's chest. I seized it and pulled it from the torso. It was heavy, and well balanced. The night watchman was nearly upon me."

He stopped speaking and rubbed his right hand. No one spoke for quite a while. Driftwood arched a skeptical eyebrow. Hubbard cleared his throat and in a high, nervous voice said, "This is pulp, right, Walter? Not real."

Gibson flexed his hand a few times, watching it critically as if it needed to explain how it ended up at the end of his arm. "Anyway," he told them at last, "I lived to tell the tale."

EPISODE TWENTY-FOUR

HE RODE unescorted to the frontier, the far western lands, as an emissary of Zuolin. Dr. Sun Yat-sen's death had not led to the collapse of the Kuomintang Nationalists as Zuolin had predicted. General Chiang Kai-shek was emerging as their leader and he was making it clear that he would use the mighty Army of the South against Zuolin rather than keep it sheathed awaiting an outside invasion as his predecessor had.

Zhang Mei was sent to the west to meet with the young leader of the revolutionary Communists, to persuade him to ally with Zuolin against the general. Another alliance, as with the Japanese, that Zhang Mei had deep misgivings about.

He had met the professor once before, at the library, early during the occupation of Beijing. The professor was not a bureaucrat; he was a scholar and Lu Zhi thought highly of him. Only a few years older than Mei, he had fought the civil wars, although on which side it was unclear. He had a fierce mind and a penetrating gaze. More importantly he had the adoration of a growing number of the restless peasants in the countryside.

Zhang Mei and the professor took jasmine tea and soft cakes filled with red bean paste under a grove of willow trees near a spring in the late afternoon as the heat of the day waned. Mei studied the man's face and sensed that he was even more powerful and self-possessed than he had been in Beijing. Although his Communist force was small—Zuolin's spies estimated that he had the ability to raise only a thousand to two thousand men-at-arms—his reputation was growing among the farmers and villagers and others who toiled for the landlords.

"Zhang Zuolin believes in your cause," Mei began. The words felt empty, as if they were the platitudes that might fall from the mouth of Mi-Ying. "He believes General Chiang means to destroy us both."

"Zuolin is a bandit," the scholar said, "and he has increased the influence of the Japanese within China to the extent that they now see our land as a colony. You know this to be true. Your true feelings toward your father's advisers are known."

"That may be," Mei replied, "but as long as China is weak, Japan will be a power here. If General Chiang launches a war against the northern provinces, the chaos will only create more opportunity for foreigners of all kinds. Not just the Japanese but the British and French as well. Even the Americans."

The professor shrugged. "Perhaps the next war will be a just war," he said. "Perhaps the chaos it will create will sweep away old obstacles—the landlords, the bureaucrats, the merchant class, the corrupt, the imperialists. Even the warlords. Then the heel would be lifted from the throat of China's sons. This would be a just war. I see disappointment in your eyes. This is not the expression you hoped to take back to your master?"

"It is not what I hoped to hear, that is true," Mei said. "But not for my father. For me. I seek to end the wars."

"Through a political solution?"

He nodded.

"War can only be abolished by war."

"Wars!" Mei spat. "Zuolin has been a warrior his entire life and while he is fortunate to have survived, he knows no other way than war. I and my brothers have been trained as warriors, ensuring that the legacy of war will survive yet another generation. I would like my son to know another way, perhaps a scholar's way such as the one you chose. Or an artist's. I do not wish to perpetuate the warrior line."

"Do you not think that the farmer wishes any more for his son? Or that the laborer any more for his? You feel the weight of the oppression of your circumstances. Does any man not feel it just as keenly? The wars you seek to end will only be eliminated through progress. Progress itself is a war, and the struggle against it is a war as well. Do you understand the inevitability of war yet?"

"I do not accept it, Professor."

"Only when men are free of class will wars end. That may happen in our lifetime. This choice is for men like you and me to make. A revolution to purge the body politic and end wars is within our grasp. Politics is war and war is politics and the only difference is the amount of blood spilled." He paused and grimaced slightly with distaste. "Just as some would wish that diplomatic negotiations can be resolved with an assassination. Do you understand?"

They sat in silence for a great while. The spring gurgled and bubbled. Mei thought that if the spring had consciousness it would think as the professor did, that as the water carved a path through the rock, it was unaware that in mere miles it would be swallowed by the vast waters of the mighty river which it fed into. In this same way would the professor be devoured by the greater armies of Chiang's Kuomintang. Mei understood the professor's true meaning about the inevitability of war. The professor would have no alliance with Zhang Zuolin. Perhaps he had already allied himself with Chiang. Perhaps not. Perhaps he would simply wait, growing stronger out here in China's farthest reaches, until either Zhang or Chiang was victorious but weakened. Then he would make his move.

"You could stay, you know," the professor said, at last. "A dragon is always necessary in war."

Mei stood and dusted himself off. Then he ceremoniously bowed to the little man, who also stood. He knew at this moment that there were archers, with bows pulled, just out of sight, waiting for a gesture to strike and bring him down. For the third time in his life he prepared for his immediate death. The professor kept his arms stiffly at his side.

"Professor Mao, my wife sends her respect," he said, "and you have mine as well."

The professor flinched slightly at the mention of his wife. He nodded his head. "Lu Zhi is a rare woman," he said after some consideration. "Her perceptions of the tales of universal balance are unique. She has done well to marry you and bear you a son. Take my greetings back to her as well."

He gestured and Mei prepared for the stabbing pierce of the arrows. The thought of his son and the sound of the spring brought him peace.

Instead, Mei's horse was brought to him, and he rode out immediately, unprovisioned. As he rode, he sensed the arrows of the archers upon his back day and night until he reached the border of the province.

EPISODE TWENTY-FIVE

WALTER COULD feel the night watchman's clammy, moldering hands around his windpipe, crushing it. He could feel the hilt of the knife shudder as the lethal blade sank through muscle, tissue, and veins. He could feel the hot spurt of blood on his hand. He could hear the creature calling out one last time for its father.

He sat up in his bunk. The train had stopped moving. Early dawn light crept through the wood slats of the blinds. He heard snoring from the guest compartments, Driftwood in one and Hubbard in another. His traveling companions had turned in soon after the conclusion of his story, for what else could be said? He wondered what Driftwood thought of him; his piercing dark eyes were intelligent and quizzical. He hadn't spoken much during the story of the night watchman. He seemed like a straight-up guy, but Gibson wondered who he really was and where he had come from.

For a moment he thought that the police had stopped the train and would be swarming in to question him. But some distant angry car horns reassured him that he was back in New York.

He had tried to sleep but it had been difficult. He had always been prone to nightmares, and living through one had made it hard to tell where his day had ended and his slumber began. He had spent the late hours of the ride at his magic work desk concentrating on spring-loaded strikers.

He lay back for a few moments. Maybe the question he should have asked Hubbard that night in the White Horse was really where does pulp end and reality begin, not the other way around. His world seemed twisted out of sorts. His life reminded him of one of those awkward first attempts at sound pictures a few years back; the moving image would often lose synchronization with the sound recording so that the actors' voices would trail the movement of their lips just enough to be noticeable and irritating. That's how he felt now. A few seconds behind his own action.

His body was sore and aching, not only from the various bruises and scrapes but from the actual exertion which had begun with carrying the coffin. He was a writer, after all, and not given to exercising much.

He could smell coffee. He got up and padded across the small chamber to the door and opened it. Chester had placed a carafe outside his door, along with some eggs and toast. He brought the tray inside and set it on the bunk. He drank his first cup, black, staring at the window. He finished his second cup after washing up and had emptied the carafe by the time he was dressed.

He stepped into the main cabin and walked over to his writing desk. He looked at the manuscript. It wasn't his best work, by a long shot. But it was probably good enough, and, more importantly, it was done. Nanovic would always prefer to have a poorly written book in on time than a late masterpiece. He drew out a brown envelope and dropped the pages into it.

He heard the galley door open. "Everything all right, Mr. Gibson?"

"I could use another year of sleep, Chester," he said. "And I already gotta get a move on. This book's gotta be dropped off."

"I called Manny as soon as we got in, so he's waiting for you. You want me to drop your luggage off later?"

"Thanks. That'd be a help." He saw the issue of *Bronzeman* and picked it up. "Congratulations, by the way."

Chester beamed. "Thank you, Mr. Gibson. I've been using your typewriter."

"I would hope so. Mind if I take this with me so I can read it?"

"Oh no, sir. That'd be real fine."

"What's it about?"

"It's about the fire. Only I turned it into a story so it wasn't so real, y'know?"

Gibson nodded. A few years ago several prisoners at the Ohio State Penitentiary had set some paint cans on fire hoping to escape during the commotion. Instead, the fire quickly spread out of control. Men were trapped in cells that wouldn't open. The guards had no evacuation strategy. The building was over a hundred years old and stuffed to twice its capacity with poor saps, most of whom had been caught by the circumstances of the Depression. Over 320 men died in the space of an hour. Many of the men who survived, including Chester, had been given an early parole. It was still no compensation for his scars.

"I'll give it a good read." Gibson folded the magazine into his coat pocket. "Just keep writing, keep writing," he offered.

"I will."

Gibson went to the door and opened it. "Listen," he said. "If those two want breakfast or anything, help them out. And if Mr. Driftwood, the new guy, wants to stay onboard a night or two before he gets straightened out, let him know he's welcome to. It's not going back to the yard until next week."

"Yes, sir. Are you still planning on going to Miami next month?"

"I'll let you know."

He stepped off the train into the chill of the clear morning air. The train yard was slowly coming to life; the shouts of teamsters and railmen mixed with the low rumble of the big engines and the occasional squeal of metal grinding against metal. He saw Manny's Checker Cab and the big heavyset man eating dunkers behind the wheel.

Manny knew his way around the city as if a map of its entire road network had been tattooed upon the back of his eyelids. In addition to his flawless, instinctive sense of direction, he seemed to be related to one half of the city and on a first-name basis with the other half. To Walter, who was originally from Philadelphia but wrote about New York, Manny was a library on wheels. It didn't matter that his knowledge was sometimes suspect; what mattered was the accent of authority he gave it. He had given Gibson a lift home once and had easily drawn out who he was and what he did. Gibson had given the man a couple of signed mags for his kids and the man was eternally grateful. From that point on, whenever he had the chance, he acted as Gibson's self-appointed chauffeur. All he had to hear over his radio was that Walter needed a lift, and there he'd be. No one else was allowed to pick him up, even if it meant that Gibson sometimes had to wait a little longer.

Manny tossed him a wave and started his engine. Gibson waved back. He stopped and stretched his sore arms over his head. The air was brisk but it was warmer than it had been in Providence. He took a deep breath of Gotham air and began to feel better. His Pullman was still hitched to the longer passenger train and people were disembarking. Suddenly Gibson froze.

He saw The Shadow again.

The Chinese man was in New York. As he stepped off the passenger car, his eyes swept the train yard like a wind that could blow dust from its every corner. Gibson stepped back between the train cars, hoping the long early shadows would conceal him so he could watch. It worked. Not noticing him, the Chinese man began to walk toward the parking lot. He parted the small crowd with what seemed to be a palpable emanation of energy. People moved out of his way without realizing they were doing so. Gibson began to follow him. The man walked with assurance; once he was certain of his surroundings, he gave them no other thought and never looked back to see Gibson.

The dark character slid smoothly into the back seat of the cab parked in front of Manny's. Gibson could see his hawklike profile framed in the window. The car headed toward the street and Gibson realized there was no way he could make it across the yard in time to get to Manny's cab in order to follow. But he had to know about this Chinese stranger who had saved his life but probably ended Jeffords's. The story had not ended with the death of the night watchman. The true ending to the story was about to turn onto the avenue.

He gave Manny a whistle and when the cabbie looked at him, Gibson ran his hand back and forth across his hat brim a number of times. Then he pointed to the departing cab. Manny nodded. Gibson watched him plop his cigar between his thick lips, and a moment later the cab spun out of the yard, gravel spitting away as the wheels dug in for traction.

Gibson rubbed the stubble of his chin thoughtfully for a moment. Every bone in his body ached to follow them. He broke out his pack of Chesterfields and lit his first cigarette of the day. The Chinese man hadn't seen him. He was positive of that. He wondered what could have brought this man to New York, and as his mind began trying to draw connections from Providence, trying to create a story, he looked for another cab. He would have loved to follow them, but the brown envelope in his hand was growing hot. No matter how much this new story begged to be told, the fact of the matter was that he still had a manuscript to deliver.

Besides, Manny had understood the meaning of his signal. While Gibson was a Phillies man, Manny was a Brooklyn Dodgers fan. During the summer his radio was locked on to Ebbets Field. Gibson's signal, the rubbing of the hat brim, was a classic Casey Stengel command to his pitcher, Van Lingle Mungo, when a man at first was preparing to steal second.

Keep your eye on the runner.

EPISODE TWENTY-SIX

C HINA WAS shattered.

All the previous wars Mei had fought in were mere squalls to the typhoon which engulfed the land from mountain to sea, and from border to border. It touched all lives. It was as if the concept of peace had been vanquished from life and memory. His son learned riding and swordplay from soldier masters as he had, and spoke of winning battles as eagerly as he had. He was only six.

Loyalties changed as often as the tides. Chiang had been ejected from the Kuomintang but had regained control. Chiang and the professor's Communists had briefly allied, but that alliance had fallen apart when Russian meddling in the affairs of the Communists surfaced.

Across the countryside Communist rebellions increased in ferocity and nipped at the flanks of the Kuomintang. One of Chiang's generals formed an army of his own and brought it against Chiang in Nanking with help from British and American warships. Mei found the shifting political landscape dizzying, as complicated as the beautiful game of chess that the Russian diplomats had once enjoyed so ferociously in the courtyards of Shenyang Palace.

Zuolin himself now commanded an army of a million men. He joked that he longed for the days when he rode with only two hundred warriors at his side. Mei had seen the burning campfires of six hundred thousand of those troops turn a valley at night into a lake of fire. Battles had been fought at forlorn places with names such as Xuzhou, Lincheng, Jiujiang, Xuehuashan Mountain, and Longtan. Yet still Chiang's Kuomintang pounded back at them with relentless force. And now, at last, Zuolin was retreating from Beijing.

The Japanese had landed troops at Jinan. Mi-Ying had assured him that they were only securing their vital national interests, but the old warlord saw what Mei had warned him of for so long: the Japanese were establishing a beachhead in order to pave the way for an invasion one day should the civil war weaken the Chinese to the point where that opportunity would present itself. Zuolin ended his alliance with the Japanese and Mi-Ying, who stayed behind in Beijing to await his next master. Or his fate. Without Japanese support, Zuolin's position as the ruler of China was untenable.

"We will return to Manchuria, the land of our fathers," the warlord told his sons. "Let them have this sewer. Behind the protection of our mountains and walls we will wait and grow stronger, and when they are weak we shall come again. We are not leaving China. China is with us."

Lu Zhi sobbed at the thought of leaving her beloved library behind. Beijing had been her home all her life and leaving grieved her. His son was eager to ride the train and see his grandfather's great palace. Mei had assured him that it was not only more beautiful than Beijing's but cleaner. The boy's eyes had glittered eagerly in the lamplight at bedtime as Mei described the wondrous things he would see in Lianoning: the caves they would explore, the mountains they would climb, the surf they would swim in, the kites they would fly, the birds they would catch, the deer they would hunt. Until the early morning when he had ridden out in preparation for the retreat, he and his wife had lain together and known love.

His men were certain that Shenyang City was secure. Some Communists had been executed and the families of the remaining Japanese were taken to the port for deportation. Flags of joy for the return of the Emperor of the Northern Lands hung from doorways and trees and flew from rooftops.

On the morning of their arrival he took a train from Shenyang Palace to Huanggudun Station on the far outskirts of the city. He had decided to surprise his wife and son by meeting them here and joining them for the remainder of the journey instead of waiting for them to arrive. Even weary Zuolin would be pleased to see him. His son loved trains. He had an elaborate collection of American tin miniatures which he spent hours with. He thought the metal dragons the most incredible inventions, and most of all Mei wanted to share in at least a part of his son's thrill in riding one.

There was a small crowd at the station hoping to catch a glimpse of their leader. The bees hung in the air much as they had a morning long ago in a distant copse at the far end of a rice paddy. He brushed the soot from his clothes; on his trip from the palace, the train windows had been open to let the fresh summer morning air in. He heard the distant whistle of the train announcing that it was clearing the final mountain pass several miles away, and his heart leapt. He could feel his Shaozu's arms around his neck, taste Lu Zhi's lips. On the horizon, a thin gray cloud of smoke mixed with steam appeared above the trees.

There was a face in the crowd, turning quickly from him as if to avoid his eyes. Mei moved his head to catch a better glimpse. The man was furtive. Mei pushed toward him, calling for assistance from his detail. The man broke into a run at the sound of his voice. Mei recognized him. Mi-Ying. There is no reason for him to be in Shenyang, Mei thought, and at the same moment he knew, of course there is.

The explosion threw great chunks of the train into the sky. They ascended so gracefully, so slowly through black ash that they almost appeared like dry leaves driven before the wild wind. Then the sound reached his ears, a mighty roar, and the power that lifted those sections of the train revealed itself. At the station people began to murmur, then scream.

He leapt upon a horse and rode in the direction of the noise and the fire. It wasn't what he thought, he told himself. It wasn't the right train, he prayed. Shaozu was special, he knew, favored by the gods. And the gods would protect him.

The woods were aflame. Great pieces of shrapnel lay in craters, smoldering. He tried to drive his horse through the flames to the twisted wreckage beyond, but there was no approach. The horse was not a soldier's mount and responded to the command with fear. It bucked and reared and threw its rider. As he fell through the air like another piece of debris, Mei knew that the bomb had been placed with devastating precision for maximum impact.

They were all dead, was his last thought as his head hit the earth. And he knew it was true.

EPISODE TWENTY-SEVEN

"W HERE THE hell is The Shadow?" Orson Welles's voice boomed through the movie theater. His ribbing cracked through Gibson's headache like an anarchist's brick through a government office window. "Is he even in this piece of crap? It's called *The Shadow Strikes.* Where's the goddamn Shadow and when in hell is he going to strike?"

The pain in Walter's head had been growing steadily since his leaving the train yard. A long morning of defending his book to Nanovic hadn't helped anything either. Nanovic must have gotten a good night's sleep because he had torn into Gibson's writing as if the formula for writing these stories was so simple that anyone but Walter B. Gibson could write them. He knew that Nanovic sometimes did that when he wanted to feel more like a writer and less like a glorified proofreader. Since the appearance of Kent Allard and the debacle which had followed, Nanovic had taken great pains to drag a fine-tooth comb across each page, questioning Gibson's every word choice. He was taking great pains to see that nothing like that was ever going to happen again.

After the meeting Gibson had placed a call to the Providence police department and told them he suspected some kind of dustup at the medical lab down by the docks. There had been a long silence at the other end, and then the voice said, "So?"

"Don't you think you ought to look into it?" he had asked.

"It's looked into," the voice replied. "What's your name?"

Gibson had hung up. Seemed like old Aunt Annie had been right again regarding the competence, if not the outright complicity, of the Providence police force.

He had met Welles for lunch at the Automat. Welles had grumpily complained about how he wanted to go to Reuben's for one of their eponymous sandwiches: corned beef, sauerkraut, Swiss cheese, and Russian dressing toasted under the broiler. But too many magicians lunched there. Reuben's was very popular with the crowd who patronized Tannen's Magic Shop. Guys like Tommy Hanlon Jr., who worked with Orson at his theater; Herman Hanson, who had understudied Thurston and was so good at impersonating him that when the master had suddenly died of a stroke during an intermission last year, Hanson had taken the stage for the second act and anyone in the audience would have sworn that he had seen Thurston; and Joe Kavalier, a quiet artist who had a fascination with Harry Houdini and prodded Gibson for an anecdote every time they came together. Welles knew all those fellows as well. He was a proficient amateur magician and admired their talent. He constantly pushed Walter to star in his own show. Walter always retorted that he'd star in a show when Orson started writing pulps.

Gibson could not face too much scrutiny from the brotherhood. Not as long as he was having an affair with one of its members' wives. The group prided itself on its closely held age-old secrets, so it was hard to keep a secret from them. He knew that there were already whispers.

He'd had to explain this situation to Welles to get him to stop grumbling so peevishly about the sandwich that Gibson had so cruelly deprived him of. Fortunately the only thing which improved the young man's mood more than food was gossip, and the storm clouds of despair which had overshadowed his normally exuberant and optimistic nature had parted instantly.

"You're breaking up a marriage?" Welles had asked, conspiratorially. "And she's fifteen years younger than you? I must meet this Salome!"

"I'm not breaking up a marriage," Gibson had replied. "And if you think I'm too old for her, he's nearly sixty! He married her young to lock her up. And now he's loaning her to Blackstone anyway."

"Well, it's obvious she has her type. You've got to admit that. Let's say she likes her men somewhat experienced, shall we? Wasn't she the bird who used to have a chicken act?"

"Still does. But she's moved on to mind reading now and retired China Boy except for the kids. She's a hell of a mentalist too, I gotta tell ya. She picked a few things out of my head I didn't know I had up there."

"What happened to the chicken?"

"You're in the theater district a lot. Keep your eyes peeled. If you see a beautiful girl wearing a big floppy hat and carrying a basket with a black rooster's head sticking out of it, that's my gal."

"I shall look for nothing else." He had plunked another nickel in one of the cases and removed a second slice of apple pie. "Where do you think this can go, Wally, my friend? Do you think she'll leave him? And think about this: do you really want her to? What would you do with her if you had her? Hm?"

"I want her," Gibson had said without hesitation. "No. I don't know. I want to see her. That's all. If that means that I'm in love with her, I don't know. I just want to go get her."

"So go get her."

"It's Monday. The theater's dark today and she's not at her hotel. I sent her a telegram, though. Told her I want to see her again."

"Then you must make her leave him and damn the consequences. And by God, make sure she brings that chicken."

"She won't. She just won't. Have you ever been out with a married woman?"

"Of course! Married women are the most in need of someone to love and admire them. Single women get that from every man. Married women get it from none."

He hadn't told Welles about the Providence experience. It was an easy topic to avoid. Welles had wanted to hear gossip about Blackstone's opening night party, which had been at Mamma Leone's, the au courant Broadway restaurant where patrons could fish for their dinner from a trout-filled brook or converse with Mamma's horse, which lived in its own special stable with Dutch doors that opened onto a vast dining room.

They had finished their lunch and made their way to the movie palace to catch this week's chapter, the fifth, of the two-reeler serial adventure adaptation. Walter had written the first draft of *The Shadow Strikes* last October and sent it off to the Alexander brothers at Grand National Pictures in Hollywood. Welles and Gibson had eagerly sought out the serials for the past few weeks to see how their character had made the transition to the screen. Changes had been made.

Welles's level of concern about the quality of the film was well placed; like Gibson, he had a vested interest in the character of The Shadow. Welles was starring as the voices of The Shadow and Lamont Cranston on the wildly popular weekly radio adaptation of Walter's mag. A successful Shadow serial would create even more demand from which Gibson and Welles could profit. On the other hand, nobody wanted to be associated with a flop. Welles had made two significant contributions to the legend of The Shadow (three, if you took into account that he gave voice and life to an enigma). He had introduced a new character, Margot Lane, The Shadow's faithful friend and companion, to banter with The Shadow on his adventures and to give him somebody to rescue from time to time. The Street & Smith policy toward women in *The Shadow* may have been for Walter to stop writing about them at the knees and start again at the neck, but Welles wanted something a little sexier and he got it. Welles had also conferred upon The Shadow the power of invisibility; on his show the avenger became a frightening voice from the ether which surrounded criminals and audiences alike through the mystical ability to cloud men's minds. When Gibson, who spent long hours writing radio scripts with Welles, had initially and loudly questioned whether an audience would accept the trick of invisibility, the young man had earned his eternal respect by replying confidently, "If radio listeners will believe in a ventriloquist act they can't see, they'll believe even more in invisibility!" Gibson wrote it that way for the radio, and Welles was right—the audiences ate it up. But The Shadow would never be invisible in his mag. Not as long as he wrote it. In his mags The Shadow would always be there, if a person only knew where to look.

Despite the radio broadcasts' tremendous success, the sponsor, Blue Coal, was threatening to pull out because it found Welles and his versatile troupe, the Mercury Theatre on the Air, too difficult to work with. They often missed deadlines and refused to allow the coal-mining executives to comment on scripts. The network had assured Welles, and Street & Smith, that the Goodyear Tire Company had expressed sponsorship interest and was waiting in the wings. Should Blue Coal drop out, The Shadow would soon be cautioning drivers about the evils of driving on wet roads with unsafe tires.

"There's no Shadow in this movie!" Welles was nearly standing. Fortunately the theater was nearly empty. The Shadow as a movie character was a bust. Without the spectacle of Welles's invisibility angle, or the detailed nightscape moods of Walter's stories, what was it about? Just another detective story. On the screen, the former silent picture star Rod La Rocque, mostly famous for being Vilma Banky's husband, poked around one of the phoniest mansions they had ever seen, occasionally running into someone he suspected of embezzling eleven million dollars. "When does he become The Shadow?"

"Maybe next episode?" Gibson said, hopefully. "I know I wrote him in."

"Don't they listen to the radio? They don't even get Cranston's name right! They keep calling LaRoque Granston. Don't they read the magazines? Didn't they read the script?"

"As I recall I think they started production before my script was in."

"Don't they know what they have here? Don't they know what The

Shadow is? You know what it is, what the thing is? They don't have any respect for him. They think he's just a pulp." Welles dropped down, irked, in his seat. He shifted uncomfortably in his seat a few times and then he leaned over to Gibson. "Want to know how I'd make a Shadow movie if they gave me a chance?"

"Not a play?" Gibson asked. Welles had a brilliant imagination and a true knack for creating amazing stage scenes. Last June his *Voodoo Macbeth,* a Federal Theatre Project–WPA production, had created a bona fide New York craze. It was the event which put 125th Street on the A-train map for many white downtowners. The fashions inspired by the production could still be seen on the mannequins in the windows of Fifth Avenue eight months later. Walter had seen the production twice at the Lafayette and once at the Adelphia and been completely transported to another world. In those theaters, the rhythms of the islands had come to life and destiny moved through the fetid, steamy jungle Welles had realized in the middle of civilization. Welles had used Shakespeare to penetrate the heart of darkness. The production had made him the toast of the town. He was a sensation.

When the curtain had risen on that show, and on him, he was twenty-two years old.

"No," was the reply, "a movie. A real movie."

Walter squirmed again as Rod La Rocque lumbered through a phony fight scene. "Let's hear it."

"It will be dark," Orson began softly, in the deep performance voice he used for The Shadow. "It will be dark. Perhaps the darkest movie ever made. Light will barely penetrate the mists and darkness and when a shaft of life breaks through, it is only to shine for a moment on a brief moment of good which is to be snuffed out when it fades. Moonlight illuminates a sleeping baby. In the darkness she disappears. A man smokes a cigarette beneath a fading street lamp. When it flickers out he is mugged with a blackjack. This is the black world through which The Shadow moves.

"It doesn't matter what the story is. What matters is the world. I

195

would have The Shadow, or some part of him, in almost every shot. Somewhere. In the background, you might see a hint of his cloak, or the brim of his hat or the glint of his eyes. I'd set the story entirely in the criminal underworld. The villains would be the protagonists and The Shadow would be their antagonist. He's a force of nature. He coalesces around evil the way clouds come together along a cold front to form a thunderstorm. His glee at being summoned again, at being needed, at being alive is what makes him laugh. It's his thunder, and his actions are his lightning. My Shadow movie would be about the panic and fear he creates in the minds of the black-hearted.

"In this film, the darkness is something real, unconsciously shared and connected throughout all of humanity. It's the darkness that we all share, that you've personified, given a name. The Shadow is the champion of despair. He is a trickster unleashed by the evil that men do to restore balance. It's as if the act of evil deeds cracks the mantle of humankind and what bubbles up through the new crevasses, like a spring, is The Shadow. He can't be unleashed until the crime is committed, but once it has been, he is the opposite reaction to the criminal's action."

"But doesn't that make him part villain too?"

Welles thought about that for a moment. "Yes. Yes, of course he is! It takes a villain to know a villain, right? In some ways, the villain is even closer to him than the hero. Without the villain he wouldn't exist, wouldn't bubble up, as I was saying. He'd certainly have no purpose even if he did. The villain taps down directly into the liquid well of darkness, the sanctorum of The Shadow, and steals from him that which he safeguards, violence and fear. The Shadow manifests himself through the righteous, all his faithful agents, to retrieve what was his to begin with, that part of himself which was stolen, and to restore universal harmony."

Gibson almost blurted out that he had seen The Shadow, nearly told Welles about Providence. But Welles was a hard man to interrupt.

Welles shrugged. "The only good characters I'd present would be the agents of The Shadow—Harry Vincent, Margot Lane, Shrevnitz, the working stiffs who would be exploited by the criminal element if it weren't for him. In fact, I'd want the audience to suspect each of them—the cabbies, the construction joes, the fruit vendors, and the doormen—of being The Shadow. The audience expects Lamont Cranston to be The Shadow, so that's one place where I'd throw them off. Cranston, or Allard, what have you, he's just another agent in the end, doing The Shadow's bidding, spying on the underworld, bringing him information. The Shadow's agents are the tools through which The Shadow acts and he uses them to change the villain's world, manipulate his destiny, moving them like chess pieces, forcing the villain to react and react and react, each time thinking that he's defeated The Shadow only to find that another agent has become The Shadow and is challenging him again and again, trapping him in an illusion of mirrors, until that villain's fate is inescapable. And that fate is, of course, his doom.

"I'd never use a straight cut when The Shadow was in action. Everything would be done in dissolves so the images flow into each other. I'd pick the craziest angles I could shoot so that the audience would feel like the criminals, off balance and operating outside of normal conventions. Movies are about the interplay between light and dark, black and white. And so is The Shadow."

"Well, it's an awful lot to draw out of some pulp mags."

"It's all about the lie. The big lie. That's what our audiences want from us, Walter. From you and me they want the big lie. They want the big stories about the great things. Not for us the little tales of simple people. We have to tell the big lie. The bigger the better. As far as I can tell, the best way to lie is to use film. Everything about it is a lie. The script is a lie the writer tells, which the actor speaks, lying to convince you that the words are his. The cameraman uses light and angles to lie about how good that actor looks. Then the editor takes all the lies, picks the best ones, and stitches them together into one great lie from beginning to end. But in spite of all that, when it's done right, somehow it becomes something quite like the truth. That's what I want to do. But," he added wistfully, "you know the joke, right? How many Broadway directors they say it takes to change a lightbulb?"

"I don't know."

"Ten. One to do it, and nine to tell each other how they would have done it better."

They sat in silence for a few moments as Rod faced menace from a gun-wielding thug. They both sighed at the same time as the cliff-hanger came to an end.

"Hey! There's a one-reeler cartoon, *Hawaiian Holiday,* after the newsreel," Orson said as the Movietone logo splashed across the screen. "Want to stick around? I love Walt Disney."

"Really?"

"Absolutely. He is certifiably the only genius working in Holly-wood today."

"I knew him in France during the war. Skinny kid. Drove an ambu-lance. Who knew?"

"I can't wait to see what he does with *Snow White. Variety* says it'll ruin him; they say people won't go see a feature cartoon. But I'd bet any amount that they will if Disney makes it. It's amazing to me that the man is able to craft such a personal artistic statement in an art form that requires so much anonymous collaboration."

"I don't really follow the kids' stuff too much."

"Yeah, that's right. I forgot you're a *serious* writer. And how is your great American novel coming along anyhow?"

"I'll let you know when I start it."

"Too busy writing good to write great."

"Which reminds me, I've got another script to get to you. Inter-ested in a paper caper? A powerful news tycoon is murdered and only The Shadow can solve it."

"Interesting. But hold that thought. Stick around and I'll show you what I'm talking about."

Gibson looked at his watch. "All right," he said, "let's see what we shall see." He lit a cigarette. The silver light cut through the smoke. Suddenly the newsreel, which had been running, caught his attention.

Thunderous howitzer cannons blasted an unseen enemy. "Dateline: China! General Chiang Kai-shek, leader of the Nationalist army, has ended the civil war against Mao's Communist rebel army in the greater interest of expelling the advancing Japanese army, whose devastating invasion of the Manchurian provinces continues."

The narrator's delivery was spitfire fast over spectacular battle footage of the brave and bold Chinese fighters. They crawled through mud or manned 37mm artillery guns. "The generalissimo came late to this conclusion, and only after being kidnapped by a faction of officers within his own troops led by General Zhang Xueling."

The shot changed from weapons of war to one of a group of Chinese men in uniform. They posed stiffly, as if for a still photograph, looking all the more foolish for trying to remain motionless before the lens of a motion picture camera.

"General Chiang Kai-shek was persuaded to embrace the cause of Chinese unity at the home of General Zhang's brother and closest political adviser, Zhang Mei. Sources claim that Zhang Mei, known as the Dragon of Terror and Peril, could himself lead the Chinese government at some future time."

Gibson's hands began to tremble. He instantly recognized the eyes of the intense dark man standing behind the soldiers. It was his Shadow, the Chinese stranger. He was the only man in the group whose very stillness seemed to reflect who he was, not what he wanted the camera to commemorate.

"Subsequent to the kidnapping, while all the plotters of the conspiracy have been rounded up, the general's brother, the inscrutable Zhang Mei, has escaped into the shadows of war! Current whereabouts? Unknown."

Stunned, he felt stuck in his seat. The cartoon began and Welles immediately began chortling, then laughing.

The Shadow's laugh.

Walter sprang from his chair, not unlike his companion had when the serial had begun.

"What about the cartoon?" Orson shouted.

"I can't stay!" Gibson hollered back as he ran up the aisle toward the exit. "I've got to find a cab!"

EPISODE TWENTY-EIGHT

"DEAR BROTHER," Xueling said to him, "Manchuria needs you now. I need you now."

Snow was falling. Xueling was visiting Mei in the small house he had claimed near the outskirts of Shenyang, far from the palace. Mei scratched his hands through the long beard he had grown during his mourning.

He could see his brother's eyes moving from him to the object behind him. Some time ago Zhang Mei had sent soldiers back to his home village and had them retrieve the statue of the god whose priest he had once pretended to be. He had wanted to show his wife and son something of his childhood, and this hollow old statue was the only tangible memory he could provide them. Of course, Lu Zhi thought it silly and had banished it to a far corner of her garden. Still, he'd had artisans restore its golden glory. When he had moved from that house, the statue was all he had asked to accompany him.

"I have nothing more to give to Manchuria," he replied. "Nor to China. I have given all."

"I have lost my father, as well," Xueling reminded him.

Mei nodded but did not reply. He brushed a minute speck of incense ash from his black silk robe. "I wear the black robes of the old monk who taught us in our youth. Do you remember he once told us that in order to wear the white robes of healing, one must first wear the black robes of destruction?"

"You will find Mi-Ying someday," Xueling said. He knew Mei had been scouring the countryside on the trail of the traitor. His quest had yielded no fruit, no relief.

"I believe he has fled to the south." Mei nodded. "I will follow him there."

"I have decided to strike my father's colors," Xueling said, suddenly. "I have made this decision with the advice of my brothers."

This, at last, distracted Mei from his concerns.

Xueling continued, "The men of Manchuria are brave and determined, but General Chiang's army will overwhelm us in the end. I will order my father's colors struck at sunset tomorrow and at dawn the next day we will raise the flag of the Republic of China. Henceforth, I will be the commander in chief of the Manchurian border. It is peace. Of a kind."

"A peace with those who have killed my family? What kind of peace is this?"

"A peace that will unite China."

"I believe we should fight on forever!" Mei spat, his voice dripping with bitterness. "Hit them harder, and harder, and harder!"

"Even if many more sons and wives and fathers die?" Xueling asked with surprising tenderness. "Even if the Han race be wiped from the face of the earth?"

"Yes!" Mei felt a murderous rage sweep over him. He dashed his weapons rack to the floor. "How can I swear loyalty to a man whose heart I want to rip out?"

Xueling gestured to an aide who stood nearby, who quickly left through the door. There came the sound of low voices in the small courtyard beyond. "I thought, as we all did, that General Chiang was behind the assassination. However, one who represents interests other than China's has recently come to me with new information."

The aide reentered the small room with another man. He was white and wore the uniform of an American officer.

"This is Captain Towers of the United States," Xueling introduced the man, who bowed deeply and formally. He bore himself alertly and carried the demeanor of a warrior. "He has been attached to diplomatic relations in many other countries. He has recently brought intelligence to me of conspiracies which sought this assassination to push us over the precipice into a great civil war. Then, like vultures, the plotters would pick apart the corpse of the land. He has helped me turn away from that fall for the good of China. Now you will see who Mi-Ying's merciless allies in this conspiracy are." He turned and looked at the young captain, who stood ramrod straight. "Who has caused the death of our father? Of this man's wife and son?"

The aide began to translate haltingly to Towers but the man cut him off with a wave of his hand. Towers's eyes met Mei's and his strong gaze did not waver for an instant.

"Japan," Captain Towers, the American officer, said in Chinese. "The Japanese."

EPISODE TWENTY-NINE

"So, THIS is where it gets interestin', 'cause this is where I lost him," Manny said, hitting the brakes with enough force to bounce Gibson forward against the dashboard.

"You lost him?"

Unfazed and unmoved, the cabbie chewed on his unlit cigar stub. "Wanna know what happened then?"

Gibson sat back in his seat. "Hell, yes!"

It had taken Manny's dispatcher several hours to track him down. During this suspenseful wait Gibson had managed to convince himself that something unfortunate had happened to his affable friend. In the end, however, the familiar cab had squealed to a stop in front of his hotel. The trip down the West Side had taken only minutes. Manny had just stopped his cab by the newsstand on the Ninth Avenue IRT elevated tracks at Sixteenth Street. A young man was hawking after-noon editions of the *New York Post*. The light from the setting sun was sliced into neat slivers by the massive ironwork trestle overhead.

Manny leaned on the horn. At the sound the paperboy stopped hec-toring the commuters and, with a smile of recognition, ran to the open window on the driver's side.

"What's up, Manny?" He was a teenager, of slight build and with dark eyes. His fingers, gripping the ledge of the door, were long and thin. The hair under his gray cap was a dark mop of brown curls and his eyes were wide and street-wary.

"Mr. Gibson, this here's Kurtzberg."

"Hiya, mister." The kid shook his hand.

"Hello."

"He plays stickball with my kid out in Sunnyside. So here's what's what. I follow your fella to here and then the cab stops and he gets out. He's heading for the elevated and I want to keep an eye on him but if I leave my cab behind I'll get fired. I'm on call, my dispatcher's barkin' at me. Nothin' I can do. So I think fast. I look over and I seen Jakey selling his papers right here on that corner. I give him da sign, and as sure as Bob's your uncle, he's up the El after him. Even jumps the turnstile."

"That's right." The kid nodded.

"Where'd he go?" Gibson asked.

"Just up to Thirty-fourth Street near the post office," the teen replied. "I followed him off the train, and down at the entrance there's this guy waiting for him with a car. But he ain't Chinese. He's American. Kind of an older guy, older than you even, with short silver hair. I tried to get close enough to hear them talking, but I couldn't do it. Whatever the Chinese man tells this guy really ticks him off something fierce. He starts pounding on the roof of the car. Then the Chinese man tells him something that completely turns him around, makes him laugh. They get into the car.

"Now I can't follow him on foot and I ain't got no cab fare. But I see a pal of mine, Stanley Leiber, who works at his cousin's husband's newsstand up there."

"That's one of Martin Goodman's stands," Manny said.

"Yeah, I know him," Walter said. "Also prints *Stag Magazine,* right?"

"He's got a string of newsstands. Real bona fide operation." Jakey continued his story. "Stan's also a part-time Movietone news runner, a guy who rides his motorcycle to the site of a news story. The camera-man gives him the film and then he beats the devil through traffic back to the lab to get the film processed so it can get onto movie screens before *The March of Time.* He says it's kinda like bein' on the pony express," he added somewhat wistfully. "Plus he makes some good scratch."

"Forget it, kiddo," Manny said, "I ain't talkin' your pop into get-tin' you no motorbike. Them things are a menace."

"Anyway, I tells him to keep his eye on the runner and he sets off after 'em and that's the last I seen him."

"Great work, kiddo. I'll see you at the next game." Manny slipped him a few bucks and put the car into gear and they raced up Eighth Avenue toward the post office district.

The car squealed to a stop at the newsstand, its racks bursting with titles, an Indian scout leaning against one wall.

"Hey-ho, Stan the man," Manny hollered at the young man sitting on a stack of magazines before the stand. The young man, about the same age as Jakey, and just as gangly, nodded and rose stiffly. His face bore a fresh bruise, his fingers were dark with oil stains, and he walked with a limp over to the cab.

"Jesus, pal! Somebody rough you up?"

"Nah, Manny," the young man said, defiantly, spitting on the side-walk. "I got hit by a tuna."

"How's that again?" Gibson asked. The kid appraised him coolly.

"'S'all right," Manny reassured him. "He's the one calling the plays."

The kid spat again. "I followed that car all the way downtown. You know the Fulton Fish Market, by the water there?"

Both men nodded.

"That's where I got hit by a tuna. Some son of a bitch thrown it from a stall to a truck and the sucker smacked right into me. Forty-pounder, easy. Laid me right out on Peck Slip. Knocked the chain off my dang bike. Took me hours to get her running again. A crime too, 'cause I missed the drop from London out at Idlewild."

"Damn," Gibson sighed and sat back in his seat.

"Game called," Manny grumbled.

"Naw," Stanley seemed offended. "We got a pulp stand down there. Big Sammy the Boxer works it. You'll know him when you see him, a huge grizzled piece of meat with a face that looks like a pile of broken brick. I gave him the signal. He hitched a ride on the back of a fish truck which was heading in the same direction."

After slapping Stanley a few bucks to help him recoup the loss of the London drop, they left midtown and sped toward the waterfront. He was in it now, Gibson thought, grinning at the exhilaration of it all. The story was coming. He could feel the sense of urgent, unstoppable momentum rising up within, the same sensation he experienced when it all went well, the writing, as it went on the train when he had opened up the throttle and let the words out. He rubbed his hands—his fingers were throbbing—then leaned forward to watch the buildings flash by as the Brooklyn Bridge grew large.

Within moments they were in the midst of the Fulton Fish Market. The smell of fish permeated the car, even with the windows closed. Most of the buyers were already in business, bidding on and then distributing to local restaurants and fishmongers the day's fresh catch being brought in from the sea. They found the plug-ugly pugilist, just as Stanley had described him, sipping a last whiskey of the day in his newsstand next to the tavern that sat behind the open-air fish stalls. Two drinks later and they were back in the cab heading farther south, into the financial district, the only part of New York that could truly be considered abandoned at night.

Manny pulled the car to a stop in front of an office building. It was indistinguishable from hundreds of other New York office buildings. Six or seven stories high, no ornamentation. "This was where Sammy the Boxer followed them to."

Gibson could see lights on in the lobby and a pair of uniformed security guards inside. "Do you feel that?" he asked Manny. "The vibration?"

"Mm-hmm. Subway."

Gibson shook his head. "No. There's a rhythm to it. You catch the same sensation in the Street & Smith building. I think there's a printing press down below us. Probably in the basement. It may even extend under the sidewalk."

"What're they printing?"

"I don't know," Gibson said and then pointed to the end of the block. "But I do know how we can find out." They headed to the dilapidated newsstand on the corner. A German shepherd barked at them as they arrived.

"Easy, killer," Gibson said to the alert hound. "Sammy the Boxer sent us."

An old man in a battered fedora rubbed the nape of the dog's neck. It sat back on its haunches. The old man squinted at them. At least one eye seemed to. The other eye was long since gone.

"Yeah," he grunted with a phlegmatic rattle.

Gibson folded a bill into the tin cup the man left out for change. "You, uh, keep your eye on the runner?"

"What do you think?"

"Hey, mac," Manny said, impatiently, "you know what goes on in that building back there?"

"Well," the old man said, "if you'd asked me that this morning I'd have said I didn't know. But since Sammy told me to watch the runners and they seemed particularly interested in it, I got a customer who's a rocketeer to find out for me."

"What's a rocketeer?"

"The post office guys that operate everything coming and going through the pneumatic tubes are called rocketeers. Okay, all the post offices in the city are connected by pneumatic tubes, thirty miles of 'em or more, with cylinders about this long"—he held out his hands to indicate a span of about two feet—"that go whizzing through them all day and all night. My rocketeer wrote down his question and put it in the tube at the Church Street office and it shot up to Times Square. Then it went to the Ansonia station, then on and on to the Planetarium office, the Cathedral office, and the Morningside office, before it finally gets to the Manhattanville station on a Hundred and Twenty-fifth Street, where someone who finally knows something about the building works. Two hours later, my rocketeer's back with the answer. Ain't the modern age great?" He unfolded a crumpled piece of paper. "That building there is the American Bank Note Company. Ever hear of it?"

Gibson shook his head.

"No? They print up money for other countries. It's a foreign currency mint."

Gibson pushed the now insistently nuzzling dog away from his crotch. "Did they go inside?"

"Nope. After a little while of looking it over and talking, the car drove off. I couldn't follow that."

"Of course not." Gibson grimaced with disappointment, feeling the trail of pursuit suddenly grow cold.

"Not the car. No. But that big Chinaman, he left on foot."

"Tell me you sent your dog after him, right?"

"Hell no! Shep minds the store. I followed him," he pointed north, toward Chinatown. "Went down an alley on Doyers. The door with the red light over it."

"You know," Manny said to him as they climbed back in the car, "a red light in Chinatown? That means opium."

"I know."

Manny turned the cab into the twisted net of Chinatown streets. He pulled up in front of an alley. At the back of the alley was a door. The red lightbulb flickered weakly in the darkness.

"This fella. He owe you money?"

"Nope."

"You owe him money?"

"Uh-uh."

"Then what's he to you? What do you want with him?"

"He's got the ending to my story."

He opened the cab door, stepped out, closed the door, and leaned in through the window, placing some bills in his hand. Manny would find out later that Gibson had slipped him a hundred bucks.

"You sure you want to go in there?"

Gibson shrugged. "You know, it probably won't even be the worst place I've been in this week."

"You want I should stick around?"

"No. I might be a while."

"Some game, huh?"

"Yeah," he replied, "sure was. Really kept our eye on the runner."

He watched the cab drive away. After a night spent calling on what felt like half of New York he suddenly was all alone. He looked down the long alley to the dark door. Extra innings, he told himself, and headed toward it, his footfalls echoing softly.

"*Fook yuen? Fook yuen?*" the smoke peddler called as Gibson slipped him money to enter. He had been in opium dens before, and this was an opulent example of one. Men lying on red silk pads on pallets on the floor behind carved screens were being tended to by a few men with pipes. The thick, richly sweet smoke hung low in the air. Several musicians played odd stringed instruments, a slow, meandering melody that sounded to Gibson like the memory of a brook in spring. An ancient staircase to the left vanished into the darkness upstairs. "*Fook yuen?*" the man asked again, trying to tug him toward a low couch.

Gibson shook his head. He held up a hand for caution and slowly reached into his jacket, pulling out the long, lethal knife which he had found in the corpse of Jeffords. He presented it, hilt first, to the little man, who seemed gnarled right to the tips of his tinted, curved fingernails.

The sleek peddler's eyes narrowed cagily. Gibson stared back at him. The men slipped away behind some curtains for a few moments. Then he returned, and the knife was gone. The man drew back the curtains. Gibson could see a simple iron spiral staircase leading up into darkness. Another Chinese man was guarding it; this man did not look like the smoke peddlers, who were shifty and cowed. He stood proud and alert. Gibson placed him for a soldier. He approached the man and attempted to stare him down as well. This man wasn't going for it. After several moments he smirked at Gibson and turned and climbed the staircase. Gibson followed.

The staircase opened onto a landing. Another Chinese man was guarding the door. This man appeared to have had his jaw broken recently. It was swollen and purplish and pushed about an inch too far to its right. A red bandana was wound tightly around his head. The pain must have been significant but he stoically held his post. The first man spoke to him. Through his clenched jaw the second man uttered a sound which could have been a chuckle. Then he opened the door.

Gibson instantly recognized where he was. It's the backstage of a theater, he thought. Indeed, the flies and drapes and boards were still intact, though covered with dust. The front of the stage was blocked by a great tattered backdrop. Seen in reverse, it appeared to be a Chinese temple scene. There was even a statue in front of it; he could see its shadow on the painted muslin.

There were stacks of long crates which were much cleaner, much newer, and the footprints and slide paths surrounding them showed that they had been placed here recently, probably by the small group of Chinese men who were right now sitting or leaning on them and looking at him. Some of them cleaned their knives. Some of them cleaned their guns. All of them glared at him.

"Zhang Mei," he said loudly. "I want to speak with Zhang Mei."

A voice rolled toward him from the shadows behind them; it was deep and melodious and fluidly inflected. It was a voice Welles would have admired. "Who are you?" it asked of him, simply.

"I'm your biographer." It just came to him. There was long pause.

"Who are you?" The voice was more quizzical now.

Gibson took a few steps closer to the Chinese group. He still couldn't see the speaker. He now stood in the midst of the Chinese. "I am a writer. I write for the pulp magazines. Popular stories."

"Who are you?"

"I am Walter Gibson. The man from the docks in Providence. You saved my life."

"Who are you?"

"My writing name is Maxwell Grant. I am the best-selling writer in this country." His eyes were adjusting to the new, darker wing of the stage. He could make out a black figure now. "You have reached out your hand from your land and touched this land. Already your name is known here. But not your life's story."

"My life speaks for itself," the shape said.

Gibson knew that he had been dismissed. He felt the men behind him begin to stir. It would only be another second before a knife slid between his ribs, or a thin metal thread was pulled tightly around his throat.

"Al Capone!" he exclaimed. "You've heard of Al Capone."

Even for a man from the other side of the world, that legendary name still had resonance. It gave the men creeping up behind him pause. The black shape before him shifted, and he realized that the man he had been speaking with had had his back turned to him the whole time. The figure stepped into the dim light and Gibson could see that this was indeed the man he'd been looking for. His eyes were glittering and hard but there was something in them that Gibson recognized. Something that again gave him the feeling that he might be looking into the eyes of his own creation.

"I was his biographer. And when he dies, his story will live on. He gave me what I wanted and I gave him what he wanted."

"What is that?"

"Immortality."

Zhang Mei smiled. It was a dead, mirthless smile. But it wasn't menacing. Gibson had simply amused him to the extent that he was able to be amused.

"If you stay you cannot leave without it being my will. I may never will it so."

"I know."

"And you will have to write fast, then. For my story is long and our time is brief."

"Well," Gibson said with some modesty, "in addition to being the best-selling writer in America, I'm also the fastest."

Zhang Mei nodded and the men fell back with soldierly ease and went about their crate-shifting exercise. Gibson took out his notebook and pencil. Gibson noticed that Zhang Mei had a delicate teacup filled with steaming tea and he wrote down that detail, accompanied by a note that the tea smelled like jasmine. Zhang Mei took a sip of the tea. "Well then, biographer, where should I begin?"

"Start with your parents," Walter said, already writing his lead sentence. "Who were they? What were they like?"

"I never knew my father," Zhang Mei said. He thought for a moment longer and then he spoke, and as he spoke, Gibson wrote. "The man who would be my father was a Manchu and he rode from the west, from the Nulu'erhu Mountains, across the windswept, snowy plains of the Lianoning Province, behind Zhang Zuolin, the warlord."

Issue 4:
HELL GATE

EPISODE THIRTY

S HE COULDN'T sleep. Lester didn't seem to have the same problem. He was slumbering away in their bed. His snoring managed
to be reassuring and irritating at the same time. She left the room and
padded down the hallway to the living room to get another book from
the shelf. Other books, which she had been poring over in an attempt
to find some history of her statue, were strewn across the living room.
It would require some explanation, she realized, as the room hadn't
looked like this when Lester had fallen asleep only hours ago.

They had been making love since their return from Chinatown the
night before. She had thought they would be too tired, or overwhelmed, for passion, but in fact it was just the opposite. They stayed
in bed and ate leftover Chinese food and made love over and over. It
was the first time since sometime before the pregnancy ended. It was as
if the excitement had ignited her need for him.

She added several of Lester's research books to her of-interest pile
and then her hand fell upon a German travel guide. Slowly she pulled
the book down. The book fell open to the page she knew it would: the
crease in the spine was permanent. She looked at the photo of the
palace of Ludwig II, the mad king of Bavaria. Deep under his castle

nestled high in the Alps was rumored to be a treasure guarded by a hall of mirrors so devious and fantastic that it could make someone mad within hours. This book had been in her purse last year in Switzerland. It had been the book she referred to when she begged Lester to take her just a little bit over the border, only twenty miles. She had even spoken with some locals and knew of an unpatrolled border crossing they could drive their little Citroën over. Lester hadn't wanted to, but he did it.

She closed the book and put it back on the shelf. What the book didn't say was that the palace had been turned into a Nazi troop bivouac. Books could be useless like that.

She spent some time cleaning up the books, putting them away. There were no answers to be found in them. No treasure clues.

She climbed back into bed. She could still hear the ringing voice of the young Nazi soldier who approached them as she leaped out of the car. She could hear Lester urgently asking her to get back in. Why had she stubbornly argued with him?

She lay back and curled up against him, pressing hard into his body, resting her leg over his, laying her head on his chest, rousing him. He wrapped his arms about her and kissed her forehead. "I think we're going to miss church tomorrow. Today. We'll go next week."

"Mm-hm." She toyed with the hairs on his chest. There were a few gray ones she hadn't noticed before. "Why did you tell that cop your name was Kenneth Robeson?"

"Did I do that?"

"Mm-hmm."

"Really? I don't remember that. I guess I felt more like Kenneth Robeson than Lester Dent."

She could almost hear him thinking about the events at the restaurant, reliving them.

"I nearly got you killed twice."

"Not bad for your first time out."

"Don't joke about it," she insisted. "I get us in trouble."

"I'm not joking." He sat up. "Can't we go out to dinner at our favorite restaurant and not have an adventure? You went into the theater without me. You mouthed off to that cop. It wasn't quite as bad as getting us chased over the Alps with the entire German army shooting at us. But it was close."

"Why don't you stop me?"

"Because you're a hard woman to say no to." She rolled away from him onto her other side and was quiet for a while.

"I always get us into these things and you have to get us out. Don't you get mad at me for it?"

She heard him exhale in frustration. "Maybe you're just the kind of person that things like this happen to. You know, some people have good luck, some people have bad luck, some people have money luck or romance luck. Maybe you've got adventure luck and these things find you. And one of these times your adventure luck is going to run out and I'm not going to be able to save you, because you don't let me protect you."

"I thought you did a pretty swell job in Chinatown."

"It could have gone the other way on a dime."

"There are things you can't protect me from, Lester. There have been and there will be."

"I'm aware of that. But at least I feel that in some ways, I'm a good counterbalance to your adventure luck. I have a touch of protection luck. But only a touch. In the hospital, for example," he went on. "Turns out you and I have the same blood type and I could give you a transfusion. But I couldn't protect you from losing the baby."

"You're right," she sniffled and then blew her nose on what she thought was rough for a handkerchief, but was really soft when it turned out to be a sock.

"So okay," she said. "I'll try to watch out for my adventure luck. I love you too much."

"I love you too," he said, and she wondered if he had heard her and understood her. It occurred to her that married people use "I love you" to convey a variety of meanings from "I'm sorry" to "I'm right, but . . ." to "This is great" to "I'll do exactly what you say from this day on." She thought he might be reading that very interpretation into her expression, when what she really had meant by "I love you" was that he was her man. But her emphasis had slipped at the last moment.

"I love you too," she said, meaning that they didn't have to continue their conversation right now. She knew the doctors had told Lester that she would never be able to carry a baby to term, and that he wanted to talk about what that meant for their life together. Lester may have finally been able to get her to leave the apartment, and that was a big step in the right direction, but she wasn't ready to talk about their never having a child together. She rolled over and looked up, trying to distinguish his features in the dark. She helped him glide a hand up her side to her breast, sliding her thigh against his. She parted her lips and kissed him.

The night after crossing the border back into Switzerland, they had made love the same way as they did now. She couldn't smell him or hear his voice, not to mention look at him, without wanting to be enveloped by him. She could remember the way she felt when they had exited the Citroën and had seen the angry, punctured metal in the bonnet, torn through by the machine gun's bullets.

It was a month after their return from Europe, after the day in Bavaria and the nights in the Alps, that they had discovered she was pregnant for what would be the last time.

EPISODE THIRTY-ONE

LIGHT BROKE apart through the Rose Window and scattered in dappled fragments of color across Norma's hymnal.

The pastor read from the Gospel of John, "Jesus said to Nicodemus, 'Most assuredly, I say to you, unless one is born again, he cannot see the kingdom of God.'"

Holy Trinity Church was a Gothic structure on Central Park West. It was far bigger than the small Lutheran church she and Lester had attended back in La Plata, and sometimes she felt overwhelmed by its great presence: the elegance of the triptych of Christ rising behind the alabaster altar, the Louis Tiffany stained-glass windows, but especially the great pipe organ. Their old church had had a donated upright piano which had been lovingly tuned once a month. Holy Trinity incorporated much more music into its services than her old church had, and she loved that.

"Nicodemus said to Him, 'How can a man be born when he is old? Can he enter a second time into his mother's womb and be born?'" She watched Lester's fingers tap silently against his thighs, writing another book or transcribing the pastor's sermon, she wasn't sure which. He didn't like church very much but he dutifully went along with her every Sunday. During a very busy period it could be the only time during a week that he stopped moving. He stifled a yawn. Almost.

"And Jesus answered, 'Most assuredly, I say to you, unless one is born of water and the Spirit, he cannot enter the kingdom of God. That which is born of the flesh is flesh, and that which is born of the Spirit is spirit. Do not marvel that I said to you, "You must be born again." The wind blows where it wishes, and you hear the sound of it, but cannot tell where it comes from and where it goes. So is everyone who is born of the Spirit.'"

The organist began to play and she looked down at the words on her page: "Come, Oh, Come, Thou Quickening Spirit." She felt Lester touch her hand and she smiled at him as he intertwined his fingers with hers. He was too shy to sing out loud, even in a great mass of people, but he enjoyed listening to her sing. The hymn brought tears to her eyes.

On the steps she and Lester stopped to shake the pastor's hand and thank him for the sermon. As they parted, a voice called out to them, "Excuse me!" They stopped and saw a couple, their age, a few steps up from them. A little boy in his Sunday suit held on tightly to his mother's hand. Norma recognized both the mother and the son. The mother was new to the city and their church. Her husband had died and she had moved up from somewhere in the South to live with her sister. Norma could see that the little boy held something tightly in his hand. "We're so sorry to bother you, Mr. Dent," the mother said. "But last week one of the boys in Sunday school told him that you were a writer. Would you mind . . . ?" She helped the little boy take a step toward them. He unfurled the object in his hand. It was the latest *Doc Savage* issue. "He's such a big fan."

Lester grinned. "Of course," he said. He pulled a pen from his pocket and took the magazine from the little boy's hand. "*The Sea Angel.* One of my very favorites. What's your name, son?"

"Bruce," said the little boy.

"Okay, Bruce." Lester scribbled down a quick message on the cover. "For Bruce—Remember to strive every moment of your life to make yourself better and better, that all may profit by it. —Kenneth Robeson." Then he wrote, in parentheses, "Lester Dent." He handed the book back to the wide-eyed youth. "That's the first sentence of the Doc Savage oath," he said gently. "Do you know the other lines?"

The little boy nodded. "By heart," he said and quickly rattled off all four lines of the oath so it sounded like one long sentence: "Let me strive every moment of my life to make myself better and better, that all may profit by it; let me think of the right, and lend all my assistance to those who need it, with no regard for anything but justice; let me be considerate of my country, of my fellow citizens and my associates in everything I say and do; let me take what comes with a smile, without loss of courage; let me do right to all and wrong no man."

Norma and Lester burst into proud laughter and Lester tousled the boy's hair. The child's mother thanked them profusely, embarrassing Lester. Then she politely pulled her little boy away.

They stood alone on the steps; all the other churchgoers had moved on to the rest of their Sunday. The pastor closed the doors to the church. A strong wind rustled the bare trees across the street in Central Park. Norma sighed and Lester put his arm around her.

"I'm getting better about it," she said. "I really am." She meant it. In the past week as she had put aside Dutch Schultz and turned to researching the golden statue she had seen in the theater, she had had to admit to herself that she just wasn't feeling as bad.

"I know," he said with a reassuring pat on her hand. "Come on and let's walk over to the Tavern on the Green. I'll buy you a Manhattan."

She nodded and they began to walk.

The Chinese men seemed to appear out of nowhere (although afterward she would recall that they had been lurking on the outskirts of her awareness all morning) and surrounded them before they knew it.

"What the hell?" Lester said loudly. It appeared neither of the men spoke English. They were dressed in suits. The man in charge nodded his head politely toward a sedan, which Norma now realized had been idling in front of the church as they had come out. For a moment she thought that this was her retribution for breaking into the theater, until she suddenly recognized him. She felt Lester's arm begin to slide from her body.

"Wait," she said to him. "This man works for Mr. Yee. He's his cook!"

The man nodded, recognizing Yee's name, and gestured at the car.

"Is something wrong? Has something happened to Monk and Ham?"

The man gestured again to the car. She looked at Lester. He shrugged. "I don't like it," he said.

"I'm going."

"Then so am I."

They climbed into the back seat of the Buick. The two men slipped into the front seat and they pulled away from the curb.

They drove downtown. Lester and Norma tried various ways to communicate with the men but were met only with patient smiles. Finally they gave up and watched the city pass by their window. In no time they were entering Chinatown. Norma could see the tall pagoda roof of the bank on Canal Street. The car pulled to a halt in front of a building she recognized as one that Lester had pointed out to her last week.

"It's the Hip Sing Association," he said to her.

The two men got out of the car and opened the passenger doors. Lester and Norma stepped out. It was as busy as any day in Chinatown. They were escorted into the building.

Inside the small lobby stood Mr. Yee. He was elegantly dressed in a white Chinese jacket and pants. Instead of buttons the jacket had toggles made of knotted silk which slipped through loops. The lobby was festooned with regal decorations in advance of the upcoming unity parade which was to end here with a great feast.

"Yee," said Lester, "we're being kidnapped!"

"Oh, no!" Yee said, looking surprised. "My cooks refuse to learn English."

"Is everything all right?" Norma wanted to know. "Are Monk and Ham all right?"

"Yes," he said. "I'm very sorry to have upset you like this. This is a very special day." He snapped at the cook in a burst of spitfire Chinese which Norma figured probably translated along the lines of ". . . or at least it was supposed to be until you ruined it!"

"Why?" asked Lester.

"Because I am repaying my debt to you."

"What debt? You don't owe me anything."

"You have been my friends for many years and you stood up against that policeman. He came in this week and actually put money into the China fund. For this I am so grateful and as a Hip Sing man I am able to show my gratitude by welcoming you into the brotherhood as my brother." He looked at Norma. "I'm sorry the Hip Sing does not extend the same honor to women, but you will understand that my appreciation flows from your husband to you as well."

"Really?" She felt a little stab of disappointment.

"Yee," said Lester, "I don't know about this."

She took his arm with both hands. "My husband is honored by this." She turned her smile from one man to the other. "We both are."

"I didn't know that a white man could join the Hip Sing." Lester was still hesitant.

"On occasion and only to a certain degree," he replied, smiling at how well his surprise was playing out after all. "For example, you will never be called upon to marry a dead man's wife or return his bones to China. Will you follow me upstairs?" As he spoke he handed Lester clothes similar to his. "You will put these on when we enter the temple."

"Temple?"

"You will see."

The building had several floors. The doors on every floor were closed to them. The stairs were wide—a dozen men could easily stand shoulder to shoulder on the staircase—and the ceilings were tall. The air was fragrant with aromatic incense. The walls were lined with photographs and newspaper articles depicting the history of Chinese in America. Norma saw images of men working on the great railways, huddling together in alleys, gambling in saloons.

225

They reached the landing before the last staircase and at last saw another man. A Chinese warrior stood, bare-chested, at the top of the stairs. He had both hands on the hilt of a sword with the biggest blade Norma had ever seen. The point of the sword rested on the floor. They looked up at the man and he looked down at them.

"Mr. Yee," Lester asked, "is there any pain involved in becoming your brother?"

He shook his head. "No," he said. Then he added, "Just death."

"What?"

"It is merely a ritual death."

"Is that a better kind than regular death?"

Yee led Lester up the stairs. "Please lower your head when I tell you to. But quickly." Lester stood in front of the guard, who raised the broadsword to his shoulder like a batter.

"Now!"

The sword passed cleanly, with a whisper, over Lester's bowed head. Norma breathed a sigh of relief. The guard smiled at them both.

"Death is the necessary step on the road to enlightenment. Come," urged Mr. Yee, "Mock Sai Wing awaits."

"Who's that?" Lester asked.

"My uncle. He is a very important man. Your newspapers sometimes refer to him as Mock Duck," Yee said, with a proud smile. Norma made a mental note to remind herself to ask Lester why that name had caused him to stammer and go pale.

The guard opened the large double doors and led the two men under the arch into the joss house, a temple on the top floor of the building. It was as if a treasure chest had been opened in front of her eyes. Light streamed into the room from all sides through floor-to-ceiling windows. Red banners hung from the ceiling and posters decorated the pillars holding up the vaulted ceiling. There was a large statue of Buddha at the far end of the room and incense burned before it, filling the air with the smell of jasmine. Norma counted a dozen men in the room. They were all dressed, as Mr. Yee was, in elegant white silk pajamas. The men broke apart and formed two lines as

Norma and Lester entered. At the far end of the gauntlet they had formed stood an aged man. Norma recognized him as the old man who had been dining in the restaurant with them.

Lester looked around. There was nowhere for him to be modest, so he disrobed and dressed in full view of the other men.

"That's some scar on your uncle's neck," she said to Mr. Yee.

"Many years ago an assassin came right up to him in the street and shot him at point-blank range. And yet he survived. There is an old Chinese joke about Chinese men being bad shots. Not funny. But true."

Lester turned, dressed in black silk.

"Very good. Black is the color of destruction. After you are destroyed you will then be given the white clothes of healing."

"Okay."

"They will ask you many questions and I will translate and then help you respond. Are you ready to stand before Shen Yi, the Sun-God, and receive his arrows?"

"Ritual arrows, right?"

"Yes."

"I am."

Mr. Yee indicated that it was time for Norma to leave. Frustrated, she took a few steps back, letting the guard close the heavy, carved doors. She stepped up and put her eye to the seam and found she was still able to watch. Lester's eyes were sparkling with delight as he was escorted to the head of the gauntlet. Mr. Yee left him there and walked around to join his uncle at the end of the line. The men raised swords. As Lester walked down the line, each man lowered his sword and gently tapped Lester against the back of his neck. Norma breathed a sigh of relief as he reached the end and the last man. Then the two lines of men closed ranks behind him, blocking him from her view. She could see the top of his head nodding solemnly and hear his deep voice repeating Mr. Yee's soft responses. But she couldn't make out any details.

She was put out. She and Lester were partners in so many things they did. She wasn't used to being sidelined and didn't appreciate having the strictures of five thousand years of culture applied to her. She was pleased that Lester would have a new experience, but she wished she were having it with him. So it wasn't so much that she was bored or indifferent but more that she was a little jealous when she turned away from the ceremony for a few moments to look at the wall of old photographs behind her.

Many of the photos were of men who must have been members and the places they came from. One photograph in particular caught her attention. She recognized it as San Francisco's Chinatown, reduced to rubble in the aftermath of the great earthquake.

Her self-pitying indignation was swept away by a great thrill at the sight. Sitting placidly, untouched amidst the devastation, as if the walls of the surrounding temple had collapsed directly outward only to reveal it and the devastation as far as the eye could see, was her golden statue. As small as it was in the picture, it still leered horrendously at her. The delicious tingles of discovery swept down from the crown of her head. She wanted it. She wanted to go back to the theater and bring the world to see it. She wanted to grab Lester and show him, but he was in the middle of drinking some symbolic blood. At least, she hoped it was symbolic.

The ceremony ended with a great "*Ho!*" resounding from the room, which Mr. Yee later told her translated as "Good!" The great doors opened and she was invited to enter. Lester was beaming with pride. The men surrounded him and clapped him on the back. He changed back into his church clothes. Then, as a single mass sweeping her husband along, the men headed downstairs to celebrate.

Norma motioned for Mr. Yee and when he came to her she showed him the picture.

"What's that?" she asked.

"That is Tai Yi Jiu Ku Tian Cun," he replied. "The Judge of the Dead. The highest ruler in hell. He is carried forth by ten monks who represent the ten Lords of Death. Upon death all souls must appear before Tai Yi and be judged."

"Well, that Tai Yi," she said, unable to say the rest of the Chinese words, "that's the statue I found in the theater. I guess I didn't describe it well enough for you. That's my treasure."

He pursed his lips for a moment. "He is not a treasure to be found. He is an omen of great death and destruction. He is not something you should ever hope to see for real in your lifetime. He judges men and gods alike."

"Well, of course. I'd never want to see him for real. He sounds very unpleasant. But I'm talking about this statue, not the real god. This is a statue made of gold. Like this one in this picture of San Francisco thirty years ago. I'm sure of it. I'd love to take another look. I'd just love to! To just know."

His gentle dark eyes grew cloudy with worry for her. "You must not go back to the theater. You must not look for Tai Yi. Tai Yi comes when there is misery and sorrow and troubles, and many dead to judge. Look closer at the picture, Mrs. Dent. You say it is just a statue. How would you know a god if you met one?"

EPISODE THIRTY-TWO

"**D**EAR EDITOR,'" The Flash read to Driftwood from the latest issue of *Astounding Stories*, "'This is to notify you of the official commencement of the Iowa City Science Fiction Advancement League at the Iowa University Law School. We wish to express our utmost appreciation to the publishers of *Astounding Stories* for the creation of such a worthwhile literary genre, adding many hours of enjoyment to the average Iowa law student's hectic life. The ICSFAL consists of seven full-time members—six students and one faculty member. In particular we wish to stress our admiration for the scope and detail of John Campbell's essays on the latest knowledge of the solar system. They are accurate and exciting and full of insight into OUR UNIVERSE NOW. Your articles show that good science writing can be as entertaining as good science fiction writing. Also, we are an organization wishing to grow and support science fiction, *our* fiction, and we are looking for new members in the Iowa City area who wish to join us or like-minded organizations across the country who share our mission and would like to establish larger communications. For us the living, I am, Randolph Farmer, Iowa Law Commons, Iowa City.'

"And there's three other science fiction club announcements just like it." He tossed the latest issue of *Astounding Stories* onto the table, where it began soaking up the dribbles of beer. "I'm telling you, Otis, there's a real gold mine in this science fiction. Something huge is happening here. It's bigger than Walter Gibson money or even Edgar Rice Burroughs money. I'm talking about publisher money. Tycoon money. A law student doesn't have time to scratch his own ass or chase girls, but he finds time to get a group together in a dormitory basement and spend an evening talking about rockets to the moon?"

"They're crazy?" Driftwood suggested. He picked up the magazine and thumbed through it. He had been staying at The Flash's hotel. The Flash had fronted him some cash until his disability checks were forwarded from California. The Flash didn't know exactly why he was trusting this stranger (after all, what kind of name was Otis Driftwood?) but he had taken a liking to the fellow and wanted to lend a hand up. Driftwood was a caustically cynical and suspicious son of a bitch, but he was funny and The Flash (who wasn't funny at all but admired people who were) enjoyed his company. After a morning spent writing he had gathered up Driftwood and hit the newsstand for the latest issue; then they had made their way to the White Horse for Dutch courage.

The brutal cold spell which had followed them down from Providence had lifted somewhat, though the warmth of the fireplace was still welcome. Few people had drifted in this afternoon: two boys barely old enough to drink were rifling through some papers in an open portfolio at the bar, and a tired drunk, whose head was slumped down on his chest, was drowsing near the drafting door.

"In the beginning was Hugo Gernsback and he begat *Amazing Stories*." The Flash sighed wistfully. "Now there's a guy who could have had it all. What he must take to bed with him at night!"

"What happened?"

"He saw it all coming and he reached for the brass ring and missed it, that's all. Old Hugo was the ed on *Amazing Stories* and he saw that the mags that sold the best were the ones that had a science fiction story in them. Usually it was just a Welles or Verne reprint, but every month he'd have some new stuff. Well, a competitor to *Amazing Stories* was *Wonder Stories,* and it was on the verge of folding. Old Hugo scraped together every dime he had and he bought out the old *Wonder Stories* title and he started to publish mainly science fiction stories and it really took off.

"Then he started the SFL, the Science Fiction League, and sold club charters through the magazine. He made money off the stationery and stamps and pins and membership dues. So he's building something akin to the Boy Scouts, y'know? A nationwide network of fans who communicate with each other through his magazine and take their marching orders from him.

"Now the thing you gotta realize about the fans is that there are two types. There's the group that'll read science fiction and other stuff as well, but then there's this core group that takes it so seriously they won't read anything else. And you better get the science part right or you're going to be hearing it. And the core members in different cities start communicating with each other through the letters column and they're complaining that the mag isn't publishing their kind of stories, don't feel like they're being taken seriously enough, don't have enough of a voice in the rules or the charter of this club, and they revolt!

"Some of the core fans in Brooklyn announce the formation of the International Scientific Association, the ISA, a completely fan-run organization. Now old Hugo should have just let them have their moment in the sun and it would have faded away, probably. But instead he treated them as if they were important and he announced, in print, that they were officially expelled from the SFL. This turns them into revolutionary heroes in the eyes of the other core fans, right?

"Well, in protest, all these clubs start rejecting the SFL and *Wonder Stories.* This means money out of Hugo's pocket. So he has to sell the magazine to keep the club going. But what he doesn't realize is that without the mag he's got no way to talk to its members. He got shut out and the fans took over."

"Amen, brother!"

"Hear me out! Science fiction magazines are the only mags on the newsstands today where the sales numbers go up every month! So when I say there's big money to be made in this science fiction writing game, I mean there's big money there, Otis. It's virgin territory. That's what John Campbell believes. And I do too. I have high hopes of using science fiction to smash my name into history so violently that it will take a legendary form. I am going to write science fiction stories until my fingers drop off. And I tell you what. It's gonna make me rich."

"From writing?" Otis sipped his beer. "How many rich writers do you know? I guess a fella could do all right peddling hokum, but I don't know about rich. And speaking of hokum and malarkey, do you think he's full of crap?"

The Flash was confused. "Campbell?"

"No. Gibson."

"About what?"

"About the night watchman. Was that some bullshit?"

"Well, it does seem a *little* pulp."

"A little? I don't know, brother. Chinese murderers, and poison gas, and monsters?"

The Flash hesitated. He felt he had to defend Gibson. This guy, this stranger, had no idea what Gibson was really about. Not the way The Flash did. Who was this Otis Driftwood, anyway, to doubt a great pulp writer like Walter Gibson? If Gibson said there had been a chemical incident at the Providence Medical Lab, then a fella had to believe him, right?

"Well," he replied, drawing his words out in a hesitant manner, "real or pulp, I guess it doesn't matter. It's a hell of a story and I wish I had dibs on it."

"Sure, but . . ."

"I'm going to get the next round," The Flash interrupted, because obviously Driftwood wasn't going to and he didn't want to keep arguing about Gibson. He shook the kinks out of his legs and strolled over to the bar. Was it possible that Gibson was still tweaking him the way he had tweaked him with that Sweet Flower story? He leaned against the bar and ordered.

While he waited for the bartender to draw his beers, he looked over the shoulder of the two teens going through their portfolio.

"Funny pages?" he asked them.

"Kind of," said one. It came out *kaand uf.*

"Sort of," said the other. It came out *sert ef.*

"You boys are from Cleveland, right?"

They nodded.

"We're trying to sell a comic book story," one of them said. He had jet-black hair. "Comic books are the next big thing. We came all the way in for a meeting with some publishers."

"We got turned down," the other one said.

"We got another meeting tomorrow," the first one said, none too optimistically.

The Flash looked over their shoulders. As far as he could tell it was a comic strip, even though there were a lot more panels on the page. The crude drawings seemed to show a muscular strongman in circus tights chasing some crooks. "Is he actually wearing a cape?"

The boys nodded.

The Flash shrugged and paid for the beers. "Seems to me as long as people can buy a book full of words and stories by real writers they ain't gonna want to pay the same price for a book of pictures," he said. "People like to read, boys. It's the most popular form of entertainment there is! If the movies and radio haven't got people to stop reading books, then nothing will. And by the way, at least Alex Raymond's stuff looks good."

Feeling pleased with himself for defending his chosen profession so vigilantly (but aware that he had just taken out his anxiety about Gibson and Driftwood on these two poor saps), he left them there and sauntered back to the table. He plunked Driftwood's beer down in front of him.

He was just settling back into his seat when the old drunk from across the room lurched up to their table.

"Aw, come on!" The Flash said. "What are you drinking? You smell like ammonia!"

"Hey, bub!" Driftwood asked the man. "You all right?"

The man wasn't as old as The Flash had thought he was at first. But if it were possible for a man to be a human shipwreck, then The Flash was looking at one. He was thin, thinner even than Driftwood. His skin was waxy and jaundiced, and The Flash was nearly certain that he could see the veins underneath.

"I used to be a writer," the man said. His jaw seemed locked in an unsettling position while his lips continued to move. This made it appear as if his voice was not cooperating with the movements of his mouth. The Flash had never seen anything quite like it before. Certainly not from any rummy. "I'm a writer."

"Of course you are. Everybody is," Driftwood said. "Have a seat here, brother, I'm gonna buy you a drink and you're gonna tell us a story." The Flash wished that Driftwood wouldn't encourage the stranger; he was getting an unsettling feeling about him. But Driftwood seemed to really enjoy the whole my-down-and-out-comrade routine, and The Flash could tell that he was getting earnest about speaking with the drunk. The bar was empty at the moment. The two boys from Cleveland had packed up and left as soon as The Flash had finished speaking with them. The bartender was outside arguing with a shopkeeper from next door about a truck which had been blocking his store for two days. The bartender was maintaining that he'd had no delivery scheduled.

The man eased himself slowly into a chair. "Hot in here," he said. "Too hot."

"Because of the fireplace," The Flash pointed out sarcastically, really hoping now that the man would move along.

Driftwood shot him a look he wouldn't have expected from a man who owed him as many beers as he did. Then Driftwood looked back at the rummy and said, "You all right, friend?" His tone was genuine; he was concerned. But there was no response except the man's slow breathing. After a moment Driftwood shrugged, stood, and said, "I'm going to hit the head. When I come back we'll get this guy to the hospital."

The man seemed to be catching Driftwood's comment on an echo, lifting his head to watch him depart after a long moment of distracted thought. Hubbard smelled ammonia again. And something else. What was that other scent? Then it suddenly hit The Flash where he had smelled this before, this combination of ammonia and lavender.

"Christ in a handcar!" The Flash would have leapt out of his chair if the man's hand hadn't reached out and curled tightly around his wrist. His clutch was ice-cold. "You're a Christ almighty dead man!"

The thin gray man attempted to smile; at least the skin around his lips folded back to reveal some teeth. "Almost," he whispered.

"How? How? How?" The Flash's heart was pounding.

"Cool air. Ammonia. Certain elements, military elements, which help maintain the viability of life without life. It came to me, lurking in the shadows of my dreams. It's my own new science. Bionecrology. What do you think? I'm thinking of endowing a chair at Providence College. If I had left any money." He tried to laugh; it sounded like a cat retching.

"This is impossible. We buried you," The Flash said.

"You came to my house. You talked with my aunt. I heard one of you say you came here. So I've been waiting." His head drooped to his chest momentarily and when, with great effort, it rose back up, it hung to his right and stayed there, awkwardly. "It's too hot," he said almost apologetically. "Watched you all at my aunt's house but couldn't talk. Wasn't sufficiently reanimated."

The Flash looked on in disgust as a thin black fluid dribbled down the back of the hand still gripping his arm. He clapped his hand over the bony wrist. He instantly realized there was no pulse. And yet he could not remove himself from the clasp. When he pulled his hand away there were bits of flesh clinging to it. The Flash asked in horrified amazement, "Are you rotting?"

The man's body jerked with a spasm. He put his hands with their long spidery fingers on the table to steady himself. "Is Walter Gibson coming? I wanted to see him. I tried to call him." He looked up at them with a pathetically desperate and haunted look in his eyes. A piece of flesh tore free of his cheek, and an eyeball began to sink into its socket. The Flash could see the revealed muscle contracting. It began to turn gray even as he looked. The Flash shook his head and the other man managed an expression that resembled sadness.

"What happened?" Hubbard asked. "Tell me about the lab. Tell me what happened. Tell me about the gas."

"The gas. That's why I'm here." He seemed to draw some energy from rediscovering his mission. "In its day it was so new that it wasn't even given a name. It was just known as 'the gas,' or sometimes 'that shit.' It's only effective as a gas for a very short time. It's extremely volatile in its liquid form, which makes it doubly effective as a gas and an explosive, so even though it dissipates quickly, it covers a lot of ground before. Reaches a lot of troops. In its gaseous state you definitely have to inhale it for it to kill you. It might burn your skin a little, but the gas won't kill you if you don't breathe it in. If you do get a full lungful, it kills you fast. So fast you end up looking like you froze where you were. That's the best death you can hope for.

"Say you're a little farther back from the gas when it's released and don't inhale it at full strength. It will still kill you, but instead of fast and painful, it's slow and even more painful. It'll make you wish you had just taken a deeper breath. Days, or even weeks. All the liquid is slowly drawn out of your organs as you dehydrate from within. Your skin turns transparent and you can practically see the muscles and veins beneath. Through it all, you never lose your mental acuities. Your mind stays as sharp as ever, which is how you want it as your body melts like a candle from the inside out. That's what happened to me.

"But it's while it's in the liquid state that it is particularly horrifying. It seems that there is something about its nature, when it's concentrated into that form, that really lets it get into a person in a horrible way. Only a small amount coming in contact with the skin seems to drive directly toward the central nervous system. Your mind goes before your body does. Imagine the worst case of rabies madness you've ever seen in a dog transferred to a man. There was a watchman at the lab; I fear for his soul."

"Where did the gas come from?"

The man nodded in his dreamlike way. "Colonel Towers came to us one evening just after the new year with a discovery he had made in some old army files. A record of a weapon lost and forgotten over twenty years ago."

"Who's Colonel Towers?"

"A frightening man, Colonel Towers. There must be men like him in every army throughout history—the kind of soldier the army can't do without but fears one day will turn against it. The kind of officer who leads a coup. A Caesar. A Cromwell. Extremely erudite and well traveled. I know he speaks a dozen languages and there hasn't been a war on this globe in the past thirty years, no matter how far-flung, that he hasn't observed on behalf of his masters. He journeys wherever the winds of war are blowing. He's an instigator and a meddler. He doesn't really have a command, but neither does he seem to be commanded. He's a man to be regarded with respect, even though he may be of the most villainous nature. A man like Towers needs to be at war, needs a war of his own. I believe that is what he has sought all these years. That's what led him to discover the gas. And its whereabouts.

"Harmony Isle. A little outcropping of Perdition on earth. Towers and Jeffords hired the *Zephyr* and went. I think Towers must have already known the power that was within his grasp and he began to erase his tracks even at that moment, for when they returned, the crew, good local men I had grown up with and worked with, had been left behind. Jeffords insisted there had been an accident. But I think they were abandoned there. It was left to us—the few researchers at the lab, myself, Towers, Jeffords, and the night watchman—to bring the deadly cargo into the lab. Into our lives. Back into the world.

"Jeffords and his crew worked diligently around the clock. Towers wanted a neutralizing agent, an antidote. Some key which would allow him to open his demon box safely. Meanwhile, he would leave for long stretches at a time. Finally, several weeks ago, I transcribed the fruitful results of the research. A formula. We had discovered Towers's key.

"I've seen that at the moments of greatest triumph in life, the moments of greatest disaster are not far behind. The metal drum that the chemical was transported in was old and had been rusted by its exposure to salt air. The researchers had taken great care to remove only the amount they needed to work with, so that it needed to be touched only when absolutely necessary. But still, as they say, accidents happen. And then I saw why Towers wanted this abomination. I saw firsthand, in an instant, what it could do."

He coughed, unable to clear the rattle from his throat. "Afterward, when I realized I had time to live, I destroyed every bit of our work. I thought that would be enough to stop Towers. That without the neutralizing agent he would be unable to use it. I thought it was enough and I thought I could do more. But I should have known better. And I was so afraid. Of dying." He tried to laugh and it turned into a seizure which convulsed his body, and he doubled over, his head hitting the table. He brought himself upright, the skin peeling away from his skull where it had impacted upon the wood. The black fluid streamed down his face.

"What can I do?" Hubbard asked.

The man slid The Flash's magazine around to him. "Never got published here," he wheezed. "Barely ever got published. Not leaving much behind." He picked up a pen and scribbled something on its cover. He set the pen down. "My last story," he said. "Get this to Walter Gibson. He'll get it to someone who can stop Towers before he uses more of the gas. I know he will."

He collapsed on the table with a moist thud.

"Holy hell! What happened?" Driftwood was back. The Flash felt barely able to breathe. One by one he lifted the dead man's fingers from his arm until he was finally able to remove the hand.

"Is he dead?" Driftwood asked. Driftwood reached out and gave the bony shoulder a shove. He nodded at The Flash.

"Goddammit!" exclaimed the bartender, bursting into the room. "Some ass drove an ice truck all the way down here from Providence and then just abandoned it in front for two friggin' days." He looked at them. "What the hell's going on here? Is that guy dying in here? People can't die in here. We'll get a reputation!"

"Relax, Pete," said The Flash to the bartender. He picked up the magazine, looking for meaning in the last words the man had written. But all he could see scrawled was cockeyed gibberish. "If it means anything to you, he didn't really die here."

EPISODE THIRTY-THREE

THE URGENT pounding at the door startled her.

She had been reading a letter to Kenneth Robeson from a little boy in Beavercreek, Ohio, who was nine years old. He had just read his first issue of *Doc Savage* and had fallen in love with it. This little boy wanted to be a writer when he grew up, just like Kenneth. Norma answered all of Lester's fan mail. She had a stack to her left and they were all similar to the one she had been reading. As she had reread the letter she heard the young boy's voice speaking of his hopes and dreams for a meaningful life of excitement and adventure as embodied by Doc Savage. These were Lester's boys. She had wondered if he ever really knew what an important part of these lives he had become. But she knew when it came down to it that no one understood better than he.

When she opened the door, there stood two young men she didn't recognize. One of them was short and stocky and had a loose mop of curly red hair on the top of his head. The other was tall and slender and handsome with deep, dark eyes. The redhead was wild-eyed, as if he had just come from an exciting ball game. The other man kept his eyes down and seemed uncomfortable.

"Lester," she called, and the sound of typing stopped. "You have company."

"Well. That is some story, fellas," Lester said at last, looking up from his coffee and giving Norma a sly uplifted eyebrow. "It ends like it should, with the cops taking a body away."

"It's not my story," Otis said. The two men sat across from the Dents at their comfortable little kitchen table, which had once belonged to Norma's grandmother. He seemed reluctant to speak and she gave him a smile of encouragement. "Ron's the one saying he's who he says he was. Maybe he's just been hiding out in Providence this whole time while Gibson's gas was killin' him slowly, but before it did he came down to New York. Don't I know that it's easy enough to go underground. And that it's easy enough to go crazy while you're doing it. All I know is some poor son of a bitch died in a bar, pardon my French, ma'am."

"That's all right," she replied. "I'm fluent."

Lester cleared his throat. "And you haven't found Mr. Gibson?" He rose and went to the bookshelf while they answered.

They shook their heads simultaneously. It was almost comical how perfectly they were matched, she thought. Like Laurel and Hardy except that Otis was much better looking than Stan Laurel. More like Leslie Howard. But together they were quite a pair.

"Absolutely not, Mr. Dent. Absolutely not. We actually tried to find him, but we haven't had any luck. We've been to his apartment and the doorman said he hasn't been there in days," Ron said. "And Nanovic told us that he missed a couple of story meetings for the first time. We went by his train. We can't find him."

"If this is something Walter Gibson is involved in," Norma said crossly, "then we want no part of it." She folded her arms defiantly and looked at the two men. "His is not a welcome presence in my home."

"I . . . I'm sorry, Mrs. Dent." Otis looked at Hubbard. "I thought you said they were friends."

The word made Norma laugh. "A friend? Walter Gibson? I can

think of a lot of things that Walter is, but a friend is not one of them! Do you know that he nearly ruined us once?"

"Look, Mr. and Mrs. Dent, I'm really sorry about all this." Otis lit a cigarette. His hands were trembling. "I don't really know Mr. Gibson. But it seems to me that whenever his name comes up, it's always in relation to something that's almost impossible to believe."

"Hey!" Hubbard sat up.

"Listen, brother. I wasn't there for the night watchman. I wasn't there for any of the talk you had with that rummy, and that's what I'm calling him, 'cause that's what he was. I do know, however, when I came back he was dead. But for all I know everything else is just a big lie."

"Or a pack of lies?" Lester asked, still at the bookcase. He held a large chart book of northeastern waters and was thumbing through the index.

"Exactly!" affirmed Otis with satisfaction.

"Well. In the absence of Mr. Gibson, one way to find out whether this is pulp or real would be to find Harmony Isle."

"Uh . . ." Otis seemed confused. "Okay."

"But there is no Harmony Isle in Long Island Sound." Lester studied a page closely.

"Are you sure?" Ron said, sounding disappointed.

"Well, this is a pretty comprehensive survey of the coast from Nova Scotia down to the Outer Banks. There is no Harmony Isle."

"Damn!" Ron slammed his hand down, rattling the coffee cups on the kitchen table.

"Nope. Like I said. No Harmony Isle." Lester said, shooting Norma a sly grin. "But there is a Haimoni Isle." He put the chart on the table and pointed to a tiny isle between Long Island and Connecticut. "*Haimoni* sounds a good bit like *Harmony* when you think about it. Doesn't it?"

Both men nodded. "When you put that New England accent behind it, it could," Otis said begrudgingly. Norma found herself wishing that she could introduce him to some of her friends back in La Plata. The unmarried ones.

Lester thumbed quickly through another book and found what he was looking for. "Haimoni. I thought it rang a bell." He snapped the book shut. "The Haimoni Indians lived in hut villages along the coast of Connecticut thousands of years before the Pequot and Quinnipiac tribes took over the area. Haimoni Isle was the site of their sacred stone. It was an altar upon which their shaman would perform ritual human sacrifices to the fishing spirits.

"According to legend, a shaman once refused to sacrifice the woman he loved upon the altar. That night a storm raised the waters so high that they tipped the stone on its side. The entire tribe was swept away in the flood. Long after they vanished, the legend of the Haimoni Stone lived on and the other Indian tribes considered it a cursed place. Evil."

"Oh," said Driftwood, "*that* Haimoni Isle!"

Norma took up the chart and studied it. She traced her finger toward the little speck on the map and she could see her fingernail quiver as she did. "We should go," she heard herself blurt out. The men turned to look at her. "We should go there."

"Norma, it's the middle of the night in the dead of winter."

"It's the only way to know for sure."

"But isn't this Mr. Gibson's problem?"

"Oh, to hell with Mr. Gibson! What could he possibly know that we don't know? Don't you want to go see? I want to go see."

"It's an easy trip from Providence," said Lester. "Not so easy from New York. The *Albatross* is docked at Seventy-second Street. She'd have to be brought around the bottom of Manhattan and up the East River to get into the sound. If the winds prevail from the southeast it could take a day and a night's sail just to get there. And that's if I get her through Hell Gate in one piece."

"Mr. Dent," Otis said in a reassuring tone. Norma found herself resenting his earnest charm because she found it so hard to resist. "I am an Annapolis graduate and a retired officer of the U.S. Navy. There's no vessel I can't sail and no sea I can't sail her through."

"Now you want to go?" Lester asked.

"I'm gonna wait for you to come back and tell me another story?

Maybe this one will be about Atlantis! No. I'm going to see for myself what's pulp and what's real."

"I'm sorry," said Ron with a nervous note in his voice. "Did you say something about something being called Hell Gate? You're actually considering sailing a boat through something called Hell Gate to get to a cursed Indian island? Maybe it's just because I'm a pulp writer, but does any part of this sound like it might be a bad idea?"

"Come on, Hubbard!" Otis replied. "Weren't you the one telling about all your great sailing voyages on the USS *Nitro,* from Shanghai to Guam to Hawaii to Seattle on a three-masted corvette? From lookout to first mate too. Never saw a man rise that fast in the U.S. Navy. So I'm going to let you have the helm."

"I'm skipper," Dent muttered, "that's my decision."

"I recommend L. Ron Hubbard for the helm, skipper," Otis said.

"Sure," Lester grunted.

"No, wait!" Ron jumped up. His face was deep red. "I can sail. I can. That particular trip that, that there, my parents paid for."

"It was a cruise?" Driftwood was shocked.

"Of a serious nature. And there were times when I performed a mate's duties, bringing the coffee to the deck in the morning. And I did get to go up to the crow's nest several times in calm seas as long as there was a sailor already up there." He chewed on his finger. "I was fourteen."

"You made it sound like it was a year or two ago."

"He's young at heart," Norma rushed to his defense. Otis smiled and for her sake decided to stop haranguing Hubbard, for the time being.

Lester, still concerned, asked Ron, "You do have a boat, right? You do sail a boat?"

"I day-sail a sixteen-footer."

"Then you're on winches."

Ron's face was still red. Norma noticed that Ron was so mad at his companion that he couldn't bring himself to look at Otis. Otis, appearing self-satisfied, pretended not to notice. She made a small show of pouring a fresh cup of coffee for him, adding sugar lumps and stirring it for him. When Otis rattled his cup for coffee, she left the pot at the side of the table and he had to cross Ron to get it.

Thump! Lester put his index finger heavily down on the map at the point where the East River merged into the Long Island Sound. "This is Hell Gate," he said. "You see the East River is not really a river. It's a tidal estuary. So it doesn't really flow so much as it just sloshes back and forth like soup in a bowl. This spot right here is where the edge of the estuary flowing back and forth one way meets the currents of the sound flowing crosswise against it, which causes the water depth to change unpredictably. Which only matters because there are shallows and rocks which can sometimes spring up and slash a ship's hull open. Meanwhile the wind is bringing additional pressure to bear on the irregular currents and sometimes opens a whirlpool. Hell Gate is an open water cemetery. In 1904 the steam ferry *General Slocum* on a Lutheran picnic outing caught fire and became trapped in the swirling waters of Hell Gate. Over a thousand women and children went down right there in broad daylight in full view of Manhattan, Queens, and the Bronx. An entire New York neighborhood was destroyed in a single moment." He tapped the ashes out of his pipe and gazed into the empty bowl for a moment.

Norma took his other hand. "We've been through Hell Gate before. Several times. Just the two of us."

"Not at night with ice on the water." He rose and put the chart back on the bookcase.

She took a cigarette from Otis's open pack and lit it. The two young men both looked at her with surprise. Evidently they hadn't been prepared for Lester Dent's wife to show much interest in their goings-on. *Am I up for another adventure?* she thought to herself. *No*, was the answer. *No. Don't leave the house. Don't leave your safe cave. There are grocery lists to prepare and biscuits to cook. You don't need adventure to make Lester look at you the way you used to like him to.* She rose and went to his side and spoke comfortingly to him.

"We'll have two more able-bodied seamen. We might find some proof, and then what a story you'll have!"

"And if not?"

"Then at the least we'll have had a bit of an adventure."

"I thought you didn't want any more adventures."

Wrong, she countered in her head. I need adventure to make myself look at me the way I used to like to. "This will hardly be an adventure. More like an outing."

"Okay." He nodded but he still looked gravely concerned.

She gave him a quick kiss. "Ain't adventure luck the goddamnedest thing?"

Episode Thirty-Four

"Is it always this rough?" Hubbard hollered back from the bow of the *Albatross*. He was lying on his belly with his head hanging over the deck above the water and shining a light into the foam below.

"Are you kidding?" Driftwood yelled back from the helm, the wheel ever so slightly under his hand. "This is some of the best sailing weather I've ever seen."

"Keep that torch on the water," Dent roared from belowdecks where he was reading charts. "It's the only way we'll see the rocks coming."

Hubbard whipped the beam of light back onto the water. "And icebergs!" he shouted.

"Ice drifts!" Dent bellowed. "There are no icebergs on the East River!"

Driftwood smiled as he imagined what Hubbard was muttering to himself. From what he had seen of the man in the little time he had spent with him over the past week, Hubbard considered himself quite the dashing adventurer, so it was amusing to see how high-strung he turned out to be in what was admittedly a tense situation. The man could handle himself around a boat, though; Driftwood had to give him credit for that.

He felt great. The wind was brisk and smacked his face like the northern Atlantic waters he had sailed only a few years before. The *Albatross* was a beautiful ketch: a forty-foot blue-water sailer with a clipper's prow, which he adored on a boat. They had reefed in the jib and the mainsail, and with a little help from a sturdy engine she sliced through the East River at a handsome twelve knots with barely a groan from her solid planks as she heeled to port. Chunks of ice flowed by at a distance on either side.

"It's four a.m.," Mrs. Dent said. She stood next to Driftwood in the open, the collar on her oilskin turned up. Her cheeks were flushed with windchill and excitement. Her blond hair spilled out from under her black wool cap. Under the pretense of thoroughly checking his sail trim, he snuck looks at her. She was a damn beautiful lady, he thought. She had those steel-gray eyes he loved in a woman, and the beautiful breasts he loved even more. She was tall, and from what he had seen she had some pair of legs as well.

Between the silver mine and his time on the run, he hadn't given much thought to women; that wasn't his style in general. But now being this close to one who was as pretty as Mrs. Dent was really distracting. Fortunately he had the upcoming Hell Gate to keep his mind focused. Not to mention Mr. Dent.

But did she have to have that low, come-hither voice as well? "You know there's a fortune in treasure right below us?"

"Hm?"

"The *General Slocum*'s only one of many ships that went down here. In 1780 the British war frigate the HMS *Hussar,* a privateer, sank here. Not only was she carrying the gold and silver for the payroll of the British troops in America during the Revolutionary War, but on the crossing she had seized one French ship and two American ships and taken their wealth. Then she had rendezvoused with another British treasure ship and its contents were transferred to her as well because her ribs were considerably stronger. She was supposed to deliver this fortune to the payroll office on Cherry Street. But upon entering the East River, her captain received intelligence that two French frigates were hot on her tail.

"The ship was too weighed down to make it back into open water, so the captain decided to sail into the sound and seek the protection of the British forts and fleets which were stationed there. On her way through Hell Gate she hit a rock and sank like solid gold stone. No one's ever been able to recover even a farthing, but they say that in today's market the value of the treasure would easily be over one hundred million dollars. Only there's no way to get at it." She sighed and looked longingly down into the deep, dark water. "Can you imagine? All that treasure is probably less than sixty feet away."

"When you talk about treasure you get some look in your eyes," he managed. "A glow." He suddenly felt like he was falling in love. It was the best part of a romance, that falling. He tried out one of his most charming smiles on her as he slipped the wheel a few degrees against the deceptive currents. "You come alive."

"Thank you, Mr. Driftwood." She smiled back, but her smile did not seem to acknowledge the magic of his smile.

Driftwood. He hated lying to these nice people about who he was, hiding his identity like Paul Muni in *I Am a Fugitive from a Chain Gang.* He'd love to tell Norma all about himself, see how he measured up in her eyes against her husband. But he was scared. That's what it came down to. Fear. He didn't believe that these three people could betray him to a murderous gangster back in California; it wasn't about them. It was about never letting his guard down, not even for a moment.

"Don't we need an expert up here?" Hubbard shouted back.

"Just keep her in the main channel for now," Dent answered, already sounding distracted. This was followed by a brief racket.

"Lester?" Norma called.

"I'm okay."

"I'm sure you are. What are you doing?"

"Getting some gear together."

"I don't believe you'll need your metal detector out here."

"We might."

"I don't think so. Now how about coming up and helping out like you said you would?"

"In a minute."

Otis caught her amused, affectionate smile and felt a spike of jealousy stab up through him. He was suddenly glad Lester was below. He gently pinched the boat up a couple of degrees and saw what he had been looking for.

"Wake!" he called and the boat bobbed roughly over some small waves smacked back from the shoreline. He heard a crash from below, as of pots and pans clattering from cabinets, and an oath from Lester. The sudden list upset Norma's balance, causing her to pivot and slide against him. He caught her and steadied her, feeling a hint of her body through the heavy fabric.

"Watch those waves, sailor!" It sounded like Lester was extracting himself from whatever mess had been made.

"Aye aye, Cap'n," Driftwood called back, sounding as seriously innocent as he could. Norma secured her footing, though she remained close enough that he could sense her warmth, and he returned his hand to the wheel. "Sorry about that," he said, sincerely. "Little rough out tonight."

"Does your wife know where you are tonight?" she suddenly asked him, touching the tanned ring finger on his left hand, right below the knuckle. It would be years before the sallowness of that thin band of flesh disappeared completely.

Her directness caught him off balance just as his ship maneuver had, he hoped, caught her. Her eyes, which had seemed so placid and reflective moments ago, now snapped with electricity, focused on him. He felt as if he were the sole focus of her world, and his mouth went dry. When she arched a curious eyebrow, his resolutions about exposing himself vanished. He would answer any question she asked. He'd even give up his name. If she'd ask.

"Actually, I'm divorced," he said. "My former wife went crazy."

"Most men say that about their wives."

"Yeah, well, mine really did. I'll give you the address of the asylum."

She blinked and he searched her eyes for any new meaning, empathy,

251

compassion, comfort. The cold air was playing hell with his weak lungs and made his chest ache. He cleared his throat. "It all happened while I was away in the navy. She didn't come out of the basement for weeks. They had to break the door down to get to her. Her parents wanted to help more than I could, and she responded to them better than to me. We found a judge who could divorce us so they could have more control over her care. You probably think that makes me a real heel."

"Oh, no," she said. He was hoping she'd put a hand on his, but she didn't. Well, there was time. Since they were obviously on a snipe hunt, he could look forward to a long and leisurely sail with lots of easy time to talk with the missus while her mister was playing Wolf Larsen.

"Anyway, she's better now, I hear. She's been out of the hospital for about a year. But she's never forgiven me for the divorce. And I think she never will."

"Ahoy, Ron!" Dent interrupted from deep in the vessel, thumping on the cabin ceiling.

"Try and give us a little more warning on those wakes, Otis, all right? Some of us get banged around more than others." Norma said it slowly and softly. Driftwood could feel her gaze on him drift away, but he felt that she hadn't yet decided what to make of him. But she had called him Otis. The next conversation he had with her would be about her marriage, and he already knew where to start: how could someone as graceful as she be married to such a great lumbering ox and an obvious coward to boot? She'd had to practically drag him out tonight, when anyone who truly loved her would have risen to the challenge in a moment, inspiring her passions and arousing her spirits.

"What? What?" Ron's voice was thin and strained.

"You know how you were asking on the way to the marina whether I had any tricks to writing pulps?"

"Sure. But . . ."

"I've got a little thing I call the master plot." Lester poked his head out of the cabin vent. It was a little like watching a cuckoo pop out of a clock. Driftwood focused on a smokestack on the Queens side of the river. "It's a formula, a blueprint for any yarn. It's guaranteed, surefire,

bulletproof, works every time, and you're on the boat to prove it."
Then he dropped back below.

"Oh, you don't have to go into that right this minute."

"First." Lester was moving back and forth, and with each trip he
piled more gear onto the deck. As he moved, his voice faded, then grew
louder in a rhythm which ran with the surge of the sea. "You need to
come up with a different murder method for your villain, a different
thing for the villain to be seeking, an exotic locale, and a menace which
hangs like a cloud over your hero."

"No, really! Les!"

"In the first line or as near thereto as possible, introduce your hero
and swat him with a fistful. Just shovel that grief onto him. Something
the hero has to cope with, like an incredibly difficult physical conflict."

"Like a huge God-blasted ship?" Hubbard practically screamed.
"Right in goddamn front of us! Is that enough of an incredibly difficult
physical conflict for you?"

Lester dropped his gear and sprang swiftly to the forestay. Hubbard
clumsily used the sheets to steady himself as he met Dent there. Driftwood stood tense at the wheel, years of naval training filling him with
the preparation to instantly execute an incoming order from his senior
officer.

The freighter was black, and running without lights. She rose up
out of the murky waters like an ancient leviathan risen to the surface
for a great gasp of air. Driftwood now realized that he had been sensing
the thrumming of her engines for some little while as it had grown
closer, without knowing what it was. "Her helmsman can't see us!"
From where he stood, the other ship appeared motionless in the water.
Which meant that they were on a collision course.

"Ship ho!" Dent called. "Ship ho!" Even his deep voice seemed overwhelmed by the dark ship. There was no response. Hubbard shouted
and waved his flashlight at the ship, to no effect.

"I'll get on the radio," Norma said to Driftwood and started below.

"Don't bother," he replied, and she paused. "Not enough time," he
said with a shrug.

"Come about!" Dent was moving quickly aft toward the rigging, Hubbard following on the port side.

"Coming about," Driftwood rolled the wheel over, feeling the sensation of the rudder flexing against the boat's motion. The *Albatross* skidded in the current like a sled which had hit an ice pond at the bottom of a steep snowy hill. The slope of the deck pitched over a few degrees and the bow began to head to starboard. Dent finished wrapping his sheet around the winch. Then he slid across the cabin roof to Hubbard's side. He grabbed a gaff stick. "Hubbard," he shouted. "Get behind me." Hubbard moved behind Lester. "Get ready to fend off!"

"What do you mean?"

"I mean that if that ship gets too close we're going to have to use this stick to push away from her. Here, grab the end."

"Against that?"

Lester resolutely braced himself. Holding the long shaft, prepared to plunge it against the side of the rising blackness, he appeared to Driftwood like a harpooner of old preparing to strike boldly against some giant, wrathful whale. The freighter was less than its own length out. Hubbard's flashlight beam played upon her prow; streaks of rust and age had not entirely corroded away the letters stenciled there years before: *Star of Baltimore.*

"Ready!" Dent shouted to them all.

Driftwood realized that none of them, not even Norma, were wearing life vests. He could now see the motion of the freighter; the rushing gap between them was closing. Its great black hull loomed over them. Dwarfed into insignificance by its massiveness, Hubbard instinctively stepped back from the rail. Driftwood hung on to the wheel, fighting the turbulence as the *Albatross* thumped heavily into the *Star of Baltimore*'s bow wake. The sailboat shook from stem to stern; he heard the contents belowdecks slide across the galley floor.

Dent stabbed the gaff at the black hull, and as it made contact, he braced himself against the cabin. Driftwood slid the throttle of the weak engine up as high as it would go and felt the *Albatross* surge in response. The gap between the two vessels, measurable in inches, held steady. He had to keep the stern from sliding into the *Star of Baltimore* as the bow turned away. A foot of space opened between the two boats. The metal hook on the end of the gaff caught hold of something and was ripped from Lester's grip. Two feet. Norma grabbed Otis's arm. With a glance he could see that she was watching the action unfold with pure carnal delight; her eyes glittered even more brightly than when she had spoken of treasure. Three feet. As the gaff slid past him, dangling in the air, he could see that the hook had snagged the latch on the watertight hull door. Dent had speared his Leviathan.

They cleared the stern and skittered across the last of the foam and turmoil churned up by the ship's big prop. To Driftwood, the impact of the final heavy bounce seemed right beneath his feet; at the same instant he felt the throttle go lifeless in his hand, the steady vibration suddenly ceasing. He looked behind him, to starboard; almost as quickly as the ship of mystery had appeared out of the elemental darkness, she had allowed herself to be swallowed back up into it. Almost simultaneously with its disappearance, he felt the currents settle as they made the transition from the murky, icebound waters of the East River to the calm waters of Long Island Sound.

He felt warm, soft lips against his cheek. The flush was gone from Norma's face; she was ashen, but the intensity of her eyes was still stirring.

"Good job," she said.

He nodded. She took one of his cigarettes from his jacket pocket, lit it, and handed it to him. He shook his head. His hands were stuck to the wheel. She stuck the cigarette between his lips and he inhaled deeply.

"Damn Sunday drivers," he muttered grimly. She smiled, just as grim. "I think I killed the engine."

"It's okay."

"Do we go back?"

She shook her head. "No."

Hubbard sat heavily on the cabin roof. "It was the ghost of the *General Slocum,* right?"

Dent stood above him, leaning against the mainmast for support, and staring at the wide, long wake of the vanished vessel. "That reminds me. The most important writing tip of all?" He turned his eyes toward the east, the sound. He lit up his pipe and grinned. "Avoid monotony."

EPISODE THIRTY-FIVE

L IFE ON the water had its own rhythm, which they became a part of easily.

Lester and Hubbard spent time below with the engine, but while it was not leaking fuel, and the bilge pump was functioning properly, its silence remained beyond their ability to divine without dry-docking the vessel and giving it careful attention. They both suspected the jamming of a piston; perhaps one of the rods had snapped as the boat had been tossed about. Nevertheless, the wind was strong and steady and they forged ahead through a day that was bright and clear. Dead reckoning and the sighting of landmarks along the Connecticut coast to confirm their location on the chart came easily to all of them, confirming their steady progress throughout the day.

In a bleary fog at the end of her noon shift, when she should have curled up in the warm spot Lester had recently vacated, Norma laid out roast beef, a beefsteak tomato, lettuce, mustard, mayonnaise, and home-baked bread which she had brought from the apartment. One thing marriage had taught her was that there were few things a man better liked to be in control of, and few things that gave him a greater sense of control, than the creation of his own sandwich. She set the platter aside on the galley table and set about refreshing the coffee. Then, feeling a little more in control herself, she climbed into their bunk.

As she lay between consciousness and sleep she could hear the men above discussing airplanes; Lester loved to fly and Hubbard was claming to be an accomplished pilot who had flown on expeditions over China, India, and Tibet.

"You look really good for your age," she heard Otis crack wise. "It'd take most men forty or fifty years to do all the things you say you've done."

Dent roared with laughter while Ron protested the veracity of his claims. As the young man, who did seem prone to exaggerating, launched into a detailed biography of his life, she heard someone come down the ladder. Moments later, Lester crept quietly into the cabin and slipped under the sheets to lie next to her. She could feel the cold air flowing off his body and she pressed against him to give him warmth.

"Getting any sleep?" he whispered.

"Sure," she said. "Sounds like the boys are getting a little testy. They may not get their milk and cookies later."

"What about me?" he asked, snuggling closer.

"No," she said, slapping his thigh lightly. "Because then you'll just want to sleep through your watch."

When she went on deck later for her shift, Ron was sulking. She began talking to him about his children and soon his dark clouds began to dissipate. His mood became downright giddy when, several watches later, he was the first to lay eyes on their destination.

The small island rose out of the fog to meet them in the gathering gloom of nightfall. Its shores were high and rocky. Here and there they could see trees clinging to the top of the sea cliffs.

"It looks as if there's a deepwater mooring on the windward side." Lester said, looking up from the charts. Otis turned the wheel appropriately while Ron let out the sails.

Norma kept her eyes on the water looking for rocks. The water was black, with a prismatic oily sheen glistening on top. "There's a dock," she shouted. The wood was old and untended, and there were planks missing, but it was obvious from the length and width of the dock that it had been built to support large, oceangoing vessels. Without an engine to help they had to retry their approach under sail several times before Hubbard was finally able to leap to the dock and make the spring lines fast. Night had fallen heavily across the sound by the time Norma finally set foot upon the creaking wood of the dock. She could see the lights from distant dwellings twinkling far across the water, beckoning her to come out of the lonely cold and back to the warmth of home.

The rocky shore blocked the wind and all became silent and motionless. A dank stink of decay rose from the ground, as if seaweed and more had been washing into the isle's rocky crevices for hundreds of years and rotting. Upon everything was a haze of oppression, a miasma of the unreal and the grotesque. The large, bare rocks which formed the isle swept up in odd angles away from the waterline, until some fifty yards above and ahead of them the party could see the twisted shapes of small, ugly, leafless trees which struggled to survive here.

"Stygian," said Ron.

"Cimmerian," Otis agreed.

"Like Skull Island in miniature."

Norma saw Lester tuck his pistol into his coat pocket and realized that this was what he had been rummaging for earlier.

"Got one of those for me?" Otis asked.

Lester shook his head. "Sorry. Let's go." He led them down the short way to the end of the dock, where the wood met the outcropping. "Look at all these fresh scrapes," he said. "Someone's been here recently."

"A lot of fellas by the look of it," Ron added.

Carved into the rocks was a smooth, narrow path which ran quickly uphill and disappeared in a small grove of those gnarled trees. They set off up the steep, moss-lined trail, their flashlight beams looking nearly solid in the dank mist. The trees in the grove were low and withered, their branches spread out just above the explorers' heads and occasionally snagging the taller men, Lester and Otis. At one point, Lester held them up and urged silence. They each strained to hear what he had heard, but if there had been a sound, it was not repeated. They clambered on.

"Hey, Otis," Norma heard Ron whisper nervously, "who's your favorite writer?"

She could hear the tension in Otis's voice as well. "Can we close the writing salon for the time being?" he snapped. "This place is giving me the willies."

"Sure," said Ron. "Not a problem. You can all keep playing the heroes. I'm still just a pulp writer." She could hear him muttering a list of writers to himself, as if summoning them and the spirit of their tales to ward off the dangers of this night. "Of course, Jack London sets the standard for all of us. Hemingway? Honestly, I don't get the big deal. He couldn't handle real pulp. The Brits? Kipling, Doyle, and Conrad. Stevenson and Wells. Are the Brits better at pulp than we are? Maugham. Did I say that right? How do you say *Maugham,* really? Is it with an f sound or an h or is the gh completely silent?"

He grew silent as they crested the top of the hill and the path leveled out. The trees were sparse up here and craggy boulders jutted up from the gray ashy dirt. They could see the ocean on all sides from this vantage point.

"I can see the Empire State Building." She pointed out the distant light to Lester. "It looks like a star on the horizon."

"I wonder what's worse when it comes down to it?" Hubbard's nervous monologue began again. "Is a bandit worse than a brigand? Is a crook more dangerous than a thief? Why do we have more words for *villain* than *hero?*"

At the entrance to the clearing was a rusted chain-link fence clinging vaguely to leaning ground posts. The remains of an old gate hung desperately to a pole. Otis swung his flashlight around the clearing. The fence had once encircled its perimeter.

Lester lifted a rectangular piece of metal which lay to the side of the path and flipped it over: PROPERTY U.S. DEPT. OF THE ARMY. NO TRES-

PASSING. The small date stenciled at the bottom of the sign read August 1918.

"I'd hate to be the private that got assigned this sentry post," Otis said.

"I think they forgot about this place," Lester replied, tossing the sign back to where he had picked it up.

"There's something up ahead." Norma pointed her flashlight.

They walked past the gate toward the low structure. Concrete walls on three sides rose only as high as their waists. There was a wide cement staircase beginning at the top of the open fourth side and descending a short way into the earth, where it was stopped by a metal door. The door hung ajar several inches, exposing only darkness.

"An underground depot," Otis explained. "Looks like Uncle Sam wanted this sealed up but good."

Lester pulled the gun from his coat pocket. When the others gave him raised eyebrows, he shrugged back. "Better safe than sorry," he said. He took Norma's flashlight in his other hand and descended the steps. He reached the floor and nudged the door open with his forearm. Then he shone the flashlight inside.

"It's a room," he told them. "A big storeroom. A big empty storeroom. Wait a sec. There's something in the corner."

"Lester?" Norma called, but he had already entered the bunker. There was a long moment of silence and then she heard him swear, something he never did. He came out a moment later and leaned heavily against the doorjamb. She started to slip past him to see for herself but he grabbed her roughly and held her.

"Bodies," he said, shaking his head. "About a dozen dead men. Sailors by the looks of 'em." He looked up at the other men. She felt him suddenly stiffen and stare at a point behind her. She spun around and couldn't contain the horrified gasp which leapt from her throat.

There were two of them, appearing from behind the scrub trees which lined the path. Their eyes had a cunning, merciless, brutish glint but without a glimmer of human intelligence. Each of them had sallow skin glistening with oily liquid oozing from the broken pustules

261

covering their face and hands. Clinging to each of them were the scraps and remnants of peacoats, wool sweaters, dungarees; one of them still had a knit cap clapped loosely to his head.

"The sailors from the *Zephyr*!" Driftwood whispered through his gritted teeth. "That's why Towers marooned them. They're contaminated exactly like the night watchman."

"So now you believe him?" Hubbard whispered.

"Hell, yeah."

Lester has the gun, Norma thought. We'll be all right. She saw him start to leap up the stairs while at the same time another creature materialized from the rocks overhanging the door to the bunker, arms outstretched. In an instant the contaminated sailor had its arms around Dent and they tumbled against the steps, the pistol flung forcefully from Dent's hand. Ron and Otis had intercepted their attackers and each now grappled furiously with an opponent.

A fourth slavering monster appeared from behind a rock pile and flung itself at Norma. Its moist hands closed around her throat. She grabbed its wrists and her fingers sank into the soft flesh without effect. All the man's teeth were gone and she could see the bloody gums in its gaping mouth centered in its horrible black beard. Its breath smelled of rancid fish.

She tumbled back under the force of its weight and landed heavily on her back. The impact knocked the wind out of her and she began to struggle, desperate to get the creature off her so she could catch her breath. She clawed at its face with her fingernails and it pushed away from her in pain. The texture of its face reminded her of the yellow wax beans she had prepared as a little girl. Gasping, she pulled herself to her feet. Looking around quickly, she could see that Ron and Otis were on the ground. She couldn't see Lester but she could hear the sound of his fight by the bunker door. The creature which had attacked her jumped in front of her, enraged. On its face were bloody stripes left by her fingernails. She saw a blur at the bunker wall, yet another man. Her small party was now outnumbered.

Her attacker sprang at her with a howl at the same instant that a sharp crack rang through the night, echoing off the rocks. The creature seemed to suddenly curl in midair, its trajectory changing. As it flopped heavily to the ground, Norma stared dumbly at it. Blood spurted with each beat of a weakening heart from a hole which had cratered open in the side of the beast's head. The shocking sound of three more successive blasts made her tear her gaze away from the twitching corpse, and she looked up to see Otis and Ron pushing dead creatures off them.

"Lester!" She ran to the bunker and nearly tumbled down the stairs trying to help him. He was leaning against one of the concrete walls trying to catch his breath. The biggest creature, by far, had attacked him. His shirt was ripped open and his chest was scraped and bloodied beneath it. He threw an arm around her and she kissed his face. The creature who had attacked him lay in a heap at his feet. Chunks of its brains were leaving bloody tracks as they dripped down the heavy door.

"Thank God you got to the gun!" she said.

"No," he said. "He did."

She looked up to the top of the wall, to the fifth creature she had seen out of the corner of her eye rushing to join the fracas. He stood on the rim of the wall, the smoking pistol hanging with easy familiarity in his right hand. The wind swept his long duster around him while the moon behind him bathed him in its silvery glow. The man pushed his battered ten-gallon hat back on his head, revealing a handsome young face ringed by long, loose blond hair. He seemed as untouched by any old military chemicals as the island trees themselves were untouched by the color green.

"Ain't those boys full of some fiendish shit?" No doubt, he was a Texan in drawl and swagger. "I sure am glad y'all decided to show up." He twirled the pistol back and forth expertly on his finger the way she'd seen only expert rodeo shooters back in La Plata do. "I'm even gladder y'all decided to bring a pistol along. Even if it is kind of small."

"You're glad!" she exclaimed.

"You folks mind if I ask if y'all got any grub?" His grin was bright and charming. "There ain't nuthin' to eat out here 'cept fish. An' I hate fish."

EPISODE THIRTY-SIX

"THANK YOU, ma'am," the cowboy said as she handed him another opened tin of William Underwood's deviled ham. He had already scooped the meat out of four other cans and he proceeded to do the same to this one.

Otis and Ron were on deck piloting the yacht back into the sound as the sun came up. The strong wind continued to hold steady. Lester sat across from the man. Norma guessed him to be about the same age as the boys on deck, somewhere in his twenties.

"You're a long way from home, aren't you, friend?" Lester asked.

"Not as far as I been," he replied. "Once I gave up prizefightin' and caught a ship out of New Orleans, I been to Rio de Janeiro, Capetown, Fiji, Marrakesh, Singapore, Borneo, Egypt, Zanzibar, Panama. Not bad for a cowhand from North Dakota. An' it's a damn sight better 'n being punched in the face."

He tore a hunk of bread from the loaf and chewed it greedily. She poured them all some fresh coffee. Then she took the pot on deck and freshened Ron and Otis's cups as well.

"We're making good time," Otis said to her from behind the wheel. His left eye was swollen shut from the attack. The skin on the back of

Ron's knuckles was scraped off where he had tried to hit one creature. "We should be back around midnight." Otis winked at her reassuringly. Even after having taken a beating, he still had it in him to flirt with her.

She rewarded his efforts with a tired smile. "That's good," she said. "Either of you want some more Bayer?" The day was breaking in scarlet streaks across the sky.

They both nodded and she handed them the bottle. Ron chewed his dry. "The stranger giving up anything useful yet? Like a name?"

"Lew," she said, then paused at the stairs. "Actually what he calls himself is 'Lew No-Less-No-More,' so we're just calling him Lew."

"I don't trust him," Otis said, crossly.

"He saved our lives. Those things would have killed us."

"I'd almost put mine down," Otis said with a shrug.

"You're just jealous that he got to rescue us and Mrs. Dent," Ron said, gleeful.

"Can't you work on the engine again?" Otis asked, giving the throttle his undivided attention.

Below, she took her seat next to Lester. The cowboy nodded at her and continued his story. The pace of his eating had slowed to dabbing at the juices at the bottom of the tin with his finger. "Ever been to Formosa?"

"No."

"It's a Chinese island out there in the Pacific. Nothin' but fish markets and skeeters. We put in there about three months ago. Had to run the Japanese blockade to do it, so it was really some tough going. Docked in Keelung harbor and unloaded some cargo. Guns. Weapons. That whole side of the world's at war but you wouldn't know it back here so much, I 'spect.

"Then, after a few days of doing what sailors do in port, we took on some passengers. Chinese men. About two dozen or so of the meanest cusses you ever saw. Bastards each and every one of 'em. Stayed belowdecks the whole trip back, smokin' butts, playin' cards, fightin', cookin' up food that smelled like manure, and prayin' to this big ugly statue of a god which they brung with 'em. Wasn't the first time we

265

smuggled human souls from one place to another. I ain't proud of that, but it's true.

"There was one American came aboard with 'em. Army fella. He's the one what seemed to have the arrangement with the captain. He didn't stay below with them others. He took quarters with the captain and the mate. Spoke fluent Chinese. He put off in Honolulu with one of the Chinese. Big fella. Seemed to be the boss of all the others. I drove 'em to the airport where they had a plane, and some other men, waiting to take them stateside. Seems like they were in more of a hurry than what our boat could provide for. One of the things that went with 'em was that unholy statue. I was glad for that.

"We headed on through the canal after that, and most days, even though it was infernal hot, you wouldn't even know there were men down below. They got real quiet once them others left. Just did their business real quiet. To be honest, I near forgot about 'em. We all did."

He drank some coffee and continued, "A few nights ago we sighted the Montauk lighthouse and come around the point at dawn on the tide. Late in the day we put in at Crap Island. Then he takes us straightaway up the path to the storeroom. Now as you saw from the looks of the place, there ain't been nobody set foot there in a genera-tion. But Cap'n had the key to that door from that army guy. I got it now, along with all the other keys to the ship. Cap'n throws open the door. 'That's our cargo, lads,' he says. 'Let's get it aboard.'

"That bunker was full of fifty-gallon metal drums. Those eggs were older than dirt. Rusty old tins full of some liquid. There were about three hundred of 'em, all told. And that's what we did all night was haul them drums down the hill to the hold.

"I was ashore with half a dozen of my shipmates when we heard the shootin' start. Quick as a stuck bull those Chinese had taken over the ship. They killed the men that were aboard. They had all the guns. They opened fire on us and drove us up the hill and there was nothing we could do. We watched them steal our boat. Our home. It's a strange feeling to be marooned on a deserted island within sight of New York City. Only, as it turns out, the island wasn't really deserted after all.

"All the time we were loadin' the drums I kept feeling we were being watched. Soon after the ship was away, a man appeared on the beach. We hailed him from the bluff and asked where he was from. 'Providence,' was all he shouted back. We ran down the beach to him thinkin' that he must be a fisherman and must have a boat. But when we got closer to him we could tell that he wasn't exactly all right. And then his three friends came out of the scrub and ambushed us. We headed back up the hill to the bunker but I was the only one what made it all the way."

He idly set one of the empty tins spinning on edge. "I couldn't very well leave my buddies out there, even though they were dead. They wouldn't have left me behind. So I started sneakin' out and draggin' 'em one by one back to the bunker."

"Wasn't that dangerous?" Norma asked.

"Otherwise I would have been bored to death. Once you knew they were out there it was easy to keep away from them. I tried a time or two to sneak up on 'em and kill a couple but that didn't happen either. I couldn't kill them and they couldn't kill me and we left each other alone for a day or so. It was just the surprise of 'em that got my cap'n and mates killed. Schooly Pete. Crooks. Sammy the Smoker. Hey Tony. Q. And Irving. Good men. I wish I could have done more for 'em. I ain't never spoke a bad word about a man because o' his race but if I ever get my hands on any one of those Chinese sons of bitches there'll be hell to pay."

His hands were rough and coarse from years of hard labor and sport. He drummed his fingers on the table. "I missed you all comin' along 'cause I was on the far side thinkin' about whether or not I was desperate enough to paddle a log across to Connecticut."

"Glad you didn't have to find out," Lester said.

"Oh, I coulda done it. I just wouldn't a been happy about it." He yawned. "Y'all don't mind if I stretch out for a few moments and get some shut-eye, do you? I haven't slept good in days."

Lester and Norma left him in their cabin and went up on deck, where they told the story to Ron and Otis. The rest of the trip was uneventful as they nursed their bruises. Their new passenger slumbered blissfully through the day into the night. Ron examined some of Lester's electronic inventions and the two of them discussed engineering plans. Otis tried to speak to Norma several times but she wasn't feeling very communicative. By the coming of night they had cleared Hell Gate and were once again on the East River.

Norma was seated on a lazarette and Lester had the wheel as they sailed between Manhattan and the southern shoals of Blackwell's Island near the abandoned smallpox asylum known as the Renwick Ruin. "I haven't felt wind this cold since Wyoming," he said. He hardly ever spoke about his boyhood. But she knew about Wyoming. She took his hand. She knew what he meant: he hadn't felt a cold wind like that since he was a boy standing on the plains looking for his mother and father to return home from their nearest neighbor, who lived over a dozen miles away. The closest town was twenty miles away. His parents were on horseback and the journey could take hours. His little horse had died a few weeks before. In the deep grip of a plains winter his father would not let him ride behind either of his parents. Two horses meant two riders. And so he had to stay behind and wait. He had no brothers or sisters. He was eight years old and alone on the plains.

Lester had been six when his father had taken it into his head to become a farmer. The three members of the Dent family had driven a horse-drawn covered wagon from Missouri to their home in Wyoming. His recollections of his father were of a presence that always seemed to be disappointed in him. His father seemed disappointed that Lester couldn't do more to help, disappointed that Lester's mother insisted on schooling him instead of letting him help out more in the fields, disappointed that the little boy was afraid at night, disappointed that the boy disappeared to play alone for hours at a time.

The thick white snow surrounded the little Dent farmhouse. Night had fallen. Lester's parents had not returned. In two years he had become accustomed to being alone, having adventures all his own under the vast blue sky. In two years he had played with children his own age exactly four times on visits to town. But this night was different. Now the wind howled around the house and his parents were not home. He fed himself and lighted all the lamps even though he knew his father would disapprove of wasting the oil. He built a fire too. A big one. Again, he knew his father would raise Cain over the wasted wood. But he was bound to upset his father somehow or another and the fire kept him company.

He could read, of course; there were plenty of books. His mother made certain of that. But he didn't feel like reading. He felt like playing with a friend. He was lonely. He was always so lonely. So he decided to make up a friend, and this one wouldn't disappear when they were done playing. He took a pencil stub from his tin and the notepad he used to practice his cursive in, and he began to write. It was a story about a man named Jayse who sailed a ship around the world with his many friends, including his best friend, a gorilla named Mr. Harry C. Lees. At the end of the story they rescued a beautiful woman from a monster in a faraway jungle. He called it "The Voyage of the Gossamer Goose!" It was his first story and it took him all night and part of the next day to finish it. As he wrote the last sentence, he heard his mother calling to him. He saw his father's face cloud as he entered the house. But the boy stood tall and held his father's glare until the old man had broken it off, sensing a new courage in his son. Young Lester felt braver than ever before, for he knew he now had friends who would never leave him alone again on a vast and abandoned wintry plain.

Four years after he had written "The Voyage of the Gossamer Goose!"—a period in which he had played with other children exactly ten times—his father had given up on the ranch and dragged them back to La Plata. Only Lester had managed to harvest anything from that hard land. Tucked into a case that had once carried farm tools, which now lay broken and scattered across the plains, were several dozen lined tablets filled with Lester's best friends—Jayse, Mr. Harry C. Lees, and many, many others.

Norma stood and slipped her arms around him, snuggling up to him. "I don't ever want you to be that cold again," she said.

The other men came up on deck. Otis was trying to pry the origins of Ron's given name, Lafayette, out of him. The cowboy stretched, and the kinks cracking out of his body were audible. He stopped when he saw the skyline and whistled. "That is just about the most beautiful sight I ever did see," he said breathlessly.

"Yeah," Ron said. "It does look good from far away or high above. It's only when you get down in it that it turns ugly."

"Looks mighty fine to me."

"Can you imagine trying to explain New York to a Borneo wild man or an Australian Aborigine or a man from a thousand years ago? Where would you start to describe a skyscraper? Or the lights? Or the millions of people?"

"I'll be damned!" This burst from Otis, who was the only person onboard not gazing at Manhattan. He had turned his attention to the piers of Brooklyn. It took them a moment to realize that he wasn't involved in Ron's history. "That's the ship that nearly ran us down!"

The ship was berthed at an otherwise deserted Brooklyn pier. Her stern was facing them. Her heavy prow had shattered the ice choking the slip as she had docked. They could see the deck crane swinging over the dock and crew activity onboard. They were close enough to see a few men walking along the pier.

"That's her," Lew cried. Norma saw a white fury overcome him. "That's the *Star of Baltimore.* That's my ship!" He gripped the backstay.

"Toss me my binoculars," Lester said to Norma. He looked through the glasses while Otis took the wheel. "Keep your heading." The *Albatross* shuddered as a thick slab of ice careened off her side. Lester rubbed the frost off the glasses and took another look. "Well, I'll be superamalgamated. They're all Chinese all right, just as Lew said."

On the wooden pier Norma could see a cloth-covered military supply truck. Men were unloading heavy boxes from it onto a pallet on the pier, while other men motioned for the deck crane's big lifting chain to be lowered. Other men scurried up and down the thin gangplank.

"Sons of bitches!" Lew snapped, and before they realized his intentions he had flung himself over the railing into the small tender.

"What are you doing?" Otis shouted.

"What's it look like? I'm gettin' my boat back."

"You're gonna get yourself killed."

"Ya think I'm a fool? I know what I'm doin'!" He jangled his captain's keys at them defiantly. "I'm gonna hog-tie the engine so she can't go nowhere 'fore I call the Coast Guard. I know that ship better'n anybody. They'll never know I'm there."

"You can't do something like that by yourself," Norma told him.

"Mrs. Dent's right," Lester said. "I'll go with you." His face was set with the familiar Dent determination. "If I don't he's just going try something stupid like running across the ice," he said to her, grimly.

"You're protecting him now?" she asked.

"I'm gonna try. He's got adventure luck worse than even you."

"Lester, for God's sake, stay here. Stay with me. Or let me come. What about our deal?"

He gave her a rueful half-smile. It was the look of broken promises. "You can make it up to me. I know you'll think of something."

"Lew," she called. "If you go, my husband's going to go with you, and he could die if he goes with you."

"Mr. Dent, sir," the cowboy said as he pulled the tarp from the Evinrude and primed it, "your missus would like you to stay back."

"Well, Lew," said Lester, sliding into the tender. The little boat tottered and bobbed under his weight. "Let me tell you why you need my help. That's a two-stroke engine there. Makes a noise like a band saw. If you use that you may as well send them a card with your name on it that says you'll be dropping by. You want on that boat, you're gonna have to row for it. You'll find oars under your seat." He looked up at Norma. "I just gotta try and keep him alive."

She nodded. "Okay."

Moments later, the knot untied, Lester let the line slip through his fingers as if trying to hold on to the *Albatross,* and Norma, a little bit longer. Finally he tossed the rope and Hubbard caught its wet coils deftly. Lester took up the tiller as the cowboy threw his back into the deep strokes needed to move the boat ahead. Lester turned his eyes forward, away from Norma's toward their new direction. He never looked back.

Issue 5:

THE JUDGE
OF THE DEAD

Episode Thirty-Seven

"WHAT DO you want?" Walter Gibson asked The Shadow.

"To live," The Shadow replied. "To survive."

"How?"

The only answer was laughter.

Walter Gibson woke up on the floor of the truck. It was moving again. He thought they were still in Manhattan but he couldn't tell for sure; the canvas flap covering the back of the truck had been pulled tightly shut. His head was throbbing from the blow that had knocked him unconscious. It must have been the butt of a gun. He looked up at the Chinese soldiers holding tightly to the benches on either side of truck. The son of a bitch with the busted jaw smirked mercilessly at him. Of course, Gibson thought, if he had to be honest with himself, being popped in the head with the butt of a machine gun wasn't the only reason his head was hurting. The opium probably had something to do with it as well.

It turned out that he liked opium.

He thought of some of the euphemisms his fellow writers had used for the process of ingesting it over the years. Smoke eating. Chasing the dragon. Banging the gong. They could call it whatever they preferred; for Gibson it was a little like kissing heaven.

The peddlers in the den under the theater had known when to administer just the right amount so as to prevent the excruciating headaches which would occur if too much time elapsed between doses. Since he had entered Zhang Mei's circle, warm hours had passed in languid hazy dreams of serenity and universal vision. Food became unnecessary and unwanted. Sips of tea quenched the parched throat. Random fleeting thoughts became great prophecies, and the slightest musings took on profound significance. During periods of lucidity he would scribble madly in his notebook, desperate to be able to recall the vast enlightenments which came upon him, keenly aware of Samuel Coleridge's opium-driven experience of images "rising up before him" and the crushing loss of his mystical masterpiece, *Kubla Khan,* erased under the burden of sober reality.

At other times Gibson would lie on his back and stare at the ceiling and try to picture Howard Lovecraft's face, but he couldn't remember exact details, even though the drug allowed him to recall so many more obscure faces from his past with impressive precision. He attempted to communicate telepathically with Sonia Lovecraft but he never received an answer. Helplessly he would find himself hallucinating that he was Lovecraft, buried in the cold earth of Providence, his eyes gummed shut, his fingernails and hair growing, his body frozen, waiting for the warmth of spring to begin the horrors of decomposition. His dry mouth, sewn closed, begged to cry out for justice. When these hallucinations ended he would swear not to take another puff of the sweet smoke. But only the smoke itself had the power to cloud those visions from his mind.

Sometimes he would hear laughter, but not the cruel, portentous laughter of The Shadow. Robert's laughter, the peals of joy of an excited young boy. It was years of laughter, years he had missed, and he realized that it wasn't laughter, not Robert's laughter at all, but his own sobs. He had other conversations with The Shadow, who warned him that the disloyalty of an agent would not be tolerated. He was not laughing. Then The Shadow's face would melt into that of Zhang Mei, who would take an adjoining divan and continue with the story of his life. During these sessions Gibson would rouse himself to something resembling full functionality and diligently interview and transcribe the man's words.

Late one night Zhang Mei led him up the stairs onto the stage of the theater above. In the center of the stage stood a terrible statue, carved from wood and covered with gold. It was very old, Zhang Mei explained, and had traveled as far as he had. He gave it an affectionate pat, which echoed hollowly inside. Its face was fearsome and Gibson realized that the statue's cold eyes followed him around the stage, as alive as those in one of Rozen's paintings. Only this statue wasn't a simulacrum of The Shadow; it resembled nothing more than Rozen's recurrent Death visage. "I am the only priest he has left," Zhang Mei informed him, and Gibson nodded and said he understood. "I give him my breath, which is his judgment."

At other times a strange American soldier, Colonel Towers, would appear and their sphere of intimacy would be burst. Gibson was possessive about his companion and felt that Towers had an untoward influence on him. Upon the occasions of his visits, Towers and Zhang would depart the theater, leaving Gibson in the opium den beneath it. When Towers was around, Zhang was considerably crueler toward Gibson, as well as to his own men who had accompanied him from Hawaii. "I am, as your expression goes, waiting for my ship to come in," was his disdainful answer to Gibson's eventual query about his excursions.

Towers made it clear that he didn't trust Gibson, but he knew that there was no way Gibson could escape the opium den unless Zhang gave the word. There were smoke men ready to plunge knives into him in an instant. From their mysterious outings Zhang would return alone hours later, angered and frustrated. Until his rages passed, Gibson would remain silent and investigate the deep inner workings of his own being. He spent a lot of time thinking about Litzka. He had begun to realize that the chances of his seeing her again were growing slim.

Late on the night before the one that found him in the back of a truck, he had walked with Zhang through Chinatown. The streets had been cleaned and festooned with decorations in preparation for an upcoming parade. Zhang and Gibson seemed to pass invisibly by the small clusters of people. Gibson never caught anyone looking at the tall dark Chinese man and the short white man at his side; they slid by as if they were shadows.

Bright red banners hung from the lampposts. Posters proclaiming solidarity with brothers and sisters back in China were hung in store windows. The mood in the streets was celebratory, in spite of the recent news which described defeat after defeat of the Chinese army at the hands of the Japanese. Though the fall of Beijing appeared imminent, the weekend's festival would be a show of support for the homeland.

"The kidnapping was my plan," Zhang told Gibson, as they stood before posters declaring support for General Chiang Kai-shek, "to force the general to unite with Professor Mao against the Japanese. Chiang is smart. He quickly agreed to come to an understanding with the Communists and focus the fight against the Japanese. But he demanded that Xueling and I exile ourselves from China in order that he would not have to fear another threat from us.

"I laughed at him. We were in the position of power. China was ours to save. But my brother agreed to the terms of his prisoner. No matter what I said, his mind would not be swayed. I made an attempt to kill Chiang, but he stayed my hand. I begged, pleaded, threatened; his path was set. He did not want to lead the army. He did not want the future of China to rest upon his shoulders. For him, the wars were truly over. Let it rest on mine, I said to him, but again, no. You understand I could have killed my brother then? But I did not. Instead, I did what Zhang Zuolin himself would have done. I retreated. And I formed a new alliance. With Colonel Towers.

"Xueling had already exiled himself to Hawaii by the time I was prepared to leave. He took with him men who were loyal to me, who would wait for me. When I last saw the shores of China, it was a day not unlike this, cold and raining. I was on a ship bound for Formosa. I watched the horizon until the land disappeared. I was leaving behind the bodies of my wife and my son with no one to pay them honor or light the candles and incense for them. And I had been unable to avenge them upon Mi-Ying. I wept openly for all which I had lost beyond the horizon.

"It is good that the general now recognizes Japan as the true enemy and fights with Professor Mao instead of against. But the time for victory slips away. There is not enough leadership. The Japanese war machine is mighty. There is not enough money for food or for arms."

He stopped and fingered one of the red flyers taped to a lamppost. "My friend, Colonel Towers, came to me in Taipei when all seemed lost. He knew of a way to defeat the Japanese. He knew where money could be found to supply an army. He knew of a weapon which could drive them from our shores forever." He tore the flyer from the post. "He brought me hope when there was none."

Gibson looked at the photo printed above the Chinese text. He recognized General Chiang Kai-shek but the man next to the general meant nothing to him. He said as much to Zhang, who nodded.

"Of course. Why should you know the face of the consul general? Why should you know his name? He is of no importance to anyone but himself. A mere diplomat." He snatched the paper back, crumpled it up, and threw it into the gutter, where it unfurled slowly in the water from the melting snow. He added his own spit to the swirl. Then he began to walk again.

"What's in it for Towers?" Gibson asked.

They turned the corner back to the street which led to the theater and to the opium den at the end of the alley. "Colonel Towers is a complicated man. He speaks Chinese like I speak English. We have taught each other much. Like many men, Colonel Towers dreams of being a wealthy man. A powerful man. The kind of man who can influence the course of history. Though he may be an American, he is a true citizen of the world and his ambitions do not obligate him to remain in America. He will be content to be wealthy wherever his wealth finds him."

"Will you make him wealthy?"

"If he can deliver to me the power of my destiny, which I believe he can, then it will be within my power to do this for him. Yes."

A canvas-covered military truck had parked in front of the theater. The driver leapt out of the truck upon seeing Zhang and fell to his knees. Tears streamed down his sea-worn, weather-beaten face. Zhang fell upon him and the two men embraced and spoke rapidly to each other in their own tongue. Gibson was momentarily forgotten. For a moment the thought occurred to him, *Run!* He could disappear into the city. But he stood still and watched. He had never seen Zhang happy and he found it fascinating. He almost felt as if he shared in the man's joy.

Soon they were inside and the warmth of the drug filled his being once more with hallucinations of merciless Chinese statues, the red eyes of The Shadow, and the lost laughter of a little boy who loved trains.

The activity lasted all day long. He heard scraping and bumping upstairs in the theater, big objects being slid across the floor. Men came and went. Zhang barked orders. Men responded. The sounds of commotion upstairs blurred into those from the street—the preparations for the parade. Finally, at the coming of night, he was roused from his stupor by Zhang. Gibson's vision took a while to come into focus.

"Come with me, my biographer," Zhang Mei snapped, impatient at Gibson's groggy ineptitude. "There is another chapter to be written tonight." A pure formidable energy emanated from Zhang, and Gibson could see in his bearing the warrior who had slain so many men single-handedly at the battle of the river, who had led troops into battle under the banner of Zhang Zuolin. He knew in an instant that his secret sharer was gone forever. Zhang's men hustled Gibson out toward the back of the truck. One of the men flipped down the rear gate of the trunk, while another swept back the canvas cargo door.

"Jesus Christ!"

Two rusty old canisters—identical to the one he had found in the Providence Medical Lab, right down to their weathered army stencils—were lashed tightly to the bed of the truck. Hands propelled him up and on, the momentum knocking him against one of the drums. He scrambled away from them and picked himself up. The rest of Zhang's company clambered in after him. They were solemn and resolute, and they eyed him with stern silence. On the floor was an open crate of machine guns. Another held cartridges for those guns. A third box remained closed. The last man aboard dropped the canvas over the back.

He heard Zhang's voice outside.

"Zhang Mei," he cried, "Zhang Mei! What are you doing?"

But there was no reply. Moments later he heard both doors of the cab slam shut and the engine roar to life.

He had no sense of where they were when the truck finally came to a stop. The men seemed restless, but they made no move to exit. Gibson felt a rumbling sensation vibrating against his tailbone on the bench where he was seated. It was a familiar sensation and for a strange moment he thought they had parked by the loading dock of the Street & Smith building. But the instant he had that thought, it introduced another which told him exactly where they were. The American Bank Note Company lay on the other side of the canvas wall.

The gate of the truck was carefully and quietly lowered and the men filed off. One man remained in the truck with his gun in Gibson's ribs. There was a crisp, efficient order to the distribution of guns and ammo. The third case was opened and gas masks were pulled from it. Each man put one on. Gibson stared as one of the two drums was carefully lowered to the street by anxious men. The masks gave them an insect-like appearance, with bug eyes and a drumlike proboscis hanging down to their chests.

"Zhang Mei? What's happening?" he said loudly. The men looked at him. Zhang Mei gave him a disdainful glare. He felt the muzzle of the gun poke his ribs, hard, and his heart began to race. Three men picked up the drum and ran with it to the front door of the building, and he knew the guards were done for unless he did something. "Hey!" he shouted, trying to warn the men inside. "Hey!" The guards in the lobby stirred.

He felt something explode off the back of his head, and he sank to his hands and knees, bolt of pains radiating through his body like the energy waves broadcasting from the RKO Studios' theatrical emblem. For a moment he thought he had been shot, but he realized that he had been cocked with a rifle butt. Nausea overcame him and through blurred vision he saw one of the men use an implement to rip the stopper from the drum. The guards were rising now; they looked startled. One of the Chinese men took a sledgehammer to the glass door, smashing it.

White gas blew from the hole in the drum like a whale's plume, and Gibson remembered the pressure it was under. The men rolled the drum through the shattered glass. In an instant the lobby was filled with white, billowing clouds which swallowed up the guards. With the glass gone Gibson could hear their coughing screams of wretched agony. The sound lasted only a moment. They had been given no time to raise the alarm. Anyone else in the building, especially in the floors below as the gas sank, would also be dead within moments.

The drum exhausted its pressurized contents rapidly. While the lobby was still full of poison, Zhang Mei barked a command and the men followed him inside. The gas spilled out of the lobby and onto the sidewalk toward Gibson. He felt for his glasses—one lens was broken. Half blind, he dragged himself to his feet. The man who had hit him kept the gun trained on him in a way which let him know that he would not be given a second chance. The gas stayed low, like a heavy mist, and soon the truck was surrounded. Gibson snatched a gas mask from the crate and held it to his face.

The gas swirled around his feet but rose no higher and soon it began to evaporate into the air. Suddenly he felt the vibration stop. The printing presses had been turned off.

After a lengthy period of inactivity the men emerged from the lobby. Still wearing their masks, they looked like ants pouring out of an anthill. They carried case upon case, which they stacked upon pallets in the truck. The addition of the cases made the truck sink under their combined weight.

"Years ago the ruling coalition in Beijing, under my adopted father, placed an order for new currency from this place. It was bought and paid for by the Chinese people." Zhang Mei was speaking up to Gibson from the curb. His voice was flattened by the mask. "When the coalition collapsed, it became unclear to whom this money should be released. Many claimed ownership, but none could prove it. And so here it has rested these many years."

"No receipt. No money. Holy Christ," Gibson murmured. "It's the greatest lost Chinese laundry ticket joke in the history of the world."

"And here is your punch line: Your government can never admit that this money has been taken. To do so would destroy all that is left of its global economic integrity."

"How much money?"

"Enough to win a war. Enough to rebuild an empire after its invaders have been repelled. Enough to avenge my family. Enough to seat a new emperor in Beijing—one who will bring peace to China."

"But how much?"

"Seven hundred and fifty million dollars," Zhang replied. "Tomorrow night, after we celebrate with our brothers, we shall begin our journey home. Colonel Towers has arranged it so that we will not be pursued by your coast guard or navy."

The engine rumbled to life and the men climbed back on board, considerably more cramped. Zhang disappeared from Gibson's view in the commotion of moving soldiers. That's when Gibson made his break for it. He lunged for the rear gate, hoping to take advantage of the confusion.

That must have been about the time the rifle butt hit him for a second time, because the RKO antenna in his head began broadcasting pain again, and he lost consciousness. Now as he lay on the floor, looking up, he felt the truck incline gently and heard the sound of tires rumbling over wooden planks. It was the sensation any New Yorker, especially a Dodgers fan who took cabs out to Ebbets Field, knew well. They were leaving Manhattan by way of the Brooklyn Bridge.

EPISODE THIRTY-EIGHT

As THE tiny boat carried Lester and the cowboy farther away and closer to the black ship, The Flash turned to Driftwood and said, "I would have bet money that if anybody had gone overboard tonight, it would have been you."

"Me too," he muttered through his clenched teeth.

"All right," Mrs. Dent said, as the current swiftly drew the launch through the ice floes behind the freighter. "We're going to have to circle back and get them when they come back." She pointed to a wide expanse of black water, free of ice, in the distance. "We can come about in the waters between Red Hook and Governors Island."

"Sure," Driftwood replied as she went below. "Maybe they'll pick up some beer and steak from the galley on the way back. Invite some of those nice fellas on the dock to come back for a cookout."

"Why don't you take it easy, Driftwood? That's the lady's husband out there."

"And he's not coming back," he replied darkly.

The Flash felt his blood rise. "This whole trip you've been calling me a liar to my face, trying to pick a fight with the cowboy, and putting the make on Mr. Dent's missus. Now, I introduced you to them and they're nice people and I feel responsible, so show a little respect."

"You have to admit you've spun some yarns."

"I'm sure when you start telling Mrs. Dent the truth behind your whoppers, she's completely going to throw her husband over for your skinny, weak-lunged, hoboing, grave-digging ass. Send me an invite to the wedding. I'll bring something from Tiffany. Meanwhile, we got a boat to sail and you're at the helm, so sail already."

In a subdued voice Driftwood asked The Flash to let out some sail so they could pick up some speed. The Flash did what he was told for Mrs. Dent's sake, but he was tired of taking orders and tired of being on the boat.

He picked up the binoculars and could see the two men forging their way across the Stygian scene, the blocks of ice, some as small as a dime, others as big as a flat house, adding chill impediments to their progress. Below him he could hear Mrs. Dent as she tried to raise the Coast Guard, but the radio issued only static. She emerged, frustration clearly showing on her face. He handed her the binoculars.

The little boat made its way along the starboard side of the freighter to a hatch just above the waterline. It was identical to the one on the port side which had hooked Lester's gaff. "He said he had the keys," she said. A moment or two later and the hatch was open, the two men vanishing into the bowels of the ship. She lowered the binoculars and smiled slightly. The tone of her voice and the steely glare in her eyes made The Flash think that, for a while at least, Lester would probably be safer aboard the ship. She tossed the binoculars back to him and went below again.

"Coast Guard! Coast Guard! Come in, please. This is the *Albatross*. Come in, please! Coast Guard. Coast Guard? Come in. Do you copy?"

"Copy that," the radio finally crackled to life, as she fiddled with the squelch, "This is the Coast Guard. Go ahead. Over." The voice was young. The Flash imagined that the radio operator was one of his readers.

"I'm reporting a hijacked ship at the pier just south of the Brooklyn

Bridge. The ship is named the *Star of Baltimore*. There are lives in danger. Do you copy?"

"Copy that, *Albatross*." The radio sputtered again and an icy voice, nearly metallic in timbre, interrupted the conversation.

"Attention, Coast Guard." The new speaker commanded attention. Speaking softly, but with a power that caused Mrs. Dent to adjust the volume, the new voice said, "This is Colonel Towers. Do you copy?"

"Yes, sir!" The young man responded with fear and respect.

"Do you recognize my authority in this matter?"

Colonel Towers. The Flash looked at Driftwood, who acknowledged his shock with a nod and a grimace.

"Yes, sir, Colonel Towers, sir. I am fully aware of your standing orders. There is no ship. Repeat. There is no ship. Over."

"Good, sailor. Good work."

"Coast Guard!" Mrs. Dent pleaded. "Listen to me. The ship is named the *Star of Baltimore*."

The Flash looked out across the water to Governors Island, the headquarters of the United States Coast Guard's Atlantic fleet. He imagined the young signalman at his station. He chose a window in a building and decided that was where the young man was. Stu was his name, he decided. Stu, from Nantucket, who had grown up on the coastal shores of his island. Stu was one of his fans. Stu would help.

"Attention, *Albatross*," Stu spoke at long last. "There is no vessel registered as the *Star of Baltimore*. This channel is for emergency use only. If you persist in your hoax your ship will be impounded and you will be prosecuted to the full extent of United States maritime law."

"No! Please! You have to help!"

"Coast Guard, Governors Island Station, out!"

Damn you, Stu, The Flash thought angrily. The next time I write a coward who shoots men in the back, he's going to have your name. The radio remained silent.

Mrs. Dent came up from the cabin. Her jaw was clenched and roses of fury blushed her cheeks. She took a deep breath.

"It's gonna be close," Driftwood said. The Flash turned and watched the blackness which indicated open water rapidly approach. "Sure wish we'd fixed the motor."

"You up for this?" The Flash asked him. His eyes were trying to factor in a dozen different potential hazards at once.

"It'd be easier with an engine."

"Well, we don't have one," Mrs. Dent snapped at him. "And if you don't feel like you're up to it, just step aside and let me do it."

"That's okay," Driftwood said, cowed. "I can do it."

The Flash looked into the frigid, swirling waters. Once, fishing as a boy in the early Montana spring, he had slipped in the mud and fallen into the Missouri River. The runoff from the winter snow had been colder than anything he could have imagined. His head slipped only briefly beneath the surface of the water but his breath had been snatched away from him by the cold. His diaphragm would not expand even as he struggled to inhale, and panic had set in almost immediately. The stabbing of a thousand chilling needles in his flesh, the vicious, ruthlessly gripping current, turned him into a violent thrashing animal, a wolf with its paw in a trap. All he knew, had ever known, would ever know, was that this cold death was so fast, so powerful, so overwhelming. Only his clawing hand, reaching for a low-hanging branch, had secured his rescue. Only the feeling of his hand on that branch, that security, had restored his reason, had allowed his rib cage to expand with air in spite of the water's viselike grip.

He knew exactly what it would feel like to die in the water.

"Ready to come about?" Otis asked. His voice was thin and tight.

"Ready!" Mrs. Dent stood ready to cast her sheet off.

The Flash grabbed the handle and prepared to coil his sheet around the winch when the sail was tossed free. "Ready to come about!" he shouted.

"Coming about!"

The boat heeled over in the opposite direction and The Flash braced himself against the cabin. He felt a solid thump as ice cracked against the hull. They were right up against the ice shelf.

"We're aground!" he shouted. "We're on the ice!"

"I know!" Driftwood grunted, wrestling with the wheel. "I know!"

From his angle he could see only ice below. The boat scraped against it with a crackling shriek. He secured his lines and the sails filled with wind, the *Albatross* trembling as it ground against the outer edge of the ice.

"Get ready to jump to the ice!" he yelled to Mrs. Dent.

"No!" She shook her head. "She'll make it. You hear me?" she hollered to Driftwood. "She can make it!"

Suddenly the *Albatross* shook with a thud as it knifed back into the water, free of the ice and heading back up the channel. The Flash sank against the cabin to catch his breath. Mrs. Dent reached for, and he gave over, the binoculars. She looked for a long time and he peered at the ship, following her gaze. He thought he saw the blur of a figure ducking behind a vent at the front of the ship, near the cabins, but he couldn't be sure. She swore and lowered the glasses. He took one look at her face and knew something terrible had happened.

"What?" he asked.

"It's Lester," she said. "He and the cowboy are up on deck."

Episode Thirty-Nine

G IBSON HEARD the sound of lapping water. He had been concentrating so hard on making the pain in his head go away that
it took him a few moments to realize the truck had stopped moving
and the engine had been shut off. Zhang Mei's men filed off the truck
as before, unconcerned with the prostrate white man.

He staggered to his feet, using the bench for support. Through the
cargo flap he could see glimpses of Manhattan across the water. He
parted the canvas and looked out. The truck had backed down a large
wooden pier, much greater than the one he had explored in Providence.
He made his way cautiously off the truck. To his right loomed the
Brooklyn Bridge. To his left a great black ship—blacker even than the
putrid water beneath its hull, a ship old and carrying the scars of
decades of battle against the sea and elements—soared high above him.
There were still more Chinese men on board the ship, speaking excitedly with their comrades on the dock as they lowered a gangplank
down. Zhang Mei led the ascent, embracing the men on the ship as he
reached the deck.

Gibson began to back away, hoping to steal off down the dock, but a
hand shoved him forward. It was his old friend, the soldier with the

busted jaw. Overhead, the deck crane had been brought roaring to life. Its arm swung out over the truck and the operator slowly lowered the hook at the end of the steel cable toward the truck. Men helped guide the heavy hook inside the cargo truck, where the hook was fastened to the chains binding the crates of money to the first pallet. Then, with men shouting directions, the operator began to winch back, soldiers inside the truck guiding the pallet out as the slack went out of the cable, then the pallet swung free and began to rise. The first load of lost Chinese loot began its journey home.

Gibson's escort forced him on toward and up the gangplank. He heard the sound of grinding gears and saw that the great doors to the hold in the center of the ship were being winched open and the pallet was being lowered into its depths. Zhang Mei watched from the edge of the hold, arms crossed in satisfaction. Gibson was allowed to sit on a crate and smoke. The men worked efficiently and quickly, but even so, Gibson grew weary.

Finally Zhang Mei beckoned to him. He rose and walked to the hold, wary of the yawning opening. "America is a young country," Zhang Mei said, "but one thing they have become better at than anyone else is the art of killing."

Far below them, arranged like neat little clusters of eggs in a country farmer's stall, were dozens upon dozens of the ancient army drums. Thousands of gallons of malevolent death waiting to be spilled across distant battlefields.

"You can't use this," Gibson said, horrified. "It's obscene."

"Once wives and children become the targets of war, that word loses its relevance. I will use this gas to drive the Japanese from every inch of the Middle Kingdom, then I shall take what's left of it and bring it to their shores. By the time the summer flowers bloom beyond the walls of Shenyang Palace the war will be over. And I will once more be able to lay those same flowers upon the graves of my wife and my son." He leaned in close to Gibson and whispered his final thought before sweeping away from Gibson's side and vanishing down the gangway.

Walter Gibson felt the weight of his life upon his shoulders and was unable to move. The shouts of men and the grinding of the crane gears receded along with his sense of the rest of the world. He knew that he was about to die and suddenly all he craved was the sight of one more dawn.

Across the great distance that seemed to separate his unmoored mind from reality he heard a sharp crack, as if some ice on the river were breaking up. He looked up and saw the engineer operating the crane stagger from his cab, a hand against his bloody face. Something seemed to strike him and he fell back against the control levers. The arm of the crane suddenly dropped down with tremendous speed, crashing against the deck with tremendous force; he could feel the entire boat shudder. The pallet that had been dangling near the hold opening fell to the deck, then was yanked with great force by the falling crane across the deck. It skidded away from where he stood and smashed into the gangplank, dislodging and shattering it. Together, the pallet of heavy cases and what was left of the gangplank toppled to the pier, exploding through the wood into the water. The cable, still attached to the pallet, was drawn taut before snapping; it sailed into the air with the crack of a whip, then fell across the ship. The recoil of the cable springing back was enough to send several heavy iron beams that had been part of the crane structure hurtling into the hold. Fascinated, horrified, Gibson watched as the debris slammed into a bundle of canisters, crushing them like tin cans.

The men below never had a chance. He looked down into hell. Gas jetted out through the hold in a horrifyingly wide spray. Great feathery plumes spurted up into the night sky, then fell back to become part of the roiling gray mass, devouring the luckless men trying to escape it. It spread to fill the floor of the hold and then rose up, like a tub filling with water. So quickly, he thought. The sight of onrushing doom was paralyzing; he was rooted to the deck.

Robert. I'm sorry.

For a moment the turmoil below seemed to coalesce into a giant form in which he could see the rage of The Shadow, his Shadow, his dark angel of retribution, sweeping up toward him, eyes ablaze with wrath. The mass spilled out onto the deck, flowing over his shoes.

Litzka. I'll try to hold my breath for you.

He felt the impact of a body slamming into his side. The impact lifted him off his feet, knocked the wind from his lungs. He had the dizzying sensation of motion, of being swept down the deck by a great force, of arms around him. Someone was dragging him. A man. Not The Shadow. The gas poured across the deck toward him. He was at the bow. How had he arrived here? There was a thunder in his ears.

Then he felt himself being lifted up against the rail. His mind finally seemed to uncloud and he looked at the man forcing him up.

"Dent?" he said, amazed, and then began the long fall into the black abyss.

The pain he felt was immense beyond measure. It was as if all the pain he had ever felt in his life had revisited him all at once. As a writer, he never believed that words could fail him, yet this was a pain beyond describing in any sense that could be conveyed to another person.

It was a complete and resounding agony.

EPISODE FORTY

THE FLASH could never have imagined that bodies could fall so fast.

"Oh my God," Mrs. Dent cried. "They're in the water!"

The midsection of the *Star of Baltimore* disappeared beneath the thick, lethal fog billowing from its hold. A light breeze stirred the gas to starboard; it flowed heavily over the side almost like a liquid, sizzling away as it made contact with the seawater. Behind the ship Lester's head emerged; then, within a moment or two, the form of the other man he had thrown over the ship's bow appeared several yards from him.

"Is that the cowboy?" Driftwood yelled to them.

"I can't tell," The Flash hollered back.

Dent swam to the limp form as the current pulled them both away from the freighter and the roiling gas.

"Get them," Mrs. Dent commanded to the both of them. Driftwood angled the *Albatross* to intercept, while The Flash grabbed the life ring. Suddenly they heard a low roar, like a bow being drawn along a bass fiddle.

"What's that?" The Flash yelled. "What's that sound?"

"That," Driftwood said in a choked, hoarse voice, "is the sound of a machine gun."

With the excitement on the ship The Flash had forgotten about the men on the dock. A half dozen or so men stood there now, amidst the gangplank wreckage and the debris from the pallets. The air around them was alive with fluttering slips of paper. A man in a long black coat stood in their midst towering over the other men. While the men on the dock pointed at Dent in the water, this man stood still with his face turned away, looking back at the ship. Another one of the Chinese men gripped a machine gun and fired bursts into the water. Lester struck out against the water with one hand while supporting the other man.

"No way in hell am I going near those machine guns!" Driftwood's face was white, drained of blood.

"You have to! That's my husband up there."

Driftwood kept his eyes focused on the water in front of him. The Flash realized that Driftwood was terrified. Beyond terrified. He was panicking. He slid down the deck to the helm as the sails began to luff.

"It's all in your head."

"Get away from me." Driftwood looked at him angrily. He was almost beyond reasoning with. "You ever stare down a machine gun? I'm not dying that way."

"It's just in your mind. You need to get control of it. Get your monkeys in order."

"Monkeys?" The seeming randomness of simians' being introduced into the conversation caught the edge of his attention. Just as The Flash had intended.

"The monkeys in your head. The ones that are running in a million different directions. You gotta get them running in one direction. That way!"

Driftwood pushed him roughly away. The Flash slipped to the deck by Mrs. Dent's feet. He pulled himself up and looked at Driftwood, who was staring at the dock. At last he looked up and met The Flash's eyes. For a long moment The Flash couldn't tell (and afterward he was never sure) whether Driftwood at that moment was completely sane or completely insane. A sardonic smile twisted across Driftwood's face, making his mustache twitch. "Monkeys!" He gave the wheel a tremendous spin; the sound of the spoke smacking into his hand when he finally stopped it sounded like wood cracking. The sails filled again with a steady breeze. The Flash felt the *Albatross* heel again. He slid to the other side of the deck as the boat swung around toward the *Star of Baltimore.*

"What the hell! If we're gonna die, we're gonna die!" Driftwood shouted as the sail snapped across the boat. "That's what my monkeys are telling me!" He barked out a laugh. The Flash's side was aching where he had fallen against the hold door. He rubbed it. Driftwood looked at The Flash. "All monkeys reporting for duty."

"Good."

Driftwood made a quizzical face, his eyes rolling up. "Hey! You little bastards better clean up your crap when you're done."

As the yacht drew near to Dent, the wind changed again and what was left of the gas began to flow the other way, toward the dock. It dribbled down the side of the ship and the Chinese men broke and ran, clambering over the wreckage and shattered planks to reach the truck. Finally, the tall man in the long coat turned around and looked out to the river. He was Chinese, his face fierce and strong. His eyes glittered like carved obsidian, and The Flash could feel his rage radiating across the water toward them. Thin tendrils of gas crept across the dock toward his feet. At last he broke his gaze and spun rapidly away. He moved with the athletic deftness of an animal across the broken pier, leaping aboard the truck as it roared down the pier and into the night.

The last of the gas dissipated across the waters and a strange silence fell across the river, the stillness of a big city on its way to dawn. Not a pure silence. A silence that vibrated with life and energy in a single, inaudibly low tone.

Lester struggled feebly as Otis expertly brought them alongside the hull. Hubbard threw the life ring out to Dent's upstretched hand, and within minutes the two men were finally back on the *Albatross.* Norma threw herself against Lester, feeling the cold water soak into her jacket. He was shivering uncontrollably and his lips were blue. Ron emerged from belowdecks with blankets and she wrapped Lester as he sat on the deck. He grinned at her.

"Don't try that Dent smile on me," she said. "I am not in the mood for charm." Slips of paper about the size of dollars bills were plastered against his hair. She was not gentle about slapping them off; in fact they seemed to require the extra effort. "You just had to go up on the deck of that ship, didn't you? Protection luck, my ass."

He tried to look sorry. He tilted his head so his eyes looked even guiltier. "If it makes you feel any better, you can cross jumping off a ship into icy water off my list of things to do before I die," he managed, through chattering teeth.

In rapid succession she slapped the last few pieces of paper from his head. "You're an idiot. You'd just better hope you got a good story out of it, that's all I have to say. 'Cause that one might cost you. It might cost you some toes. It might cost you a marriage."

Ron hurried up from below with some more blankets.

"Who is that?" Norma asked Ron as he covered the second man.

"That's Walter Gibson. He writes The Shadow."

"I know what Walter Gibson writes, thank you, Ron," she said icily, snatching a blanket from him and wrapping it around her husband.

"We're taking on some serious water. I'm going to tie us up to the dock," Otis said. "Before we sink," he added.

"Okay," Ron answered, standing to prepare the dock lines. "It looks clear."

"Ahoy below!" A voice hailed them. Standing on the bow of the *Star of Baltimore* and looking down at them with a curiously worried expression was Lew, the cowboy. "Everyone all right?"

"Appears to be the case," Otis shouted back. "How'd you stay alive?"

"I can tell which way the wind blows, pard. Gas heads that way," he pointed starboard, "I heads this way." He pointed to the prow. "It's all evaporated now."

"Get down and help us tie up."

"Sure," Lew called back. "I reckon everyone's dead up here. How're them fellas?"

"Little cold. Little wet. Little closer to a divorce."

Lew found some cargo netting, tossed it over the side and scrambled down to the wrecked dock.

After some careful negotiation they managed to get the yacht into what Otis and Ron agreed was a safe berth. Lester emerged from below in a dry set of clothes and was able to lend a hand. He had stuffed as much sailcloth as he possibly could into the crack in the hull, stopping the flow of water for the time being.

Upon stepping foot on the dock, Ron eagerly scooped up a fistful of paper. "Chinese money," he said, examining it. "Worthless." He flung it away, exasperated. "Just my luck. When money finally falls from the sky it's useless to me."

"What the hell happened up there?" Driftwood demanded. "I thought you were just gonna disable the engine."

"It was my fault" Lew replied. "I just wanted a look up top. The crane operator, he saw me. He shot first." He tossed Lester his pistol back. "Thanks for the loan."

"We need to get Mr. Gibson to a hospital," Norma said.

"No," a weak voice said. She turned around. Gibson was sitting up. He coughed. "Just take me home."

"You need a doctor."

"Mrs. Dent, right?"

She nodded. "Please?"

"Well, Mrs. Dent," he said with a cough, "I'm either gonna die or not and there's not a thing any doctor can do. Just take me home and I'll find out."

"Mr. Gibson," she began, "there's something I've always wanted to say to you if ever we met. You are a damned piehead!"

"Mrs. Dent, I've never heard it put exactly that way before but that sounds about right."

"Fine. Now we'll take you home."

"Hold on a split second," said the cowboy, "I'm afraid this is where we say adios."

"You're not coming?" Lester asked.

"This here is my ship. I lost her once but I ain't losin' her again. I'm staying with the old girl until the police come by. Somebody needs to tell 'em this story. Might as well be me."

"Okay. Otis, would you mind staying with the *Albatross* until I get back?" Lester asked.

"Can't Hubbard do it?" Driftwood asked.

"Why me?" Hubbard said. "It's not like you've got to be anywhere. And you know her so well, now."

"Fine. I'll do it."

"Hey," said the cowboy, twirling the pistol. "I'm all out here. Got any more bullets?"

Lester shook his head. "I never thought I'd need more than six."

Norma approached the young man and hugged him gratefully. "Thank you," she told him. "You never did tell me your last name. So we can look out for you."

The man hung his head bashfully. "Aw, ma'am," he said, "it's kind of embarrassin'."

"Don't be silly. Tell me."

He whispered it softly into her ear and she smiled and laughed and kissed him on the cheek. "I love it. I absolutely love it."

"You think?"

"Absolutely. Much prettier than Dent!"

As she helped Lester and Walter change into warm clothes below she could hear Otis and Ron up on deck. They had discovered what was left of a bottle of Lester's Cuban rum and were already spinning their recent adventure into tales, as if they hadn't been at each other's throat only a half hour before. There were things she would just never understand about men.

They disembarked and moved around the gaping hole in the pier, Ron and Lester supporting an unsteady Walter. Soon they were able to hail a wandering cab on Joralemon Street and were on their way back over the Brooklyn Bridge and into the city. Through the suspension cables they could see the two boats and the smashed pier in the distance. Then they lost sight of them altogether.

"Walter," Lester finally asked, simply, "what the hell happened?"

Walter Gibson stared back at him and life seemed to come back into his eyes. "Let me tell you a story. You can decide what's real and what's pulp."

EPISODE FORTY-ONE

H E HADN'T given them every detail. For instance he didn't tell them about his surprising fondness for opium, or about having seen The Shadow in gas. It was his story and he told them what they needed to know.

"What'd he say to you?" Lester asked, as the cab pulled to a stop before the Hotel Des Artistes. "I saw Zhang Mei whisper something to you before he left you to die. What did he say?"

Gibson rubbed the palm of his hand across his chin, feeling the growing stubble. He gave a little snort. "He said that perhaps I wasn't a biographer of great enough stature for his story after all. He felt he needed to find Ernest Hemingway. Can you believe that he said that to me? Me?"

"Well," said Norma, even as Lester tried to shush her, "he is a well-regarded author."

Gibson looked mortally offended. "I could outwrite Ernest Hemingway any day of the week. Name the weapon. Spikes and stone? Clay tablets and straw? Pen quill and parchment? Hell, straight bourbon and blarney, and I will tell the story straight and clear over Ernest any day of the week in any land under any weather. 'A Clean, Well-Lighted

299

Place,' my ass! Try that against 'I Rode the Black Ship of Death with the Dragon of Terror and Peril!' Huh!" A coughing fit ended his grand speech. As he caught his breath, weakened by the exertion, they helped him out of the cab. The crisp night air and the feeling of Manhattan *firma,* known to all, far and wide, as the most stable land in all the world, the rock that will be there for you to walk on, to run on, to chase after another pair of feet running away from you on, to ride the subway through, to fall on, to sleep on if you're desperate, slip on, spill on, urinate on, spit on—to feel his feet stake their claim seemed to imbue him with the ability to draw himself to his full, and expansive, five-foot-eight-inch height. He looked at his three concerned companions and, sweeping his arms up and to the sides, proclaimed grandly, "Anyway, I have lived to tell the tale." The exertion made him cough hard enough that they all had to turn away. "For a little while."

The first thing Norma noticed when the doors opened on his hallway was the chicken. It was a healthy representative of the species and it fixed a suspicious eye upon the four people in the elevator. She felt that it demanded a response from her so she greeted it with a casual "Hello," as if she were used to stepping off big-city elevators and being greeted by chickens every day of the week and twice on Sundays. The bird clucked at her. Then there was a shriek from one end of the hall and a beautiful young woman had rushed past them and thrown her arms around Mr. Gibson. Norma had never given any thought to Mr. Gibson's private life and she found herself surprised that such a stylish and attractive young woman might be Mrs. Gibson. Norma had seen her hairdo in *Harper's Bazaar* only last month.

"I knew that something had happened," she said to him, kissing his face. "I knew it. I knew it!"

"He needs to lie down," Norma said to her; the young woman nodded back, and in that gesture, polite though it was, she let Norma know that she would now be tending to Walter.

She led them through the open door into Mr. Gibson's apartment, which was large and full of books and magazines and magical apparatus. The chicken followed them in. Framed posters of Houdini, Blackstone, Porter Hardeen, and others were hung on the walls. The young woman opened another door for them and then followed them into the bedroom. Lester and Ron lay Mr. Gibson gently on the bed. His body was limp and his eyes remained closed. Unconscious or asleep or somewhere in between—Norma couldn't tell which.

"I'm going to get him some water." The young woman swept out of the room. Her motions and movements were light and graceful.

"What do we do now?" Lester asked Norma. Even though he was speaking as softly as he could, his voice bounced around the room. Hubbard leaned over to hear the answer. "He lives or dies and we wait and pray and try to help out his wife."

"Oh, he's not married," Hubbard said discreetly, as if he was surprised that they didn't know this.

"Who is she?"

"Well, from what he told me on the way up to Providence, she's some kind of trouble."

"Ah," she said. "Should we keep an eye on her?"

Hubbard looked down at his feet, a little embarrassed.

"A different kind of trouble," Lester said with a faint smile.

The young woman came into the room again with a bowl of water and a washcloth. The two men excused themselves from the bedroom, Lester to get some coffee brewing and Ron to slip out and get some Bromo. The two women went about stripping Gibson and making him comfortable.

Norma was reconsidering all the thoughts and feelings she had let build up inside her about Walter Gibson over the years. In her mind he had taken on the bearing of a giant, because of the way he had loomed over her and Lester. It was shocking now to see how short he was. She carefully placed his glasses on the credenza next to the bed. She looked around his room. It was clean and the furniture was well chosen. Walter Gibson was short, and wore glasses, and lived in a nice apartment like theirs, and someone seemed to care for him. He was not some malevolent villain bent on destroying the Dents. He was just a writer. A man.

"My name's Norma Dent," Norma introduced herself.

The young woman tucked the sheet under Walter's chin, then tucked a wayward lock of hair behind her ear. "I'm Litzka. Do you think we should call a doctor?"

"He won't have one. I didn't know Mr. Gibson was married," Norma said, indicating the ring on Litzka's finger.

"He's not," she replied, returning Norma's quizzical gaze coolly. "I am."

"Oh."

"Well, he's not going to die. I won't let him." Litzka sat on the edge of the bed and rubbed his arm with her hand. Then she took his hand in hers. He opened his eyes and saw her. He smiled, slipped his hand from hers, tenderly touched her cheek, and retucked that lock of hair, then put his hand back in hers again.

"Hi."

"Hi," she answered. "I missed you."

"I missed you too."

"What happened?"

"I got myself into a little trouble." He closed his eyes and sank back upon the pillows. His breathing was shallow but even and some proper color had returned to his face. "I'm sorry I acted like such a"—he smiled—"a damned piehead."

"So am I," Litzka replied.

"Well, you're here now."

"I am."

Norma left her caressing Walter's hand and slipped out as quietly as she could. Lester drowsed on the sofa. The chicken scratched at the magazine on the floor. Ron had had it in his coat pocket and had tossed it onto the sofa when they arrived. Lester must have knocked it to the floor. Norma thought Ron might not appreciate having his magazine scratched up by a chicken, so she shooed it away and picked it up. On the cover of the *Astounding Tales* magazine yet another tentacled beast menaced a lingerie-wearing damsel. Someone had taken a pen to the cover and scrawled some letters but they appeared to her to be gibberish: GZXUVG HKRRGJUTTG VRAY/SOTAY NEUYIEGSOTK.

She sat down, feeling rather helpless, on the sofa, and thankfully, Lester wrapped a comforting arm around her. She settled in against him and closed her eyes, still holding the magazine.

Ron came in a while later with a big blue bottle of Bromo Seltzer and a *New York Post*. While he and Lester exchanged their stories of the events, he prowled around the apartment looking at the magic equipment and giving the chicken a wide berth. Eventually he picked up a wicked-looking dagger. It had a curved golden hilt and the long blade comprised three sides forming a triangle, each one having a razor edge. He pressed the point gingerly into the palm of his hand.

"That was a gift Harry Houdini gave to me when he returned from Egypt," Mr. Gibson said from the doorway. He had put on an undershirt and a fresh pair of pants. He coughed but held himself up. Litzka stood anxiously behind him.

"Is it magic? Does it retract or something?" Ron still pressed the point into his hand.

"No. It's just very, very sharp." Hubbard had just come to the same conclusion and put the knife back quickly.

"You know, I always wondered how he escaped from jail cells when he was naked." Ron remarked, stanching the blood flowing from the tiny cut in the palm of his hand.

"Easy. He'd take a lock pick kit. Like this." Gibson picked up several small, thin strips of metal. "He'd roll it in soft wax until it formed a pellet. Then he'd stick it up his ass. Enter the jail cell, and abracadabra! Magic!"

"Glamorous," Ron muttered with a disillusioned tone.

"You should be resting, Mr. Gibson," Norma said.

"Please, call me Walter. Or Walt. Wally even."

"Walter, then."

"And there'll be plenty of time for resting," he said, with a cough. He looked at Lester. "I could hear you telling what happened on the *Star of Baltimore*. It's got a good ending. You save my life." He stepped unsteadily into the room. "As long as we're on the subject of endings I'd like to give another story a new and better ending. I'd like to apologize about *The Golden Vulture.* I guess it comes as no surprise to you that after I read it, I had Nanovic squash it. It was not my finest moment. I was afraid of losing The Shadow. If it's any consolation, I did it because it was obvious you were a natural pulp man and you had written such a great pulp."

"It really wasn't a good Shadow story," Lester replied. "Too much story and not enough atmosphere." Norma could see no trace of the anger which Lester had held for Mr. Gibson.

"Still, I'm sorry."

"It's all right, Walter," Norma said, turning to look at the weary man. *"The Golden Vulture* did have a happy ending for us. It led Lester to Doc Savage." She was suddenly distracted by a tug on the paper in her hand. The chicken was pecking again at the mag cover.

"China Boy!" Litzka admonished him and he turned sheepishly. "He knows better."

"That's my mag," Ron noted. "I got it from Lovecraft."

"Lovecraft?" Walter looked shaken to hear that name.

"Long story," Ron answered. "He tried to write something on it but it's just garbage. I couldn't read his writing when he was alive and I guess I can't figure it out when he's dead either."

"Let me see that." Norma handed the magazine to Walter. He looked at it for a moment and then his face lit up.

"Code," he chuckled. "It's my code." Gibson eased himself into the armchair. "But without the offset number I can't decode it."

"Offset number?" Norma felt a thrill stab through her.

"It's the number which tells you how many letters to move forward in the alphabet to find the correctly corresponding letter. There's no point in writing something in code if nobody else has the key. How'd you get this?"

Ron started to tell him the tale of the dead man who came to the White Horse Tavern. Norma picked up the mag while Walter and Litzka listened incredulously.

"Well," Norma said as Walter reached the point where Lovecraft began to melt, "this monster has seven tentacles drooping from his face. Couldn't that be the key? Seven?"

"Seven?"

"I'm pretty good at finding treasure clues," she said proudly.

Gibson rifled through an end table drawer and came up with a pencil and something which looked suspiciously to her like a decoder ring. "Read the letters to me." He went to work fiddling with the ring as she read and scribbling on a notepad, stopping occasionally to cough violently. Finally he looked up at her, eyes gleaming. "Atropa belladonna plus/minus hyoscyamine."

"That sounds like some sort of compound," Ron said with a tone of indifference. He had been reading the paper while they worked and now he looked up. Norma wasn't certain but she thought he was a little sore that he hadn't been the one to figure out the code. "You'd need a chemist to know for sure."

"Maybe it's an antidote for the gas?" Norma said.

"Good boy! Good China Boy! See Walter? China Boy loves you! He's trying to help." Litzka picked up the chicken and hugged it while it clucked contentedly in her arms.

"Anyone know a chemist?" Gibson asked.

"Sure," Ron replied, turning another page of the paper his nose was buried in. "We all do."

"What?"

"Dr. Smith. He's one of us. He's a pulpateer." He realized that they were all staring at him. "What? You don't like the word *pulpateer*? I just made it up."

"No," Walter said as slowly and as patiently as he could manage. "I want you to find Doc Smith!"

EPISODE FORTY-TWO

"Is it just me?" the cowboy asked Driftwood. "Or is Mrs. Dent one helluva damn fine dame?" They were standing on the stern of the *Star of Baltimore* watching the sun come up over the East River.

Driftwood felt a surge of possessive jealousy. "Yeah. She's all right." He had taken a strong dislike to the cowboy and didn't like his speaking about Norma in that way.

"Shoot. Just all right! I'll say. First of all, those stems of hers are dynamite. And could you imagine waking up with those gray eyes looking at you from across the pillow? Or running your hands through that hair? I do love the blondes, y'know."

"Hey, I think she's spoken for, so why don't you just step off that high horse you're on about her and let someone else have a ch—I mean leave her to her husband. I saw her first anyway."

"Hell, I know she's spoken for, pard. What I want to know is where can I find one just like her that ain't spoken for. I been at sea a long time and marooned on a desert island. I'm ready for a real woman. A mate of mine told me about a cathouse down in Chinatown," he added in a slyly conspiratorial tone. "Y'know, after once the police get here."

"You were marooned for how long? A few days?"

"I wrote a poem for her." The cowboy lit a cigar stub he had found on the dock. "'On the sea is a memory of dreams that have gone. Of oceans of sorrow and fathoms of fair hair.' What do you think?"

"Seems a little personal."

"I think she kinda likes me too," he added. "Something in the way she comes in real close to talk to you, y'know?"

"Well, since you shot up the *Star of Baltimore* we'll never know, will we?"

"I could say the same about you cracking up her boat, pard."

"None of that would have happened if you'd stayed on it."

Driftwood was relieved to hear automobile tires rumbling along the planks of the dock. "I think the cavalry's arrived."

He walked to the wreckage of the gangplank, leaving the cowboy at the stern.

"The cops sure do drive nice cars up here, don't they?" the cowboy called to him.

The sedan was one of the most elegant cars Driftwood had ever seen. As it stopped, five men climbed out and stood upon the dock.

"There's good news," the cowboy said. "Somebody sent in the marines."

"That's U.S. Army," Driftwood said, feeling his old friend, that sinking feeling, clutch at him. "And that *ain't* good news."

The other men drew their sidearms. The last man out of the car was an officer; Driftwood recognized authority when he saw it, even when it wore a non-issue overcoat. The man wore his silver hair in a crew cut. His skin was nearly brown from years spent in tropical climes. He picked up a piece of paper and crumpled it. He flipped his head up, his gunmetal eyes blazing at them from under his furrowed eyebrows. In an instant Driftwood realized that he knew exactly what the man's voice would sound like. He had heard it over the radio of the *Albatross* less than an hour ago.

"Run!" he shouted at the cowboy.

The cowboy had good preservation instincts. Not needing further prompting, he dashed down the deck. Driftwood last saw him scurry into an exhaust vent. He swiveled his head around. The crashed crane on the deck made it impossible to advance to the bow. Driftwood turned and saw the hold behind him. The only way out was in. He leapt into the opening, landed on a crate, and using the crate and drums as steps down, he moved quickly to the floor of the hold.

Trying to ignore the disturbing sight of the contorted dead men on the floor, he scanned the four walls looking for an exit. A metal water-tight door was set into the wall opposite his position. Far away. He heard the soldiers clambering up the cargo net. Damn, he thought, damn me for not pulling that up when I had the chance. He snatched up a fire axe. It gave him a momentary sense of power which faded into futility when he realized how useless it actually was. The soldiers had guns.

He sprinted across the floor hoping to reach the hatch door, leaping over the corpses, feeling vulnerable and exposed to the great sky above. He reached the door and threw back the metal bar which held it fast. The room was dimly illuminated by a thin beam of light from the win-dow in the hatch of the far end of the room which seemed to lead to a corridor. He took a step into the room, then saw something that chilled his blood. He forgot all about the armed soldiers above and froze in-stantly.

Not all the Chinese sailors had been killed when the bullet punc-tured the drum. A handful of them had made it this far and managed to swing the door shut behind them. But they had been just a little too slow. One of them swung its head around to look at him now. The skin of its face had pooled around its jaw like melted wax from a candle, pulling clumps of matted hair down along with it. Drool mixed with blood foamed from its toothless maw. They must have been hit with a liquid burst of the chemical before it became a gas.

With a guttural howl, the creature threw itself at him, while the others, alerted to his presence, followed on its heels. He stumbled back into the hold, swinging the door shut as he did so. He threw the fas-tening bolt. He felt the creature slam into the door and saw its enraged face through the glass as it tried to gnaw its way through the porthole.

Homicidal soldiers on deck and slavering monsters below. Scylla or

Charybdis, he thought. The lady or the tiger. Okay, put a plan together. I could . . .

"Down below! Hold it right there! Don't move or I'll shoot."

One of the soldiers had Driftwood in his sights. Without hesitating Driftwood raised the axe over his head. The nadir of its trajectory was the top of a one of the barrels. "Anyone moves and I'll split one of these eggs wide open!" he shouted. "Have you seen what this shit can do? Look around. You won't have time to piss yourselves."

"Hold your fire!"

"Hey, son? " He heard another voice. It was kind and fatherly and concerned. "Hey! Can you hear me?"

"Yes," he replied. He kept his arms raised and tense and his eyes focused on the drum.

"My name is Colonel Towers," the voice continued.

"I know who you are."

"No one needs to get hurt here."

"I couldn't agree more."

"Why don't you tell me what happened here."

"Well, Colonel, it all started when I followed a white rabbit down this hole."

"That's very funny," said the colonel.

"Yes, sir. It just keeps getting curiouser and curiouser."

"Your arms getting tired there, friend?"

"No, sir. I could do this all day."

"I'm sure it won't come to that. I can tell by the way you call me 'sir' that you've seen service duty. What branch?"

"I'm part of the Fredonia Freedom Fighters."

"We're not going to get very far if you don't start cooperating."

"I don't really feel the need for cooperating, Colonel. I just want to get out of this alive."

"All right, then. Now we've found something we both want. I'll let you off this boat if you just step away and let me have my cargo."

"Can't do that, sir."

"Why not, friend?"

"Driftwood. Otis P. Driftwood. Lieutenant Driftwood."

"Okay. Why not, Lieutenant Driftwood?"

He could feel sweat trickling down the back of his neck and his palms were getting slick. He was back in the silver mine again. Only this time there was no cover and the man with the gun knew where he was. "Because we both know that this gunk is supremely deadly and we wouldn't want it to fall into the wrong hands."

"Lieutenant Driftwood, those barrels were forgotten about when you were still in short pants in whatever backwater you come from."

"So it's okay to give 'em to the Chinese to use against the Japanese?"

"This weapon will end a conflict and save tens of thousands of lives."

"Or it could escalate that conflict and cost hundreds of thousands more. Only not just soldiers. Innocent women and children. Either way, if these canisters are opened, more people die. If I can stop you from letting that happen, I will." He heard footsteps clattering on the other side of the wall and realized that the colonel had sent men into the ship. They would reach the outer hold door soon.

The colonel, stalling for time, sat down on the edge of the crane. "I first heard about this chemical more than a dozen years ago from one of its creators, an old officer much like myself who felt like confessing. I assured him of his absolution. In spite of what he told me, it was incredibly difficult to find. No one seemed to know where it had wound up. If I could have pursued it full-time, then I might have found it in half the time. As you can see, I've got a job.

"But I kept coming back to it. Found a journal notation here. A chart there. But no antidote. Never an antidote. So once I found it, even though I knew where it was, I had to wait and see if an antidote could be developed. I got so damn close, but that asshole Jeffords up in Providence could fuck up a free lunch! You know one of his morons actually burnt the antidote?"

"Guess you can't use it, right? So we can all go home, right?"

Towers barked a short, cruel laugh. "Hell no! I was thinking about it all wrong. I just decided I didn't need an antidote after all. First we are gonna use it against the Japanese. And then we're gonna use it against the renegade Chinese to bring them in line. And if a few Chinese soldiers get killed in the cross fire, who's gonna even care what happens on that side of the world? They've got scientists in China too. They can figure this stuff out. Make more of it. I can see us sailing into Tokyo Bay with a shipload of this stuff and conquering Japan without firing a shot. Who knows after that?"

"Russia's just a steppe away."

Towers laughed. "But I'm not a warmonger. I want peace. It's going to be hard to enjoy a vast fortune if I'm constantly at war."

Driftwood shifted his weight.

"The police aren't going to show up to save you, you know. No matter what happens out here, my connections will keep them from showing up. I pulled in all my favors. Dug up all my best threats. Looks like you pulled a very long watch. Bet you'd like a cigarette?"

"Yeah. I'm dyin' for one. What happens to you if this goes up in smoke, Colonel? What's the army going to do to you when they find out about this?"

"There's still time to put all this right," was the reply. "This ship will sail. It may not be carrying as much money as we had hoped. But it will still tip the entire balance of power in the Pacific. In my favor."

Driftwood heard a clang from beyond the door and then there were screams, and a single shot was fired.

"What's that?" Colonel Towers asked. "What's going on?" His confident tone wavered.

"Your boys just met some more of your boys," Driftwood said. "You should be very proud. It's a family reunion."

The shrill scream of a man in terror penetrated thinly through the heavy door. A spurt of crimson blood jetted thickly across the porthole glass. Then the sounds stopped.

Towers raised his gun and clicked back the hammer. "Okay, Groucho, I've had enough of you."

"The name's Driftwood."

"And I saw *A Night at the Opera* too!"

311

"Yeah? Remember the scene where Margaret Dumont falls off the patio into the pool?"

"No."

"Too bad. Because you might have remembered that she didn't fall, she was pushed."

The colonel's flat expression registered a touch of exasperation as he made certain of his aim. That was the look that Driftwood never forgot, the way he remembered Towers forever, because the man's expression never changed even as the cowboy broke a wooden plank across his back. The pistol dribbled from his fingers and he took a step forward, then stumbled over the edge, his body twisting as he fell. He crashed heavily onto the crates above Driftwood's head. The sound of the impact was so sickening that Driftwood was actually surprised when he heard the man begin to groan.

Driftwood lowered his aching arms. "Jesus Christ! Am I glad to see you."

"Yeah." The cowboy grinned as he threw down a rope. "I figured you'd be dead by now."

The bitter end of the rope fell in front of Driftwood. The muscles in his arms screamed as he picked it up. "My arms are kind of deadwood."

Towers continued to moan.

"Wrap it around your forearms and I'll pull you up."

Driftwood listened and watched, feeling helpless, as Lew dragged a block and tackle across the deck and hung it from a twisted piece of the crane wreckage. He began to loop the rope through the pulley.

Driftwood looked down from the figure of the cowboy to see Colonel Towers scrambling over the edge of the crates toward him, his face a moist, shapeless, bloody mess. Except for the eyes. The eyes were gleaming with fury and murder. The colonel skidded down the stack of crates, the rough wood edges tearing cloth and flesh from his body.

The rope still felt slack. Behind him Driftwood heard the pounding on the hold door suddenly increase as if the creatures on the other side had suddenly grown more frantic.

Somehow Towers landed on his feet on the floor of the hold, and staggered with clumsy determination toward Driftwood, what was left of his teeth now gritted and showing as his lips peeled back. He raised his hands toward Driftwood not as if he were going to punch him, but as if he were going to claw him apart, rip his throat and his eyes out, dig out his heart and his bowels.

"Damn me," Driftwood muttered to himself.

His arms were yanked up abruptly, and the pain snapped through his body with the force of a whip. His feet were leaving the ground. He felt the rush of air as Towers leaped for him and missed, and then he was several feet above the colonel and still levitating. A look of desperate frustration snarled across Towers's face, and Driftwood knew that this man would never stop coming for him. His eyes never leaving Driftwood's, Towers put his hand on the hold latch. Driftwood could hear nothing on the other side.

"I wouldn't," he cautioned Towers.

"I'll meet you on deck," the man snarled back. The latch slammed back and he threw open the door.

Driftwood caught a glimpse of the room beyond the hatch, gore and viscera as in a butcher's shop. He would never eat a rare steak again. He saw Towers freeze in the doorway. Then the colonel turned and ran back into the hold. Driftwood watched him scramble madly upon a pallet of gas-filled barrels in the center of the hold. His quick glimpse of a rush of creatures slithering and mashing their way into the hold was suddenly obliterated by the brilliant sunlight as his head was raised above the level of the hold.

Driftwood grabbed at the deck and Lew helped him roll over onto his back. He lay on the deck, breathing deeply. The warm sun was shining on his face and he could hear seagulls crying in the air. The sea air smelled delicious. The pain was receding from his arms and he was alive. He began to chuckle, helplessly.

"What is it?" the cowboy asked. "Why are you laughin'? Damn it! What's so funny, Otis?"

"Bob!" He shouted into the cool morning air, "My name's Bob! I'm Bob again. Bob. Bob. Bob!" Then the laughter came on again and it all seemed so sublimely ridiculous. He couldn't stop laughing or saying his name; to say it now seemed so simple and so funny. *Bob.* It was the funniest sound in the universe. In a little while, the sheer giddiness of it left him and he was able to speak again. "It feels so good just to hear my own name again after so many months of lying about it. Bob. My name's Bob Heinlein, Lew."

"Pleased to meet ya, Bob."

"Yeah. Yeah. Likewise." The deck metal felt cool against his back. It felt good. Everything felt good again. "I didn't think I was gonna get out of that hole alive. I feel like I've been in that hole a very long time."

The cowboy nodded.

Heinlein sat up, slowly. "I don't think I've ever felt so good in all my life." He smiled and drank in the feeling. "There's only one thing that could make me feel any better, y'know?"

"A woman." The cowboy nodded again.

"Or two." He closed his eyes and tried to imagine it.

"Well, Bob. There was that little place down in Chinatown I was mentioning earlier."

He opened his eyes. "What about him?" The sounds of Towers trying to kick the creatures off the barrels had reached his ears. He thought about looking into the pit to see what exactly was happening, but he knew he didn't need to see exactly what was happening. The creatures would be swiping at Towers like lions in a zoo trying to pull a carcass from a meat hook.

"I reckon he might have other things on his mind than a few loose women."

"Throw me a rope," they heard him scream.

"Sorry, Colonel," Driftwood said, as he rose to his feet, in a voice far too low for the colonel to hear. "I think your ship has finally sailed."

Towers began to scream as the two men climbed down the cargo netting. By the time they reached what was left of the dock, the screams had turned to distant gurgles. And as they gingerly picked their way across the wrecked boards to safety, silence fell upon the *Star of Baltimore*.

EPISODE FORTY-THREE

"THERE WAS death afoot in the darkness.

"The eerie fog still gripped Chinatown and the red flag of war still flew from the top of the highest building. And while the cops and the On Leong tong had placed men all around the old hotel to protect Ah Hoon, what they forgot to watch was the rooftops," Lester Dent told Walter Gibson. "Two Hip Sing men made their way furtively across the roofs, from one building to another. They stayed low because the fireworks were illuminating the sky and they didn't want to be caught in the glare.

"Their meticulous trip took them several hours and it was early in the morning when they finally arrived at the building next door to the old hotel, the one with the windowless wall. Seven floors below them, on the opposite side of the gap, Ah Hoon sweated out the night. They had carried an old wooden chair with them and when they reached the building's ledge, they tied some rope around it. Then one of the men tied the other man into the chair. He looped the rope around the chimney and lowered him down the wall.

"Remember, there was only about a three-foot gap between the buildings, and a lethal abyss waited below, so the man in the chair had one helluva lousy ride. When he finally reached the level of the window, he pulled out a rifle that he had carried with him and rested the barrel on the windowsill so that that the bullet wouldn't shatter the glass. The little comic must have heard that small sound, that frightening tap. He sat up in his bed and slowly looked to the window. His eyes met those of the man dangling beyond the glass and he recognized his assassin. What he saw was Mock Duck, bound to a chair and dangling precariously outside his window like a side of Peking pork ribs in the window of a Chinese chop suey shop. Ah Hoon knew that Death had found him, but the sight of his once-feared antagonist's face covered with flop sweat and glowing red from the tightness of the ropes, his clothes torn from the bouncing scrapes against the walls and his eyes wild from the terrors of the descent, was too much for the comedian. He showed his approval for the comedic efforts on his behalf the only way he knew how. He began to laugh.

"As Ah Hoon broke into his first peal of laughter an enormous sky-rocket exploded overhead. The blast from its charge rattled the windows of buildings for blocks and its glittering flames drew all eyes. Under the cover of its storm and stress, Mock Duck pulled the trigger. The look of astonishment the police found on Ah Hoon's face the next morning was the look of a man who found his own death ridiculously funny. Which is an appropriate epitaph for a comic.

"That one shot was all it took to end the reign of the On Leong tong and bring victory to the Hip Sing. The On Leong were crushed, demoralized. That one shot ended the Sweet Flower War and signaled the ascendancy of the Hip Sing. By noon of that day, as the menacing mist dissipated, the flag of war was lowered, and to this day it has never flown over Chinatown again.

"And that," Kenneth Robeson told Maxwell Grant, "is the story as I got it direct from the horse's or, in this case, the Duck's mouth."

Even as he sat across the dining room table from Lester Dent, Walter Gibson could feel his body craving opium. The coughing fits were killing his chest, and his throat was raw. He didn't want to worry them, especially Litzka, but he was struggling to keep his words from slurring and his hands from shaking. Every time he closed his eyes he instantly envisioned the gas roiling up at him. Still, his mind felt more alert than it had in months, and he had the sensation that a weight had been lifted from his shoulders.

Smith's wife had informed them that the writer had already left but that he breakfasted every morning at a coffee shop in the vicinity of his doughnut laboratory—in order, she said, to see what doughnuts people favored. Hubbard had been dispatched to scour the area. While they waited for him to call, the conversation had turned to writing. Walter actually found it pleasant to have a conversation with Lester Dent. Dent was the only other writer in the pulp game who could understand the kind of pressure Gibson operated under.

"How much do you hate not being able to use your own name on *Doc?*" Gibson asked.

"Almost as much as I hate not being paid a percentage of the sales. John Nanovic showed me a list of house names to choose from and said take it or leave it. I picked Kenneth Robeson because it sounded rugged and adventurous, yet vaguely cosmopolitan," Lester told him. "What about you?"

"I came up with Maxwell Grant from two friends of mine. One was Maxwell Holden, who had just retired from vaudeville to open a magic shop in New York. He had a hand shadow act in which he formed life-size silhouettes that moved across a screen. My other friend was U. F. Grant, of Pittsfield, Massachusetts, who invented an illusion used by the Great Blackstone in which he walks away from his own shadow, leaving it behind in full view.

"Since these were both devices that I intended to attribute to The Shadow in his role as an avenger, I felt that the pen name of Maxwell Grant would be appropriate, so I appropriated it." He sipped his coffee.

"There's something I've been wanting to ask you," Dent said. "Why did you mess with success?"

"Hmm?"

"The Allard thing? Why mess with your formula?"

Gibson thought for a moment. He hadn't been able to answer the question for Welles or Rozen. He looked at his fingers. "I wanted to try and find out who The Shadow really was," he said at last.

Dent leaned in. "And?"

"Only The Shadow knows."

Norma came out of Gibson's bedroom, having changed into the clothes Lester had brought from the boat: a brown skirt with a cream-colored blouse. She had refreshed herself with a shower. Gibson appraised her quickly, hoping her husband wasn't watching him. Old Lester had done all right for himself, that much was for sure.

He heard a cough. Litzka was curled up on the sofa reading Hubbard's *Post*. He saw her eyes flit from him to Norma. "Feeling better?"

"Much. Anything in the paper?"

"Nothing about the Bank Note building. Nothing on the radio either. You'd think something like that would at least be on the radio."

"Towers," said Gibson, simply. The two women agreed.

"*Avenger*," murmured Dent. "Now that's a good word. Avenger. *The Avenger*. I've been thinking of a new character who is a master of disguise, which is my favorite pulp trick. I have this image of this gray face, stone gray, like a dead man's. Instead of using makeup, he'd actually be able to mold his face to look like the person he wanted to impersonate. And the only way his villains would know he wasn't who they thought he was is that he is incapable of showing emotions."

"As if the nerves of his face didn't work?"

"Exactly. Because maybe some bad guy did something to him to make him that way. Only he can't keep up the disguise for very long. Just long enough to get into trouble or penetrate a group and find out evil plans. Everything else he'd have to handle with other skills. And his role would be a kind of an avenger for those who have nowhere else to turn."

"That sounds like a character Street & Smith could get behind. You should talk to Nanovic."

"Who knows?" Lester shrugged the suggestion off. "There just never seems to be enough time to write everything that needs to be written. I mean, sure, I could write *The Avenger.* But if I'm writing that, then I'm not writing something meaningful. Something great."

"*Doc Savage* is great pulp. You shouldn't put yourself down."

"Yeah, but it's not important."

"To who? To a bunch of ivory-tower longhairs? To the fellas that run the slicks? To hell with them and the horses they rode in on! I read *Doc Savage.* It's obvious how much you love writing it. You shouldn't be embarrassed about it."

"You read *Doc Savage?*"

"Of course I do. The only way to stay number one is to know what number two is doing."

"Yeah. I feel the same way about *The Shadow.*"

Gibson smiled at him. Dent pulled out his pipe and his tobacco pouch. When he unzipped the pouch, water sloshed out of it and onto the coffee table. "Damn! Sorry."

"Don't worry about it. In case you haven't noticed, the contents of this apartment include a chicken. A little water's not going to hurt anything."

"I don't suppose you have any pipe tobacco?"

"No. Just cigarettes."

Dent shook his head. "I'm a pipe man."

"Well, there's a smoke shop about five blocks down on the west side of the street. They should open in about fifteen minutes."

After Dent left, Litzka helped Gibson drink a little more Bromo Seltzer; it soothed his headache. "You know, that's the longest conversation I've ever had with Lester."

"Well, he's not much of a talker around people he doesn't know very well," Norma said, sitting down and picking up Lester's unfinished coffee. Litzka flipped to the theater section. "He didn't grow up around people, and they can make him nervous."

"What do you mean, 'he didn't grow up around people'?"

"He had a lonely life growing up. I can't imagine a lonelier life for a little boy and it makes my heart ache.

"Sometimes I see it in his eyes when he doesn't know I'm watching him, that faraway look like he's back out there in the middle of nowhere, alone and friendless and looking over the horizon and wondering if he'll ever escape there. It's one of the reasons he loves New York City so much; he likes to be surrounded by people. He likes the constant noise and the commotion and the sense that he can't ever really be alone here, no matter what."

"My family was a part of Philadelphia society," Gibson said. "There were always parties to go to and people around."

"But you looked at the horizon too," she said, "or you wouldn't be here doing what you're doing."

He nodded. "I guess you're right."

"What do you think Zhang Mei's going to do with the gas?"

"I have no idea."

"You said there was one drum of gas left on the truck that was never put aboard the ship. What do you think he'll do with it?"

"Like I said, I don't know."

"You spent all that time with him writing about him. Think about him as if he's one of your characters."

"My characters aren't usually that deep."

"Maybe he's not either. Maybe you just wrote him that way. What would he be after if he were your character?"

"Revenge. He'd seek revenge. If he couldn't strike back at the Japanese, he'd try to find a way to strike back at Mi-Ying. But he's ten thousand miles away back in China. It'd be just as hard to get back at him as it would be to get back at the Japanese. But that's what I'd have my character do, anyway."

"Ming!" Litzka suddenly interrupted, looking up in surprise from the *Post*.

"What?" Gibson asked.

"Ming, right? You said Ming?"

"Mi-Ying."

"That's what I said," she snapped. She flipped back a few pages and then held out the newspaper. "The New York Chinese consul general's name is Mi-Ying."

Gibson scanned the small article. He smacked his forehead the way Norma had seen Lester do time and time again. He put the paper on the table. She could see one man whom the paper identified as General Chiang Kai-shek standing next to another man, Mi-Ying. "This is the same photo on the poster that Zhang Mei showed me. That's why he said he would be celebrating with his brothers. If Mi-Ying is going to be there, Zhang Mei will be there as well."

"Revenge?" Norma asked.

"Revenge," he nodded. "He doesn't care about anyone in Chinatown. Barely thinks they're real people, let alone real Chinese. If he has to open that drum of gas to get his revenge, he'll do it. But he'll want to see Mi-Ying's face when he dies."

"What happens to Chinatown if he lets the gas out?" Litzka nervously toyed with China Boy's feathers.

"Oh, my God!" Norma stood up. "Mr. Yee will be there. He's throwing a banquet for his Hip Sing Association. And he'll have Monk and Ham with him."

"Who's that?" Litzka asked.

"Friends. Children. My dumplings."

Norma grabbed the telephone but the operator was unable to connect her with Mr. Yee's restaurant or anyone who spoke English at the Hip Sing Association, and the police were lazily indifferent to her warning about a gas attack in Chinatown. "I'm going down there," she said resolutely, hanging up. "I have to warn them."

"Why don't you wait for Lester?" Gibson said to her.

"I'll be all right," she said. "I'll be back before he is."

"Let me get dressed," he insisted. "I'll come with you." He heard his front door close as soon as he left the room.

The elevator took forever to work its way back up to his hallway. The building was coming to life in the morning and people got on at almost every floor. Finally it opened on the lobby and he got out. He rushed outside and saw Lester Dent sauntering down the sidewalk, puffing contentedly on his pipe.

"Hey." Lester grinned at him. "What are you doing up?"

Quickly Gibson filled him in. Dent's face clouded over and he threw his pipe aside. A family wagon was pulling away from the curb and Gibson watched in astonishment as Dent sprang upon its running board as he had had Doc Savage do a hundred times over. The little boy in the back seat looked through the window at him in naked amazement.

"Chinatown!" Dent loudly commanded and the driver complied by hitting the accelerator like Barney Oldfield. The momentum was too much for Dent. He was flung from the car and landed in a sprawling heap in the middle of the road. Amused, Gibson ran to help him up as the car rounded the corner and disappeared from view, presumably still heading toward Chinatown.

"Okay," he said, helping Dent up. "Looks like you found another thing that only happens in the pulps."

EPISODE FORTY-FOUR

THE WALL of noise was deafening.

"A Chinese festival can last for days!" Dent shouted to Gibson over the furious storm of firecrackers. "Not like American parades at all!"

"I've been to Chinatown before, Dent!"

The festival had started at dawn; streets were closed to traffic and the cabbie had been forced to let them off at Grand Street. The day was warming quickly. The sidewalks were thronged with revelers. In the streets, two-man lion dancers from one association squared off against a longer, dozen-man dragon costume from another, while men bearing wooden drums hung from straps on their necks beat the tempo. Bottle rockets blasted into the sky and exploded over their heads. Men waved boards plastered with solemn photos of General Chiang Kai-shek, and children shouted Chinese chants of solidarity with their brothers back home. Exotic aromas from a hundred kitchens filled the air like a haze.

The gate was still down at Mr. Yee's restaurant and no amount of pounding seemed to rouse anyone from within. An old woman suddenly appeared by Lester's side. He looked down into her wrinkled face. She spoke to him but he didn't understand. Then she pointed away down toward Mott Street and Hip Sing territory. Lester grimly noted that the woman had no fingers on either hand; she gestured with a scarred knuckle-stub while she yammered urgently in Chinese.

They forced their way up the sidewalk toward the Hip Sing Association building. Lester plowed through the mass of people; his sheer bulk relative to the smaller people all around him made his progress almost unstoppable. At the same time he had never felt so powerless. He kept looking for that glint of golden hair which would be Norma, but there were no blondes on the streets of Chinatown today.

Gibson was out of breath. His face was gray and sweat poured profusely down it. He kept pace without complaining, but Dent had seen him stagger loosely once or twice as he was clipped by the elbows or shoulders of bystanders.

"You okay?" Dent asked at one point.

Gibson nodded. But he knew what the staggers meant. Exposure to that shit.

They entered the Hip Sing Association building. The men inside were formally dressed in suits or traditional Chinese silk robes. Dent recognized a man as one of those who had attended his induction and he rushed to him. The man's English was poor but Dent pantomimed and stressed the names he wanted to communicate. Was Mr. Yee here? No. Had a woman come by to find him? Yes. Where had she gone? The man smiled but could only shrug, helpless.

Suddenly something was tugging at Dent's pants and he heard a voice squeaking, "Mr. Doc! Mr. Doc!"

He looked down and there was little Ham. Monk came running up to join them.

"Hey, boys! Where's your father?"

"He's shopping," said Monk. "Mrs. Doc was here," he added as a matter of fact.

"She was. Was she with your father?"

Ham shook his head. "No. But she was looking for him. We told her that he was coming back. Then she told us not to go anywhere and she left."

"Where did she go?"

The two boys took a sullen, silent stance. They had done something wrong.

"You didn't stay here, did you?"

Ham nodded as the confession was pried out of him.

"Did you follow her?"

The little boy nodded again.

"Where did she go?"

Ham looked to his older brother. "She went to the old theater," Ham said, guiltily, at last. "She tried to go inside. But some big men came out instead and took her."

"Damn."

"You know where she went?" Gibson wanted to know.

Lester turned to Gibson. "Her and her goddamned treasure. And I'm the one who's supposed to give up adventures?" He turned to the dumplings. "Boys, this time I'm very serious. I want you to stay here. Tell your father where I went. I promise you, you won't get in trouble." He looked at Walter. "Coming?"

"Hell yes!"

They left the worried boys behind and forged back into the confusing mass before Gibson was fully able to catch his breath. They pushed their way to Doyers Street, which, being off the parade route, was not in as much turmoil. Lester burst into a sprint and arrived at the front door of the theater. He threw his weight against the heavy boards but they wouldn't budge. He turned to call for help from Gibson.

Gibson was standing, helplessly, at the head of the alley. He seemed forlorn. "There's another way in," he said, flatly. Lester joined him and they looked down the long, dark alley. A red lantern hung over a door at the end of the pathway.

The opium den was dark and appeared abandoned as they entered. "This is the place?" Lester asked Gibson.

He nodded. "Yeah. This is the place."

There was a soft rattle from the darkness; it was the gentle sound of beaded curtains being moved. Dent's eyes fell upon three men who stood in the shadows. Dent was positive they hadn't been there the moment before. It was if he had simply blinked, and in the instant in which his eyes were closed, they had appeared out of thin air. Each held a long sliver of curled steel. One of the men hissed at him through clenched teeth. Dent recognized him. It was the man he had knocked to the street during the last trip to Chinatown. The glare in his eyes showed that he was ready to settle the score. He hissed at Dent again.

Dent suddenly found himself wishing he had brought the gun from the *Albatross.* Even empty it might have menaced his attacker. For all his close scrapes he had never been much of a fistfighter and he knew his chances against this knife-wielding fiend were low. His eyes swept around for something, anything, which could be used as a weapon. But the flimsy opium pipes lying near the abandoned daises were the only possible objects at hand. The man made a threatening gesture at him. Then he grinned maliciously and raised his knife.

Walter Gibson suddenly stepped forward, in front of Dent, and held out his hands, palms toward the men. A brilliant burst of fire seemed to explode in the air just before his fingertips. The lethal attacker staggered back, blinded. The other two men drew back. Gibson thrust his hands forward again and another fireball exploded in the room, closer to them. Sparks showered upon the man who had threatened to attack Dent, and curls of flame appeared on his shirt. He dropped his knife and began pounding at them with the palms of his hands even as they spread.

"Go!" Gibson shouted at Dent. With a nod of his head he indicated the staircase to Dent's left. Dent raced up. He heard another *whoosh* and felt the heat of another one of Gibson's miraculous fire bursts. He heard a man screaming. He hoped it wasn't Walter. Then he was at the top of the staircase and entering the back of the theater.

Spots caused by the bursts of flame danced before his eyes. It took him a few moments to clear his vision and scan the stage, which was barren except for fallen bolts of aged stage cloth and the spiderweb tangles of theatrical rope which swooped up and down through the rigging. His eyes fell on one of the bundles and he realized in a moment of pure horror that it wasn't a pile of velvet. It was his wife.

She was motionless. He fell to her side. Her arms were raised over her head and a rope bound them together at the wrists. The taut rope ascended into the rafters.

"Norma?"

Her chest rose and fell but he couldn't rouse her. He patted her cheeks but there was no reaction. He felt panic rise up in him. He slipped a hand under her head and felt something warm and wet. He pulled his hand away and stared dumbly at the blood. He felt again; the lump at the base of her skull felt as large as an egg to him. Somebody had clobbered her good.

He smelled smoke and looked back; it was billowing out from the wings. He struggled with the knot but the rope was thick and the knot was fiendish. He looked around for something to cut it, but the stage was devoid of anything that could be used. He tried tugging at it, but it was fastened securely up above. He tried again with the knot; he couldn't even begin to figure out where the end was. Her wrists were chafed and scraped and her fingertips were pale blue. He pulled on the rope as hard as he could.

"You're just making it tighter."

Gibson was at Dent's side. He was breathing heavily but his eyes blazed with excitement. He squatted beside her and his fingers flew over the knots like the wings of a dove. Dent sat back on his haunches and felt her wrist; her pulse was weak and fluttery. Smoke was filling the theater.

"I think I set the place on fire," Gibson muttered.

"I don't think anyone'll care."

Suddenly the ropes fell in loose coils from her wrists and Gibson sat back with a triumphant gleam on his face. "*The Complete Guide to Knots and How to Tie Them* by Walter B. Gibson. It's still in print. You should pick up a copy."

"I will." Dent scooped Norma up. Her body was amazingly light and frighteningly limp. "Her treasure's gone," he said.

"You're right," Gibson sounded surprised. "There was a statue here yesterday."

Dent turned to the wings and the staircase, but smoke poured out of the staircase as though it were a chimney. He heard a metallic clank on the stairs and the warrior with the busted jaw stepped out of the smoke. He had ripped off his jacket and shirt. Dent and Gibson could see the fresh burns on his torso. He let an object fall to the floor. Lester recognized the metal tip of the whip chain as it hit the boards with a heavy thud.

"Any more magic tricks up your sleeves?" Dent said.

"What do you want, a grand finale?" Gibson asked.

"Got one?"

"I might."

The man unfurled the long coils of chain, slowly dragging their length through his hands. He sneered at Dent and Gibson, a desperate, enraged expression.

Dent heard a loud crash from the middle of the auditorium. A section of wood floor exploded back in a cloud of dust. The building's collapsing, he thought. An instant later a familiar face and shoulders appeared in the new hole in the floor, emerging from the dust cloud the trapdoor had stirred up like a genie rising from a bottle.

"Yee!" Dent shouted.

"This way!" Yee replied urgently. "Chinatown tunnels!"

Dent turned back to Gibson, who had bravely stepped between him and the chain-wielding man. Gibson nodded at him.

Dent said, "I'll meet you at the Hip Sing building."

"Don't be late."

"I've never missed a deadline in my life."

Dent took the small flight of side steps down to the house floor. He gently lowered Norma down to the arms of Mr. Yee, who vanished with her into the dark tunnel. The dry boards of the stage burst into flames and any path back to Gibson was cut off. Dent jumped into the passageway.

Lester made his way through the darkness following the bobbing flame he could see ahead of him in the distance. The air was fetid and the smell of smoke followed him. His feet splashed through dank, cold water that smelled of street refuse. He had to keep his head low; he found this out after running heavily into a low rafter. Above him he heard the thudding sound of the celebration as he traveled along. Periodically he would hear an encouraging shout from Mr. Yee, which kept him from choosing the wrong way at any number of intersections which cropped up along the way.

In time he saw a ladder at the end of the tunnel, rushing toward him as he ran. The hatch above it was open and light poured down in a distinct shaft. He scrambled up the steps and found himself suddenly surrounded by helpful hands and concerned Chinese faces. He felt little bodies embracing him.

"Thanks, boys," he said to the dumplings, giving Ham a reassuring hug. He was in the basement of the Hip Sing Association building.

Norma lay on the floor, still comatose, as he disentangled himself from the two boys. "She's been hit in the head," he said to Mr. Yee. "She needs a doctor."

"Follow me," his friend said.

Lester gently hoisted her up again and followed Mr. Yee up the flights of stairs to the joss house. The room was full of men, Dent noted at once. They stood at the windows watching the parade pass below them. The room was elegantly and elaborately decorated for the celebration, with red and gold banners and money gathered by the good people of Chinatown and prepared in chests to be delivered to the Chinese consulate. Mock Duck sat in a carved wooden chair and another distinguished man sat in a chair next to him. This man was being subserviently tended to by the man Mock Duck had been having dinner with the night Lester and Norma had come to the restaurant from the theater.

Mr. Yee quietly pulled a man from the crowd at the window. The man came to Dent and examined Norma's head. He clucked his tongue in worry and then he indicated that Dent should carry her body to a room hidden behind a sliding screen.

They laid her out on a small table and gently rolled her on her side. The man examined her more closely. He took a silk cloth and folded it a number of times and then placed it against her head. It instantly began turning red with blood. He placed Dent's hand on the cloth and indicated the severe amount of pressure he wanted him to apply. Then he turned and picked up a collection of small needles which lay on a red pillow. As he transferred the collection to the table he spoke to Mr. Yee.

Mr. Yee placed a comforting hand on Dent's arm. "He wants you to know there is much blood flowing to this injury which may be swelling the brain. He is going to try to decrease the swelling and slow the blood. He wants to know if you understand about Chinese medicine and acupuncture."

"A little. I've read about it. But I've never seen it."

"He says we must get started right away. The needles will not hurt her. He is a very good healer. He is the very best in America. Can you trust his skill?"

Lester thought for a moment of trying to carry Norma through Chinatown to find a hospital. There would be blocks and blocks filled with people. No ambulance could possibly get through in time. "You are my Hip Sing brother," Lester Dent said at last. "I can trust this man's skill if you say I should."

Mr. Yee gave a single nod to the healer. Then he pulled Lester aside so the man could work. The dumplings circulated around their knees, nervously. Dent rubbed Ham's hair.

"Yee?" he asked. "Who's that man by your uncle. The VIP?"

"Him? He is an important diplomat. He is the consul general. His name is Mi-Ying."

Episode Forty-Five

THE WHIRLING chain of death was mesmerizing.

The warrior spun it around with such force that it fanned away the smoke attempting to engulf him. Yet Gibson was amazed at how conservative his motions were; there was no waste of energy as he methodically built up the speed of the tip and plotted its trajectory toward Gibson's heart. This was going to be a kill that he wanted to savor.

The floorboards beneath Gibson's feet groaned as he took several wary steps back; the supports beneath them were being devoured by the growing conflagration in the den below. The man with the chain calmly adjusted his position. Gibson knew he was being toyed with. He could feel the temperature rising in the room. Glowing embers drifted up between the cracks and gaps of the planks. The whole world was going up in flames. The stage floor threatened to crack open beneath him; hell awaited below.

He shook his hands to unhinge the magical apparatus he had spent the train ride from Providence working on. From his left hand fell the squeezable pouch of flash powder, now empty. Attached to his other wrist was a modified mousetrap; the mechanism was turned on its side and reattached to a metal cuff; flint and rock were fastened to the striking mechanism. It took only a quick flick from the left hand to reset it while the audience's vision was still bedazzled and distracted by the previous explosion. Now the contraption seemed stuck to him. Maybe his sweat had glued it to his skin. He wondered what Blackstone would say about how his magic had been put to use. He would probably say something like "Rest in peace, Walter Gibson."

He coughed, and the metal spike whizzed past his moving head, tearing through a muslin flat depicting a mountain of rice paddy terraces. The blackest smoke seeped up from below and as the killer yanked back on his chain, pulling the spike free, the room grew dark, the only light coming up in thin shafts from below. Terrific, Gibson thought, now I can't even see him.

If I can't see him, he can't see me.

He slipped through the gap the whip chain had just created in the mountains and ducked. The spike punched through the muslin again, above his head, tearing another hole. Gibson heard the man cough; the smoke was growing thicker. He leaped over a row of seats and ran for cover behind the gates of an Imperial palace, a rotting wood frame of forced perspective. He heard the spike bite at the wood of the seats he had just rolled over. The killer had truly lost sight of him. He produced a scarf and held it to his mouth and nose, filtering out as much of the smoke as he could. Floorboards creaked wearily: the man was hunting for him, moving in his direction. Smoke continued to seep up into the room.

Beyond the gates where he now hid, a tattered silk scrim hung loosely from bamboo poles. Dyed upon it were the faded shapes of a court of powerful Chinese gods. The delicate fabric would have seemed nearly invisible when lit from behind. But when lights were focused on it from the front of the stage, it would have become as opaque as a wall and the images of the gods would have magically appeared, startling the audience caught under their watchful, judging gaze. In the dim orange glow of flames and sparks licking up through the stage boards, the gods flickered in and out of existence. Behind the scrim lay the brick wall and beyond it lay the dark shapes of other set pieces. On the other side of those relics was the back of the house where the doors to the street would be.

As quietly as he could while still moving, Gibson slid from behind the palace gate to the scrim, his back against the wall. He moved by inches, his hand still holding the cloth to his face, until he was behind the first deity, a thunder-faced ogre. He tried to relax his heaving chest as Houdini had once shown him. The sensation of being exposed was terrifying to his instincts; he forced himself to suppress the fear. It was one thing to know intellectually that he was concealed; it was another thing to believe it without actually being on the other side to see the proof.

He could see the killer clearly. The man stood only several yards away, fanning away the smoke that clouded his vision. He had coiled his whip chain up around his arm and the spike extended like a fang from his fist. He turned to and fro, wildly searching for a sign of his prey, snarling in near-animal frustration, surrendering to his instincts when Gibson would not.

A shower of sparks burst up through the stage. As the killer spun to look, Gibson slid farther down the wall, taking his place behind a goddess who stood holding the oceans in one hand and a ship in the other. He stifled a cough and the killer, unsure of his ears, swung his head in Gibson's direction. The man's eyes fell upon the scrim as a section of the upstage planks surrendered to the flames devouring it from below in a great crash, flames bursting through in an excited rush to fill its vacuum. The killer, staring right at Gibson, became a silhouette against the flaring light. Gibson held perfectly still, not even breathing lest he stir the silk and destroy the illusion. He looked through the eyes of the goddess, abandoning his visual focus, letting his sight grow soft, seeing it all at once so nothing could surprise him. He felt his flesh become the brick of the wall at his back, flowing out and finding purchase in the infinite crevasses like moss on a rock. He willed his mind to give no indication of its presence and as the light from the burning stage fell upon the scrim, he became invisible, the shadow of the gods.

His killer took several steps closer and cast a skeptical eye on the mural he must be seeing quite clearly on his side. Gibson was so close he could see the man's shaking hands, the tears pouring from his rage-red eyes, the black smoke smudges drawn across his face. The man spat on one of the gods. Evidently some grudges run deeper than others, Gibson thought. As the man moved to the goddess, Gibson could see through her eyes how the man admired in her form the perfection of his race. Gibson forced himself to be cold, to have no emotion about the man, the god, or their communication. With a rending squeal, the stage collapsed completely, and Gibson could feel the tremendous heat from below roil up with volcanic fury. For sure, it filled the stage with enough light to guarantee the illusion the scrim provided. His killer leaned forward to look into the goddess's eyes. Gibson's eyes were an inch away. Slowly his killer leaned in and tenderly kissed the painted mouth of the goddess. His lips were as close to Gibson's as a whisper. As he finally stepped away to take in the spectacle of the destruction of the stage, the inferno from below was raising the final curtain on Death.

The floorboards began to crack in a centerline rift, falling to the left or right, wherever their attachments were strongest. Gibson could see the backdrop of a small rural village being devoured in flames. His killer staggered back as the building shook, then raced to the other side of the room as if he had heard or sighted Gibson there. He struck several times but only succeeded in impaling a weary old wicker man-nequin.

Total clarity came to Gibson. The building would be devoured within minutes: no infant spark could ask for better tinder than what it could find here. The exit lay ahead. With his killer distracted, he ran. The floorboards were shifting, losing solidity, but weirdly seemed more alive and true to their natural origin. As they rattled and clattered against one another, they became strange leaves rustling together on a flat tree, or a windswept field of long grass. He sprinted through a sim-ple family hut, all the furnishings still set around the feasting table through intricate, patient layers of bas-relief paint. He heard a shout behind him and the rattle of chain. He leaped over a train track and knocked a hollow bookcase filled with hollow books out of his way. A cinder fell on his shoulder and he slapped a hand back against the pain. He felt the metal sliding away and realized that the fire he felt wasn't from the flame. The spike had only glanced off him but had flayed his shoulder blade open.

The impact made him stumble. He fell with his back against the wall and slid to his knees.

The whip chain spun again. He held up his forearm to shield his face and the spike drove into it with a stunning impact. The warrior grinned savagely. Gibson returned the grin. The killer gave the chain a tremendous pull with both hands, attempting to rip Gibson's arm out or fling him halfway to him. Gibson's sleeve burst open as if it had exploded. And the metal band which held the fireball device that he hadn't been able to release earlier released because of the spike embedded in the locking mechanism, and it flew back toward his killer, striking his forehead. Blood foamed forth immediately. Blackstone had always told him a secret to an old carny geek trick, "Lot of blood vessels up there. Small cut—lots of blood." Gibson could remember to tell him now, "Big cut—much more blood."

Gibson slid back up the wall. He checked out his wrist. It would be bruised, but the tip of the spike hadn't broken through the armband. He heard his killer scream at him and saw the spike flying toward him again. He slid to the left and it struck the brick to the right of his head, showering brick dust into his face. The floorboards began to collapse down the center of the room, a blazing chasm opening up between his killer and him. The spike came again and slid back again. And then again. He couldn't even see his killer now; he could only sense the angry dart seeking him out. A plaster of paris golden mountain blocked his progress finally. He fell back against the wall and something snagged the back of his jacket, pinning him.

A gulf of fire opened between the two men; it opened like a seam tearing to reveal a blasted vision. His killer launched his dart up into a beam, where it bit deeply; then he swung across the flaming chasm, landing ten feet away from Walter. He yanked on the chain, unable to free it. He smirked: his next tug would.

Gibson, struggling to free himself from the object that had hooked him from behind, found his hand upon a doorknob. He uttered a silent prayer to his goddess and gave it a twist. It opened out and he flung himself backward against it. Bright light fell upon his face and he hit the sidewalk. He instantly raised his head to prepare for the final attack.

His killer screamed and jumped into the air, grabbing the chain with two hands, hoping to let his falling weight drag it free. At the same moment the opening of the door allowed a huge rush of oxygen-rich air to sweep in to replenish the rapidly dwindling supply. Gibson actually felt the rush of the wind. The flames leaping through the gap behind his killer suddenly roared with renewed, violent vigor. In midair as this happened, the man's spike pulled free and he dropped into the center of a swirling whirlwind of fire. This horror lasted but a moment as the impact of his landing sent him crashing, with a shriek, through the crumbling boards into the roasting inferno below.

Gibson pushed himself quickly to his knees. "Holy Christ!" Suddenly from below, he saw a glint of an object flying up. The spike was driven deeply into the balcony rafter. Gibson didn't want to, but he looked down into the canyon of hell. He saw the man engulfed in flame climb his chain. One hand after another, while he screamed until his vocal cords burned away. Gibson rose to his feet. And still his killer tried, a trembling hand reaching for the wood plank, fingertips gripping. With a snap, the burning links of the chain fell apart and the man disappeared forever from view.

Gibson began to cough and it was several moments before he successfully spat, belched, vomited, and expectorated the smoke out of his lungs. He produced another silk, a clean one, and wiped the tears from his eyes.

"Walter?" He was still too close to the dark smoke and shadows of the building to see the figure in the alley. He took a step forward, into the light.

"How'd you find me?" he gasped.

"What did I warn you about falling for a psychic?" Her lips found his and she whispered, "I will always be able to find you."

When he opened his eyes finally and finished drinking her in, they ran from the alley and the burning theater and the opium den. Across the street he recognized the smug smiling face of Lafayette Ron Hubbard. Already he could hear the distant wail of the approaching fire engine. They reached the street and turned and walked casually away from the fire, which was beginning to attract onlookers from the nearby parade.

"I guess you couldn't find Smith?" he asked Hubbard.

"Oh, no," Hubbard said, and pointed out a stout man examining a window full of roasted duck. "He's already thinking about lunch." Smith heard Hubbard's sharp whistle and dashed over.

Walter shook Smith's hand. "Elmer, good to see you."

"I whipped up a little something for you," he said.

He pulled a mason jar of clear liquid from the brown paper bag he carried. "It's a decoction of deadly nightshade," he said, handing the jar to Gibson.

"Bottoms up!" Hubbard said proudly.

"Deadly nightshade?"

"*Atropa belladona,*" Smith said. "Atropine. I think I made atropine. At least I hope I did. Or something like it. It's a nerve agent counter-agent. You're supposed to inject it into your thigh, but I think this solution will have an effect if you drink it. I think. I mean, I don't know. I'm not a medical doctor; I'm just a chemist. My father wanted me to be a doctor, but I don't like the sight of blood."

Gibson fumbled with the clasp. His fingers were trembling. He handed it to Litzka. "I need help."

She opened it and held it up to his mouth. He took a deep swallow. "Tastes like vanilla," he said, "and rum." The doc puffed visibly. "Best doughnut I ever drank, Smith. How long should it take this stuff to work?"

"If it works?" Smith looked worried. "It should be pretty quick. If it doesn't, well, from the looks of you that could be pretty quick too."

They reached the top of the block. The exuberance of the parade would have shamed any self-respecting Irishman's Saint Patrick's Day spectacle. The parade was pouring through the street like a raging river with the Hip Sing building as its terminus. One after another, the bands, dragons, dancers, dogs, marchers, drummers, and fighters would reach the building and put on their finest performances for the dignitaries who watched from its great windows, open to the mild morning to keep the crowded room from growing too hot. Then they would melt into the crowd or be invited in as the men on the top floor indicated.

"Is that the ugliest goddamn float you've ever seen?" Hubbard asked them.

The platform was borne by six men, three on a side, shouldering two poles which ran through rings along its side. The men wore black hooded robes which hid their faces. A seventh man, dressed the same but free from the burden of carrying the statue, led the small procession. The cheering crowds shrank back from it as it approached, growing quiet as if in fear.

Gibson recognized the fearsome statue instantly. He had seen its grotesque visage when it sat upon the stage of the theater and glowered at him. He knew with certainty that the draped platform upon which its throne was perched was big enough to conceal a fifty-gallon drum.

The crowd silently parted as the seven men and their deadly burden entered the doors of the Hip Sing building.

"Stay here!" Gibson ordered the others. Then he began to run, pushing his way through the crowds which were beginning to congregate at the entrance to the building. The whole tenor of the crowd had changed from one of celebration to one of agitation. Gibson burst into the lobby, breathless. It was filled with revelers partaking of the vast feast. Several men, Hip Sing guards, came toward him, trying to wave him out. He barked Zhang Mei's name at them. They didn't seem to know it, but the forceful repetition of a Chinese name seemed to give them pause, as if the strange white man did have some claim to be here. He heard sounds from the staircase and bounded up them as quickly as he could.

He flew up the stairs, feeling revitalized. Smith was right. The antidote seemed to be working quickly. A large dragon costume—there must have been fifteen men inside—was swirling down the stairs toward him. He came face-to-face with the dragon. It snorted in his face and shook its whiskers. He could see the eyes of a young man peering at him through the dark opening of the beast's mouth. He put his face into the gaping maw and snorted back. The head of the dragon took a side step to the wall and the rest of the body flowed along, following its lead.

He reached the top floor, where large double doors stood open onto another world. As he walked through the opening, he felt as if he were entering an ancient court in Imperial China. The traditional costumes, the creaking tables loaded with food, the rich smells of incense, the regal decorations all combined to transport him away from New York. He revised his first impression: he felt as if he were entering a temple, a shrine, inhabited by living Chinese gods.

The crowd in the room applauded the entrance of the statue. Most of the men in the room were standing in a wide circle at the windows, which gave a panoramic view of the Manhattan skyline. This left a clearing in the center of the room for the performers to make their obeisance. At the far end of the room, opposite the doors through which Gibson was entering, was a raised dais upon which sat a number of distinguished elderly men. They all wore formal Chinese garb except for one man, who sat in the middle seat of honor. He wore a Brooks Brothers suit and a bored expression on his sour face.

The hooded men drew past the center of the room, proceeding directly to the raised platform. Expectant eyes fell upon it as the assembly waited to see what its performance tribute could possibly be. The room grew silent as the sense of expectation grew, as well as a growing sense of dread perhaps inspired by the appearance of the statue or the suspenseful, stately pace of its bearers.

The hooded leader drew to a stop before the dais. He raised his hand and the other robed figures slowly lowered their heavy burden to the floor. The leader bowed low before the man in the suit. The man replied with an indifferent wave.

"Zhang Mei!" Gibson shouted across the quieting room. "Wait."

The hood of the leader turned to look at him. From the shadows beneath its folds, Gibson thought he could see Zhang Mei's eyes, gleaming with triumph.

Zhang Mei revealed himself. There were soft murmurs from the crowd, but the strongest reaction came from the dais as the man in the American suit suddenly attempted to stand. His face had turned as white as the silk clothes the other men wore. He stumbled to his knees, begging, pleading, groveling for mercy.

Zhang Mei spoke something, savagely, to him in Chinese. Then, in a fluid movement that surprised everyone with its speed, he snatched the great sword from the hand of the Judge of the Dead, swung it through the air in a great arc of golden light, and struck the head from the man who had killed his Lu Zhi and little Shaozu.

EPISODE FORTY-SIX

L ITZKA SHRIEKED.

Mi-Ying's head fell at the base of the statue. Gibson saw its mouth open in surprise and its eyes blink in astonishment as its body took a step forward. Its hands clawed at its neck, from which a great streaming jet of blood spattered the men rushing to exit the stage. The body staggered limply off the stage and collapsed, still, at Zhang Mei's feet.

Gibson had heard the clatter on the steps behind him and he knew without looking that Litzka and Hubbard and Smith had followed him after all. He grimaced to himself, wishing that for once, just once, she had listened to him.

Outside Gibson could hear the roar of the oblivious throng as the revels in the street picked up frenzy. It was just past midday; in Chinese terms this meant the festivities had only just begun. Another parade was wending its way down the street full of entirely new participants.

With surprise he noted Lester Dent emerging into the doorway of a recessed alcove in the room. Dent's shirt was torn and soaked with large blossoms of blood; his face seemed drained of emotion. It was gray, claylike, expressionless. So, we're all here at the last, Gibson thought sadly. He nodded his head at Dent. Dent looked at him with dead eyes, as if the emotional nerves behind them had been severed, and slowly shook his head.

Zhang Mei took a step upon the platform and turned to face the assemblage. Mi-Ying's blood streamed down his face. The men who had sat upon the dais leapt away from the stricken diplomat and the sword-wielding madman. Zhang swung the sword toward the base of the statue, slicing away the curtains to reveal the old military-issue drum under the squatting statue. He cried out, harshly, in Chinese and what he said stilled the panicked room. His men moved quickly to bring the drum out from under the platform.

He spoke to his men again and they fell upon the baskets of money which had been placed at the feet of Mi-Ying. These they bore back and placed under the statue where the gas drum had been.

"A thief!" Gibson heard his own voice. He stepped into the room. "After all this, you're a common thief?" Gibson asked Zhang Mei, approaching slowly.

"If Mi-Ying were to take this money, none of it would ever reach China. With me, it will."

Gibson took a few more steps. "Last night you were the champion of China. Now you're stealing from her weakest people. Is this where the dream ends? Is this the destiny of your father?"

"I have no father," Zhang replied. "I am the Judge of the Dead."

"What about your dreams for peace?" Gibson was close enough now to see the man's mad eyes glittering. Out of the corner of his eye he saw movement. Dent was taking a few steps.

"This will bring peace to all who suffer upon the Golden Mountain."

An old Chinese man, a scarred veteran who had been sitting next to Mi-Ying, barked at Zhang Mei, who turned around. The old man was someone of obvious status in the community. Zhang Mei heeded his voice with a respectful stare.

Gibson took a few more steps. Dent did too.

The conversation rapidly grew heated. The old man's tone turned scolding and the younger man's turned sarcastic. The old man made a surprising move; with a graceful jump he flew onto the stage and attempted to strike Zhang Mei with a flurry of blows unlike anything Gibson had seen before. His fists were deftly parried and the old man was quickly knocked aside. Dent rushed to help him. When Dent looked up, the point of the great golden sword was level with his eyes. Blood dripped down the blade and fell upon the old man's wispy beard.

"Who are you?" Zhang Mei asked Dent.

"I am the husband of the wife you murdered today at the old theater." Dent's voice was as dead as his eyes.

Zhang Mei nodded. His eyes filled with something close to remorse. "I am sorry. She was unexpected. My men were defending me."

Gibson spoke. "So in the end, you are no different from Mi-Ying. A killer of children." He pointed to a pair of frightened children clinging to a man near the alcove Dent had emerged from. "And wives."

"In the end we are different because I am alive while he is dead." Zhang coughed.

Dent helped the old man to his feet. Gibson stepped before the drum. Zhang Mei stood on the riser on the other side of it. The tip of the sword suddenly flicked in Gibson's direction. He looked up the shaft to the man holding it.

Gibson swallowed hard. The edge was level with his throat. "You should have asked me to figure out this ending for you. As it is, I don't think your ending is going to work."

"What ending would you write?"

"Well, let's see. You've taken a room full of people hostage with a drum of deadly gas. You and your men have come in contact with the gas. Coughing is a sign of gas exposure." He had Zhang's full attention. Zhang lowered the sword, resting its tip on the lid of the drum. "Your ship is out of commission. Your patron is missing in action. Every person in this room wants you dead. The only plan that really matters to you, revenge, has gone off spectacularly well. Escape seems nearly impossible.

"But there is an ending and it coincides with the ending of your life's work. You wanted to bring peace. Well, you have. You have brought peace to the souls of your wife and your child. There is little more for you to do.

"I want you to know that I've figured out how your story ends."

Zhang tilted his head, curious. "Immortality?" he offered, caustically.

"Eternity."

Dent threw his arms around Zhang Mei. While Gibson spoke, Dent had maneuvered slowly behind the warrior. Zhang Mei was unprepared for an attack from someone of Lester's size. Dent locked his hands around his own wrists. Zhang's arms were pinned in front of him. They still held the hilt of the sword. Its point still rested on the top of the metal drum.

The room seemed to surge forward as men prepared to run to Dent's assistance. Zhang Mei's body was trembling. His face was growing red, as was Dent's. Zhang Mei continued to look at Gibson.

"You are right," he said through his clenched jaw.

Instead of struggling, he suddenly let himself fall forward, drawing his weight and Dent's down upon the sword. With a shriek, the sword plunged through the lid of the drum. Lester was thrown from Zhang Mei by the force of the impact and he landed heavily on his back on the floor.

Gibson heard the venomous hiss of the gas before he saw thin jets of it bursting out from underneath Zhang Mei.

"Run!" he yelled. His cry galvanized the room. Men began streaming for the exits. There was a flurry of combat in the confusion as Hip Sing men fell upon Zhang's monks, dragging them along.

Zhang Mei, placing his hands on either side of the drum upon which his chest was centered, hoisted himself up with a jerk. Blood streamed from the gaping wound beneath his torso where the hilt had gouged into the tissue and muscle of the tender abdomen. He staggered back against the platform, gasping for air.

The sword trembled against the pressure of the gas within the drum. Thin plumes feathered out around the neat incision. Gibson clapped his hands over the moist hilt, keeping the sword plugging the hole. He could feel the turmoil within the canister. It was like trying to hold back a tornado. In that moment he suddenly was able to recall Lovecraft's face quite distinctly.

"Dent! I don't think I can hold it!"

Lester gripped the hilt above his hands. Sweat streamed down both of their faces.

"Just hold it till the room's empty," Gibson spat.

Dent nodded ever so slightly, every ounce of his will concentrated upon the sword.

"Let me strive every moment of my life to make myself better and better," he muttered through gritted teeth, "that all may profit by it."

"What are you saying?" Gibson asked. The phrase sounded familiar.

Dent raised his voice so Gibson could hear. Out of the corner of his eye he saw a Chinese man emerge from the alcove carrying Norma, limp, in his arms. Outside he could hear screams and shouts as the panicked people from the Hip Sing building hit the street.

"Let me think of the right, and lend all my assistance to those who need it."

Dent was invoking the Doc Savage oath. Gibson felt a ridiculous grin spread helplessly across his face as he began to speak along with Lester. "Let me be considerate of my country, of my fellow citizens, and my associates in everything I say and do."

Dent grinned back. "Let me take what comes with a smile, without loss of courage."

A breeze swept through the room. Although the windows were open, from where Gibson stood it appeared as if the gusts came from the statue itself, as if they issued from between its carnivorous jaws. As if it were breathing. Wind, he thought, wind would be good.

The room was empty except for himself, Dent, and the corpses of the adversaries. "Go!"

"You sure?"

Gibson nodded at the gas. "I've already taken my hit. Find Hubbard. He's got the antidote."

"Okay. On the count of three. One . . . two . . . three!"

He let go and Gibson felt the full force of the gas again under his control. It was a desperate, live thing that wanted only to escape.

"Try to get everyone back," he said. "I'll hold it as long as I can!"

Dent patted him firmly on the back. The sensation was reassuring but in the end there was nothing more to say. Gibson listened to Dent's footsteps fade down the staircase. The wind had picked up now. That statue is really screaming at me, he thought. The breath of judgment.

Suddenly Gibson felt the sword jump with a new force. Zhang's hands gripped the hilt and Gibson was face-to-face with him. The two of them stood nearly nose to nose glaring at one another, the sword vibrating between them. Gibson looked deep into those dark eyes and in those eyes, at the end, he saw their fate.

"Let me do right to all and wrong no man." He grunted out the rest of the oath. Zhang Mei's teeth curled back in something resembling a cruel smile. Gibson realized that he was not fighting Zhang Mei, that the man had added his muscle and sinew, the fiber of his being, to the attempt to keep the sword in its deadly scabbard.

The poisonous vapors began spilling out in plumes from the edges of the puncture. Both the men were trembling at the effort. Gibson could feel the sword shaking and Zhang Mei's hands straining on top of his.

Gibson grinned back. Their predicament was untenable but there was something humorous about its very futility. He realized something about The Shadow that he had never understood before: sometimes The Shadow laughed because laughing in the face of Death was the only revenge against Death that a man could have. Laughter was as life-affirming, as hopeful, as spiteful toward Death as having a child. Zhang Mei seemed to understand something similar at the same instant.

"Always time to learn something new," Gibson suggested, as more gas spurted out. They each shifted their weight to try to keep the sword in.

"Yes," Zhang Mei chuckled and nodded.

"Let me strive every moment of my life to make myself better and better," he began, and Zhang Mei repeated after him, "that all may profit by it."

And then the men suddenly found themselves at the mercy of their own overwhelming laughter as the billowing white clouds of death enshrouded them both.

EPISODE FORTY-SEVEN

"How much of that antidote do you have?" he yelled to Smith. The stout little man, sweating profusely, was being towed down the stairs by Gibson's young woman. She seemed to have no hesitation about throwing an elbow jab to keep the men around her moving. Of course Smith had every reason to be scared. There was enough gas in that canister to wipe out all of Chinatown and a good section of downtown New York as well. From the window of the temple he had been able to see City Hall (he hoped the mayor was enjoying his lunch; it might be his last), Trinity Church, and the financial district, all within the cruel grasp of the poison. It was going to be a bad day for everyone south of the Hip Sing building.

He expected the gas to roil over him at any moment, but it still hadn't as he reached the next landing down. God, he thought, if you get me out of this, I promise I'll never abuse adverbs again. As if in mocking response, the man next to him on the stairs stumbled into him at full tilt. The force of the impact knocked him out of the streaming mass of humanity and onto the landing. He struggled to keep his balance but momentum did not favor him. Then his feet lost the sensation of being on the floor, he was tipping over, and he slid into an ornate screen arranged on the landing. The knock to the top of his head made it feel as if his vertebrae were collapsing into one another. Luckily his shoulder absorbed most of the impact.

After several moments of grimacing through the flare of pain, not moving, not even breathing, he opened his eyes. As he struggled to refocus, he saw a Chinese man bearing Mrs. Dent in his arms gliding smoothly down the stairs past him. At the sight of her he felt his heart breaking. Her left arm bounced lifelessly. She didn't deserve this. None of them did. But especially not her. She had been so nice to him, taken a special interest in him on the *Albatross*.

The man carrying Norma seemed to be the last person out of the temple, other than Gibson and Dent. He thought he could hear their voices in conversation, but as his senses weren't functioning properly, he couldn't seem to bring them into focus. In much the same way he was almost able to absorb what appeared to be an impossible sight, lurking in the corner of the landing. He tried to blink it away, or process it as something, anything, else. Statues. Paintings. Memories. Then, through the blazing hurt, a sort of clarity descended and what had seemed impossible a moment before became horrifyingly real.

The two young Chinese boys were terrified. The younger one, whose dark eyes were wide and fearful, held tightly to the older one. It reminded him of the way an organ grinder's monkey would cling to its master. Together they were kneeling, huddled as far back on the landing as they could go. If he hadn't fallen, no one would have seen them. He pulled himself to a sitting position as quickly as he could.

"I fell down," the younger one said.

"So did I," he replied. He struggled to his feet and snatched the little one and tucked him under his arm. He clapped his hand around the other one's wrist and helped him. The stairs were empty. Carrying one, pulling the other, he began to run.

The Flash.

In all his life he had never wished so much that he could live up to his nickname as he did right now. He'd give anything to become truly fast. He'd give up his dreams, his hopes, his wishes, his ambition, his talent, his skill, his imagination, if he could just get these boys out of the building. The flights seemed endless. He didn't remember all these steps. At one landing he dropped the older boy's arm so he could hoist the little one over his shoulder. His shoulders and head ached. He didn't want to die. He just wanted to go home to his wife. How could such a little kid weigh so much? He wasn't fast enough. The Flash wasn't going to be fast enough.

They burst out onto the empty sidewalk and the brilliant daylight stunned him. The crowd, composed of paradegoers and evacuated guests, had re-formed on the sidewalk opposite the Hip Sing building. Exhausted, he lowered the little boy from his shoulder. The older boy grabbed the younger and the two scampered across the street, vanishing into the crowd.

He couldn't take another step. If this is where the gas took him, then so be it. He had done all he could hope to do, all he had wanted to do. He sat down heavily on the curb and lifted his head straight up and back. High above him, he could see the temple floor, the silk curtains fluttering in the breeze wafting through open windows.

"Hubbard!"

He wasn't The Flash anymore.

"Hey! Ron!"

The Flash hadn't run those steps carrying those boys. He had.

"Lafayette! Hey! Ron Hubbard!"

L. Ron Hubbard heard his name. Dazed, he looked around. Two dark figures loomed over him; with the sun in his eyes he couldn't see them. Not the Chinese boys. Bigger. Men. Strong hands were gripping him, pulling him, dragging him across the street, away from the Hip Sing Association. They entered the building's shadow, and he could see his rescuers, finally. Driftwood and the cowboy helped him to his feet.

"How did you find me?" he asked them as he steadied himself and caught his breath. As he waited for an answer he began to explore the painful parts of his body, looking for blood or extruding bone, both of which he was sure he would find but neither of which he did. Both men seemed pleased to see him, to the point of genuine self-satisfaction. "What are you doing here?"

"Just had a bite of Chinese," Driftwood said, stifling a yawn.

"Best I ever et," the cowboy added. "What brings you here?"

"That shit!" he said, throwing an indicating thumb back over his shoulder.

"Aw, son of a bitch!" the cowboy said. "I seen about enough of that."

Litzka pushed through the crowd to join them, with Smith panting along behind her. Hubbard patted Smith on the back.

"Nice to see you alive," he whispered to the chemist.

Smith nodded gratefully, gasping for air. In his shaking hand he still held the half-full mason jar of decoction of belladonna, the liquid swirling around and around.

Hubbard turned to see Lester Dent standing in the doorway of the Hip Sing Association, blinking back the sunlight. Hubbard watched him scan the crowd until his eyes fell upon what he was looking for. Then Dent dashed into the street in their direction but to the right. Hubbard turned to see where the man was headed. "Oh, God."

With the assistance of two other men, the Chinese man who had carried Norma past him on the staircase was gently attempting to slide her motionless body into the back seat of an automobile. Hubbard could see instantly that any attempt they made to get her to a hospital was going to be blocked by the crowds thronging the street. With Norma in the car, another Chinese man in the driver's seat began honking the horn, pulling away from the curb. Hubbard began running to catch up to Dent, with Driftwood and the cowboy in pursuit. This time he felt fast.

The trio was steps behind Dent as he reached the car and banged on the trunk. It stopped and he threw open the rear door. Hubbard, Driftwood, and Lew ran to the front of the car, shouting and pushing people to move. All eyes were affixed to the top of the Hip Sing building; few people even acknowledged Hubbard.

Driftwood, realizing the problem, turned to him in frustration. "We're never going to get out of here."

Hubbard spun around, ready to yell at the driver to just gun the engine, when he stopped short. The door was still open and Norma Dent lay half on the seat and half in Lester Dent's arms, her blond hair spilling down to gently touch the cobblestones. The skin on her cheeks was shockingly white. He could only stare at her still, calm face.

A great and terrible murmur swept through the crowd. They all turned to look up at the top floor of the Hip Sing Association building. A cloud of white gas spilled out of the windows like a wave crashing against a rocky cliff. It spread across the sky, blocking out the light of the sun and casting a shadow over the crowd below. Wispy tendrils, pulled by gravity, began to descend.

"Son of a bitch." This Hubbard said almost in unison with the cowboy. For a moment he almost thought that somehow, in the roar of the gas, he could hear the sound of laughter, of men laughing as hard as they could, but that could only have been a strange echo because in moments it had vanished.

They all felt the wind at the same instant. It seemed to rush from the building, or from above it. It was a massive, gasping breath of air, as if the great throng, exhaling as one, had created it. It was a merciless, pitiless wind, colder than any he had ever felt in New York. It swirled skyward, sweeping up the lethal cloud.

Slowly, the deadly gas began to rise into the sky, dissipating, dispersing. The tendrils were whisked away. The wind was stiff and steady. The supply of gas within the temple seemed to reach its end. Shafts of light began to penetrate the cloud. Its solidity began to drift away in wisps. At last the sun broke through and the white haze vanished. There was a long moment of silence and then people in the crowd began to cheer with joy.

Hubbard looked at the building. The doorway was dark. Then a solitary figure emerged from the darkness into the light. It was Walter Gibson. In his hand he held the golden sword, which he tossed onto the ground with a clanging ring which echoed up and down the quiet street. The look on his face was triumphant and defiant. Hubbard knew from that look that no one else would emerge from the doorway alive. Gibson's girl burst from the crowd and dashed across the street into Gibson's arms. He caught her up in a kiss so passionate and intimate that Hubbard had to look away. Moments later they came to where Lester sat holding Norma.

"Lester?" Gibson asked, softly.

"There weren't going to be any more adventures." Dent rubbed his cheek against Norma's, nuzzling. "You promised." The others slowly gathered around the pair but it was as if they weren't there. Gibson gently placed his hand on Dent's back.

Hubbard felt the sadness well up in his throat and his eyes grow wet. Norma had seemed more alive than any woman he had ever known. Somehow this seemed impossible. He looked at her again.

Almost imperceptibly her eyelids fluttered. Then they opened. "Lester?"

With a great sob of relief, he lifted her head higher.

"Are you mad at me? Why do you look so worried?" she asked. Dent lowered his lips to hers and kissed her tenderly. She brought her hand up to his face. "Did you see I found my treasure?"

He smiled and nodded, holding her tight. She wound her arms around his neck and he helped her out of the car. As they came to their feet, Hubbard made sure that both Dents took a hearty sip from Smith's mason jar. Then he stepped back as they kissed.

A great, joyous sense of giddy relief sweep through Hubbard. He looked at Driftwood and the cowboy. They were experiencing it too. The color even seemed to be returning to Smith's cheeks. Litzka was embracing Gibson and sobbing almost inconsolably in her delight while a grateful and relieved look of thanksgiving spread across his face.

One by one Hubbard committed them all to his memory; then he took them all in at once, a great vivid tableau of a moment he was living in that he wanted never to forget. After everything he had been through with them, this is what he didn't want to see end. His friends had survived.

There was a rustle and the two little boys emerged from the crowd.

As the Chinese man who had carried Norma clapped his hands in delight, they ran straight into the arms of Lester Dent. That's gratitude for you, Hubbard thought; it's not like he saved their lives or anything.

"What's the matter with everyone?" Norma Dent asked her husband as he lowered her feet to the pavement. "At a loss for words?"

EPISODE FORTY-EIGHT

A WARM, early May breeze scattered the few remaining leaves left on the ground from the previous autumn and gently stirred the airport's wind sock as Walter Gibson stepped out of Manny's cab and onto the tarmac of Floyd Bennett Field. The dew was still sticking to the grass and he shielded his eyes from the bright morning sun, looking for the small plane.

Lester Dent and an engineer were inspecting the engine on the closed-cabin Beechcraft. Dent beamed when he caught sight of Gibson. The big man jumped lightly off the stepladder, ducked under the plane, and came toward Gibson, wiping oil from his hands onto his jumpsuit.

"Gonna name this one the *Albatross II?*" Gibson called out as he walked toward it. The wind kept threatening to pull the light objects under his arm away. "Keep tempting the fates?"

Dent shook his head. "Picked another name for him."

"Him?"

"Figured if ships are female, this fella's gotta be a male. Like it?"

"He's impressive. Heroic." He shook Lester's hand. "You're really moving back to Missouri?"

"I've got a contract for four more years of *Doc*, at least. Hopefully I can find more time to write some stories for the glossies. And maybe I can finally get around to writing a real bestseller."

"I hope you do. How about the Sweet Flower mystery? After all, you sure earned the right. You found out how it ended."

"I told you that night back at the White Horse, those literary best-sellers need to be chock-full of metaphors, analogies, and irony, and there's none of that in this story. It's too simple."

Gibson nodded. They watched the wind stir the flags near the hangars.

"You didn't have to come out to see us off," Lester said quietly.

"Sure I did," he replied, before being hit in the side by a heavy yet soft object. The impact of Norma's embrace nearly lifted him off the ground.

"Walter!" she cried, planting a kiss on his cheek.

"All packed up?" he replied, and she nodded. "New York's not going to be the same without you."

"I know," Norma said. "But I promised Lester fewer adventures."

"But if there's a Chinatown in La Plata, I'd steer clear."

"Actually"—Dent cleared his throat and gestured at the plane—"we're taking a little Chinatown with us."

"Hurry up!" cried little Ham as he leaned halfway out of the cockpit's open window. "I could walk there faster!"

His brother pulled him back inside to safety. Mr. Yee gave them an apologetic wave from inside the plane, as fathers will when their sons have embarrassed them. Gibson smiled and waved back.

"We're going to help him open La Plata's first Chinese restaurant. Norma thinks his pot stickers are a treasure worth sharing back home."

"Dumplings," she corrected him. "How is Litzka?"

"She's on the road again. Somewhere on the West Coast. I probably won't see her until the fall. If I see her again. If she comes back, I mean."

"Maybe things will work out in the future. That's what the future's for, right?"

"That's what she says. And if you can't believe a psychic when it comes to the future, who can you believe?"

She squeezed his hand. "Then trust her."

He smiled. "I wanted you to have a few things before you left. That's one of the reasons I came out here." He handed Dent a mag. "It's the next issue of *The Shadow*. With everything that happened I kind of fell behind on my writing, so I asked Nanovic to run this one."

Dent took it. He looked at it for a long moment, and when he finally spoke, his voice was thick with emotion, *"The Golden Vulture!"* He was glowing as he handed the magazine to Norma.

"Hot off the presses. And there's something else too. Since I didn't have to write this month's episode of *The Shadow* I was able to throw our idea to Nanovic. And he loved it!" He drew the board from under his arm and proudly peeled back the brown covering paper so the Dents could see it. "Says it might even get him to forget about the Kent Allard incident."

They recognized Rozen's signature flourishes on the painting immediately: a dead-faced man, wielding pistols, emerging amidst a swirl of gas pouring from the mouth of a hideously alive, golden Chinese statue. Gibson chose not to tell them that his descriptions of the hero to George Rozen had been based on the look he had seen on Lester Dent's face that one horrible moment in the temple. "Meet Street & Smith's newest hero. The Avenger!"

"It's remarkable," Norma said.

"So this is where it all winds up," Lester said, studying the painting. "In the pulps."

"Where it should stay."

Lester nodded.

"Nanovic says he'll run it. But only if we both write it. He wants us to switch off. I can write it one month and you can write it the next. If you've got the time."

Dent looked at Norma. "He'll find the time," she said, with enthusiasm. Her eyes moved from the painting to the last mag rolled up in Gibson's hand. "What's that? Another surprise?"

"Sort of. Yes." He gave a wave back to the cab and after a moment a little boy stepped out. He came slowly across the tarmac toward them. "Kind of a favor, actually."

Norma slipped her hand into Dent's as the little boy approached. He must have been about nine years old.

"This is my son, Robert." Gibson said, putting a hand on the boy's shoulder. "His mother agreed that he could spend this summer with me in New York. He's a huge *Doc Savage* fan. He was wondering if he could get your autograph."

"Hi, Robert," Dent said warmly. "Would you like Kenneth Robeson's autograph?"

The little boy shook his hand, shyly. Then he turned to his father. "Doesn't Lester Dent write *Doc Savage*?"

"That's right," Lester Dent said. "Kenneth Robeson is Lester Dent. That's me."

He autographed the first-ever issue of *Doc Savage* for the boy and handed it back.

"Thanks," Robert said, and as he read the inscription, his face lit up.

"He looks just like you," Norma said to Walter.

"You think so?"

"Those Gibson boys are handsome."

"Looks like you've got a good tailwind today," Gibson said as the wind ruffled his hair.

"Should be a quick flight," Norma replied. "If we don't stop for any adventures along the way."

"You never know," said Lester. "Adventures have a way of stopping for us."

Gibson took Robert's hand as they stepped from the airstrip to the grass. Dent slammed the door shut and Gibson laughed when he saw that *Doc 1* was stenciled in dramatic letters across the hatch. Robert clutched his newest possession tightly against his chest. Gibson rested his arm across the boy's shoulder. It felt good.

"Where's the pilot?" Robert asked him.

"Look," he said.

Norma and Lester took their seats in the cockpit—pilot and copilot. He and Robert waved and the Dents saluted them. Then Norma turned her attention to the control panel, and a few moments later, the engine roared to life. Before the turning of the plane blocked them from view, Walter caught one last glimpse of Norma speaking excitedly to her husband and pointing out something in the distance. Lester, as always, was nodding his big head in complete agreement.

With a thunderous roar the plane sped away from them and lifted gracefully into the air. Soon it was a speck in the sky, no bigger than the nearest gull as it grew closer to the clouds.

"Hungry?" Walter asked Robert.

His son nodded.

"Let's go get some lunch. I've got a story to tell you."

He looked back once, but the Dents had gone over the horizon.

"So did Zhang Mei say anything to you before he died?" asked the man they still called Otis P. Driftwood, even though they now knew his name was Bob Heinlein.

Gibson raised a forkful of steak to his mouth. "Who says he died?" he asked, and then bit into the beef. The expressions on the faces of his dining companions were ones never to forget. Driftwood and Robert, his son, were intrigued, but Hubbard looked astonished. He was glad that the two young men had been able to come to Rosoff's and meet his son. He felt a certain sadness as he realized that his circle of new friends, which had seemed so large so recently, was suddenly dwindling away. The Dents were now gone. Lew, the poet cowboy, had hopped a train to Baton Rouge in search of the ship's company's paymaster after having been evicted from the captain's quarters aboard the *Star of Baltimore* when the Department of the Navy had seized it. He felt he was owed quite a good bit of money for his services as acting captain of the vessel and he was "aimin' to collec'." Dent had made certain to retrieve his pistol before the young man had embarked upon this quest.

Driftwood would also be leaving New York in the next few days. Yesterday he had read in the newspaper that the man who had tried to take over his silver mine, the man who had killed his partner and forced him into a fugitive's secretive life, had been found shot to death in a coffee shop in Los Angeles. The cops had arrested a luckless gangster as the gunman. When pressed about what his future held, Driftwood joked that he might run for a congressional district seat that had opened up back home. Or he might become a writer. Whichever promised the most money and least work.

"You're saying he didn't die." Hubbard gaped. "But I was there."

"Were you?"

"Hell, I was! I saw the whole thing!"

"Yet you admit you don't even know what happened to Zhang Mei."

"To hell with that!" Heinlein challenged. "Did he die or didn't he?"

"How does it end?" Robert was wide-eyed and spellbound.

A vision briefly appeared before Gibson's eyes: Zhang Mei's darkly sparkling eyes vanishing behind soft enveloping veils of white gas spilling out of the canister. He could still feel the man's hands as they slipped from the sword hilt. "How do you want it to end?"

"What's the question here? Zhang Mei's dead!" cried out Hubbard.

"His lifeless body lay at the feet of the Judge of the Dead, his hand still reaching out to help contain the deadly gas, frozen forever in his final redemptive act. That's definitely one ending. But is it the right one?"

"Malarkey!" Hubbard muttered.

"Did you see his corpse? I seem to recall that you and Driftwood and Lew headed straight for the nearest tavern long before the cops started investigating. So if you didn't even check to make sure he was dead, how can you be so sure what end he came to? But if you need an ending, I'll give you an ending."

The two men set their forks down. Robert, however, continued to eat his club sandwich. Gibson felt his fingers twitch. He thought for a moment about dramatizing his story with a magic trick and then thought better of it. He would let it speak for itself.

"Zhang Mei's hands were ripped from the sword by the pressure of the escaping gas. He staggered back, surrounded by the poison, desperately holding his breath. This was enough to keep him from being fully exposed. He tried to find his biographer in the gas, but the man either had died or was lost in the haze. He plunged through the miasma toward the temple door. His head was swimming from lack of oxygen as he flung himself down the top flight of stairs and away from danger.

"He reached the lobby of the building. Outside there were Hip Sing men and On Leong men and American police. He didn't know what had happened to Towers but it was obvious that Towers had failed; whether the colonel had betrayed him, had died, or had been captured was irrelevant. What was relevant was that Zhang Mei was completely alone, a foreigner in a foreign land. But his skill was always survival. He looked around, knowing there is always a path to salvation, that there is always a way to the safety of the river. He spied the door to the basement, the stairs leading down, and rushed forward, the black fabric of the judge's robe swirling around him. In the basement he discovered that the secret hatch to the Chinatown tunnels was still open. He leapt into the opening. But it was too late. The gas had poisoned him after all, and though he struggled on as mightily as any man could, he died as the sewage swallowed him up."

"Suitably tragic," Heinlein said.

"What's the matter, Robert?" Gibson asked his son, who seemed downcast.

"It's sad."

"Most tragedy is," Heinlein replied. "And this is a villain we're talking about."

"But," Robert insisted, "he was only a villain because of what Mi-Ying did to him." He looked at Gibson. "And he was your friend, even though he did bad things. He was your friend, right?"

"So you think he deserves a better ending?"

The boy nodded.

"Good. Because there is another ending."

"There can't be," Hubbard insisted.

"There is. With the dank waters washing away the worst of the poison, Zhang Mei makes his escape into the vast network of twisted tunnels which worm their way under Chinatown. He disappears into the gloom, rats swirling around his ankles, a hundred secret doors to safety awaiting him. A hundred chances. A hundred destinies. A hundred new stories. A hundred endings."

"Is that the real ending?" Robert asked. "He's alive?"

"If you want it to be, then let's say it is. Zhang Mei lives to strike again!"

"Careful, Robert," Heinlein cautioned the kid with a wise smile. "Take any story a writer tells you with a grain of salt. Even if he's your father. Especially if he's your father!"

"I don't care if it's real or not. I just like the story now." Robert said, sure of himself.

"What I really want to know," said Hubbard, "is who's got dibs on it?"

"What?" Gibson asked.

"It! This story! Our story. It's bigger and better than the Sweet Flower story, by far!"

Gibson smiled at the redheaded writer. Even Hubbard might soon be leaving New York. He and his wife had been exchanging letters of reconciliation and Gibson knew how he missed his children. If he did leave, Gibson would definitely miss him.

"Why don't you write it, Ron? Hell, I'll even give you a title. How about *The Murder of the Shudder Man*? Or *The Terrors of Providence*? *The Trials of the Tong*? Or *Marooned on Tomb Island*? Or *The Heinous Heist*. Maybe even *The Pulp Heroes*. Lots of titles. Lots of stories. Pick one."

"Yeah, but those aren't my stories. They're yours. I can't tell those."

"They're not all mine. Some of them are Dent's. One of them belongs to Lovecraft, but he's dead. As far as we know."

"Well, I guess I could tell *The Tale of the Dead Man*."

"I was there for that too," Heinlein spoke up. "It could be my story. If I were a writer. And *The Long Watch on the Ship of Doom* is definitely mine. Definitely. For that one I just might have to become a writer."

"What happened in Chinatown was just the ending to a lot of other stories," Gibson said, looking at Hubbard. "There's lots of things that happened to us that we'll never tell each other. For example, if I tried to write about how you saved those boys' lives, I'd get it wrong. I wouldn't get your details right. The personal details, the things you were thinking, the way you were feeling. You know, the messy true things that only slow down a great pulp. Am I right?"

"Can I just use my imagination? Make stuff up? I am a writer, after all."

"There's a difference between a lie and a story," Heinlein said softly.

Gibson nodded. "Oh, you could try to tell *The Chinatown Death Cloud Peril*, but between the pack of lies you think is the truth and the truths you'll never know about, you'll be as lost as Zhang Mei in the forgotten tunnels under the streets. Unsure of which tunnel leads to freedom, you'll splash through the wet darkness, fumbling for light, hoping the path you're on is the right one, only to find yourself facing more dead ends than endings, the doors sealed shut by time and inertia and the dread that people have of the creatures that lie behind those doors."

"Do you think Zhang Mei is still down there?" Robert asked, his brows furrowed as he tried to imagine the fate that befell the adopted son of the warlord. "Do you think that he never came up from the tunnels? Maybe he decided that he was safe down there. That no one would ever look for him. And that's another ending, right, Dad? Maybe?"

"Maybe," said Gibson, and ran a reassuring hand through his son's hair. It felt just like his own. "'Maybe' is how all writers, even pulp writers, begin their stories."

His mind suddenly raced back to that day in Chinatown as they all stood together, sharing in the joy that they were all alive and, more than that, triumphant. He remembered the way he had lowered his face from the clear sky to the ground, bowing his head in thanks. He recalled the ancient grating he had noticed set in the cobblestones. He thought of the shudder that had gripped his body as he caught a glimpse, only a glimpse, of a dark and familiar face sagely gazing up at him from below the surface of the earth. If he closed his eyes momentarily he could still see the complicated look sparkling in the eyes—the rage, the fear, the loss, the knowledge, the triumph. After that, all he could recall was Litzka, warmly pressing her firm body against his, and the distant fading echoes of footsteps splashing away into dark shadows. Afterward he wasn't sure whether he had seen something or not. He told himself he would never be sure. But he was sure.

He stood up and reached into his coat for his wallet. His belly felt full of good food and beer, and a fine feeling of contentment settled over him. Spring was in the air, he would be seeing Litzka soon enough, he felt good, and he felt like writing. "Maybe Zhang Mei will remain down there, lost and lurking forever in the catacombs as the world above him marches on and remembers him only as a phantasm they think they hear below their feet at night when the city is quiet. The master of his subterranean sanctum." Robert stood up too and began putting on his jacket. Norma Dent was right, Robert did look just like him. "At any rate, my friends, my advice is to stay out of those tunnels. Because in the end you never know what you'll find or who you'll meet down there."

"Well, at least promise me that you'll never write it," Hubbard said.

"It's not my story either. I may use it. But I'll never write it. I promise you."

Gibson tossed enough money down on the table to cover all their meals, plus a little extra. "Why don't you fellas have a quick one in honor of Howard Lovecraft before you go. On me."

"You have to go?" Hubbard asked him.

"Yep." He shook their hands. "Gonna take my boy up to the top of the Empire State Building to see where King Kong fell. Then I've got to get cracking on a new story. I'm feeling mighty inspired; the presses never stop and I'm already behind." Walter Gibson grinned at his friends. "These things don't write themselves, you know."

EPILOGUE

T HE PULP Era ended.

The big presses finally stopped running, turned off by wartime paper shortages while the mags themselves were physically torn from the newsstands by Mayor La Guardia's garbage enforcers. The controversy metastasized from New York, and decency and morality oozed across the nation like black tar and old blood. Attentions and imaginations drifted elsewhere, to war, to comics and movies. And then only attentions were left to drift to television. The pulps, the pages where American myths had been born, were gone.

But some shadows of the era live on.

Why tell my story now? Survival. Emperors, like heroes, villains, people, myths, and even eras, can be forgotten. Obscurity is the true death of them, of us all. Does it matter whether my story is true or not? Not if in the end it means I won't be forgotten. The Pulp Era is dead. Long live the Pulp Era.

The people. They matter almost as much as I do.

Lester and Norma Dent returned to La Plata, where Lester continued to write Doc Savage and Avenger novels for many years. He and Norma started a thriving business in aerial photography and ran a small fleet of planes. It took him eleven more years before he was published in the glossies. In the intervening years he bought a big car with DOC 1 on the license place and patrolled his town with a big dog at his side. Their dreams for a child of their own were never to be fulfilled.

China was devastated by the war against the Japanese, although the alliance of Chiang Kai-shek and Mao held together for the duration. In the end Mao was able to seize control of China. Zhang Xueling, while hailed as a hero by the Communist Party, was forced to spend the rest of his life in exile in Hawaii, considered too much of a threat to the movement that his actions had inadvertently saved.

Dutch Schultz's treasure has never been recovered. Today it would probably be worth as much as fifty million dollars. Neither has the gold of the HMS *Hussar* been recovered from the bottom of the East River. Its value today could be as much as a billion dollars. Both are a gift from me to you. But be aware that the weed of crime bears bitter fruit. Crime does not pay.

Mock Duck died in 1943 of natural causes. So the stories say.

For years, until the tunnels were finally sealed up for good, people who were superstitious spoke of the demon who prowled under the cobblestones of Chinatown. Such people cut a wide berth around sewer grates, manhole covers, and cellar doors, while those few who weren't superstitious heard only the unsettling nighttime keenings and scrabblings of lost cats and large rats echoing up from beneath the streets. Today only a few can even remember the tales of the demon, or describe his horrible laughter.

Robert Heinlein ran in, but lost, that election. So he became a writer too. Politics' loss is literature's gain. In the end he may have been the best writer of the lot, and he was the first science fiction writer to regularly write for the slicks and to make the bestseller lists.

Howard Lovecraft was far more widely read after his final death. Fans of his formed a small press to distribute his books, which have been in circulation ever since. The creatures which haunted his imagination continue to bubble up into the imaginations of others, like a virus of mythology.

Ron Hubbard did Lovecraft's postmortem career one better. He died a few years ago but somehow manages to keep writing bestsellers. He created more than a mythology; he created a philosophy which became a religion. I truly salute his initiative in this effort.

Neither Orson Welles nor anyone else has ever made a good movie out of *The Shadow* or *Doc Savage*. And no one ever will.

My last faithful friend and companion, Walter Gibson, wrote over three hundred Shadow novels, and as if that weren't enough his contributions to the art and science of magic have placed all magicians of subsequent generations in his debt. He married Litzka, who was the great love of his life, after a suitable period in which she mourned the loss of Maurice Raymond (whom she had always loved and whom she tended until the end). They lived and wrote together about magic until the end of Gibson's life. She was the first woman inducted into the Magic Hall of Fame by the Society of American Magicians. They loved each other dearly.

I may have driven Gibson mad from time to time, but don't all the best faithful companions do that? And I was faithful to him. I do believe he returned the favor to me, as you have now seen. His mouth formed the words around my breath. I have been mute for so long without him. But now there is you.

How do I alone know the path of the tunnels, through all the dark places, to doors which lead to the right endings? And how am I able to see into the hearts of all my agents and know, finally, what stories, real or otherwise, lurk there? You have read my tale. You know.

You are my agent, my new faithful friend and companion.

Listen and you will hear me laughing and you will know I am coming.

I will always be right behind you.

Especially at night, when you will not be able to see me in the darkness.

You will hear me laughing not because you are evil and not because we are about to die but because I have you now, my dear reader, and because sometimes I just have to laugh.

THE END

ACKNOWLEDGMENTS

I N ADDITION to the voluminous works of Maxwell Grant and Kenneth Robeson, three books have fueled my imagination for over twenty-five years: *Doc Savage: His Apocalyptic Life,* by Philip José Farmer; *The Duende History of* The Shadow Magazine, by Will Murray; and *The Shadow Scrapbook,* by Walter B. Gibson himself. Other works that helped me tell this tale include *Pulp Art,* by Robert Lesser; Spider Robinson's introduction to *For Us, the Living,* by Robert A. Heinlein; *The Immortal Storm,* by Sam Moskowitz; *Man of Magic and Mystery: A Guide to the Work of Walter B. Gibson,* by J. Randolph Cox; *Walter B. Gibson and The Shadow,* by Thomas J. Shimeld; *Lester Dent: The Man, His Craft and His Market,* by M. Martin McCarey-Laird; *I. Asimov* and *In Memory Yet Green,* by Isaac Asimov; *The Futurians,* by Damon Knight; *Lost Gold & Buried Treasure,* by Kevin D. Randle; *L. Ron Hubbard, Messiah or Madman?,* by Bent Corydon and L. Ron Hubbard Jr.; *Bigger Than Life,* by Marilyn Cannaday; *Shudder Pulps: A History of the Weird Menace Magazines of the 1930s,* by Robert Kenneth Jones; *The Great Pulp Heroes,* by Don Hutchison; *The Hatchet Men,* by Richard H. Dillon; *The Encyclopedia of Science Fiction,* by John Clute and Peter Nicholls; *The Encyclopedia of American Crime,* by Carl Sifakis; *Tea That

Paul Malmont

Burns: A Family Memoir of Chinatown, by Bruce Edward Hall; *Bare-Faced Messiah,* by Russell Miller; *H. P. Lovecraft: A Biography,* by L. Sprague de Camp; the *Mock Duck/Blood of the Rooster* series by Jay Maeder for the *New York Daily News;* and *Fortean Times Magazine.* I made many online trips to Syracuse University Library's Street & Smith's Preservation and Access Project, to ThePulp.Net, HMSHussar.com, Wikipedia.org, Zoetrope.com, Writers.net, and to the site by Ah Xiang, UglyChinese.org.

Thank you to Tony Spina of Tannen's Magic for playing Walter Gibson for me once, for the gift of Norgil, and for telling me a few stories about the man you once described to me as your "best friend." Thank you also to Forrest J. Ackerman, for opening the Ackermansion and telling me some stories. My gratitude also to Robert Lesser, Mark Halegua and the Gotham Pulp Collectors Club, Tom Johnson, the Popular Publications archive at the New York Public Library, and Robert Weinberg. Of friends I must first mention the beautiful minds of Tracy Fullerton and Anton Salaks for their insights. Jennifer Levesque, thanks for opening the door. From one draft to another, Sam Hutchins, James Graham, Richard Siegmeister, Peter Bock, and Barry Crooks were the best of supportive friends, and Jerry Quartley always brought great wine. Thanks also to Chris Wickland, Charles Ardai, Albino Marsetti, and Judith Zissman for their encouragement. For early advice I turned to the generosity of Heather Swain and Kevin Smokler. I would also like to express my appreciation to the talented people it is my pleasure to work with every day at R/GA—Bob Greenberg, John Antinori, Nicole Victor, Chapin Clark, Ted Metcalfe, Ken Hamm, and Mae Flordeliza—for their forbearance.

Susan Golomb, my agent, I cannot say thank you enough to express how much I really mean it. Thanks also to your loyal and trusted sidekicks, especially Jon Mozes, but Kim Goldstein and Casey Panell as well. Geoff Kloske, my editor, thanks for joining me in the adventure and pointing out the perils and pitfalls. A heartfelt thank you goes to David Rosenthal. And to Jackie Seow, thanks for the great cover. Also at Simon & Schuster my deepest appreciation goes to Victoria Meyer,

Acknowledgments

Elizabeth Hayes, Tracy Guest, Kathleen Maloy, and Laura Perciasepe for all their hard work. And a special thank-you to Marysue Rucci.

Ed and Giulia Herbst, thanks for all the support and meatballs. Jason and Andrea, love always. Mom, thanks for the late-bloomer gene that finally bloomed. And Dad, in 1976 when I was ten, you introduced me to the Doc Savage and the Shadow you knew back in 1936 when you were ten. It was great to catch up with them again. Thanks.

ABOUT THE AUTHOR

Paul Malmont works in advertising. He lives in Brooklyn with his wife and two boys. This is his first book.